Mal [and] Chad

FOOD FIGHT!

ALSO BY

Stephen McCranie

Mal and Chad

The Biggest, Bestest Time Ever

Mal and Chad

Stephen McCranie

FOOD FIGHT!

Philomel Books 🐾 An Imprint of Penguin Group (USA) Inc.

For my mom.

PHILOMEL BOOKS

A division of Penguin Young Readers Group.

Published by The Penguin Group. Penguin Group (USA) Inc., 375 Hudson Street, New York, NY 10014, U.S.A. Penguin Group (Canada), 90 Eglinton Avenue East, Suite 700, Toronto, Ontario M4P 2Y3, Canada (a division of Pearson Penguin Canada Inc.). Penguin Books Ltd, 80 Strand, London WC2R 0RL, England. Penguin Ireland, 25 St. Stephen's Green, Dublin 2, Ireland (a division of Penguin Books Ltd). Penguin Group (Australia), 250 Camberwell Road, Camberwell, Victoria 3124, Australia (a division of Pearson Australia Group Pty Ltd). Penguin Books India Pvt Ltd, 11 Community Centre, Panchsheel Park, New Delhi — 110 017, India. Penguin Group (NZ), 67 Apollo Drive, Rosedale, Auckland 0632, New Zealand (a division of Pearson New Zealand Ltd). Penguin Books (South Africa) (Pty) Ltd, 24 Sturdee Avenue, Rosebank, Johannesburg 2196, South Africa. Penguin Books Ltd, Registered Offices: 80 Strand, London WC2R 0RL, England.

Published simultaneously in Canada.
Printed in the United States of America.
Edited by Michael Green.
Design by Richard Amari.
Library of Congress Cataloging-in-Publication Data is available upon request.
ISBN 978-0-399-25657-8
5 7 9 10 8 6

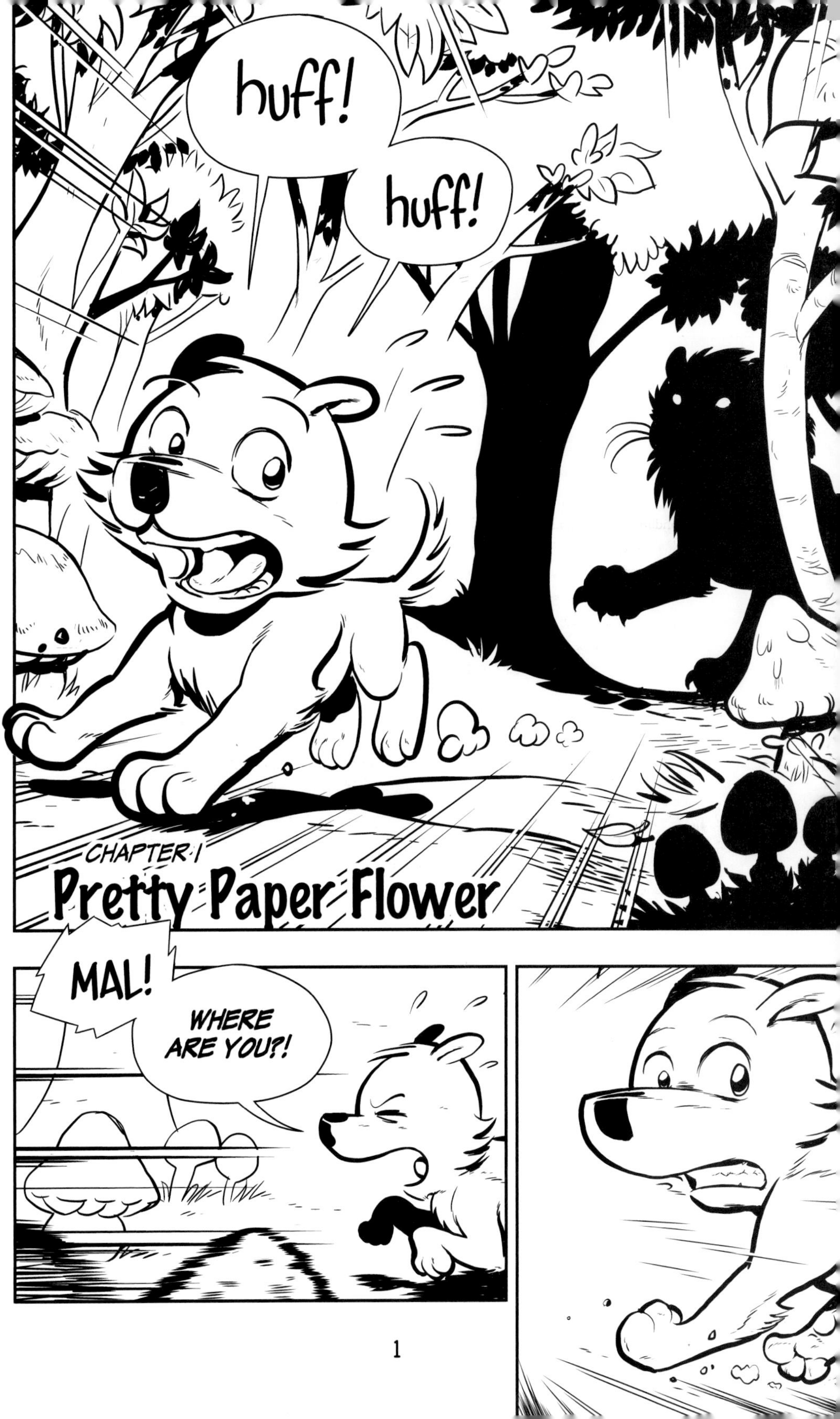
huff!
huff!
CHAPTER 1
Pretty Paper Flower
MAL!
WHERE ARE YOU?!

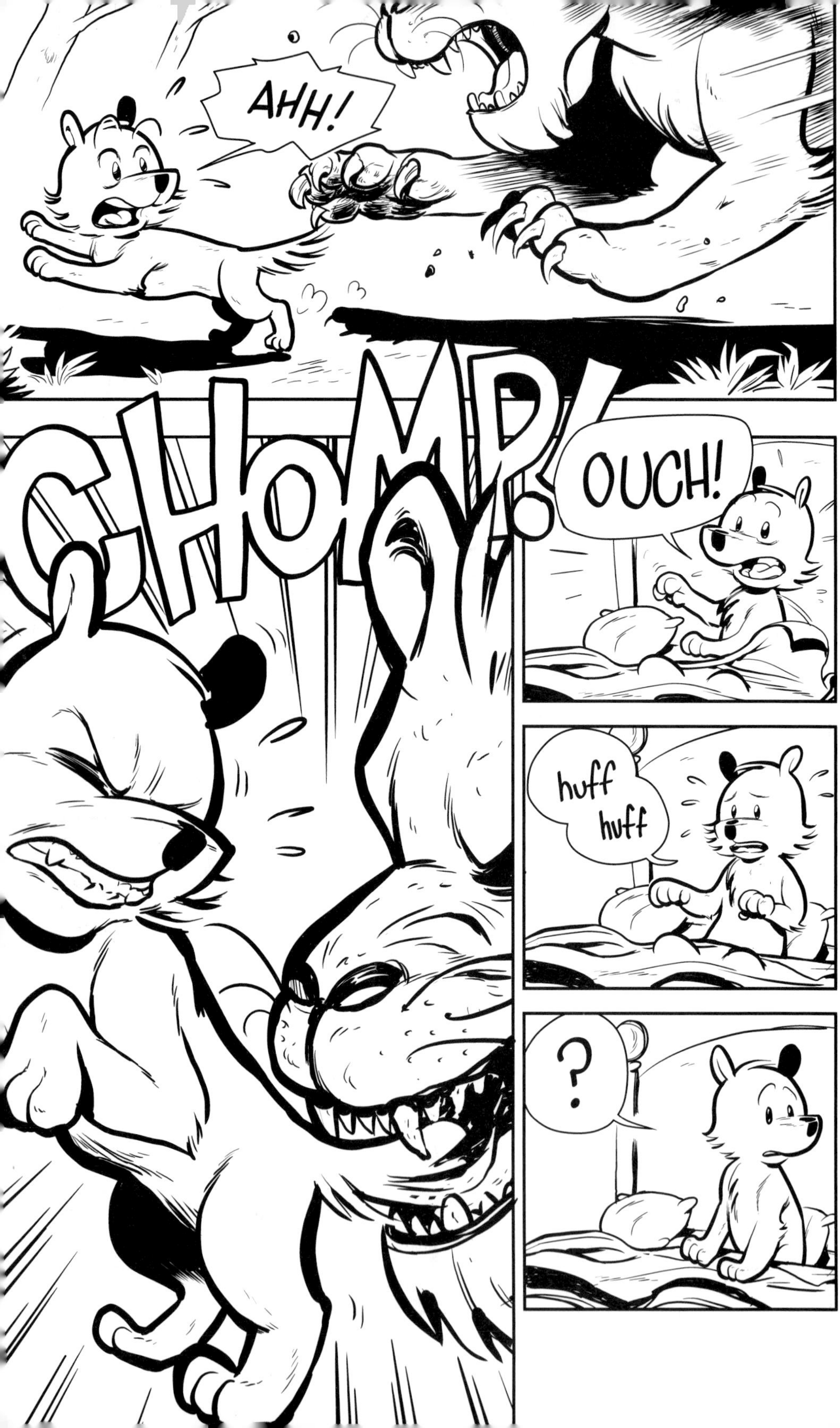
AHH!
CHOMP!
OUCH!
huff
huff
?

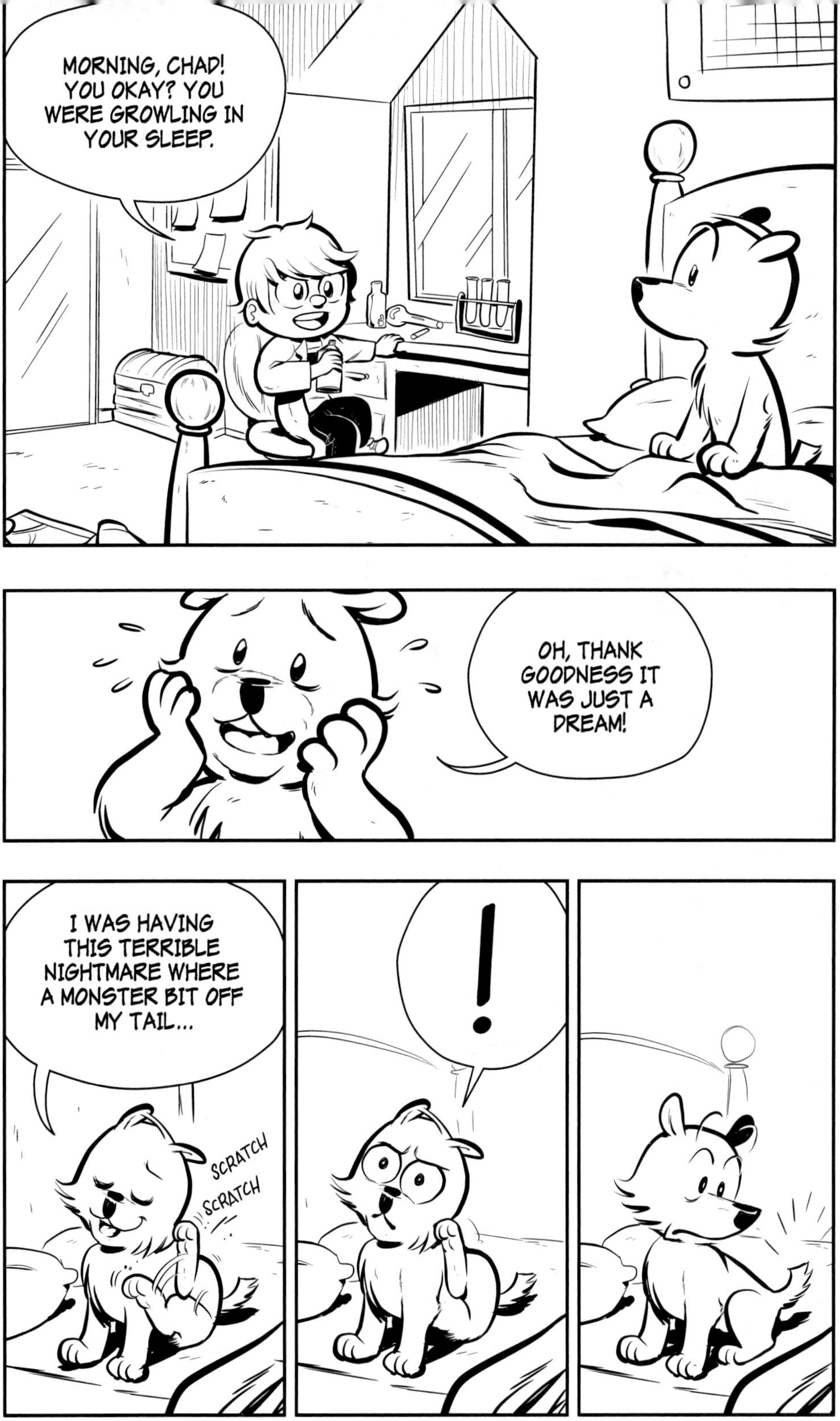
MORNING, CHAD! YOU OKAY? YOU WERE GROWLING IN YOUR SLEEP.
OH, THANK GOODNESS IT WAS JUST A DREAM!
I WAS HAVING THIS TERRIBLE NIGHTMARE WHERE A MONSTER BIT OFF MY TAIL...
SCRATCH
SCRATCH
!

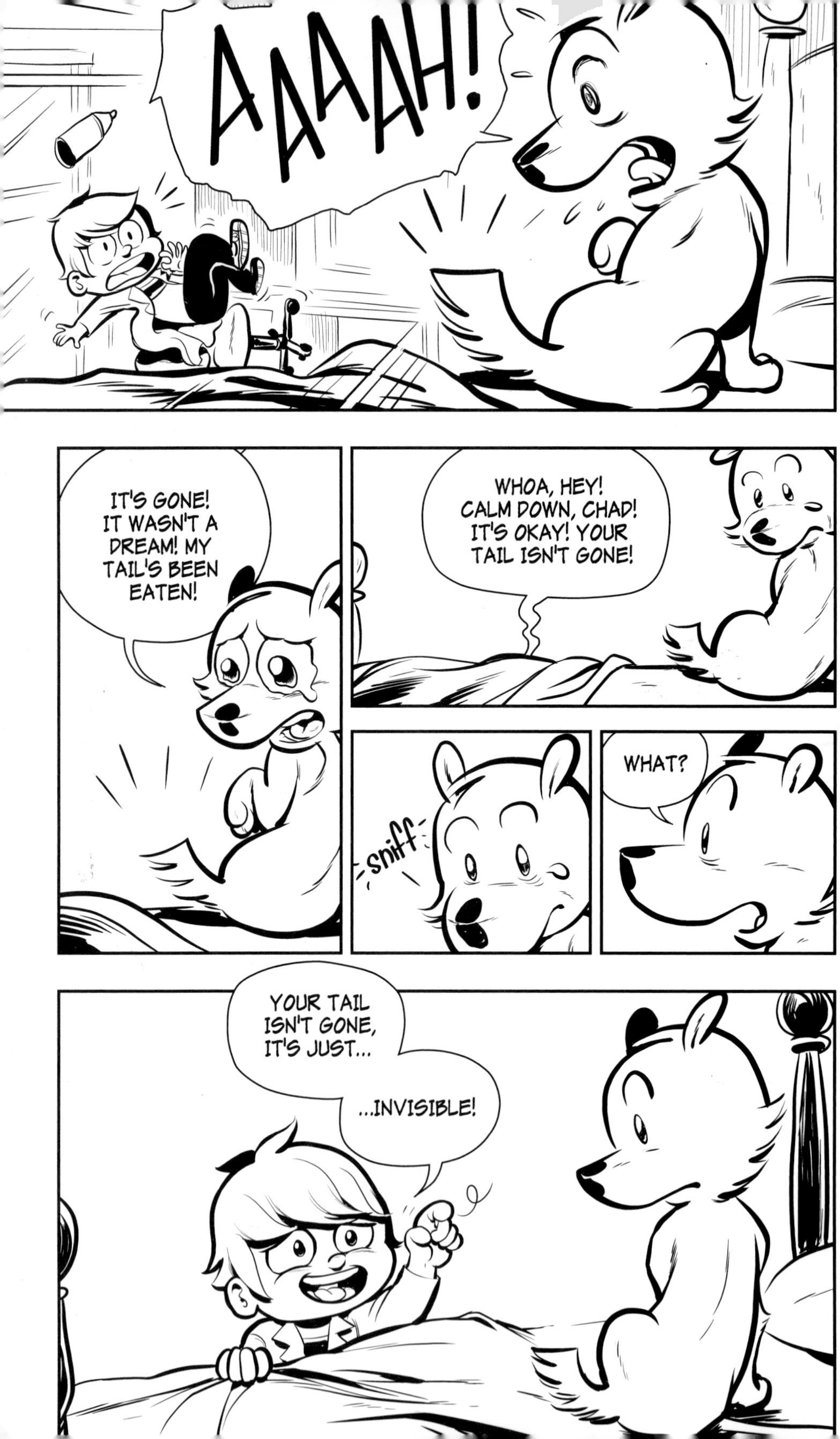
AAAAH!
IT'S GONE! IT WASN'T A DREAM! MY TAIL'S BEEN EATEN!
WHOA, HEY! CALM DOWN, CHAD! IT'S OKAY! YOUR TAIL ISN'T GONE!
sniff
WHAT?
YOUR TAIL ISN'T GONE, IT'S JUST...
...INVISIBLE!

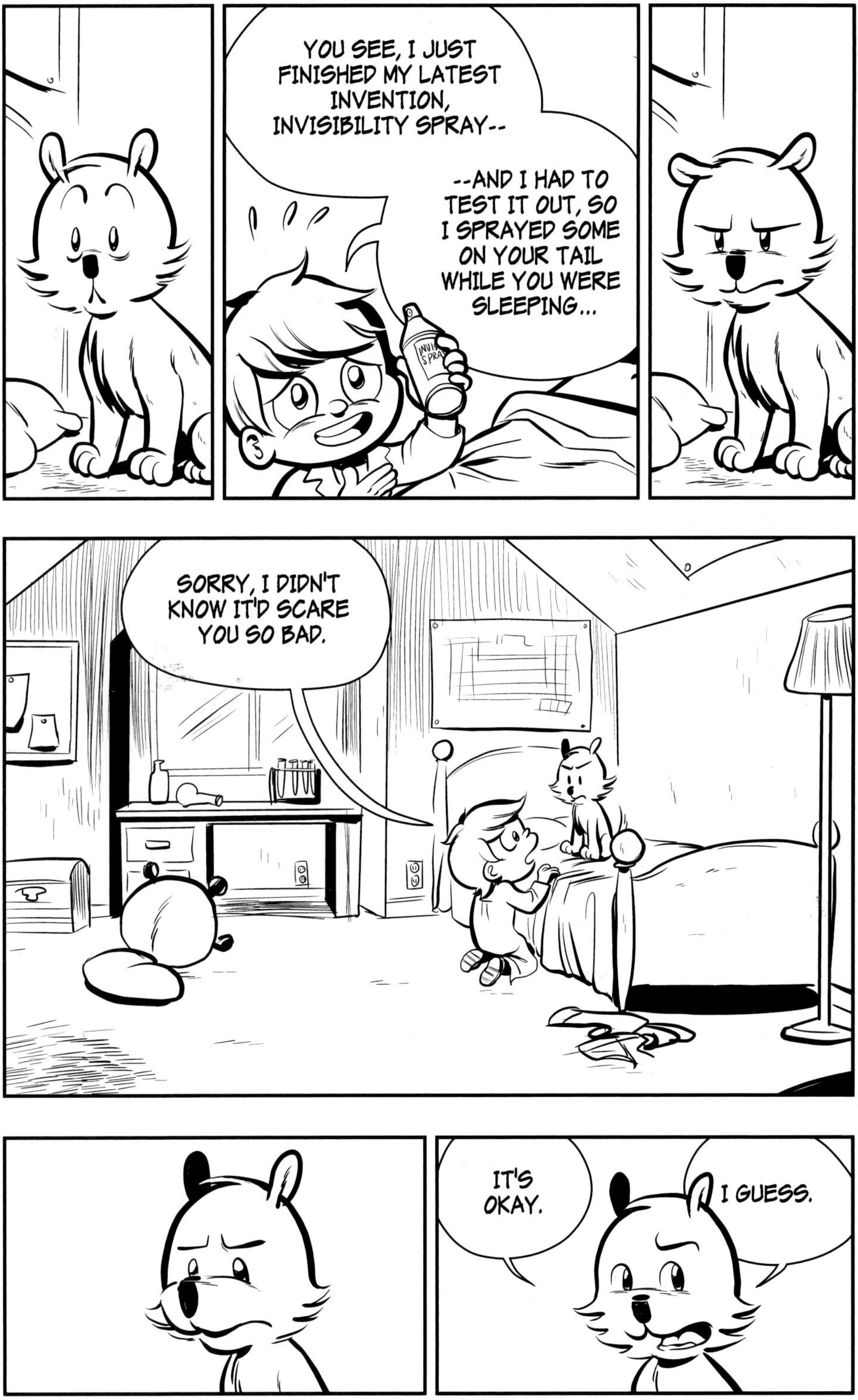
YOU SEE, I JUST FINISHED MY LATEST INVENTION, INVISIBILITY SPRAY--
--AND I HAD TO TEST IT OUT, SO I SPRAYED SOME ON YOUR TAIL WHILE YOU WERE SLEEPING...
SORRY, I DIDN'T KNOW IT'D SCARE YOU SO BAD.
IT'S OKAY.
I GUESS.

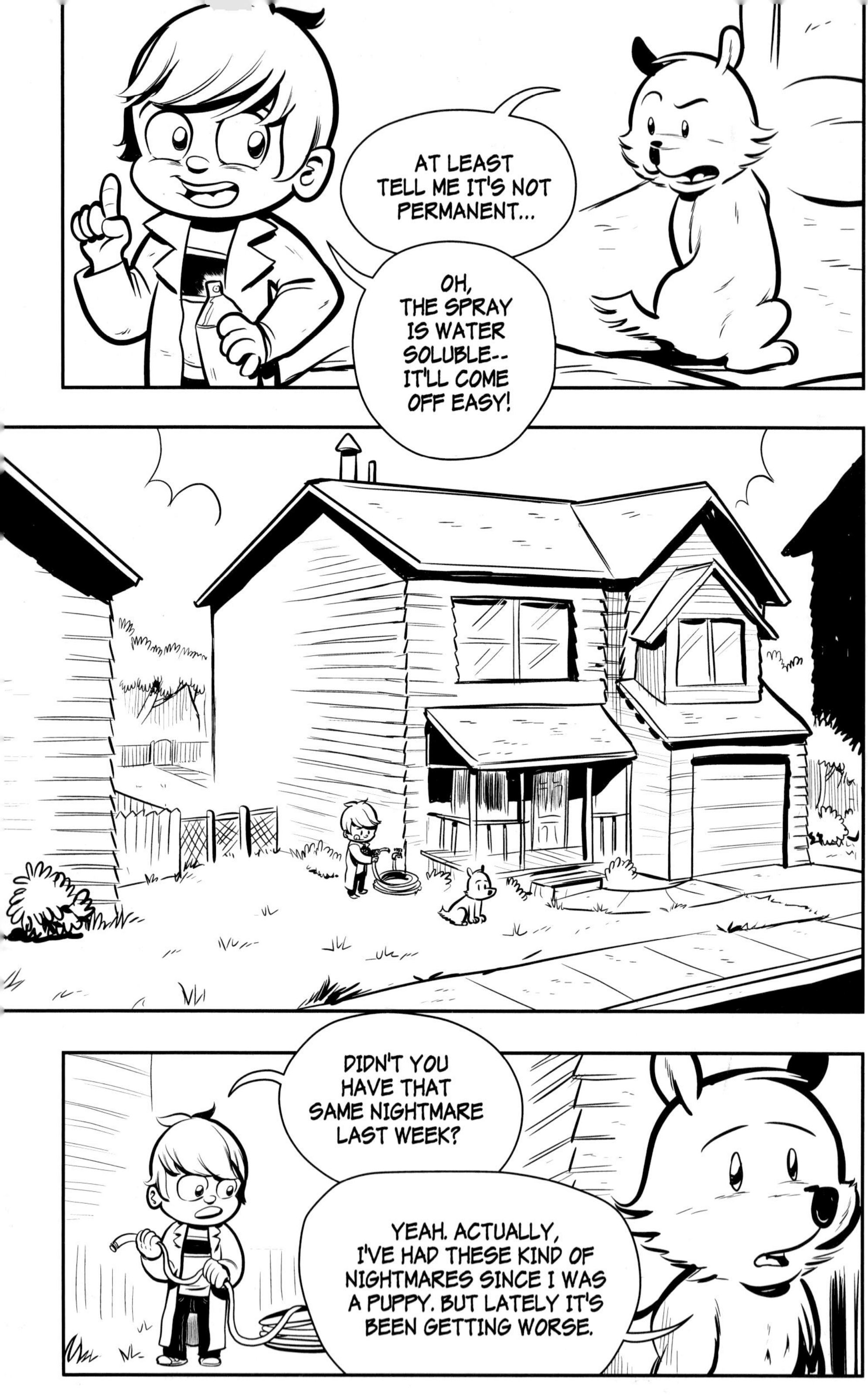
AT LEAST TELL ME IT'S NOT PERMANENT...
OH, THE SPRAY IS WATER SOLUBLE-- IT'LL COME OFF EASY!
DIDN'T YOU HAVE THAT SAME NIGHTMARE LAST WEEK?
YEAH. ACTUALLY, I'VE HAD THESE KIND OF NIGHTMARES SINCE I WAS A PUPPY. BUT LATELY IT'S BEEN GETTING WORSE.

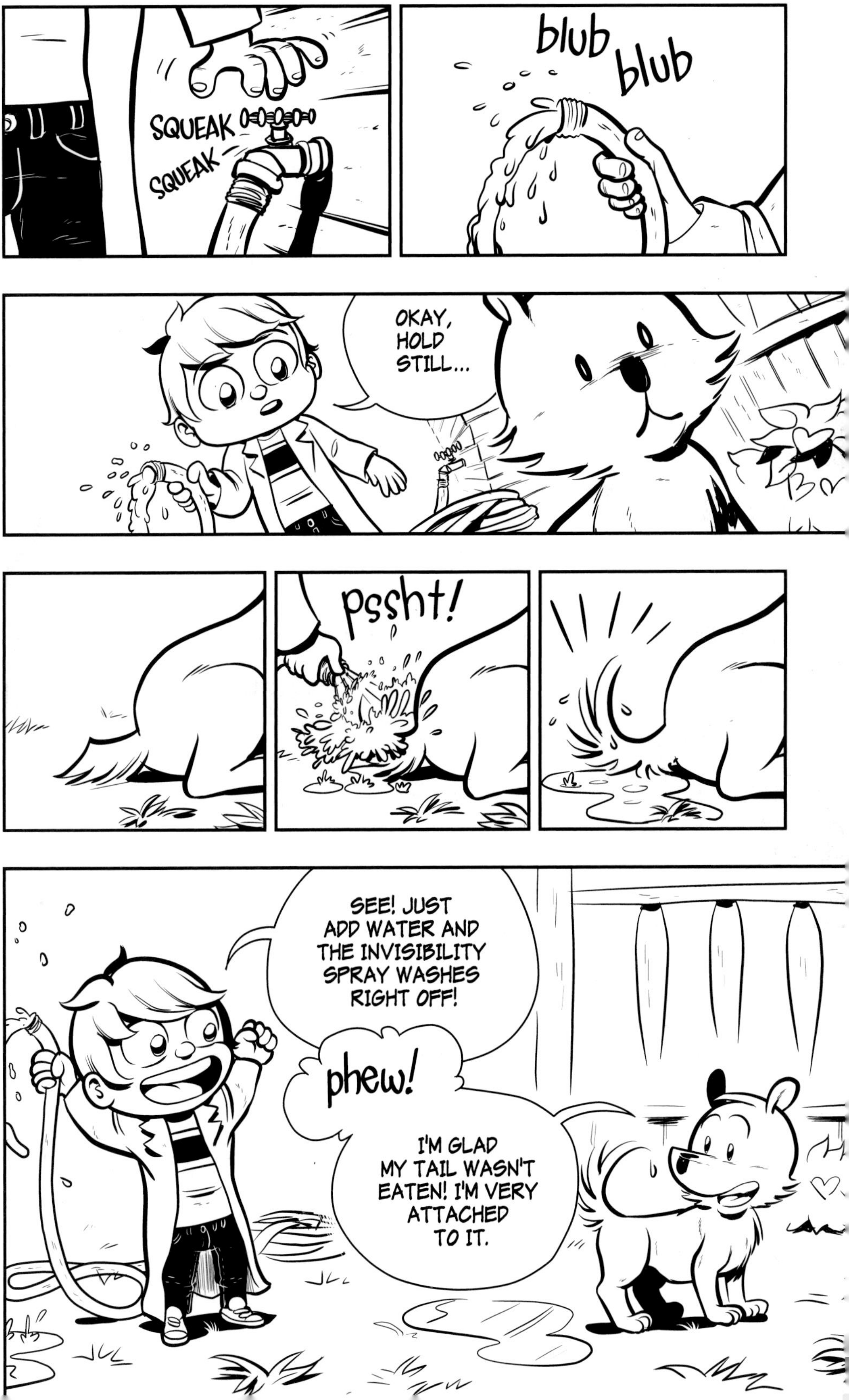
SQUEAK
SQUEAK
blub
blub
OKAY, HOLD STILL...
pssht!
SEE! JUST ADD WATER AND THE INVISIBILITY SPRAY WASHES RIGHT OFF!
phew!
I'M GLAD MY TAIL WASN'T EATEN! I'M VERY ATTACHED TO IT.

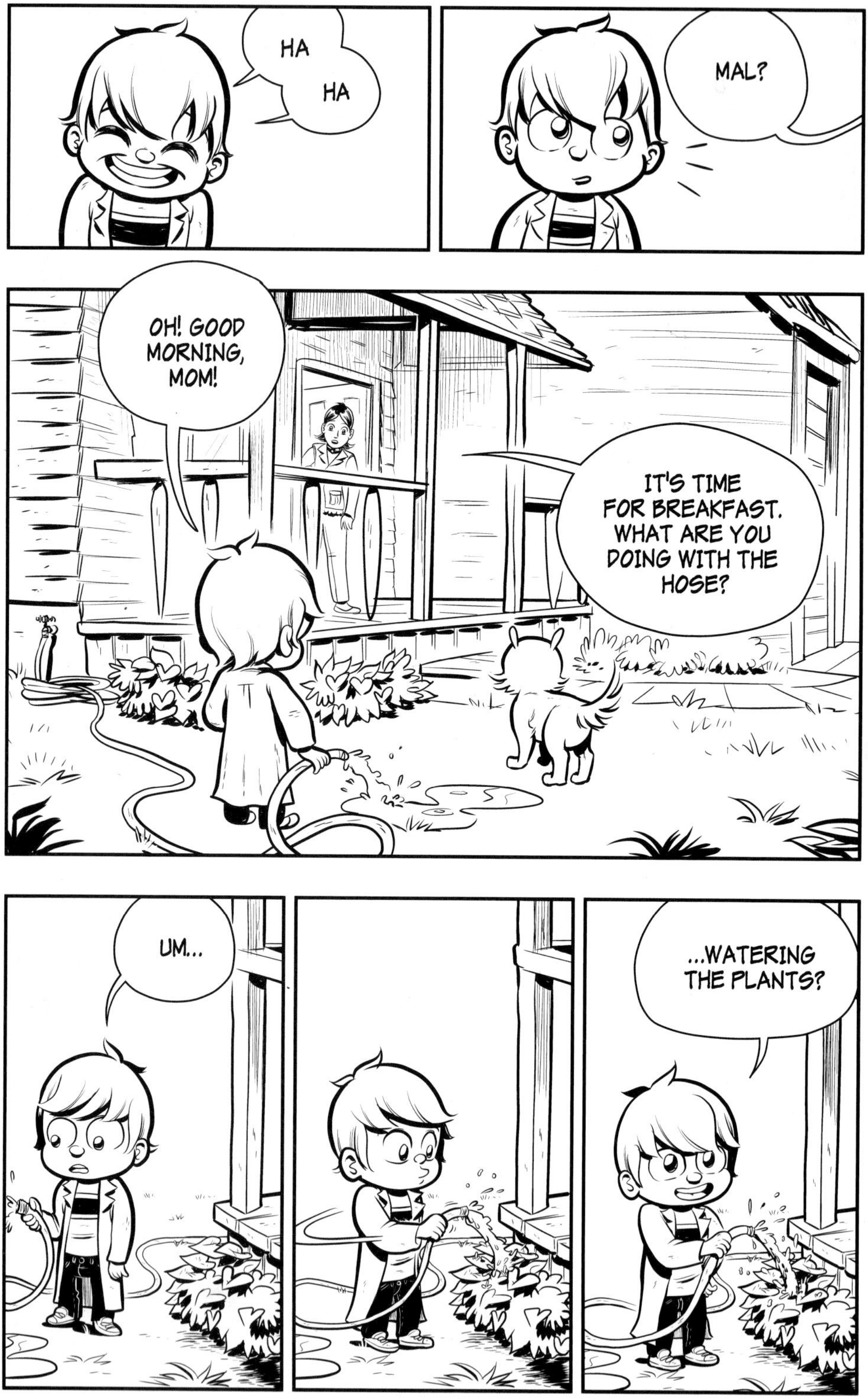
HA
HA
MAL?
OH! GOOD MORNING, MOM!
IT'S TIME FOR BREAKFAST. WHAT ARE YOU DOING WITH THE HOSE?
UM...
...WATERING THE PLANTS?

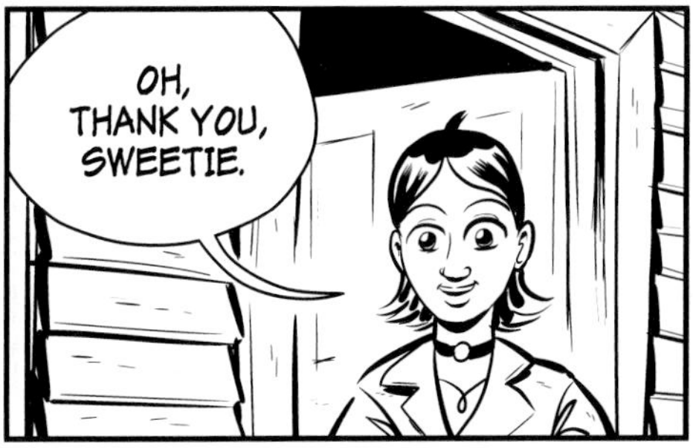
OH, THANK YOU, SWEETIE.

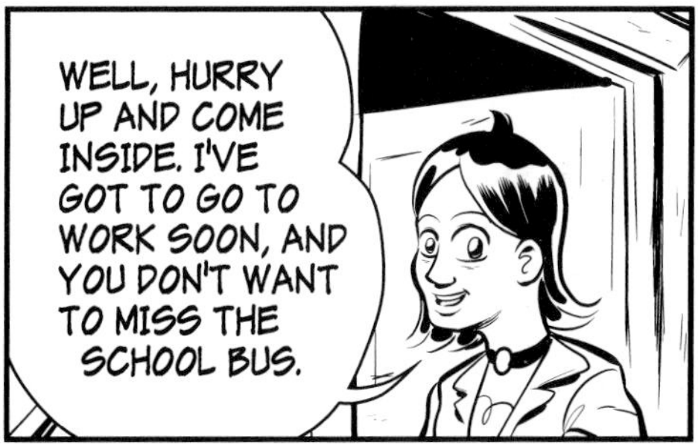
WELL, HURRY UP AND COME INSIDE. I'VE GOT TO GO TO WORK SOON, AND YOU DON'T WANT TO MISS THE SCHOOL BUS.

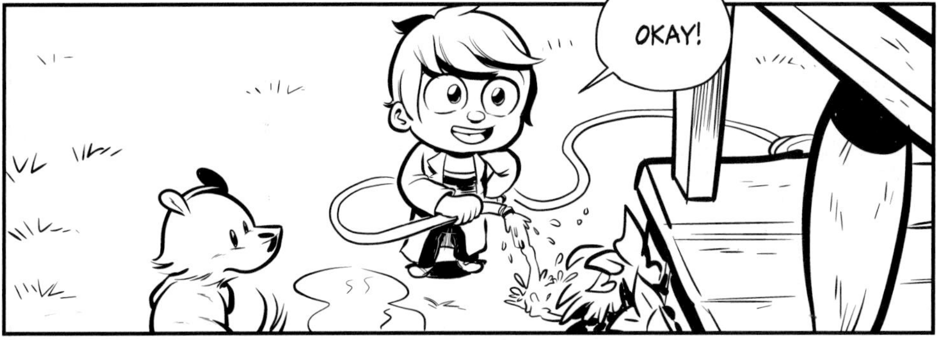
OKAY!

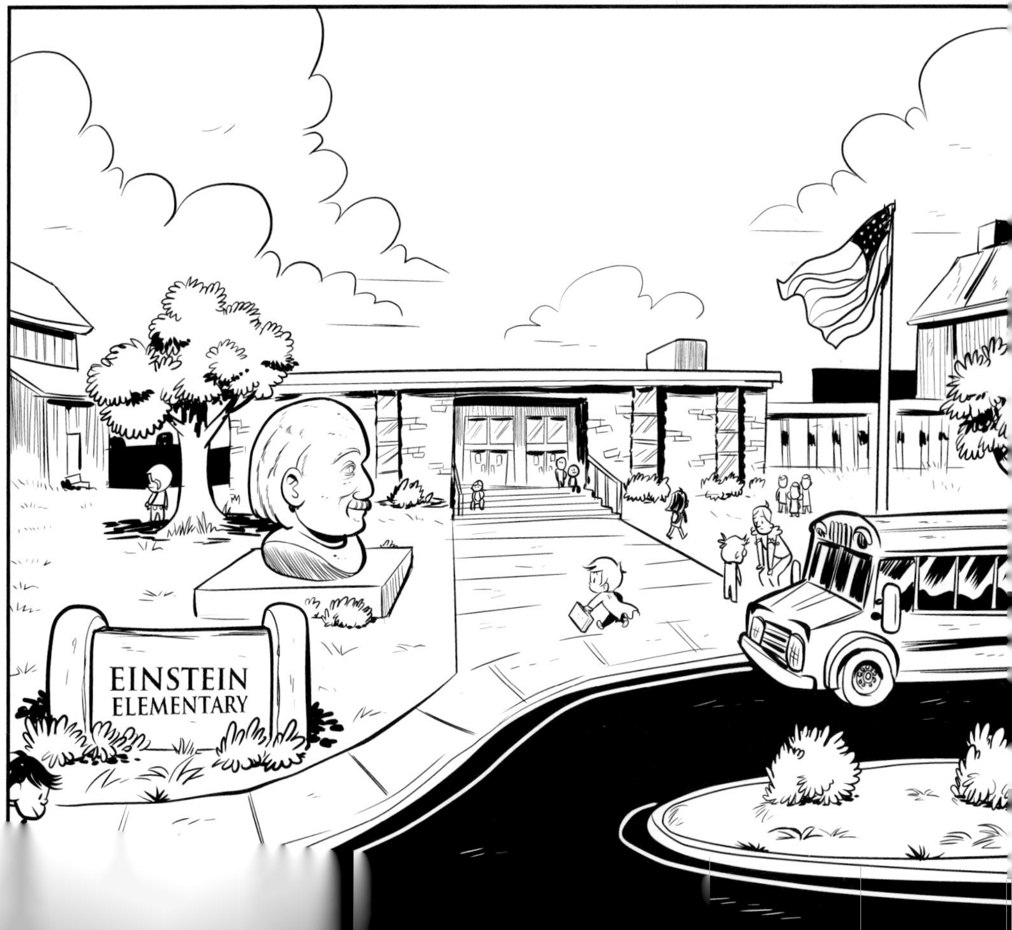
EINSTEIN
ELEMENTARY

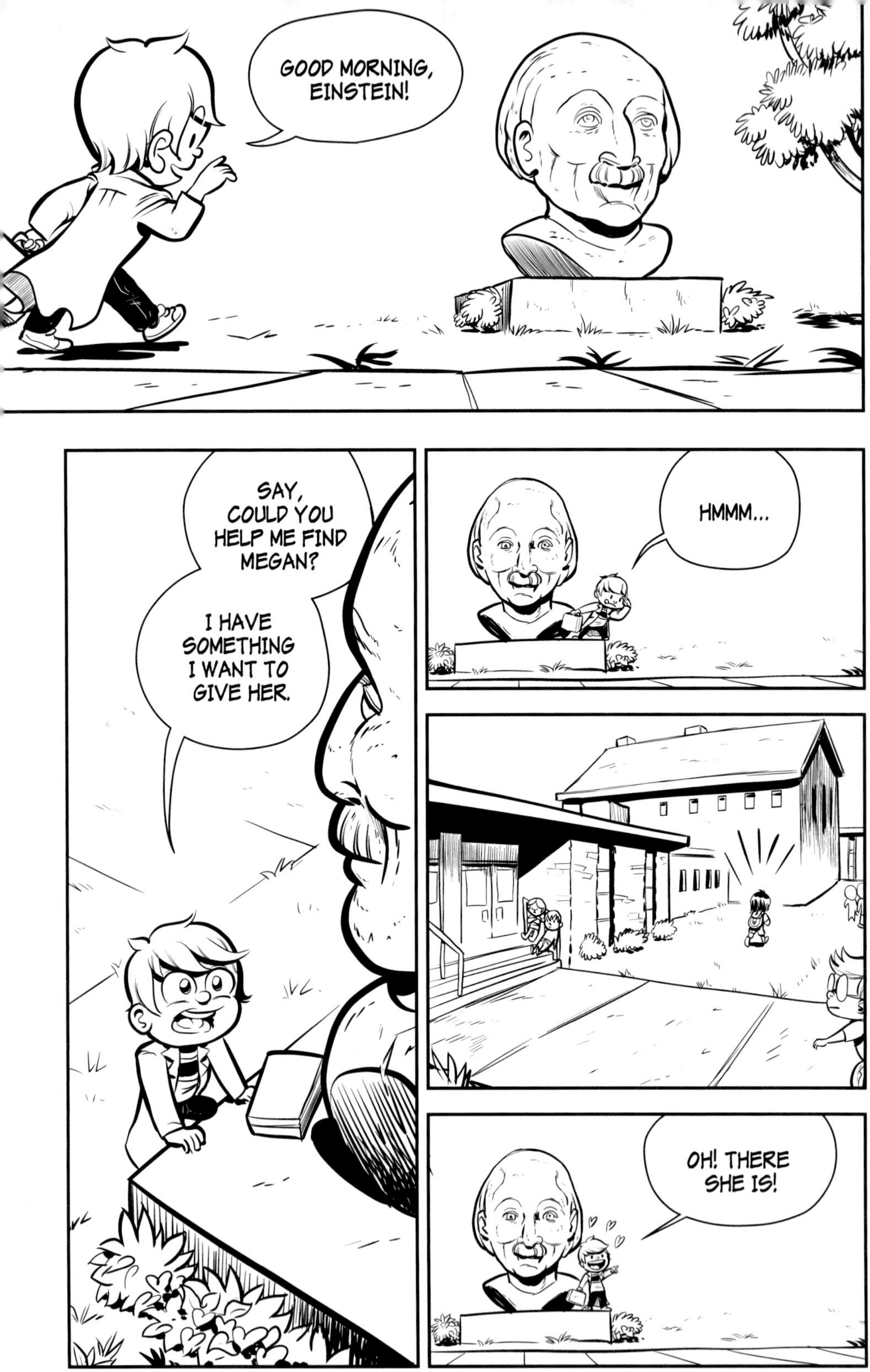
GOOD MORNING, EINSTEIN!
SAY, COULD YOU HELP ME FIND MEGAN?
I HAVE SOMETHING I WANT TO GIVE HER.
HMMM...
OH! THERE SHE IS!

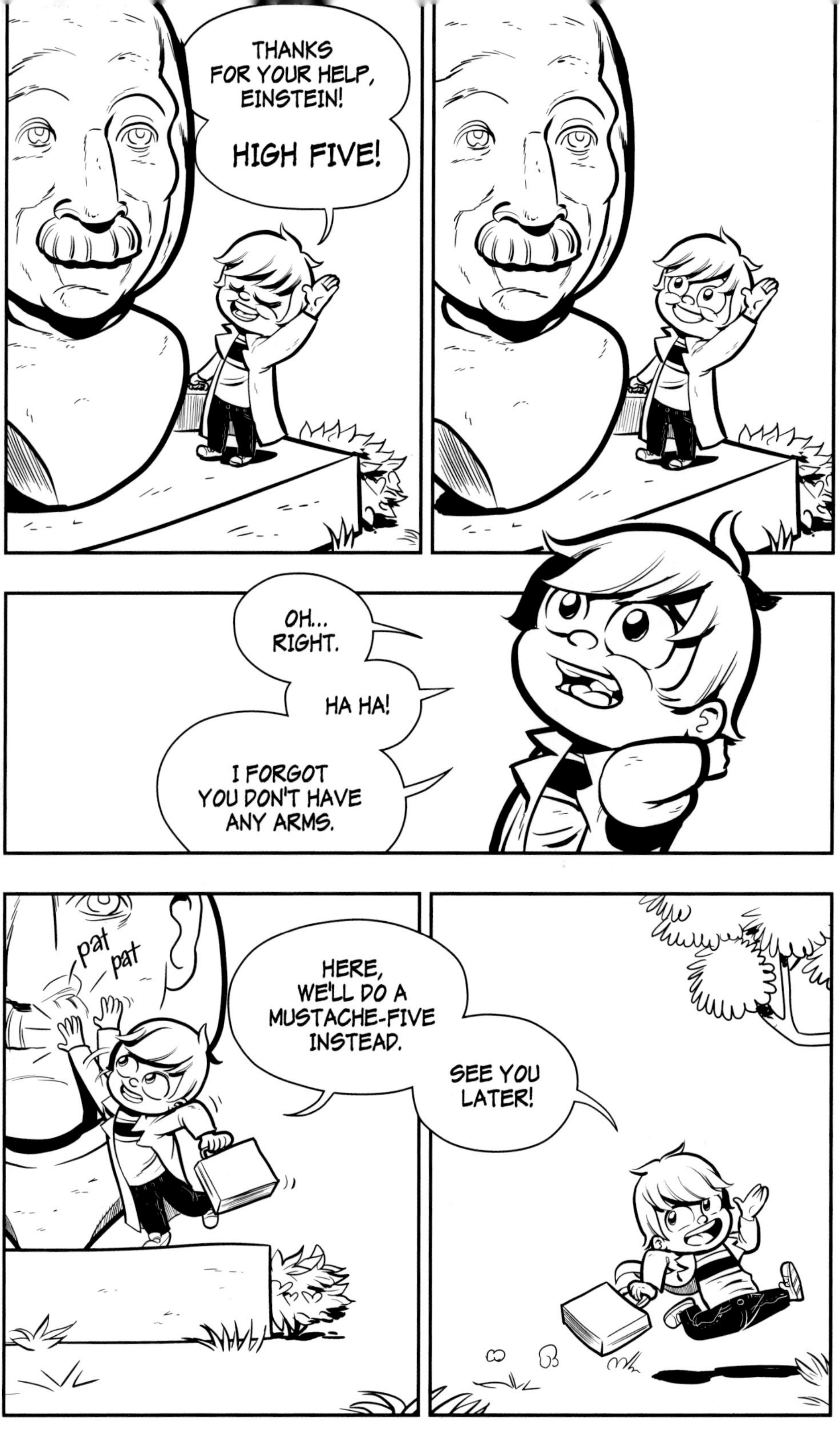
THANKS FOR YOUR HELP, EINSTEIN!
HIGH FIVE!
OH... RIGHT.
HA HA!
I FORGOT YOU DON'T HAVE ANY ARMS.
pat pat
HERE, WE'LL DO A MUSTACHE-FIVE INSTEAD.
SEE YOU LATER!

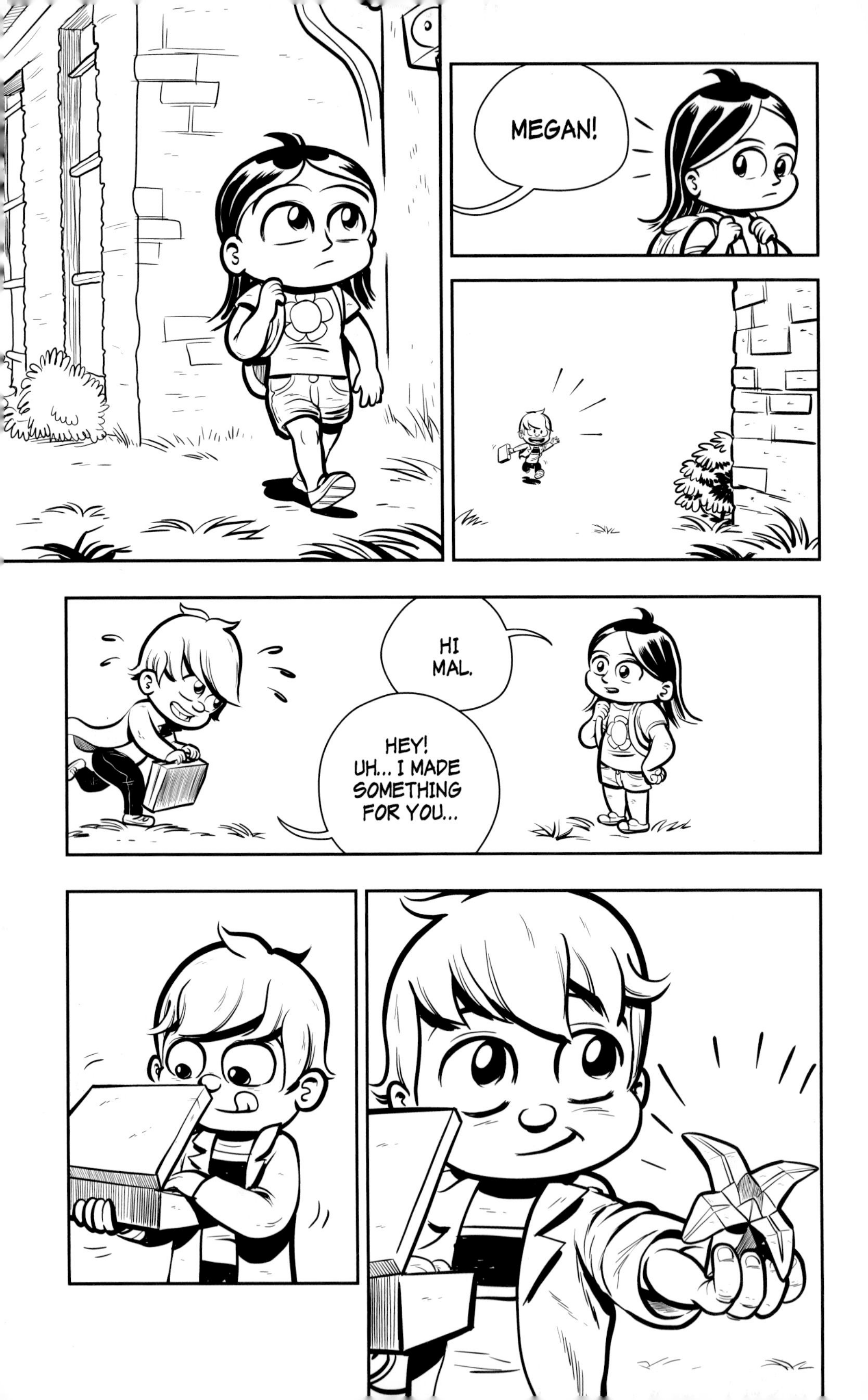
MEGAN!
HI
MAL.
HEY!
UH... I MADE
SOMETHING
FOR YOU...

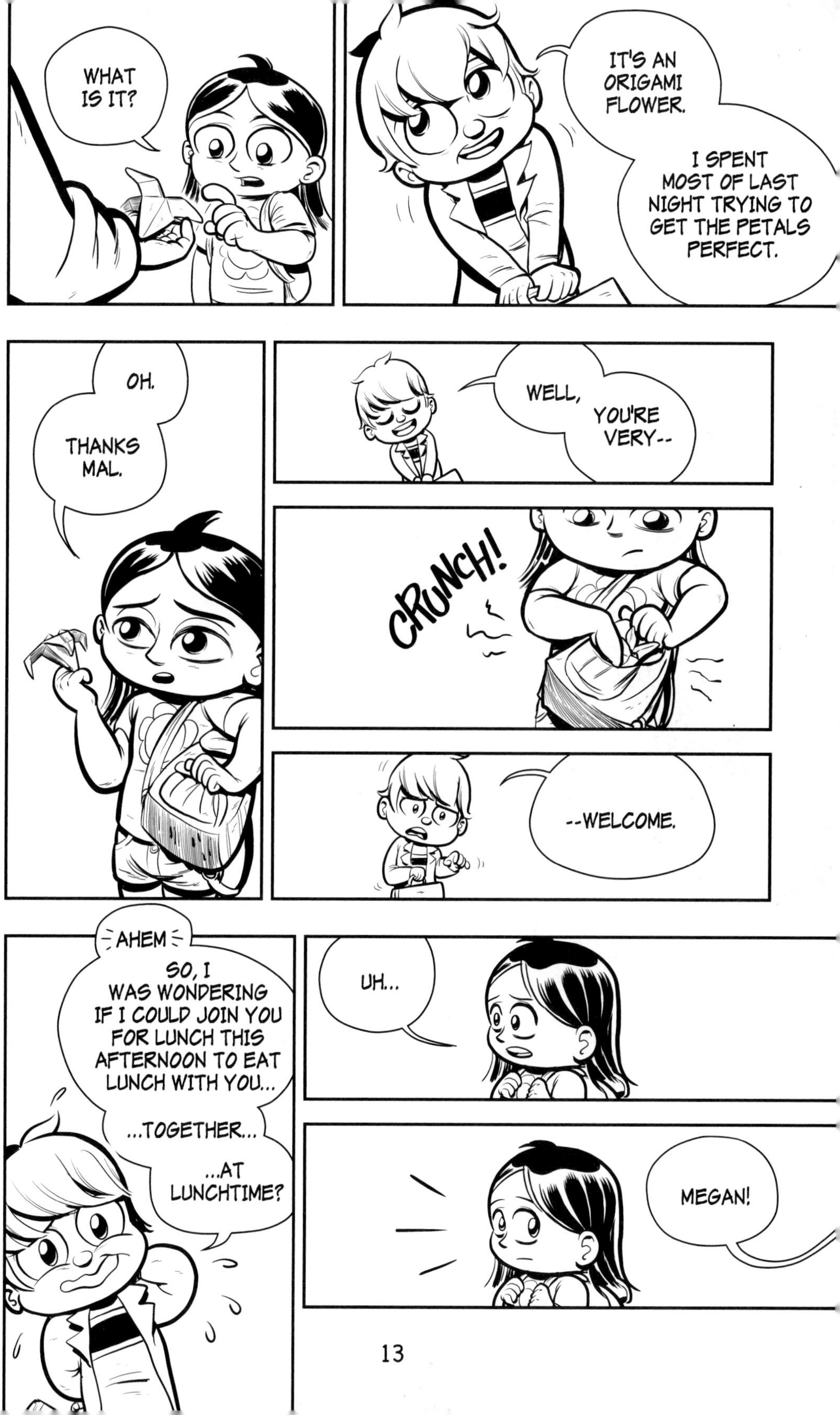
WHAT IS IT?
IT'S AN ORIGAMI FLOWER.
I SPENT MOST OF LAST NIGHT TRYING TO GET THE PETALS PERFECT.
OH.
THANKS MAL.
WELL,
YOU'RE VERY--
CRUNCH!
--WELCOME.
AHEM
SO, I WAS WONDERING IF I COULD JOIN YOU FOR LUNCH THIS AFTERNOON TO EAT LUNCH WITH YOU...
...TOGETHER...
...AT LUNCHTIME?
UH...
MEGAN!

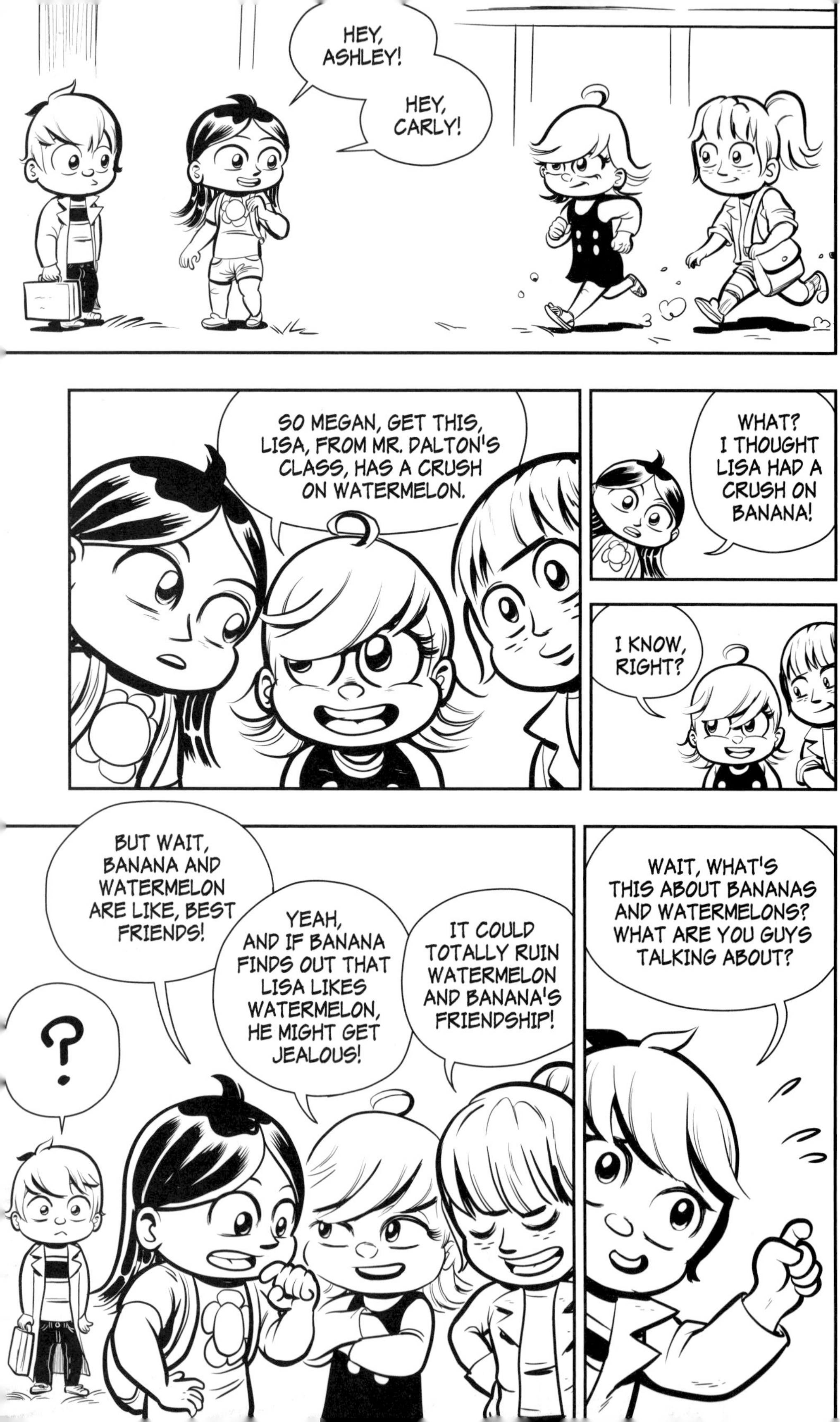
HEY, ASHLEY!
HEY, CARLY!
SO MEGAN, GET THIS, LISA, FROM MR. DALTON'S CLASS, HAS A CRUSH ON WATERMELON.
WHAT? I THOUGHT LISA HAD A CRUSH ON BANANA!
I KNOW, RIGHT?
BUT WAIT, BANANA AND WATERMELON ARE LIKE, BEST FRIENDS!
YEAH, AND IF BANANA FINDS OUT THAT LISA LIKES WATERMELON, HE MIGHT GET JEALOUS!
IT COULD TOTALLY RUIN WATERMELON AND BANANA'S FRIENDSHIP!
?
WAIT, WHAT'S THIS ABOUT BANANAS AND WATERMELONS? WHAT ARE YOU GUYS TALKING ABOUT?

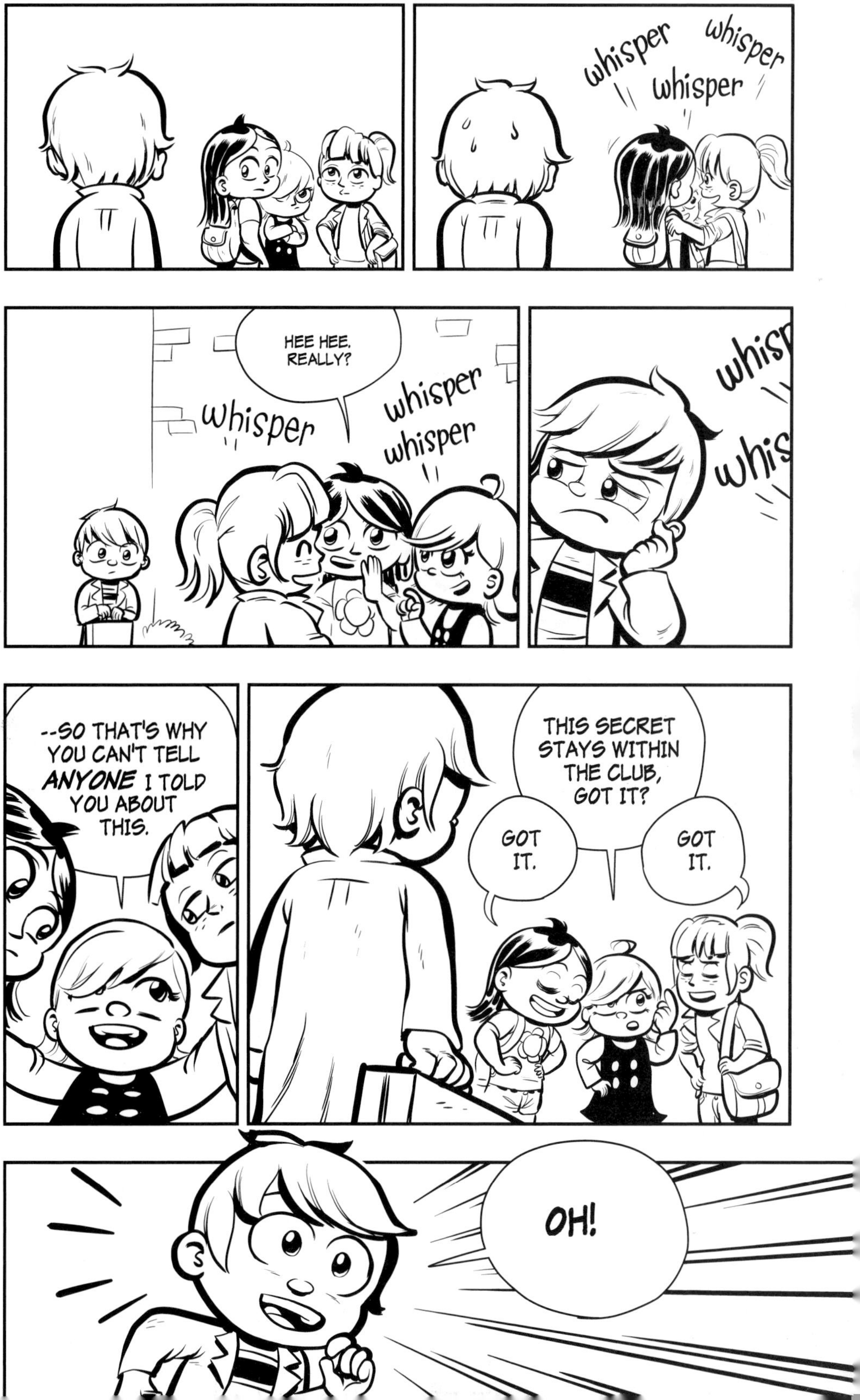

whisper
whisper
whisper
HEE HEE. REALLY?
whisper
whisper
whisper
--SO THAT'S WHY YOU CAN'T TELL ANYONE I TOLD YOU ABOUT THIS.
THIS SECRET STAYS WITHIN THE CLUB, GOT IT?
GOT IT.
GOT IT.
OH!

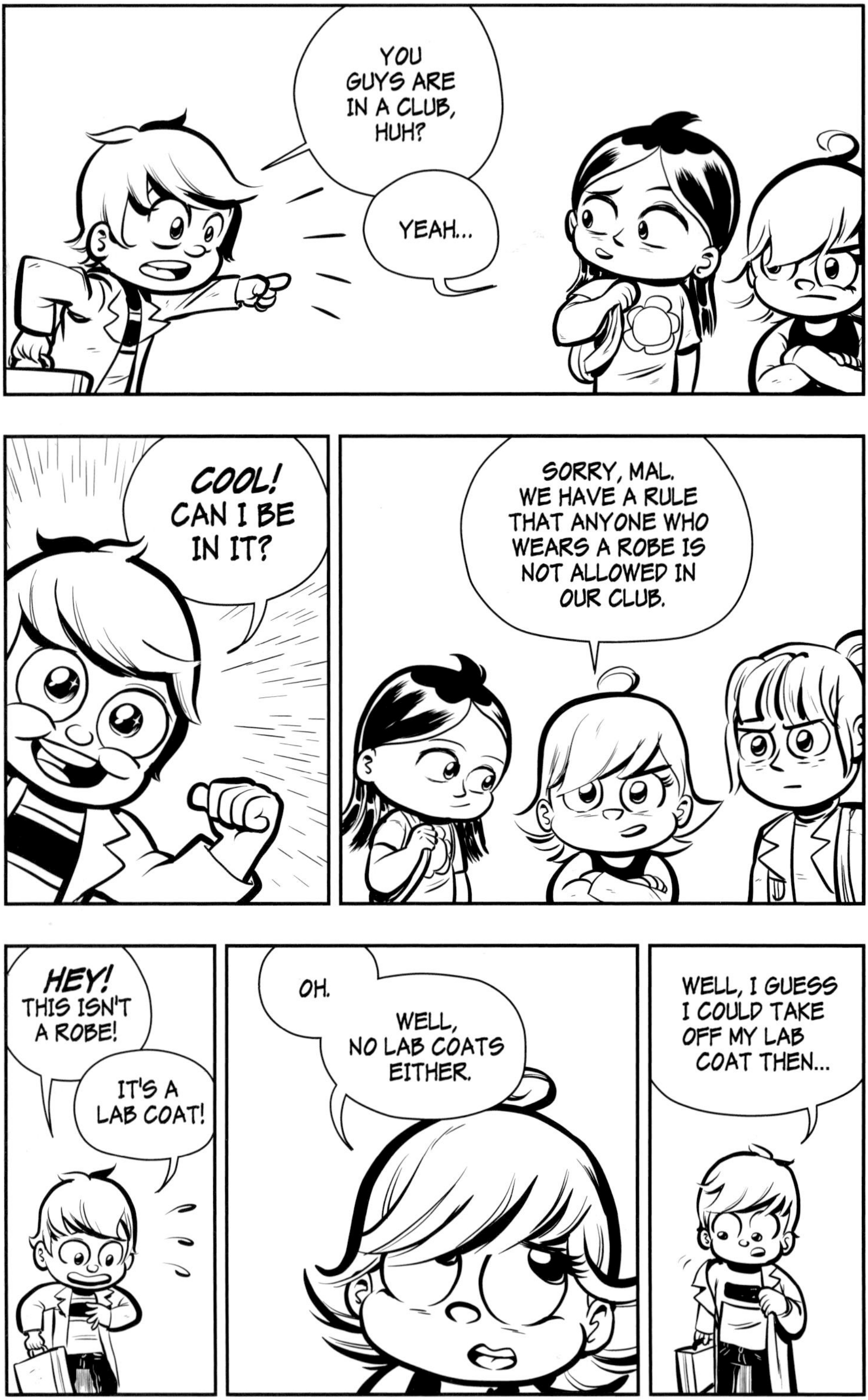
YOU GUYS ARE IN A CLUB, HUH?
YEAH...
COOL! CAN I BE IN IT?
SORRY, MAL. WE HAVE A RULE THAT ANYONE WHO WEARS A ROBE IS NOT ALLOWED IN OUR CLUB.
HEY! THIS ISN'T A ROBE!
IT'S A LAB COAT!
OH.
WELL, NO LAB COATS EITHER.
WELL, I GUESS I COULD TAKE OFF MY LAB COAT THEN...

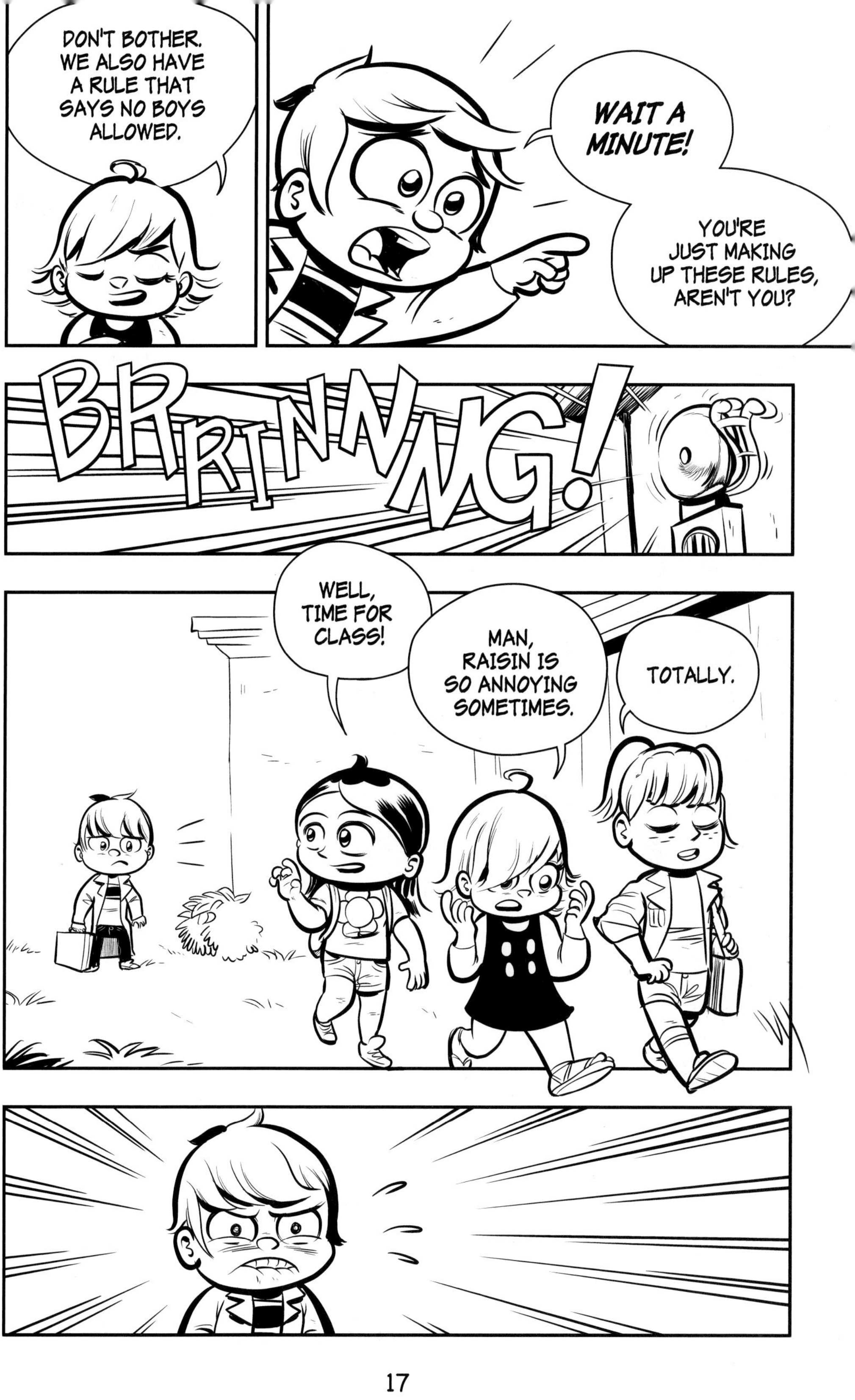
DON'T BOTHER. WE ALSO HAVE A RULE THAT SAYS NO BOYS ALLOWED.
WAIT A MINUTE!
YOU'RE JUST MAKING UP THESE RULES, AREN'T YOU?
BRRINNNG!
WELL, TIME FOR CLASS!
MAN, RAISIN IS SO ANNOYING SOMETIMES.
TOTALLY.

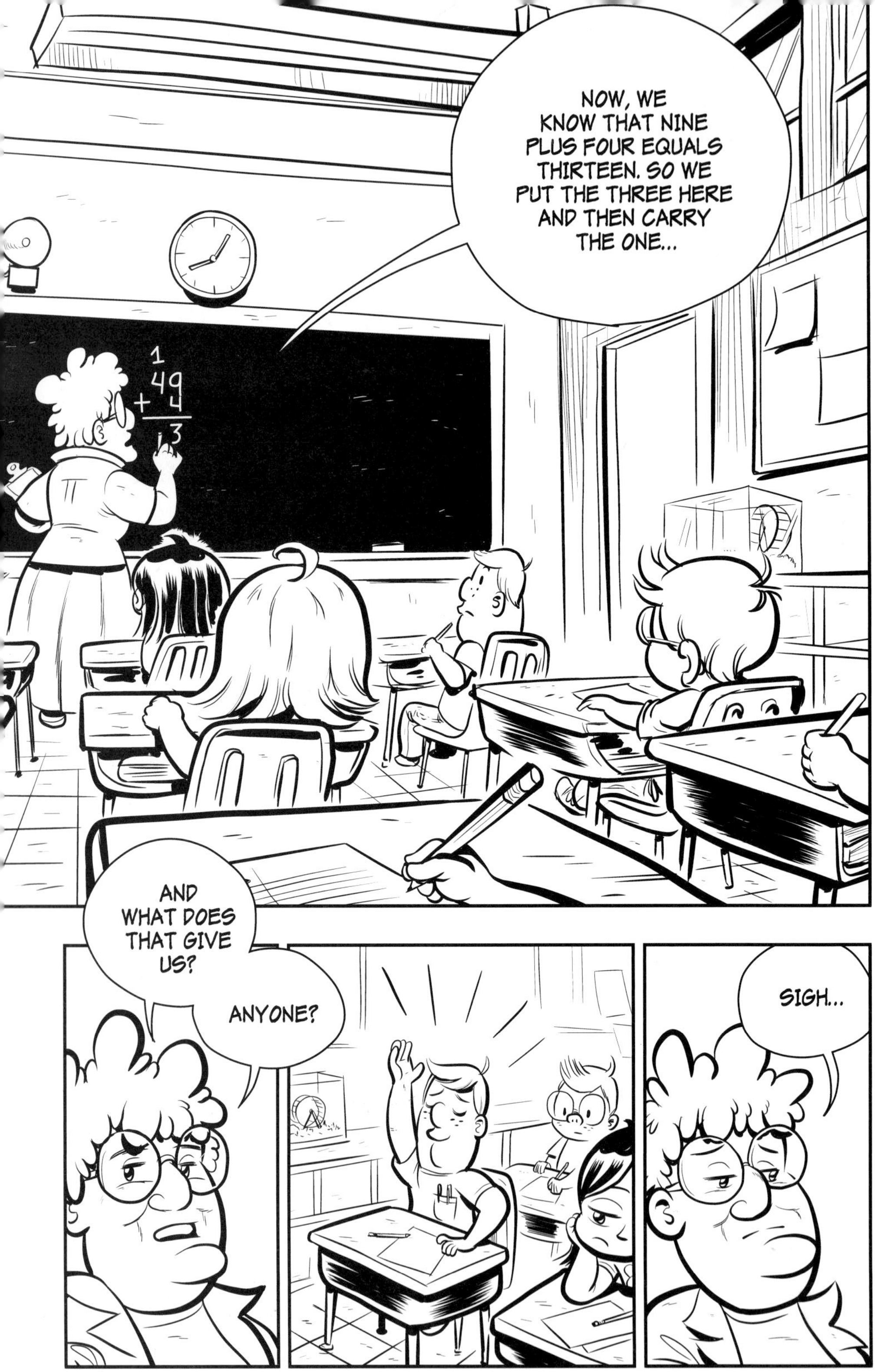
NOW, WE KNOW THAT NINE PLUS FOUR EQUALS THIRTEEN. SO WE PUT THE THREE HERE AND THEN CARRY THE ONE...
AND WHAT DOES THAT GIVE US?
ANYONE?
SIGH...

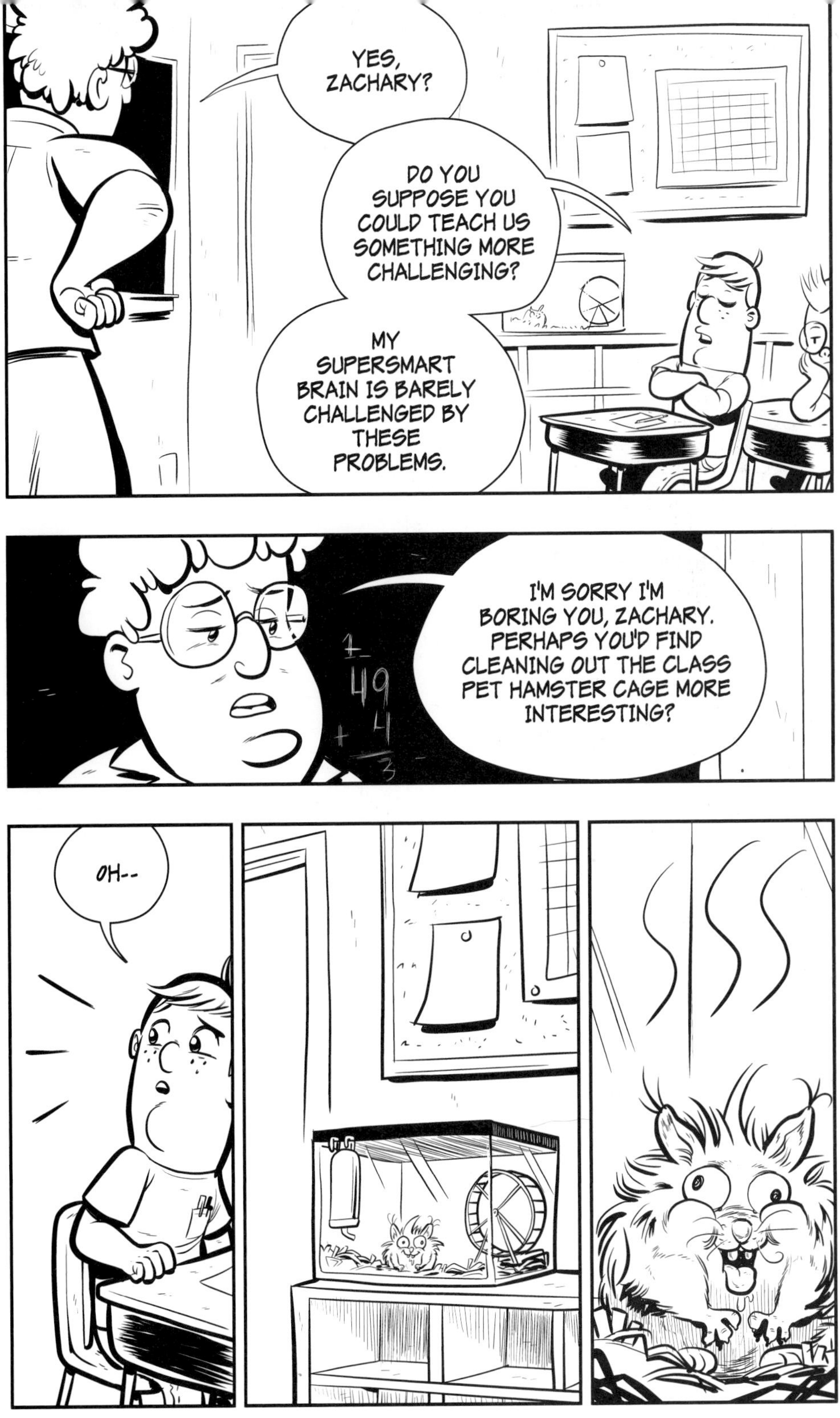
YES, ZACHARY?
DO YOU SUPPOSE YOU COULD TEACH US SOMETHING MORE CHALLENGING?
MY SUPERSMART BRAIN IS BARELY CHALLENGED BY THESE PROBLEMS.
I'M SORRY I'M BORING YOU, ZACHARY. PERHAPS YOU'D FIND CLEANING OUT THE CLASS PET HAMSTER CAGE MORE INTERESTING?
OH--

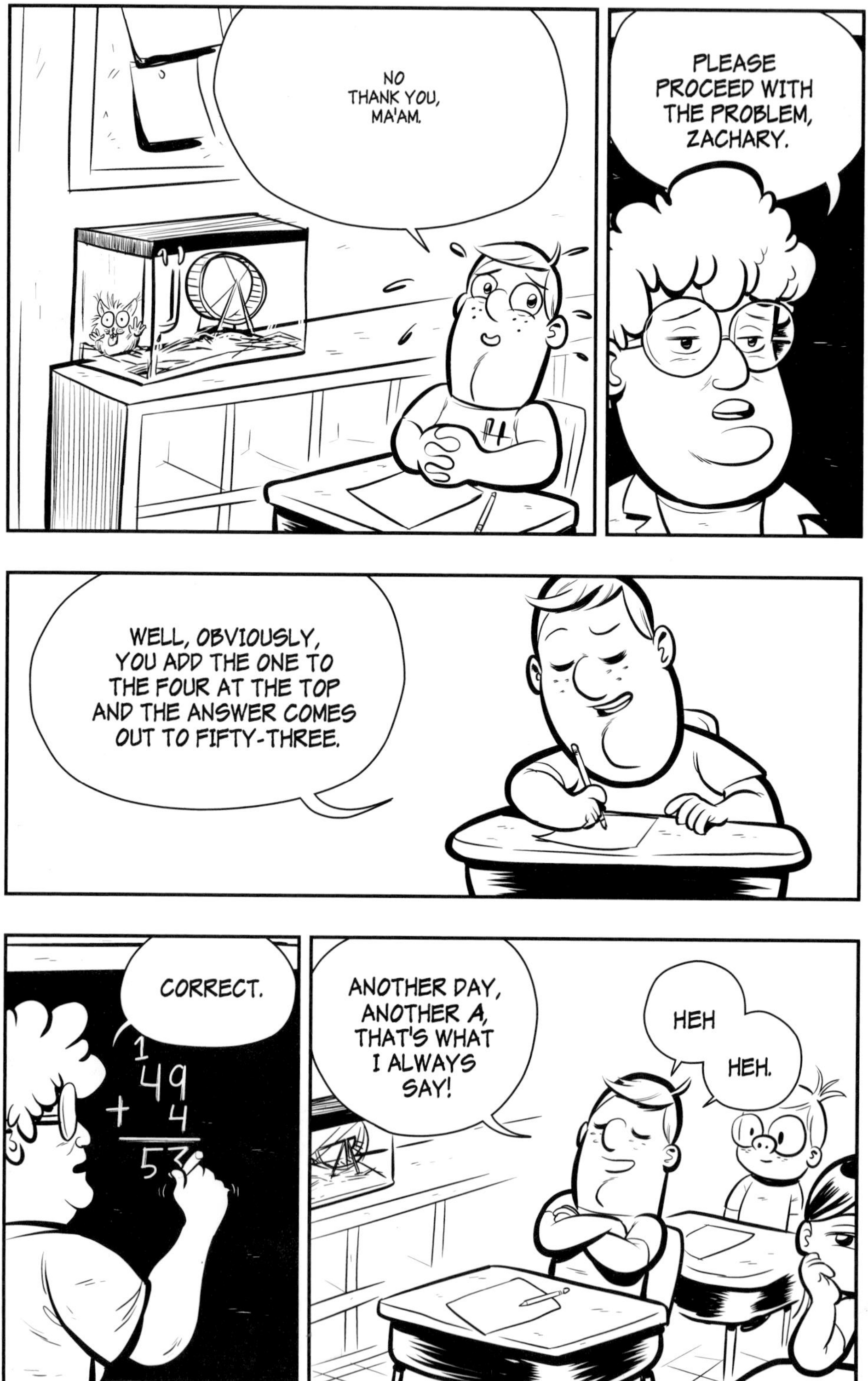
NO THANK YOU, MA'AM.
PLEASE PROCEED WITH THE PROBLEM, ZACHARY.
WELL, OBVIOUSLY, YOU ADD THE ONE TO THE FOUR AT THE TOP AND THE ANSWER COMES OUT TO FIFTY-THREE.
CORRECT.
1 49 + 4 53
ANOTHER DAY, ANOTHER A, THAT'S WHAT I ALWAYS SAY!
HEH HEH.

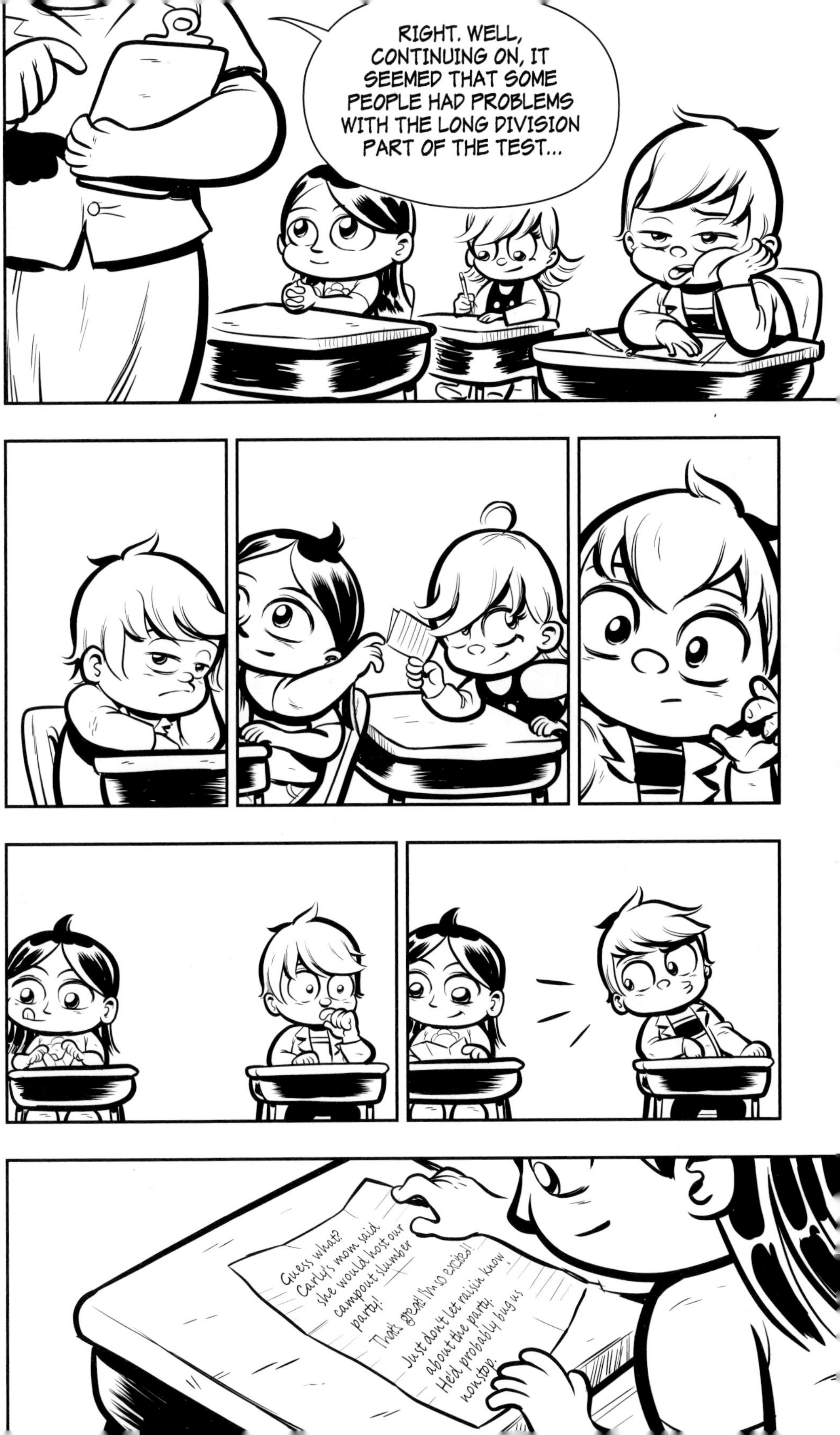
RIGHT. WELL, CONTINUING ON, IT SEEMED THAT SOME PEOPLE HAD PROBLEMS WITH THE LONG DIVISION PART OF THE TEST...
Guess what? Carly's mom said she would host our campout slumber party!
That's great! I'm so excited!
Just don't let raisin know about the party. He'd probably bug us nonstop.

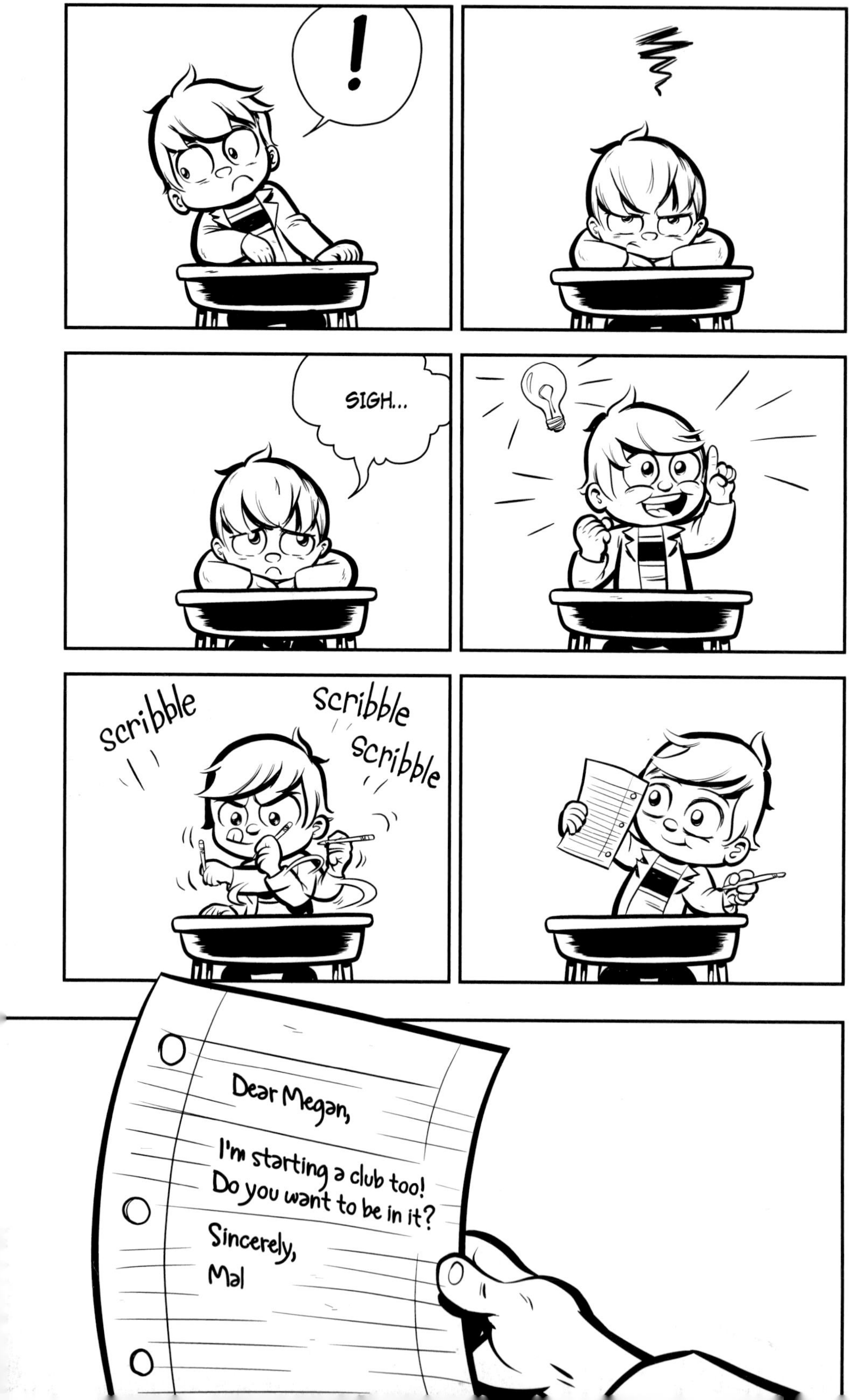
!
SIGH...
scribble
scribble
scribble
Dear Megan,
I'm starting a club too!
Do you want to be in it?
Sincerely,
Mal

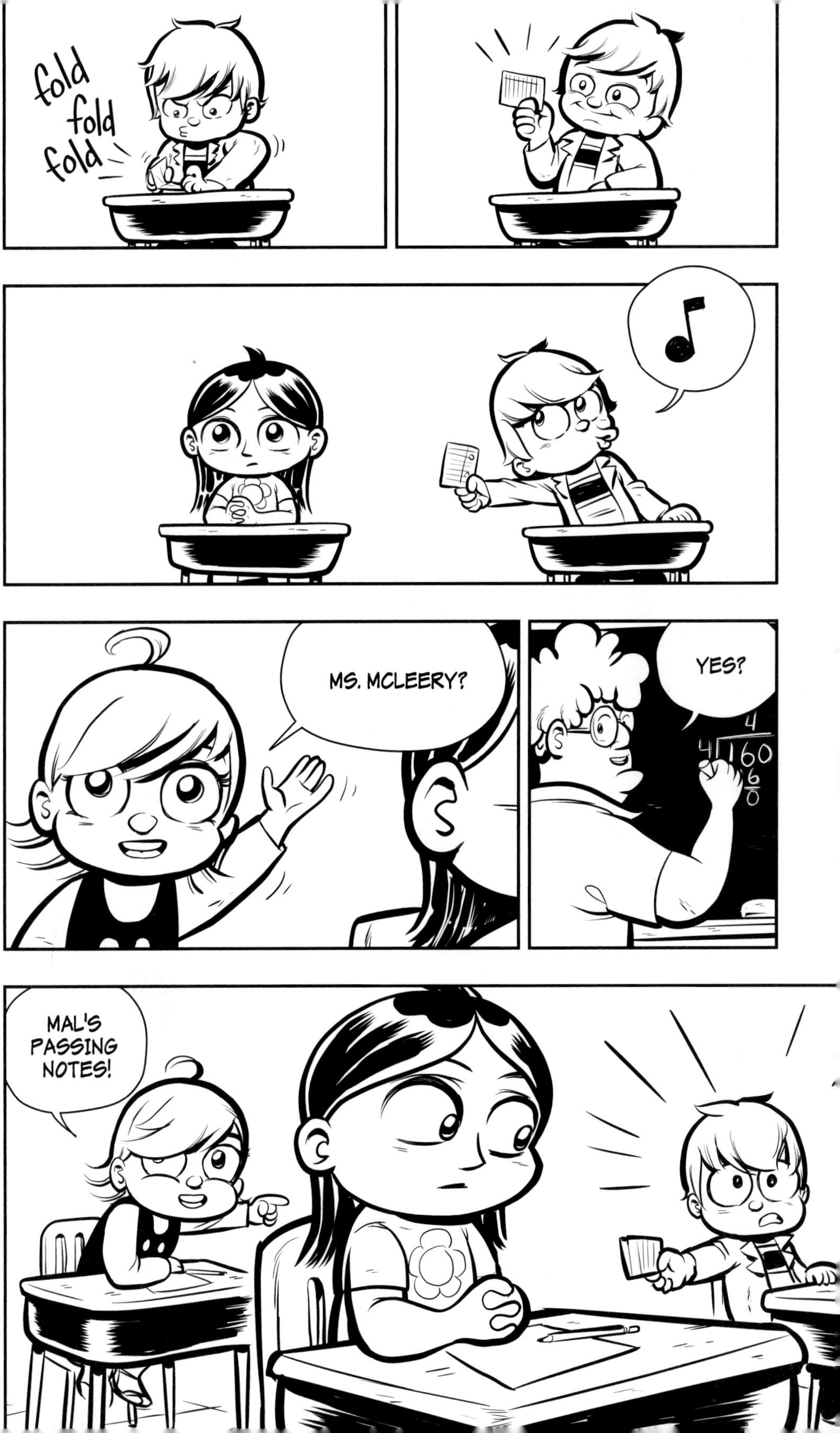
fold
fold
fold
MS. MCLEERY?
YES?
MAL'S PASSING NOTES!

MALCOM, YOU KNOW WHAT THE PUNISHMENT FOR PASSING NOTES IN CLASS IS, DON'T YOU?
gulp

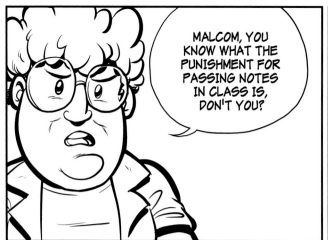

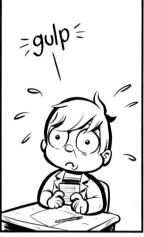

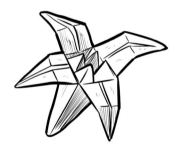

CHAPTER 2
Nightmare Monster

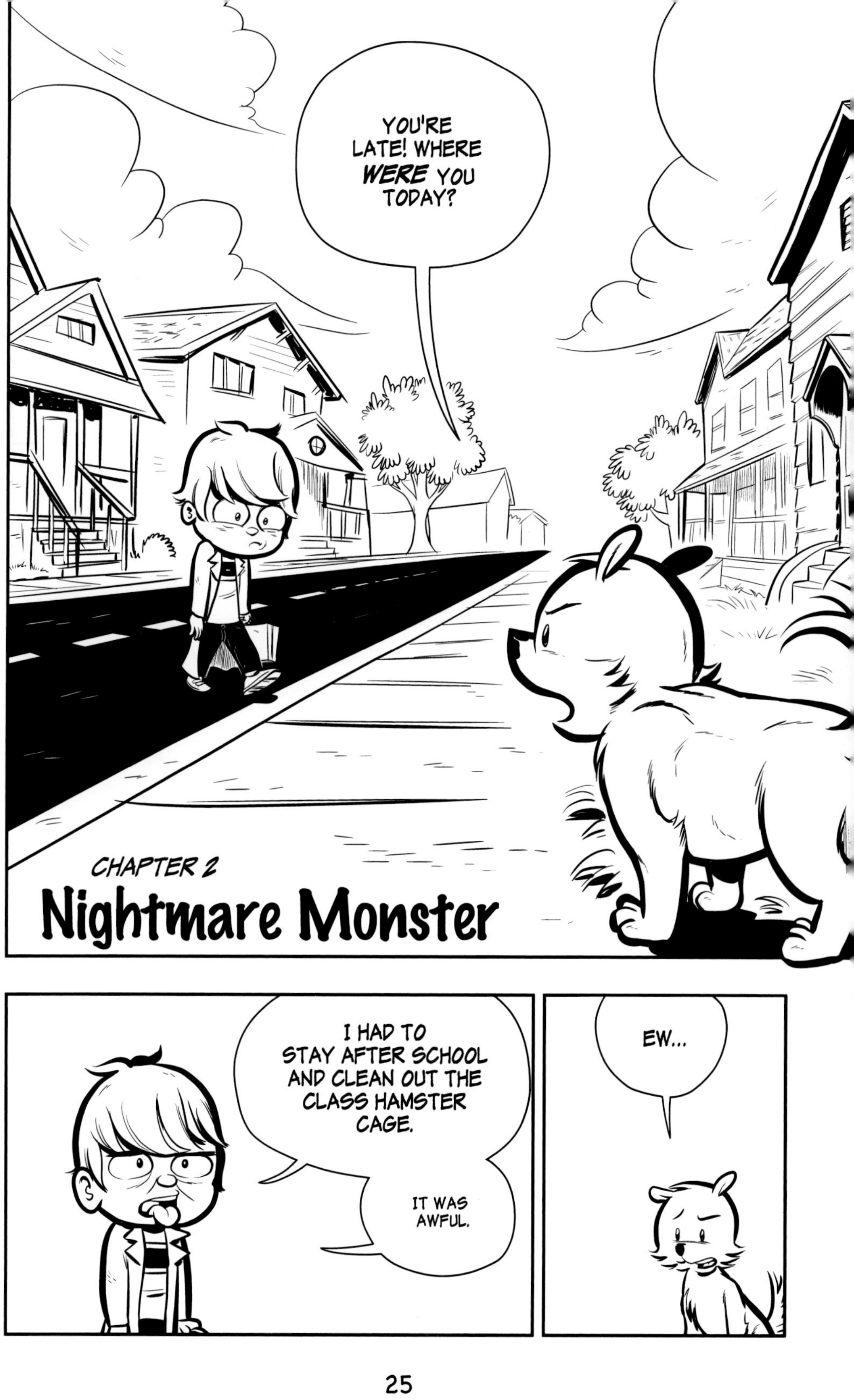
YOU'RE LATE! WHERE WERE YOU TODAY?
I HAD TO STAY AFTER SCHOOL AND CLEAN OUT THE CLASS HAMSTER CAGE.
IT WAS AWFUL.
EW...

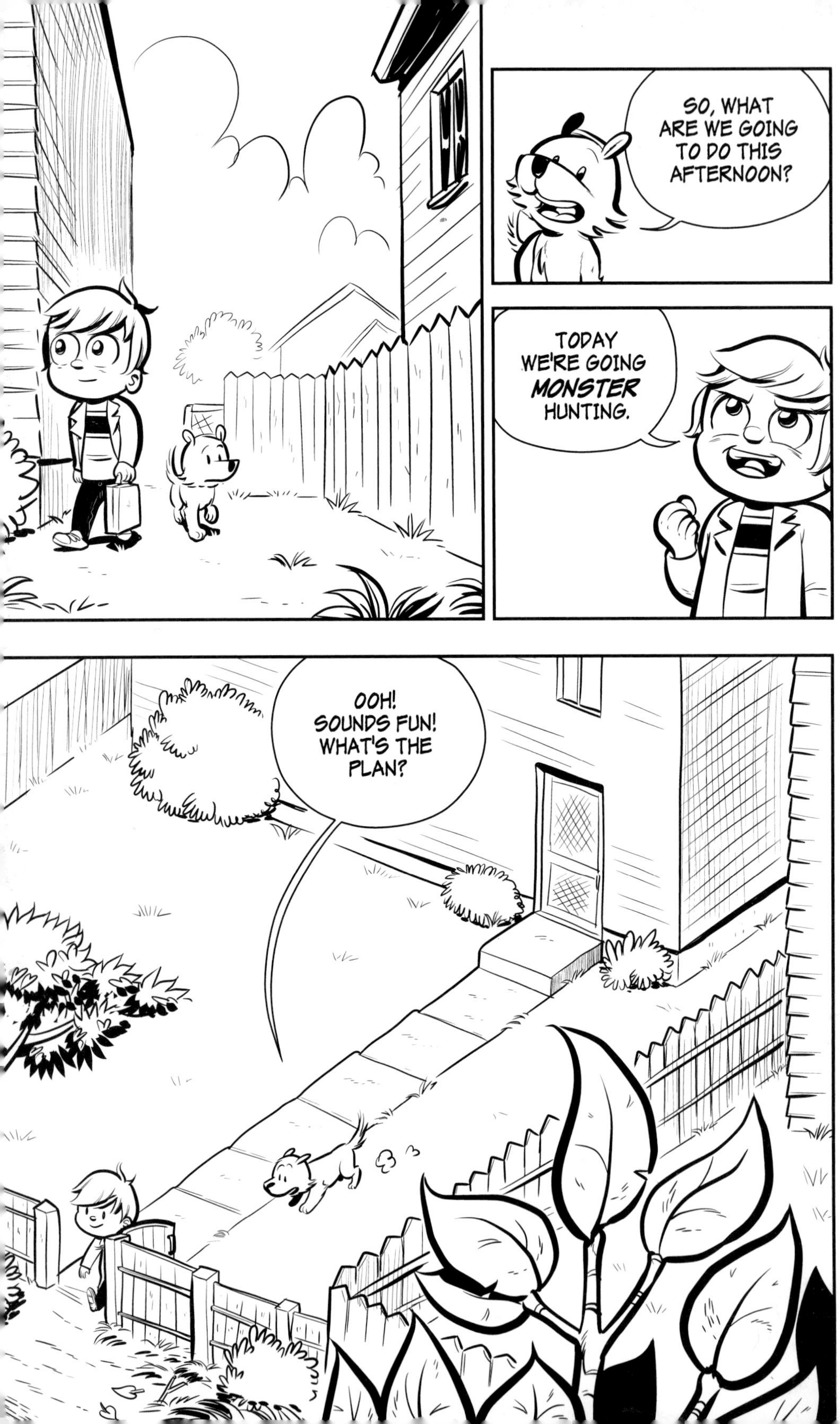
SO, WHAT ARE WE GOING TO DO THIS AFTERNOON?
TODAY WE'RE GOING MONSTER HUNTING.
OOH! SOUNDS FUN! WHAT'S THE PLAN?

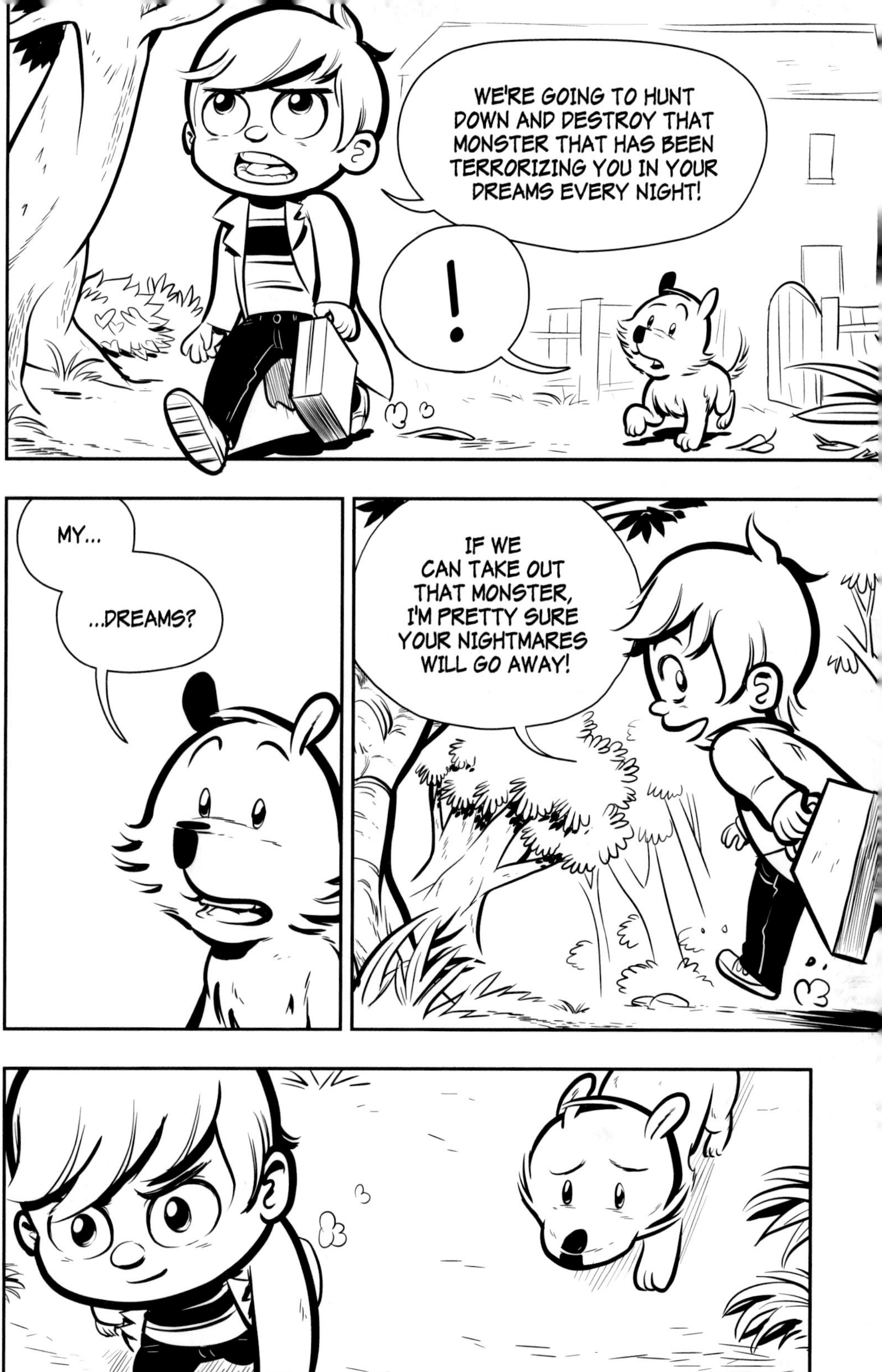
WE'RE GOING TO HUNT DOWN AND DESTROY THAT MONSTER THAT HAS BEEN TERRORIZING YOU IN YOUR DREAMS EVERY NIGHT!
!
MY...
...DREAMS?
IF WE CAN TAKE OUT THAT MONSTER, I'M PRETTY SURE YOUR NIGHTMARES WILL GO AWAY!

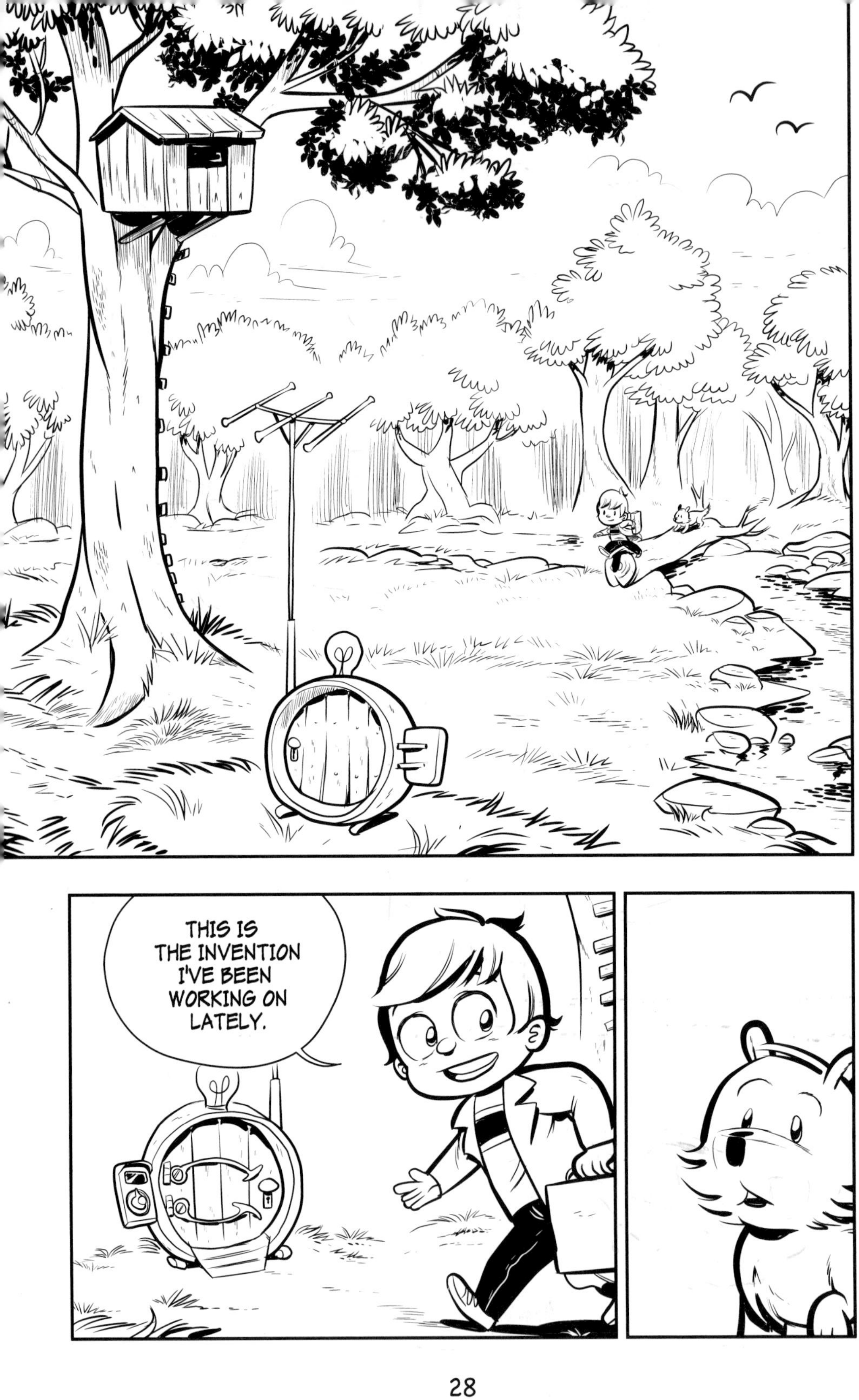
THIS IS THE INVENTION I'VE BEEN WORKING ON LATELY.

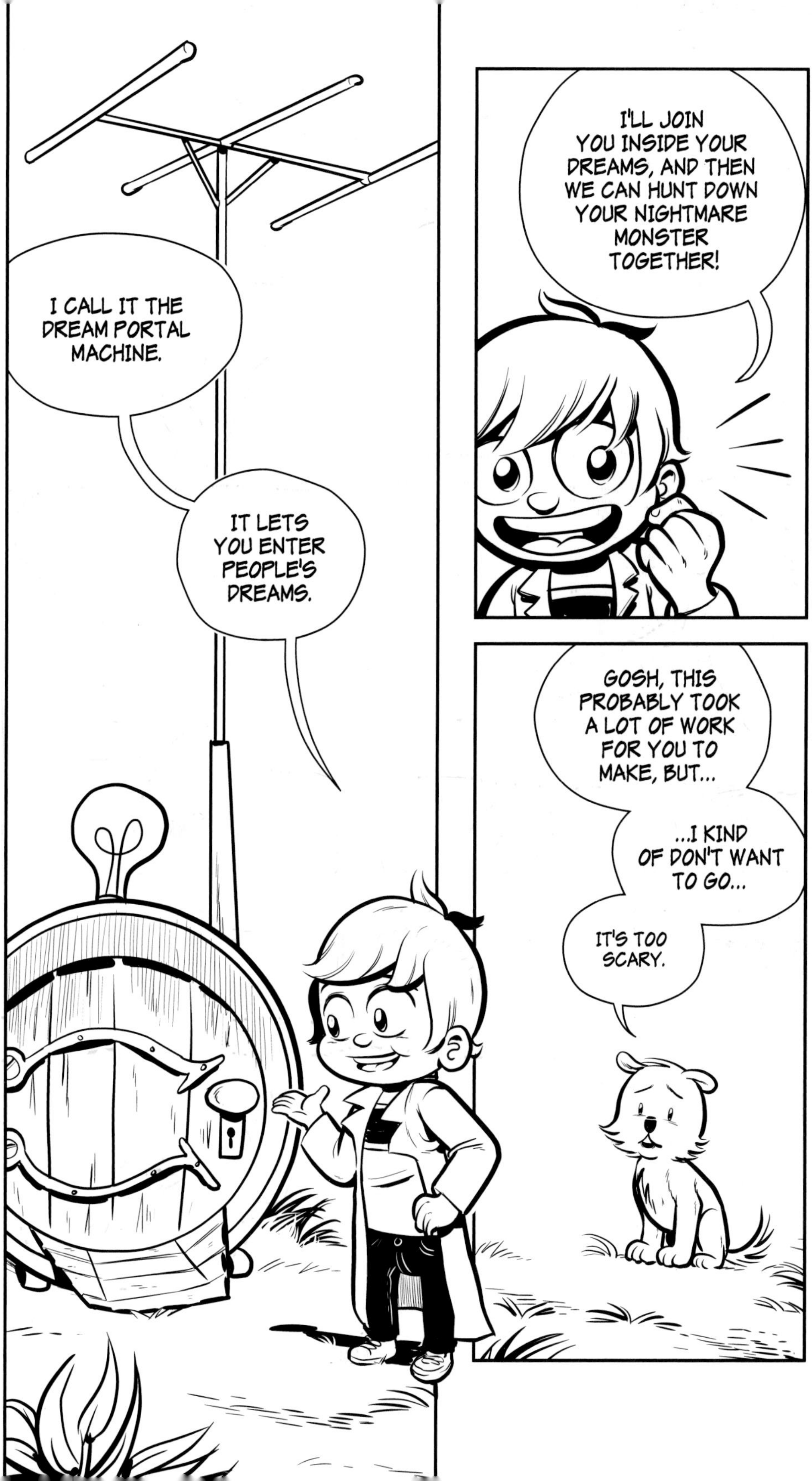
I CALL IT THE DREAM PORTAL MACHINE.
IT LETS YOU ENTER PEOPLE'S DREAMS.
I'LL JOIN YOU INSIDE YOUR DREAMS, AND THEN WE CAN HUNT DOWN YOUR NIGHTMARE MONSTER TOGETHER!
GOSH, THIS PROBABLY TOOK A LOT OF WORK FOR YOU TO MAKE, BUT...
...I KIND OF DON'T WANT TO GO...
IT'S TOO SCARY.

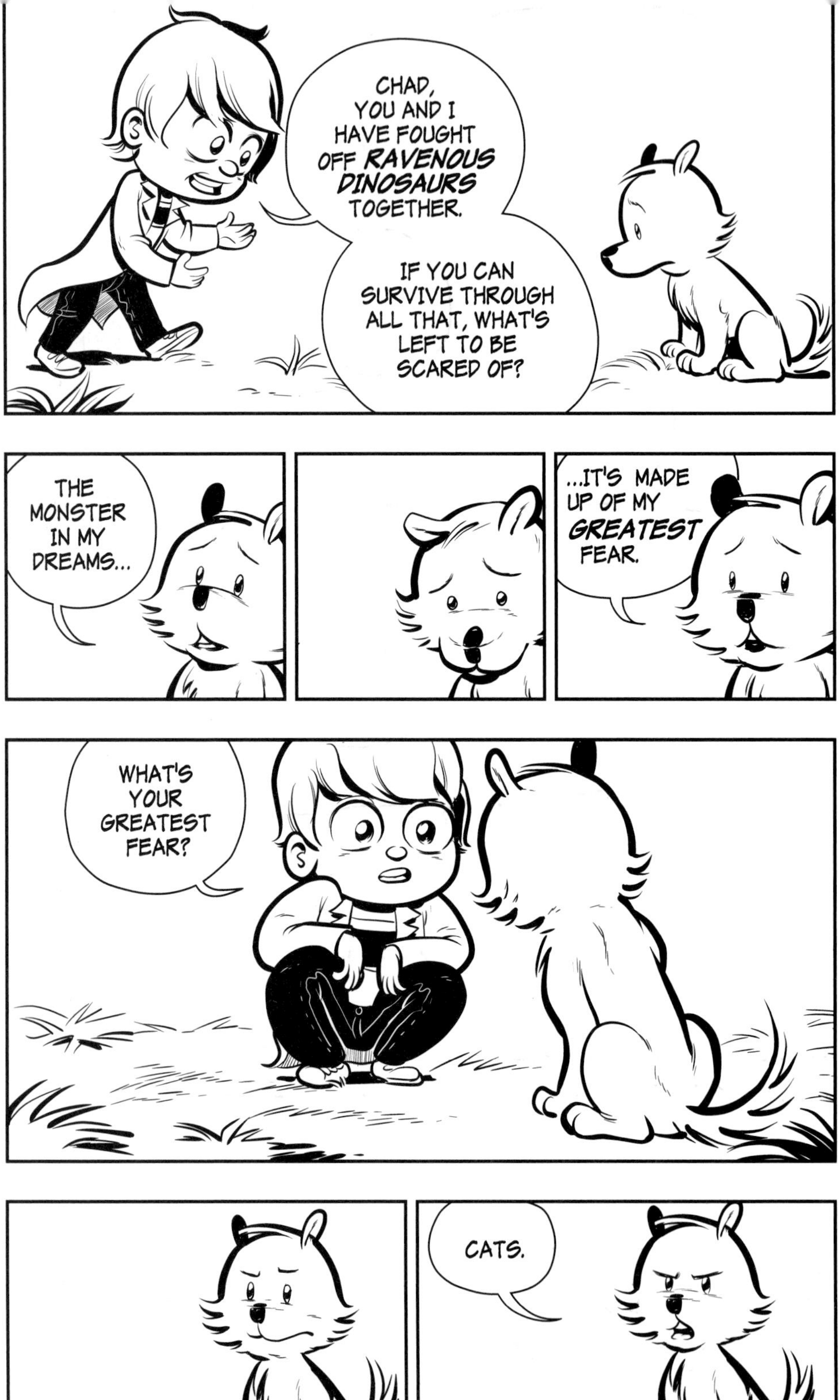
CHAD, YOU AND I HAVE FOUGHT OFF RAVENOUS DINOSAURS TOGETHER.
IF YOU CAN SURVIVE THROUGH ALL THAT, WHAT'S LEFT TO BE SCARED OF?
THE MONSTER IN MY DREAMS...
...IT'S MADE UP OF MY GREATEST FEAR.
WHAT'S YOUR GREATEST FEAR?
CATS.

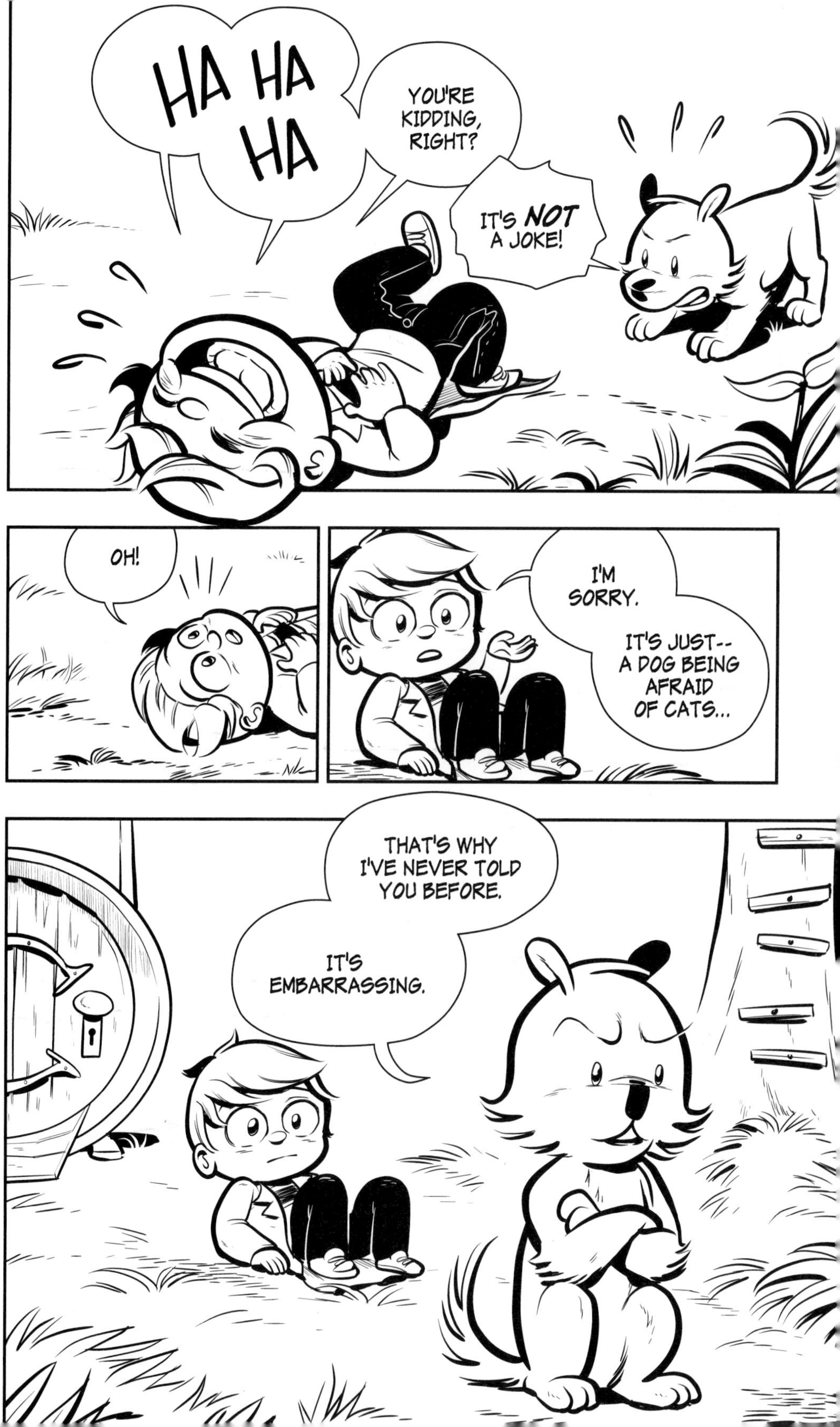
HA HA HA
YOU'RE KIDDING, RIGHT?
IT'S NOT A JOKE!
OH!
I'M SORRY.
IT'S JUST-- A DOG BEING AFRAID OF CATS...
THAT'S WHY I'VE NEVER TOLD YOU BEFORE.
IT'S EMBARRASSING.

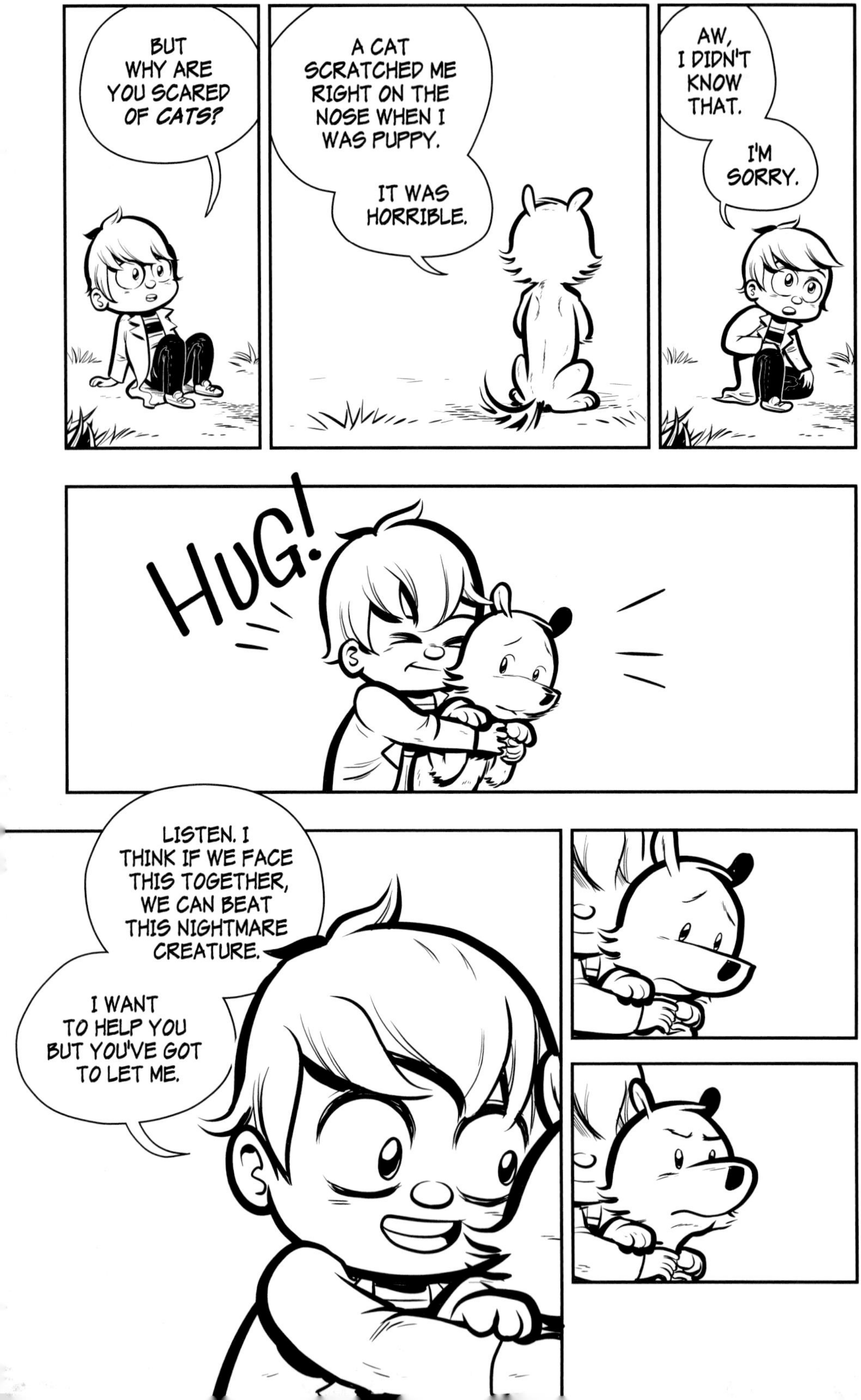
BUT WHY ARE YOU SCARED OF *CATS?*
A CAT SCRATCHED ME RIGHT ON THE NOSE WHEN I WAS PUPPY.
IT WAS HORRIBLE.
AW, I DIDN'T KNOW THAT.
I'M SORRY.
HUG!
LISTEN. I THINK IF WE FACE THIS TOGETHER, WE CAN BEAT THIS NIGHTMARE CREATURE.
I WANT TO HELP YOU BUT YOU'VE GOT TO LET ME.

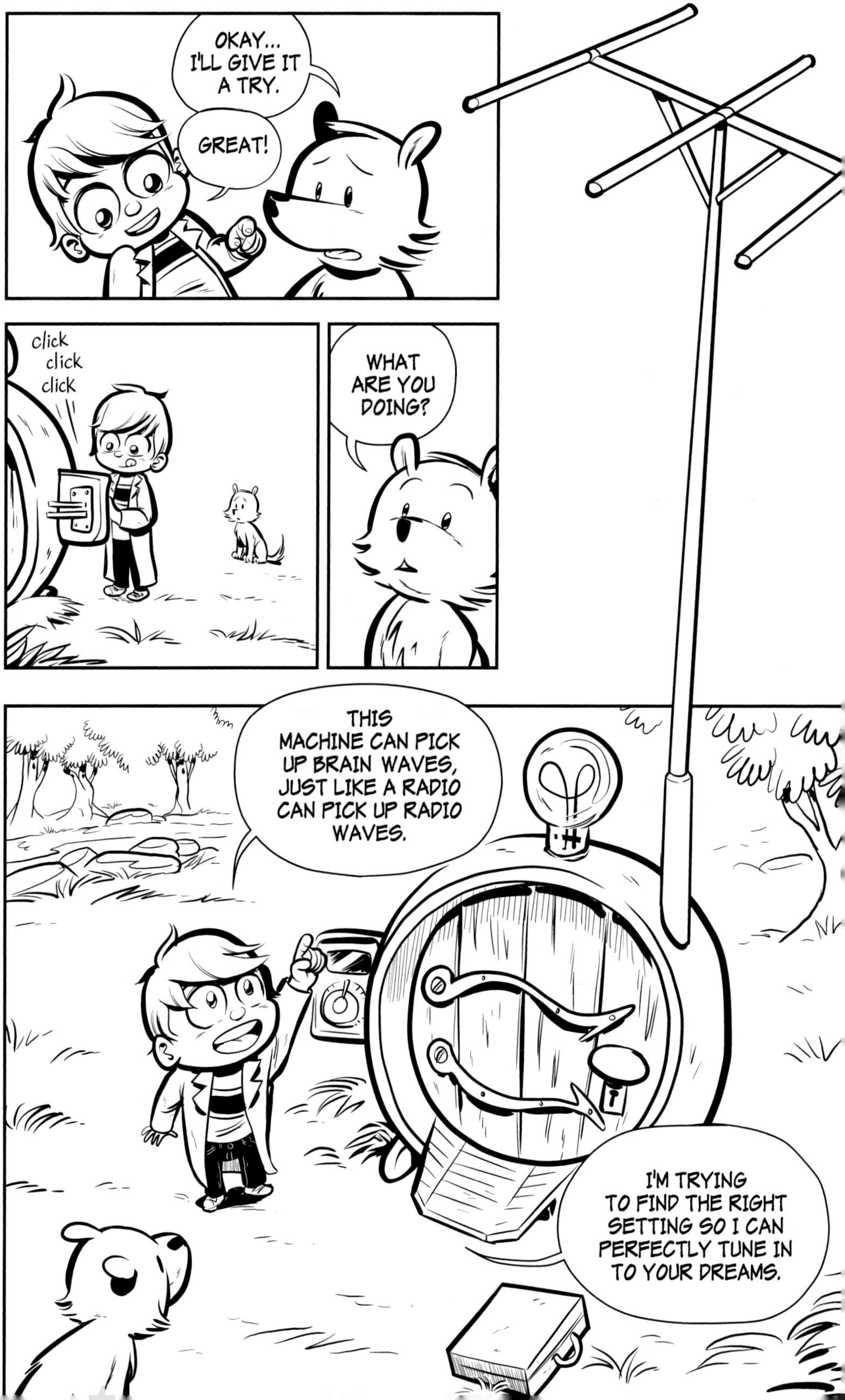
OKAY... I'LL GIVE IT A TRY.
GREAT!
click click click
WHAT ARE YOU DOING?
THIS MACHINE CAN PICK UP BRAIN WAVES, JUST LIKE A RADIO CAN PICK UP RADIO WAVES.
I'M TRYING TO FIND THE RIGHT SETTING SO I CAN PERFECTLY TUNE IN TO YOUR DREAMS.

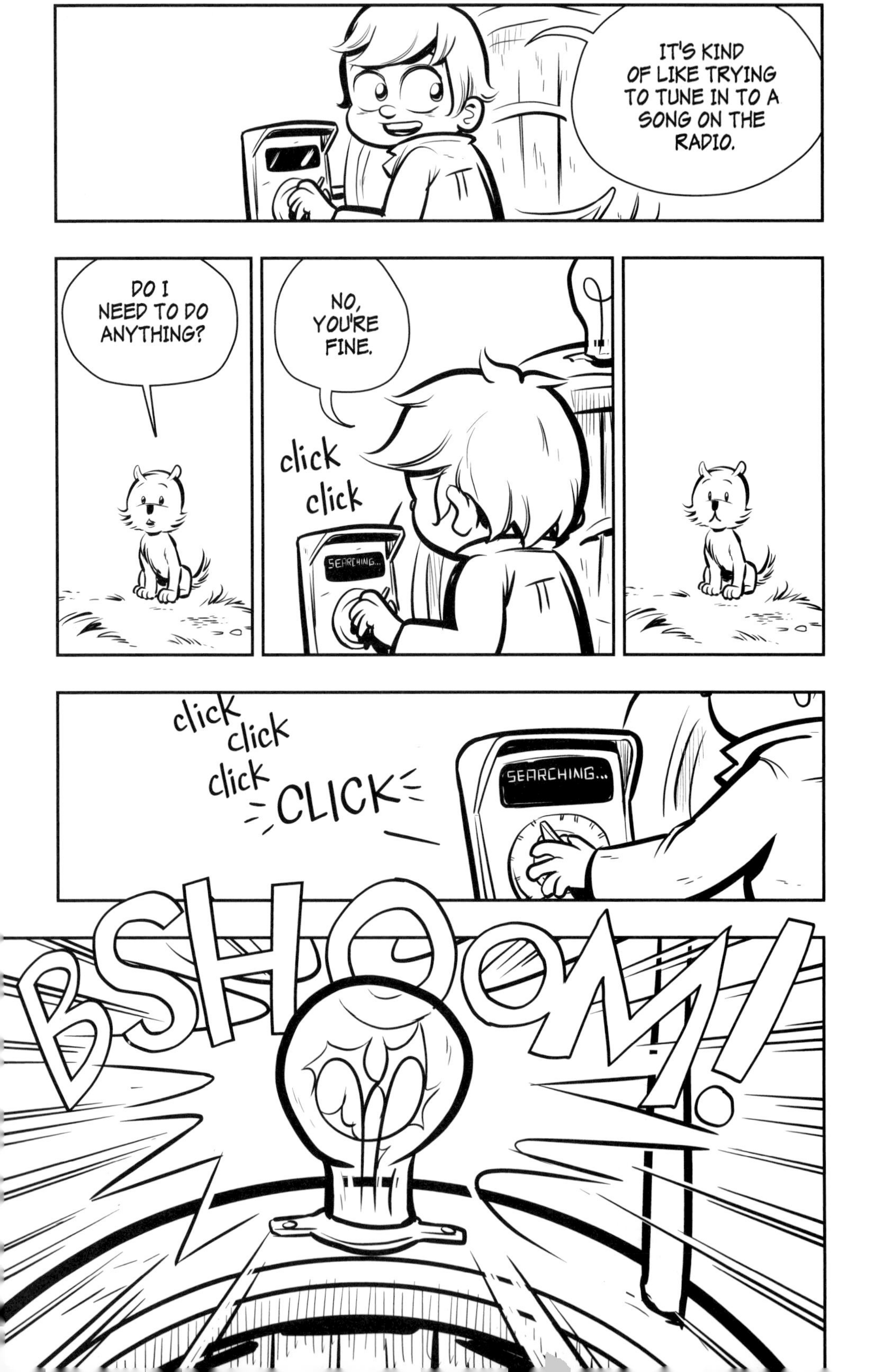
IT'S KIND OF LIKE TRYING TO TUNE IN TO A SONG ON THE RADIO.
DO I NEED TO DO ANYTHING?
NO, YOU'RE FINE.
click click
SEARCHING...
click click click CLICK
SEARCHING...
BSHOOM!

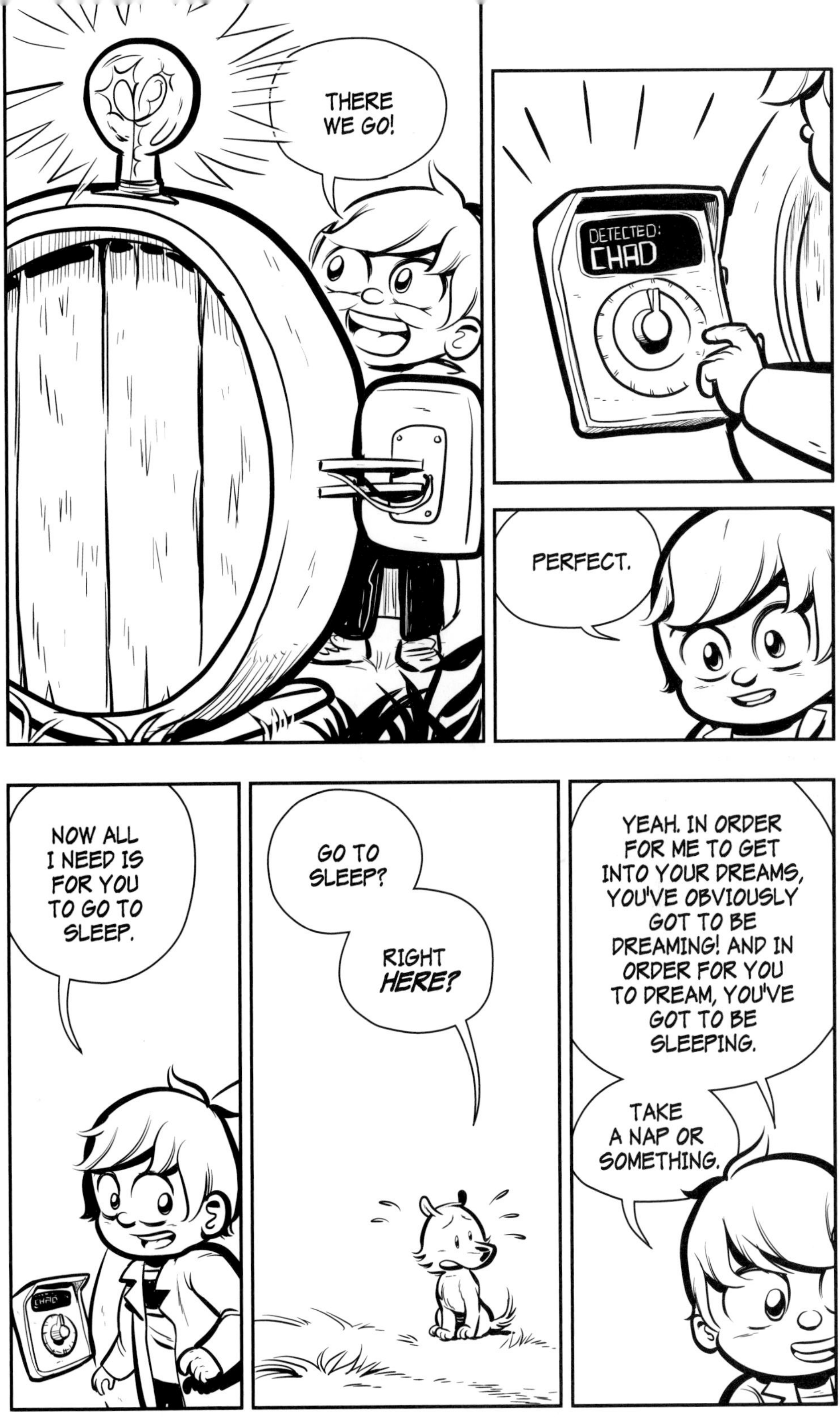
THERE WE GO!
DETECTED: CHAD
PERFECT.
NOW ALL I NEED IS FOR YOU TO GO TO SLEEP.
CHAD
GO TO SLEEP?
RIGHT *HERE?*
YEAH. IN ORDER FOR ME TO GET INTO YOUR DREAMS, YOU'VE OBVIOUSLY GOT TO BE DREAMING! AND IN ORDER FOR YOU TO DREAM, YOU'VE GOT TO BE SLEEPING.
TAKE A NAP OR SOMETHING.

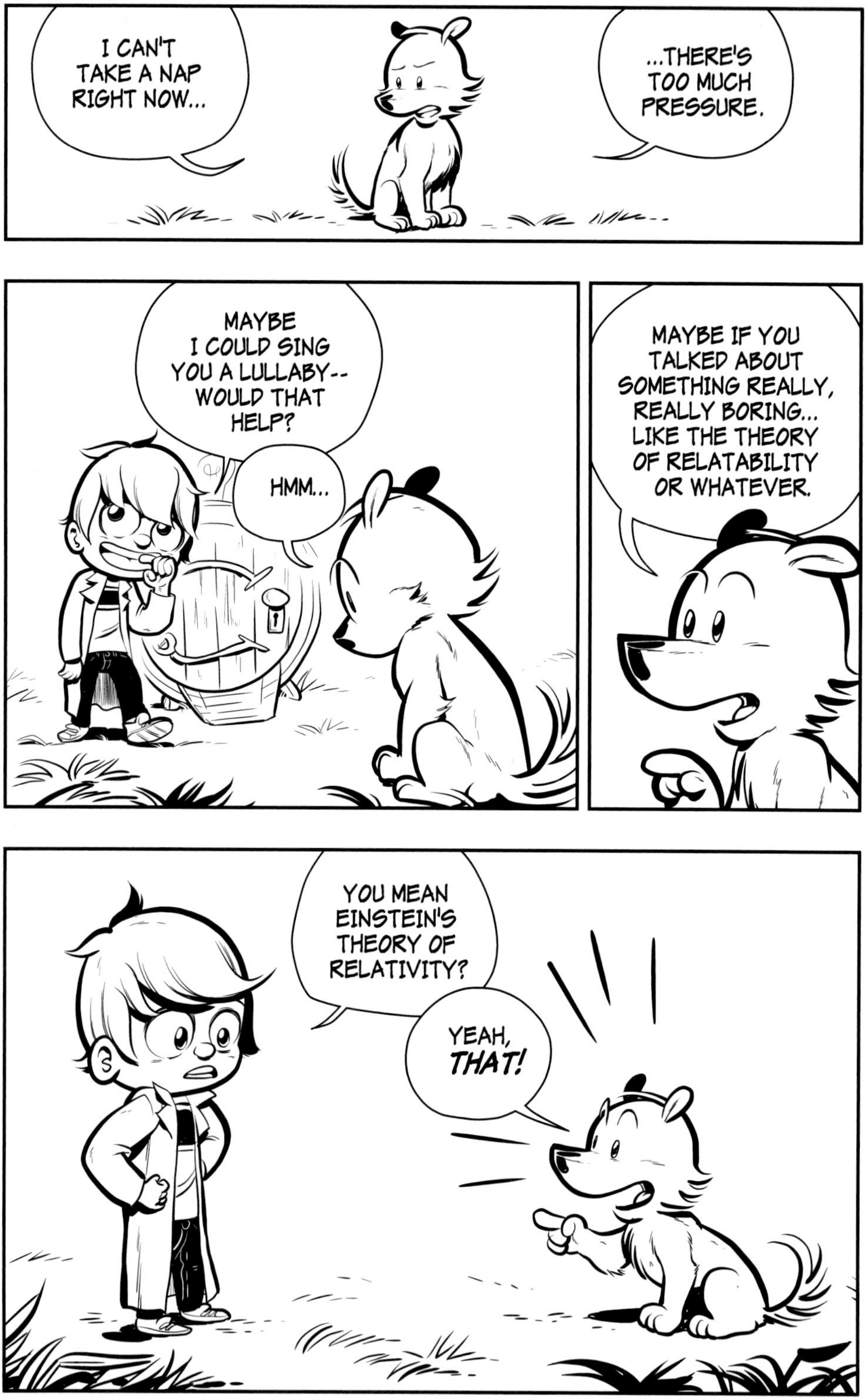
I CAN'T TAKE A NAP RIGHT NOW...
...THERE'S TOO MUCH PRESSURE.
MAYBE I COULD SING YOU A LULLABY-- WOULD THAT HELP?
HMM...
MAYBE IF YOU TALKED ABOUT SOMETHING REALLY, REALLY BORING... LIKE THE THEORY OF RELATABILITY OR WHATEVER.
YOU MEAN EINSTEIN'S THEORY OF RELATIVITY?
YEAH, *THAT!*

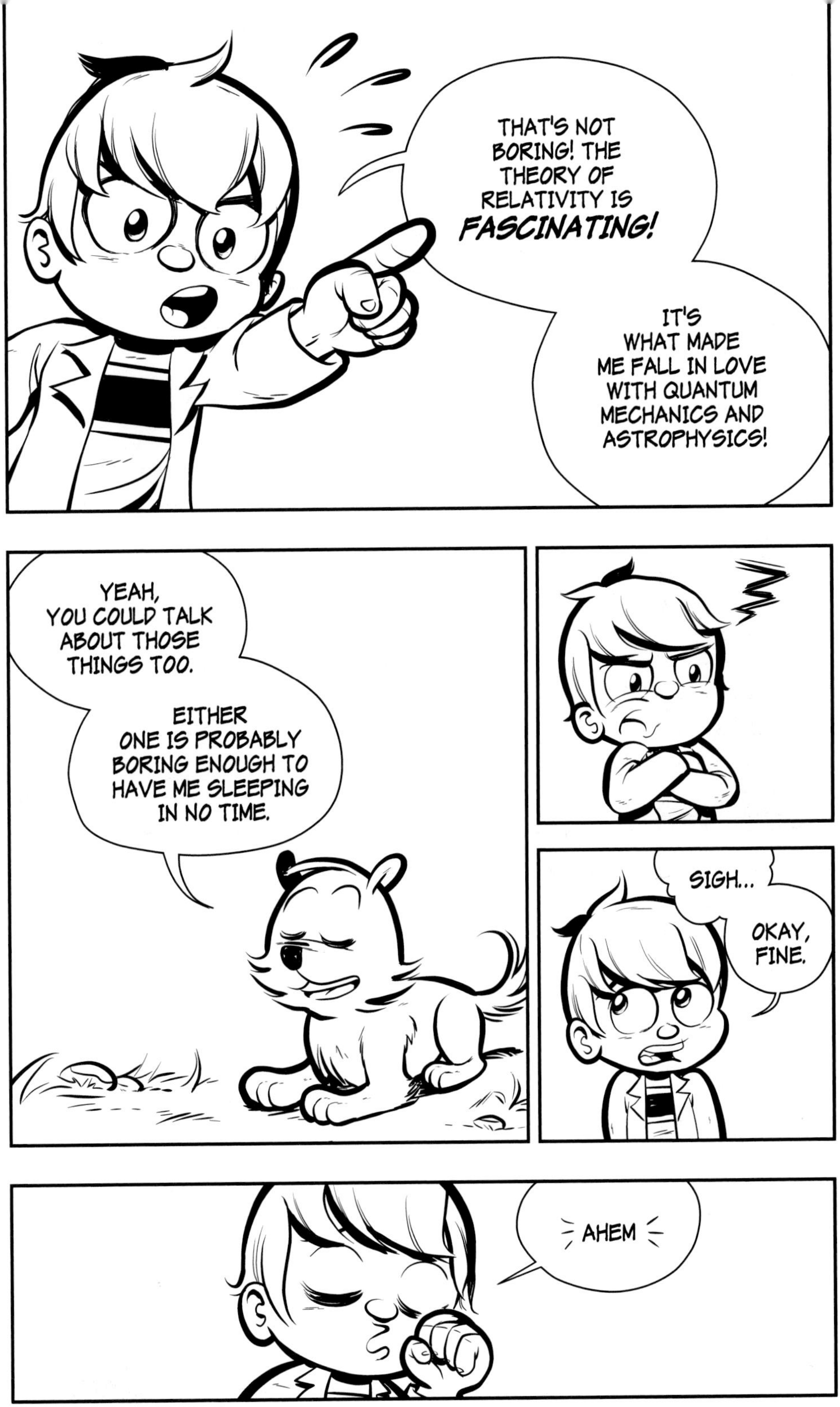
THAT'S NOT BORING! THE THEORY OF RELATIVITY IS *FASCINATING!*
IT'S WHAT MADE ME FALL IN LOVE WITH QUANTUM MECHANICS AND ASTROPHYSICS!
YEAH, YOU COULD TALK ABOUT THOSE THINGS TOO.
EITHER ONE IS PROBABLY BORING ENOUGH TO HAVE ME SLEEPING IN NO TIME.
SIGH...
OKAY, FINE.
AHEM

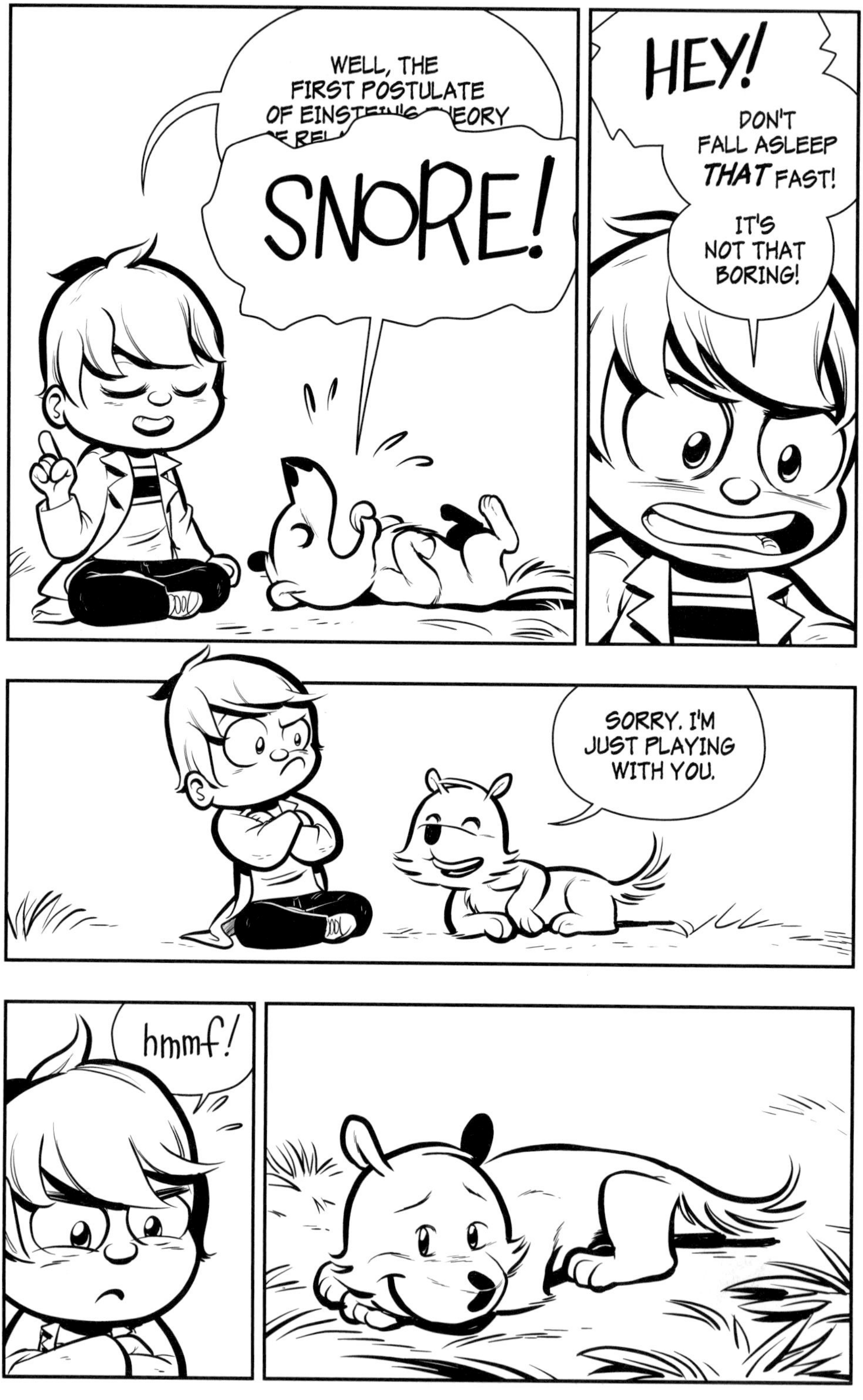
WELL, THE FIRST POSTULATE OF EINSTEIN'S THEORY
SNORE!
HEY!
DON'T FALL ASLEEP THAT FAST!
IT'S NOT THAT BORING!
SORRY. I'M JUST PLAYING WITH YOU.
hmmf!

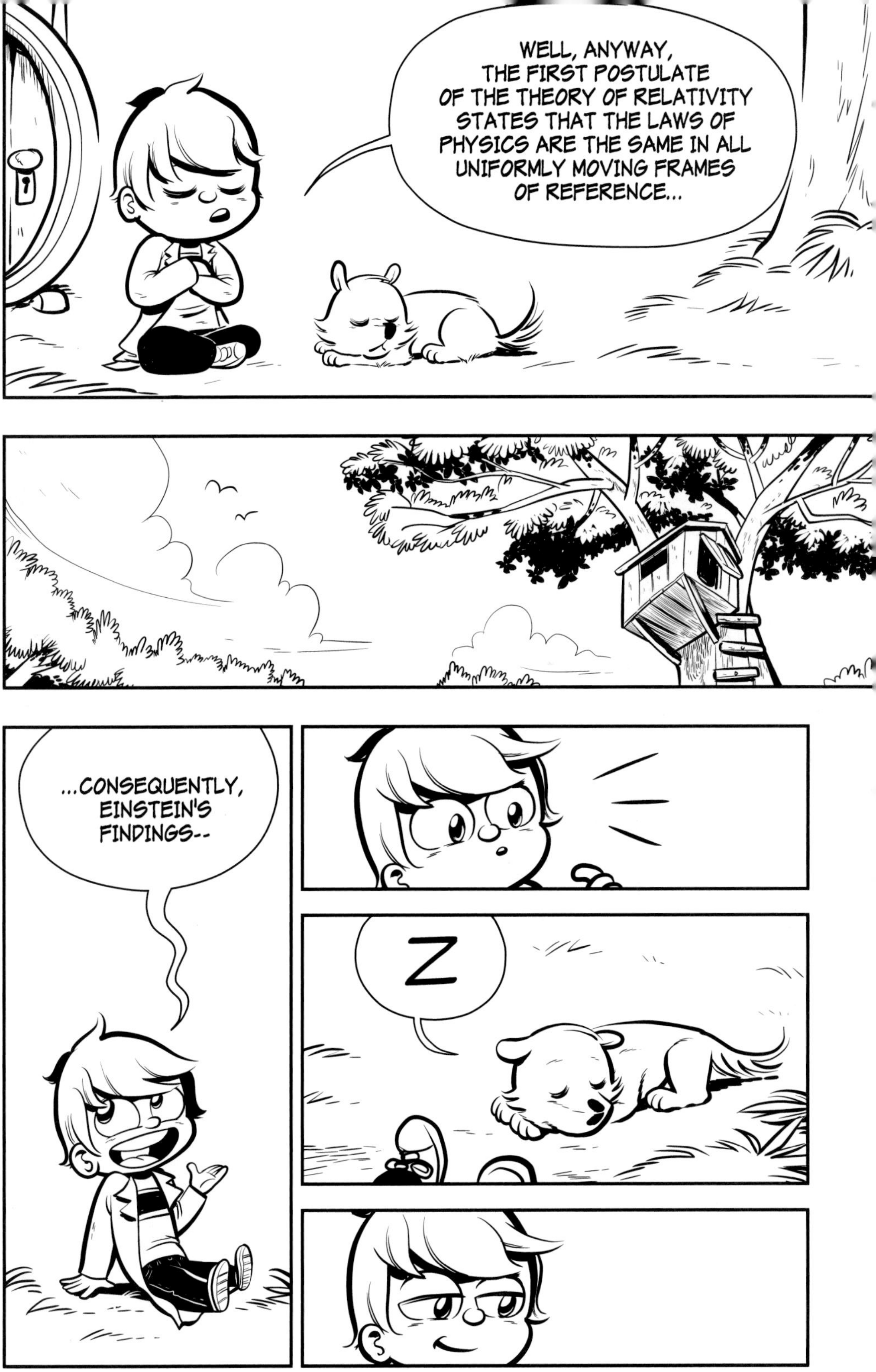

WELL, ANYWAY, THE FIRST POSTULATE OF THE THEORY OF RELATIVITY STATES THAT THE LAWS OF PHYSICS ARE THE SAME IN ALL UNIFORMLY MOVING FRAMES OF REFERENCE...
...CONSEQUENTLY, EINSTEIN'S FINDINGS--
Z

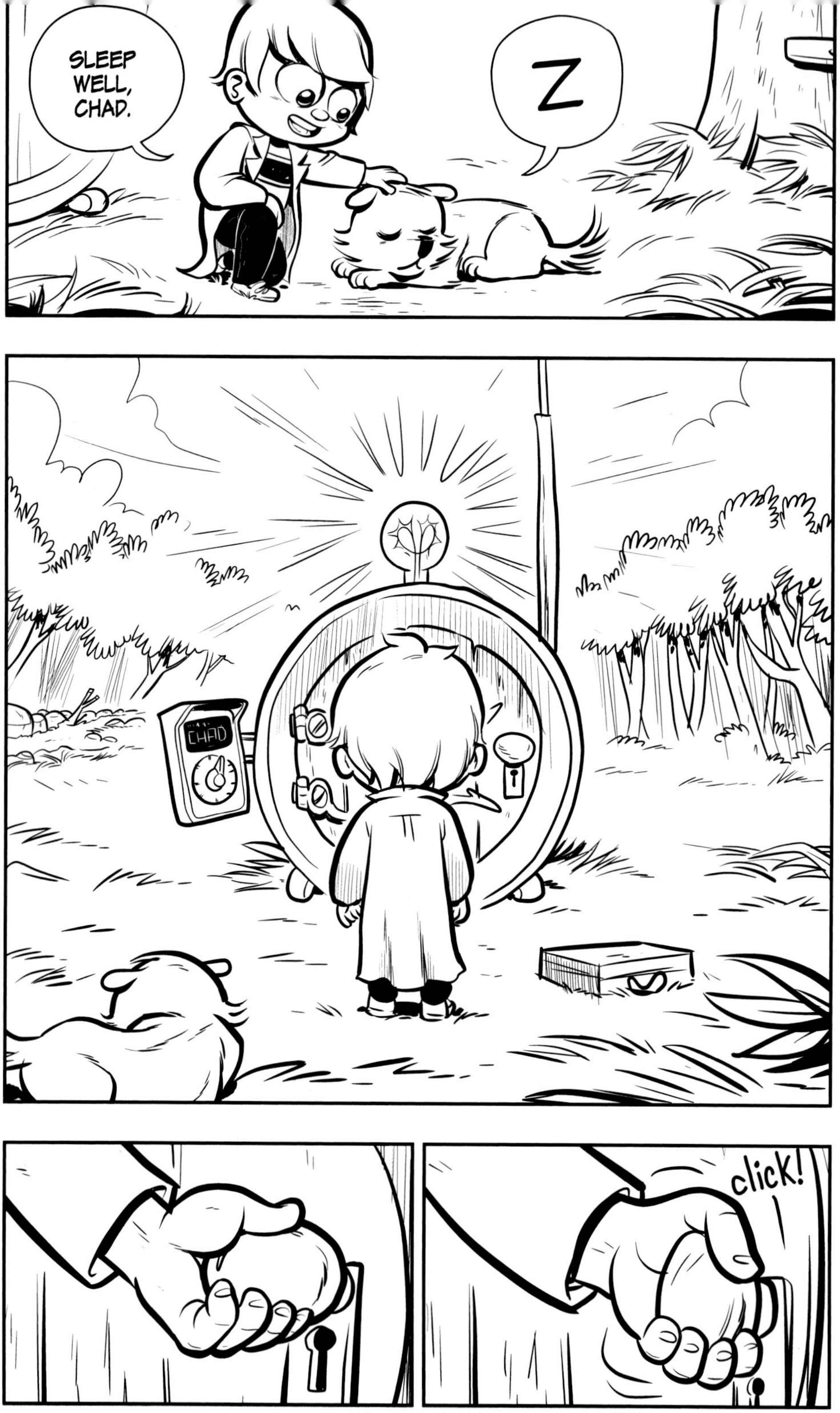
SLEEP WELL, CHAD.
Z
CHAD
click!

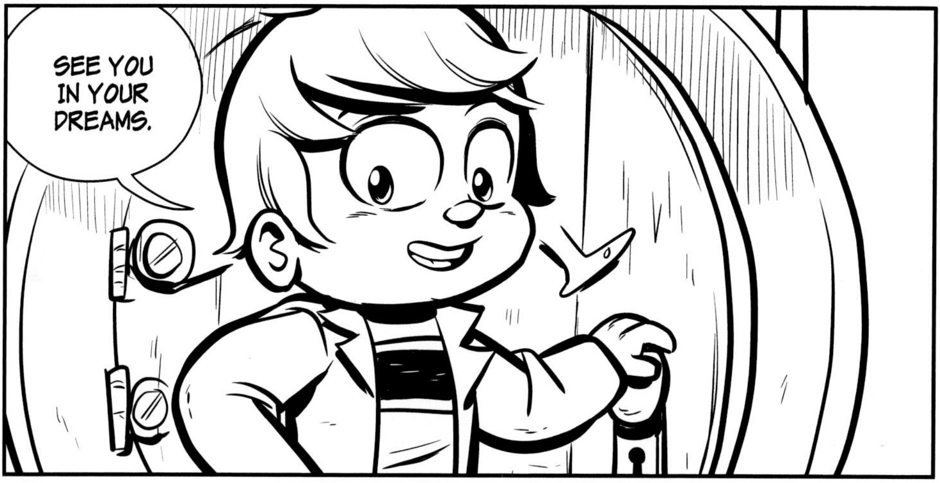
SEE YOU IN YOUR DREAMS.

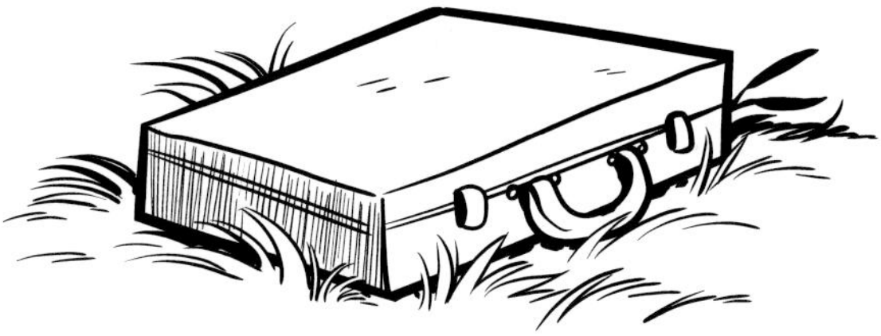

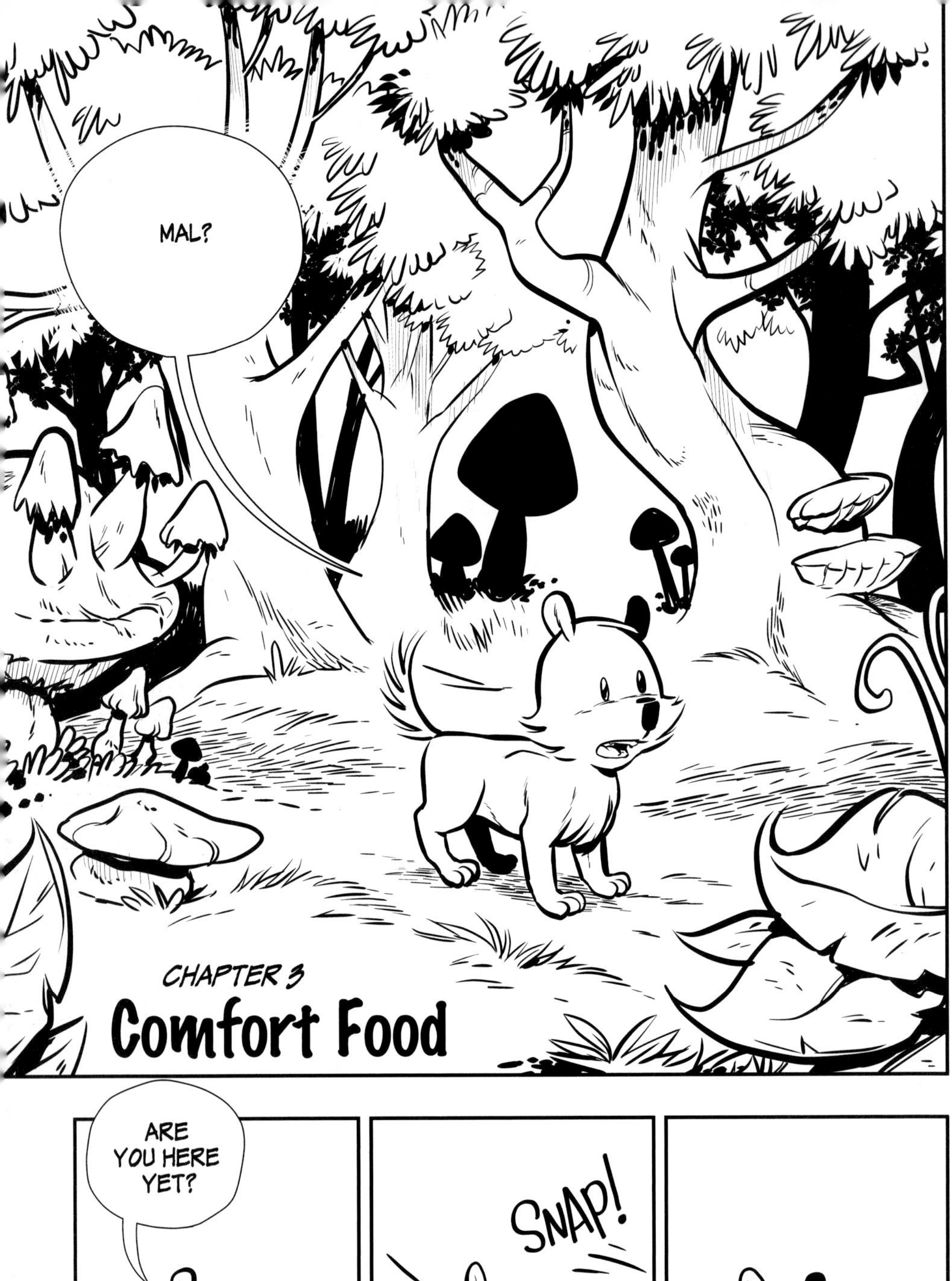
MAL?

CHAPTER 3
Comfort Food

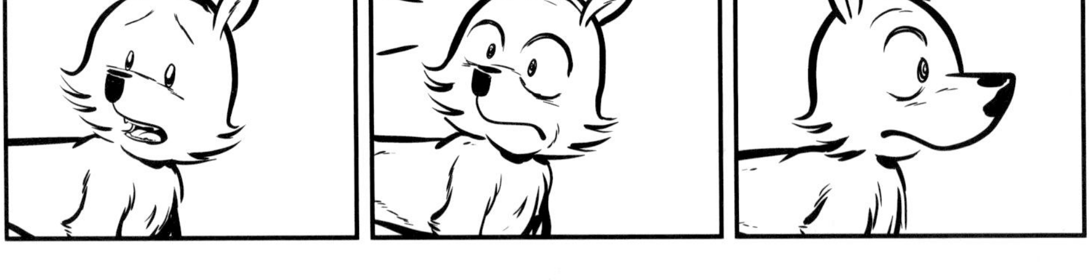
ARE YOU HERE YET?
SNAP!

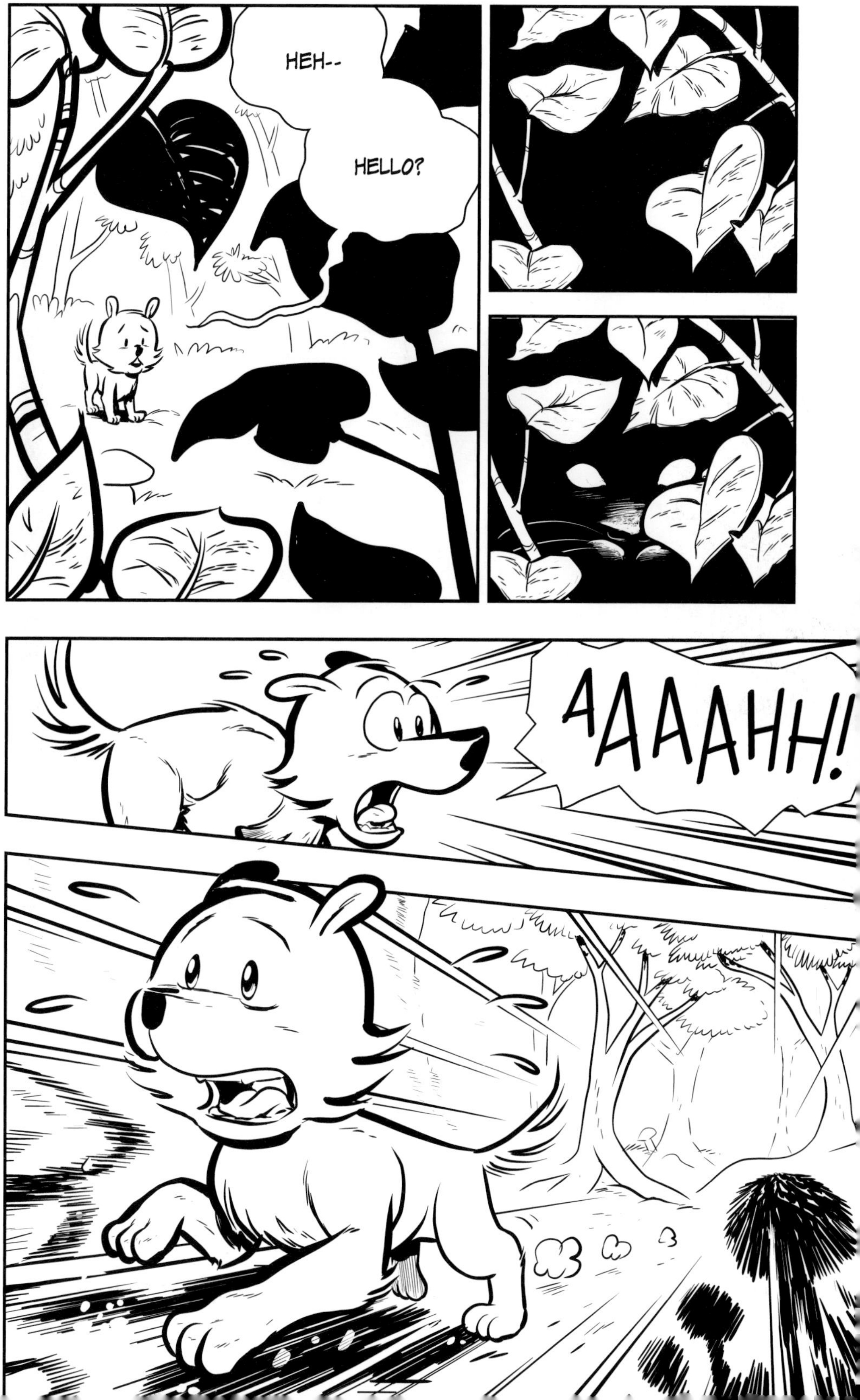
HEH--
HELLO?
AAAAHH!

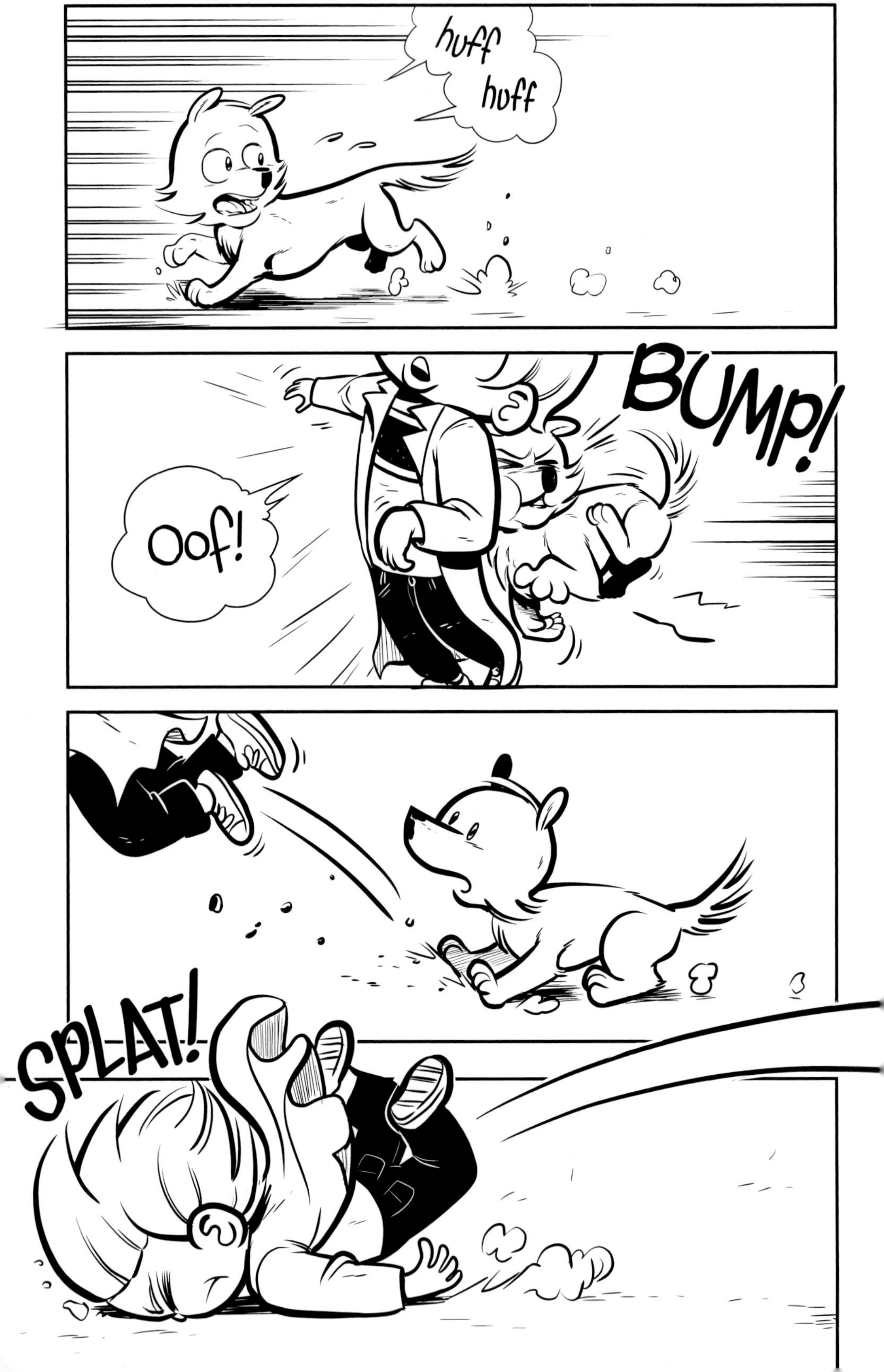
huff huff
BUMP!
Oof!
SPLAT!

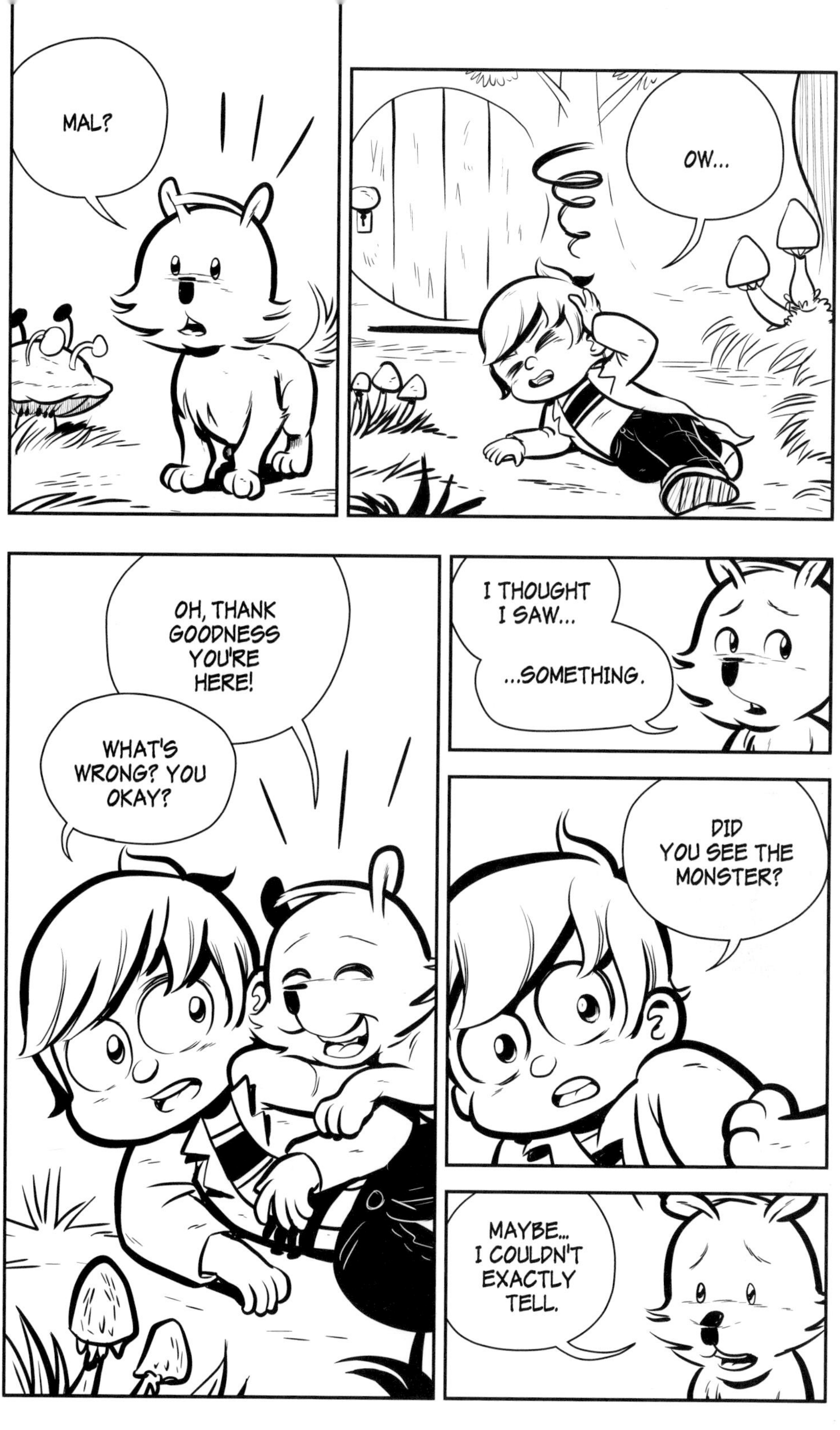
MAL?
OW...
OH, THANK GOODNESS YOU'RE HERE!
WHAT'S WRONG? YOU OKAY?
I THOUGHT I SAW...
...SOMETHING.
DID YOU SEE THE MONSTER?
MAYBE... I COULDN'T EXACTLY TELL.

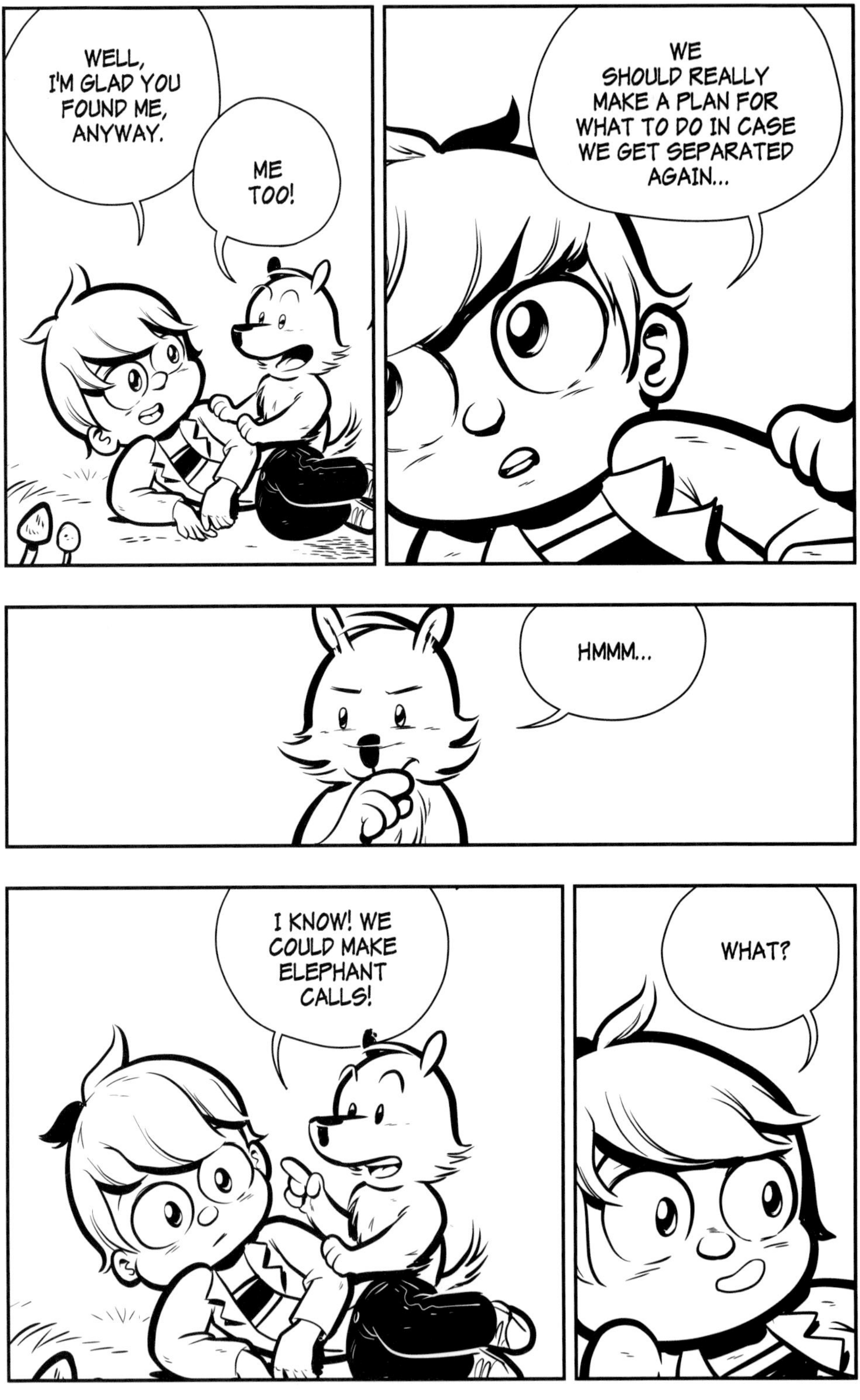
WELL, I'M GLAD YOU FOUND ME, ANYWAY.
ME TOO!
WE SHOULD REALLY MAKE A PLAN FOR WHAT TO DO IN CASE WE GET SEPARATED AGAIN...
HMMM...
I KNOW! WE COULD MAKE ELEPHANT CALLS!
WHAT?

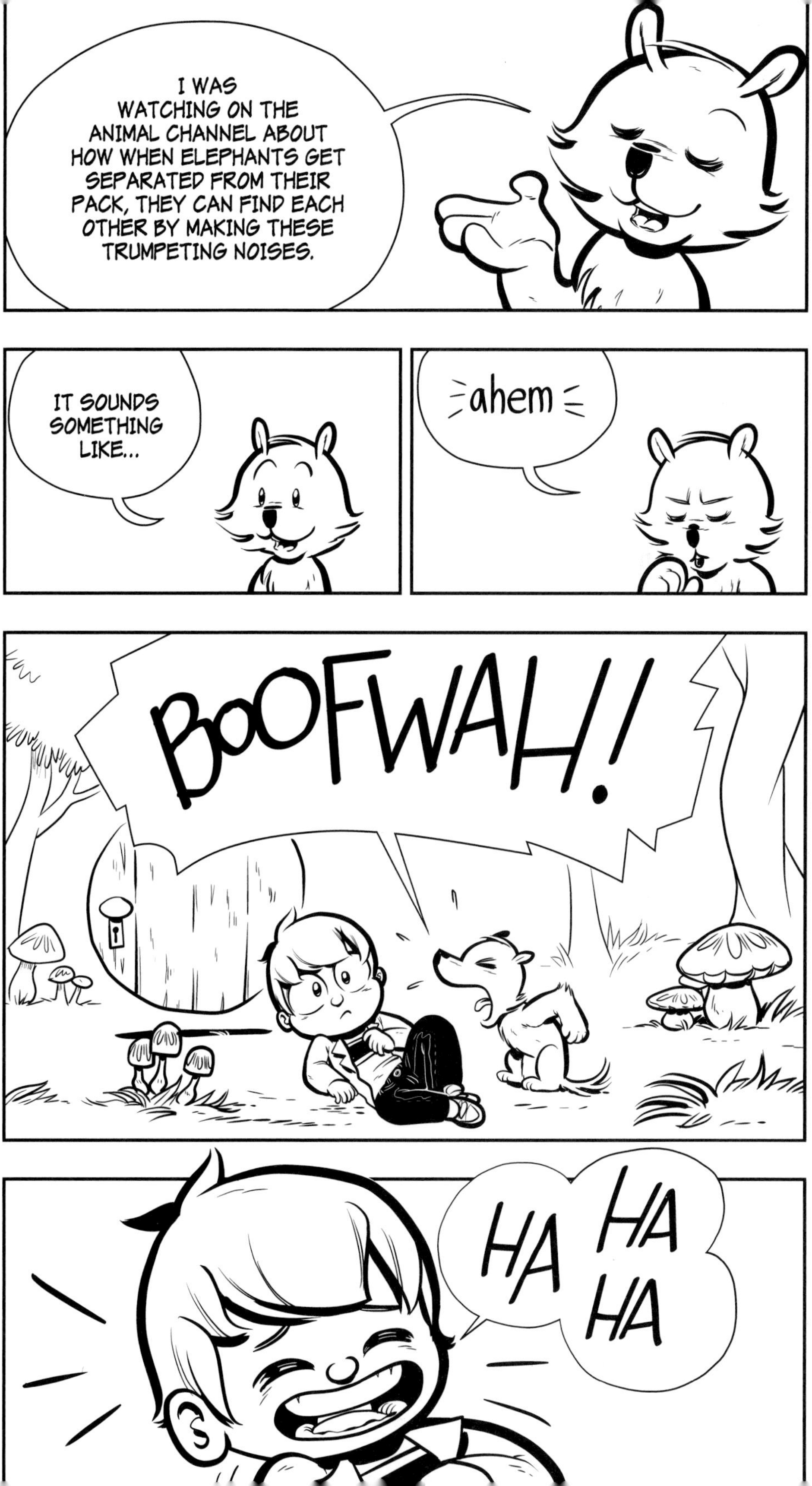
I WAS WATCHING ON THE ANIMAL CHANNEL ABOUT HOW WHEN ELEPHANTS GET SEPARATED FROM THEIR PACK, THEY CAN FIND EACH OTHER BY MAKING THESE TRUMPETING NOISES.
IT SOUNDS SOMETHING LIKE...
ahem
BOOFWAH!!
HA HA HA HA

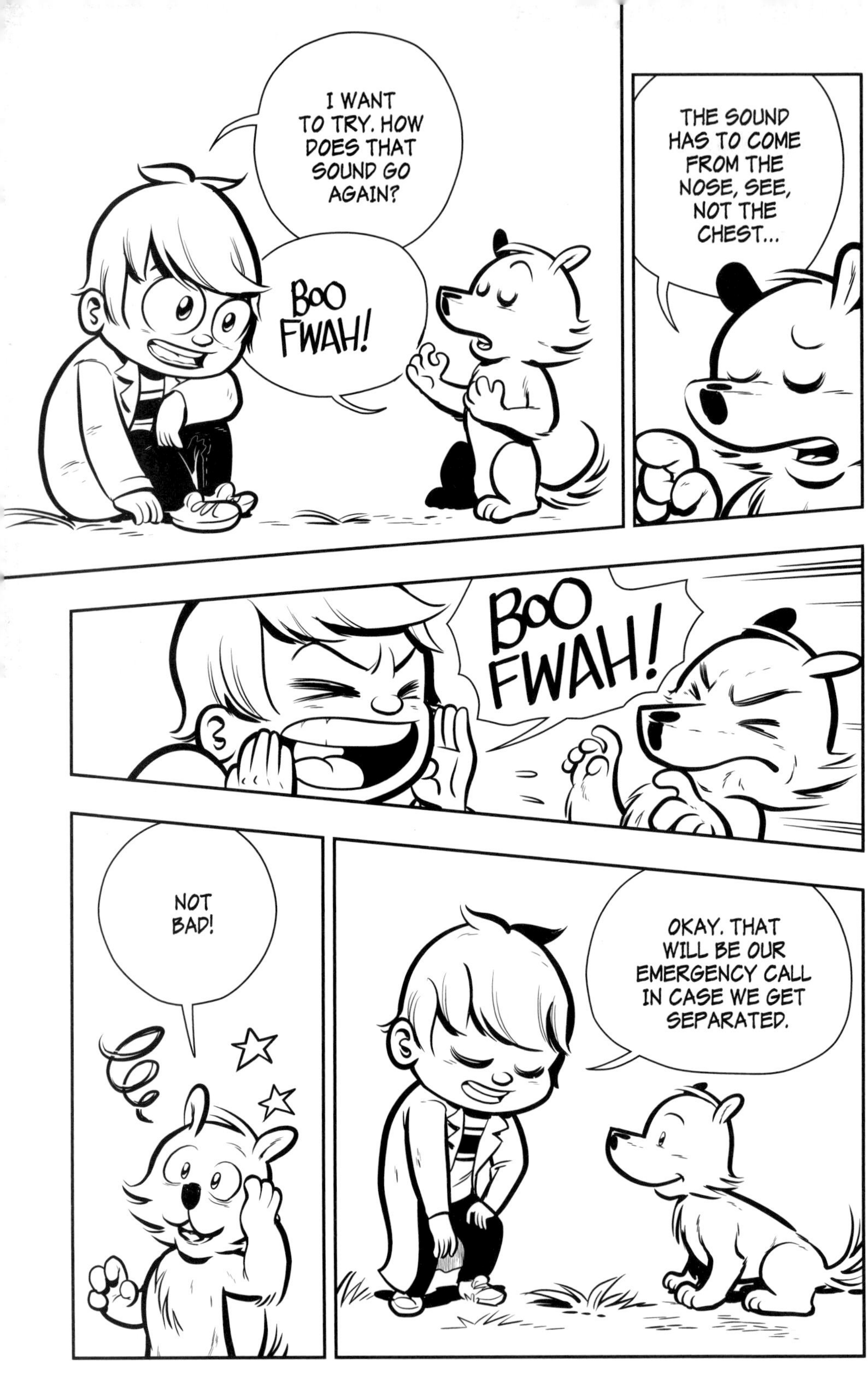
I WANT TO TRY. HOW DOES THAT SOUND GO AGAIN?
BOO FWAH!
THE SOUND HAS TO COME FROM THE NOSE, SEE, NOT THE CHEST...
BOO FWAH!
NOT BAD!
OKAY. THAT WILL BE OUR EMERGENCY CALL IN CASE WE GET SEPARATED.

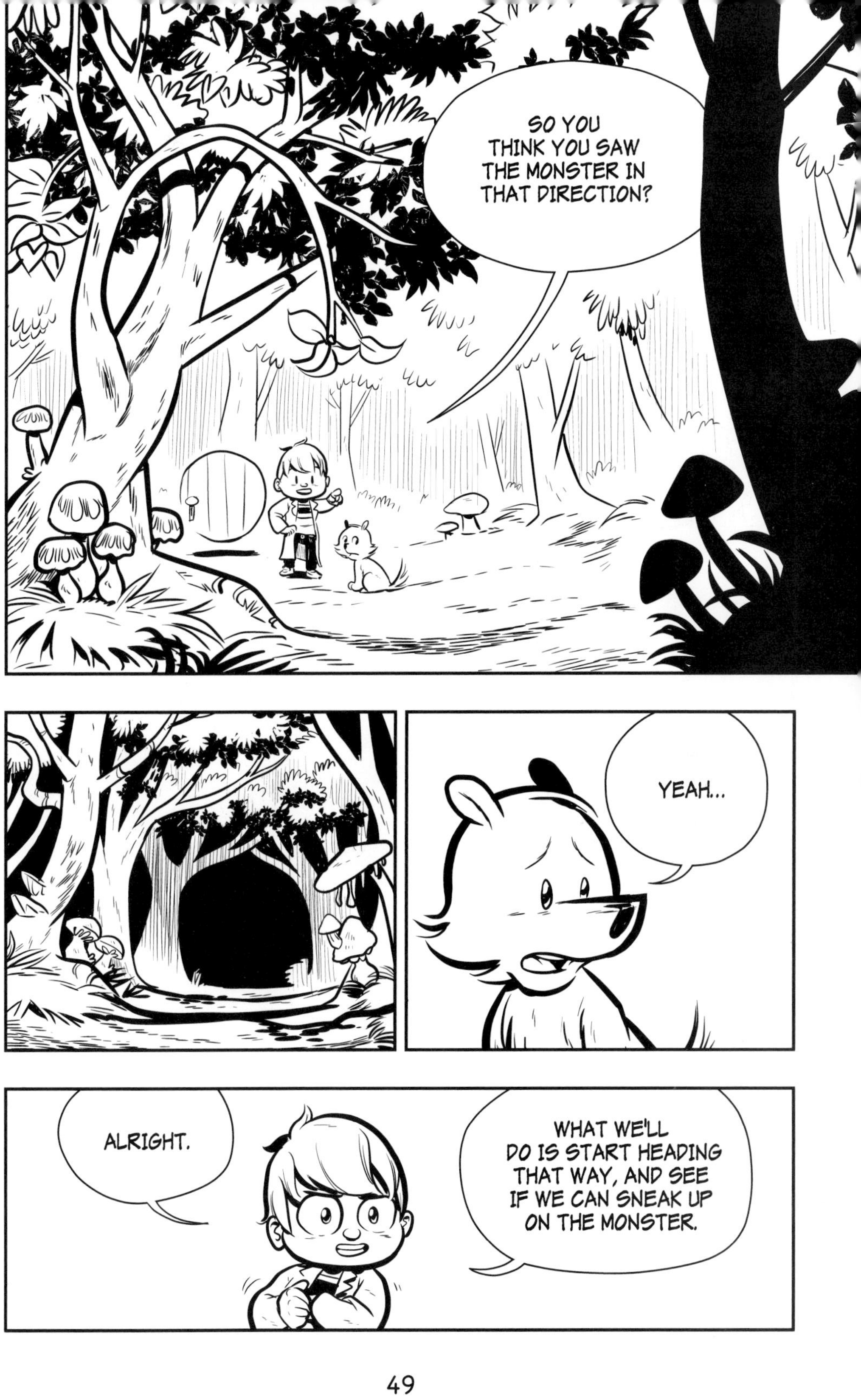
SO YOU THINK YOU SAW THE MONSTER IN THAT DIRECTION?
YEAH...
ALRIGHT.
WHAT WE'LL DO IS START HEADING THAT WAY, AND SEE IF WE CAN SNEAK UP ON THE MONSTER.

I'VE MADE THIS COOL LASSO GUN THAT CAN SHOOT LASSOS!

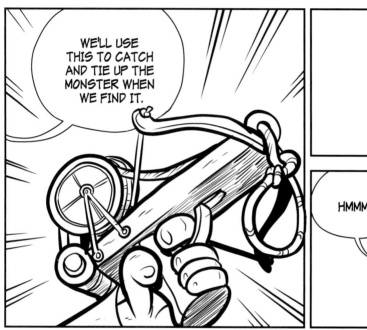

WE'LL USE THIS TO CATCH AND TIE UP THE MONSTER WHEN WE FIND IT.

HMMM...

I'M HUNGRY.

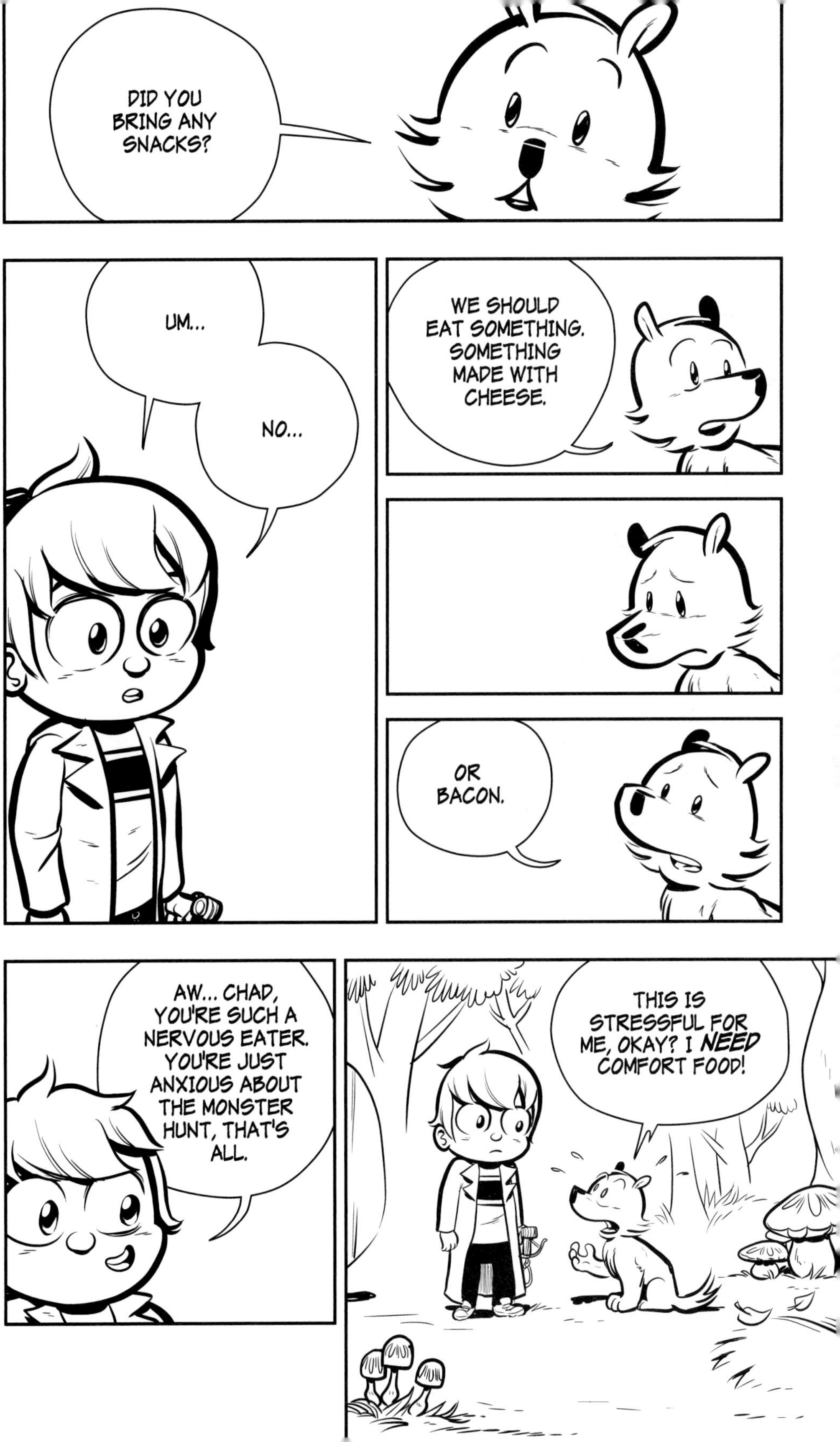
DID YOU BRING ANY SNACKS?
UM...
NO...
WE SHOULD EAT SOMETHING. SOMETHING MADE WITH CHEESE.
OR BACON.
AW... CHAD, YOU'RE SUCH A NERVOUS EATER. YOU'RE JUST ANXIOUS ABOUT THE MONSTER HUNT, THAT'S ALL.
THIS IS STRESSFUL FOR ME, OKAY? I *NEED* COMFORT FOOD!

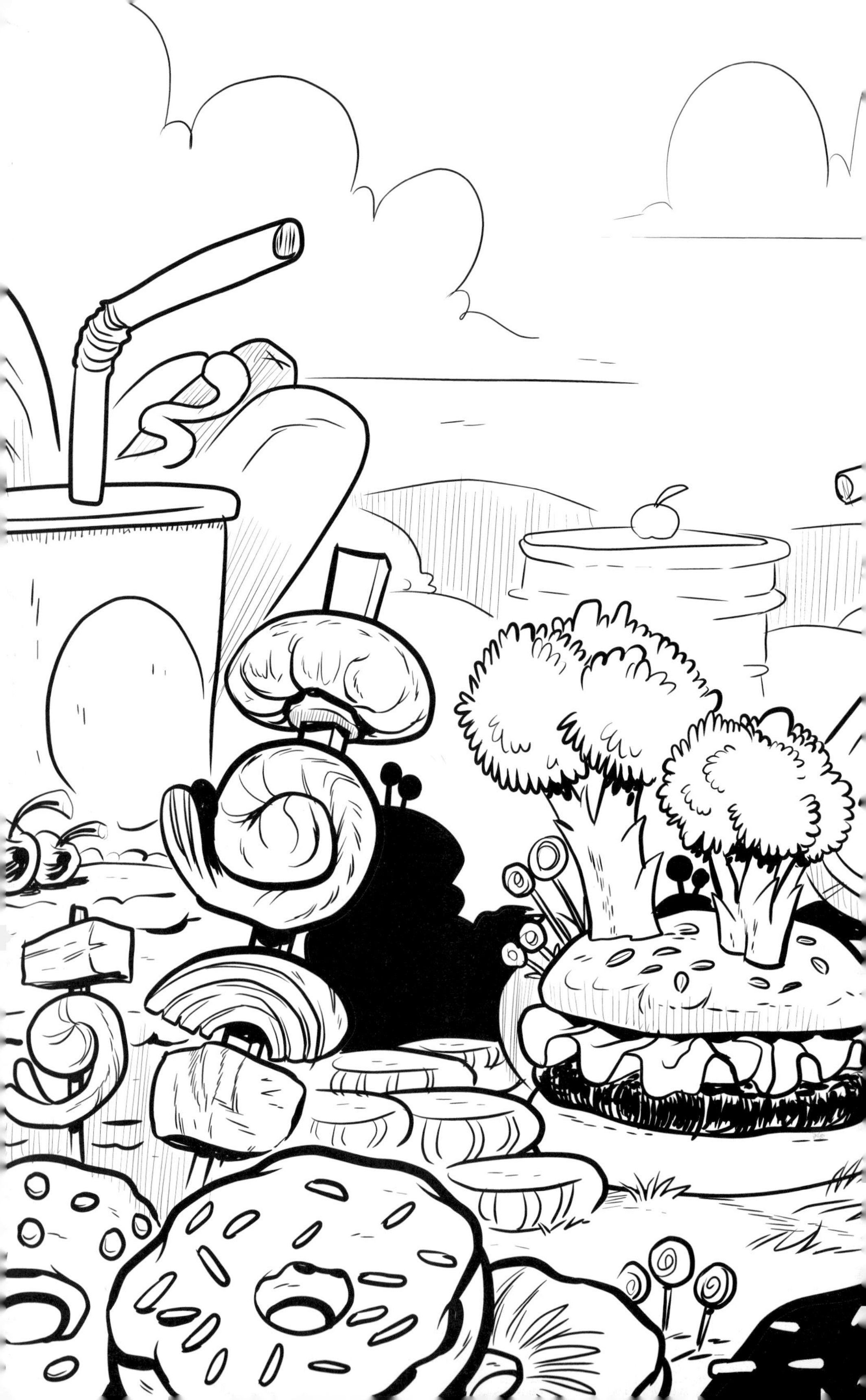

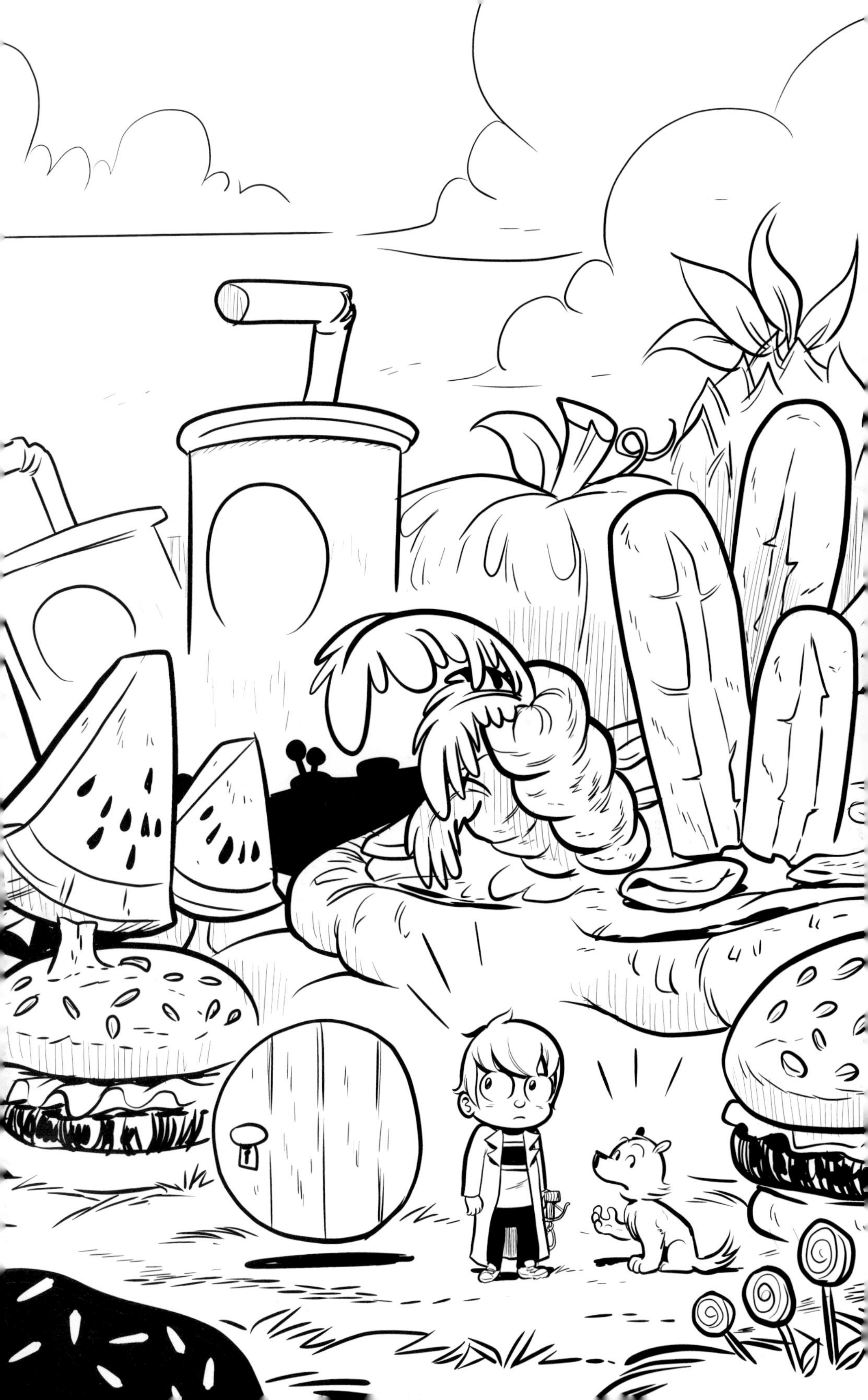

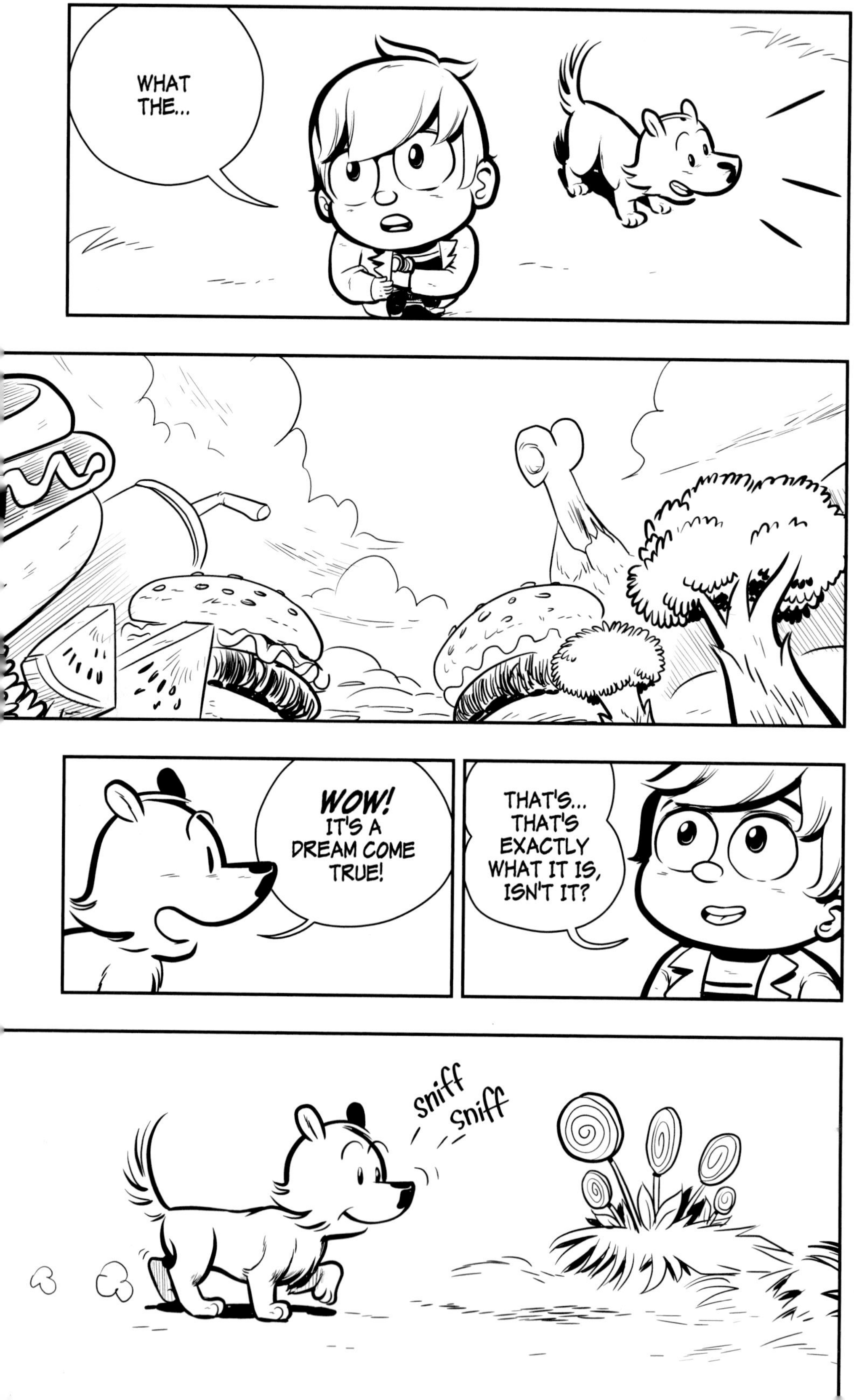
WHAT THE...
WOW! IT'S A DREAM COME TRUE!
THAT'S... THAT'S EXACTLY WHAT IT IS, ISN'T IT?
sniff
sniff

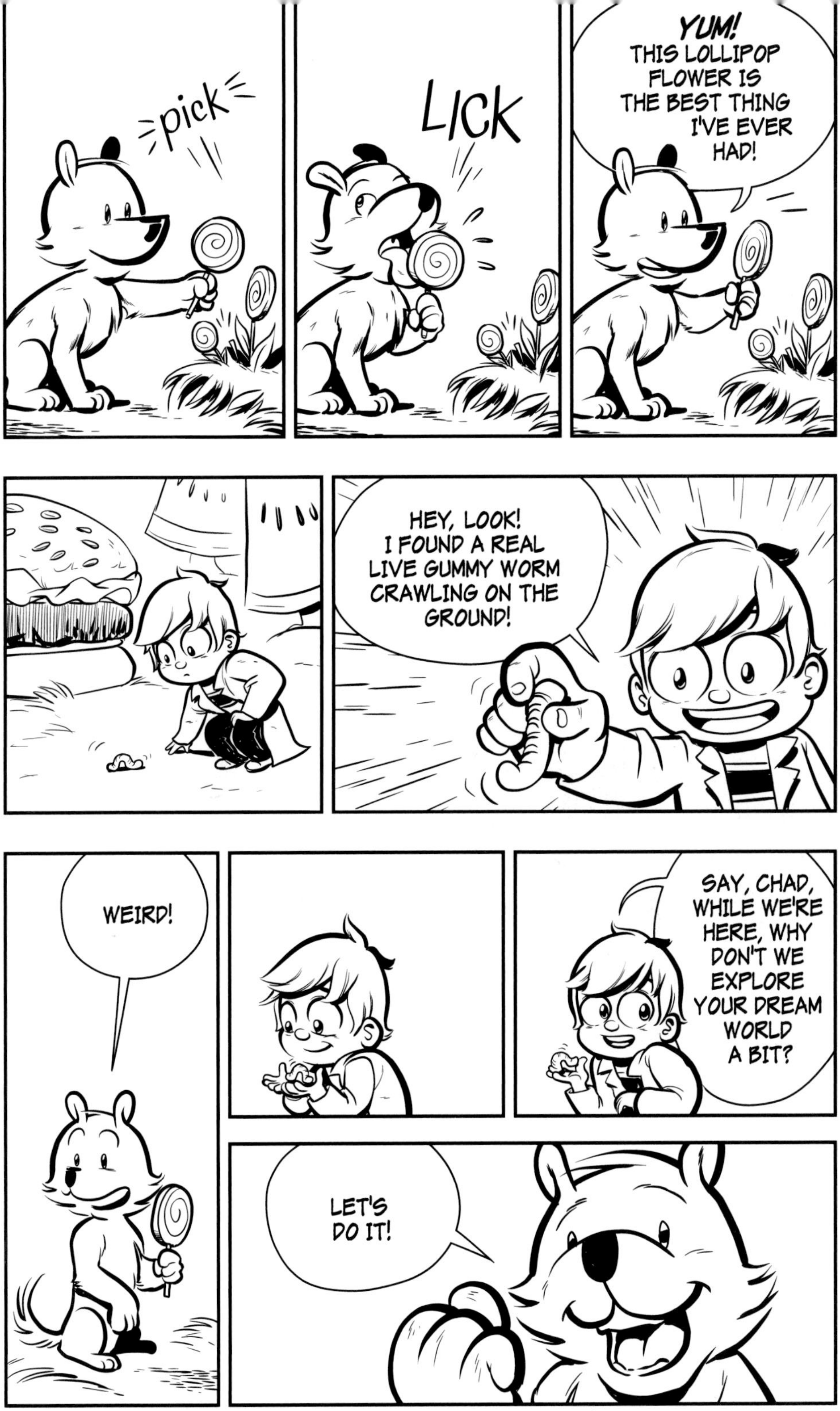
pick
LICK
YUM! THIS LOLLIPOP FLOWER IS THE BEST THING I'VE EVER HAD!
HEY, LOOK! I FOUND A REAL LIVE GUMMY WORM CRAWLING ON THE GROUND!
WEIRD!
SAY, CHAD, WHILE WE'RE HERE, WHY DON'T WE EXPLORE YOUR DREAM WORLD A BIT?
LET'S DO IT!

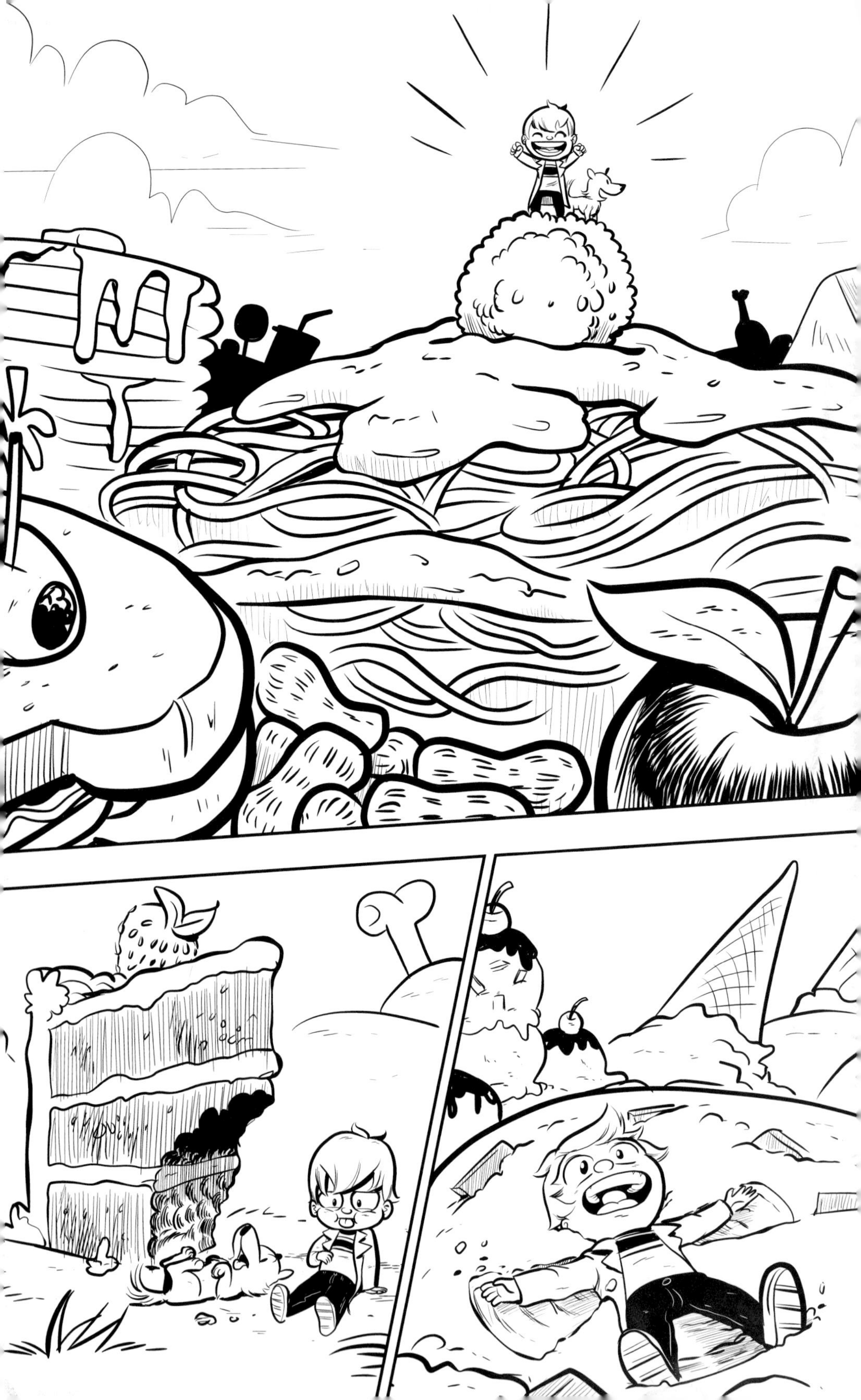

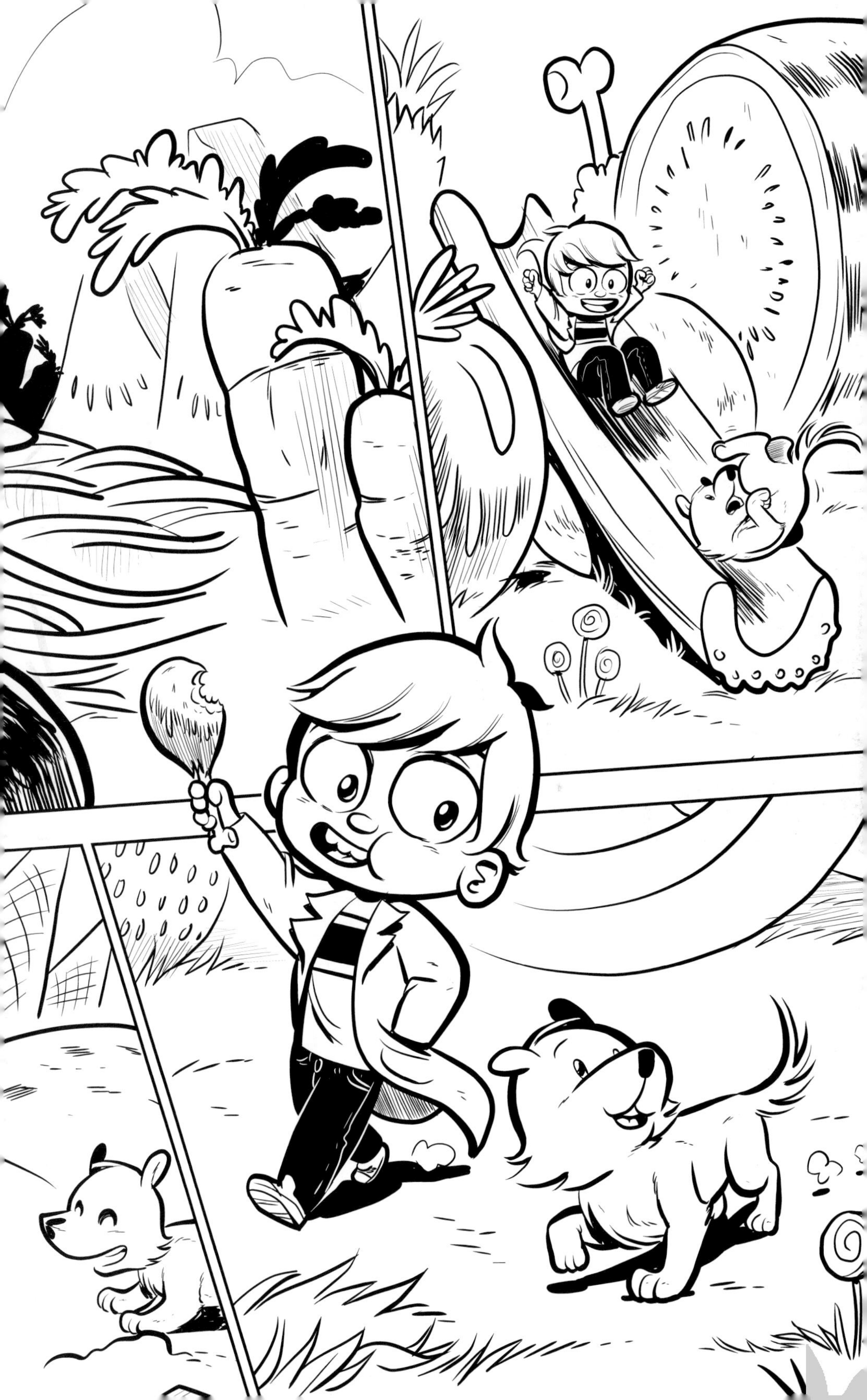

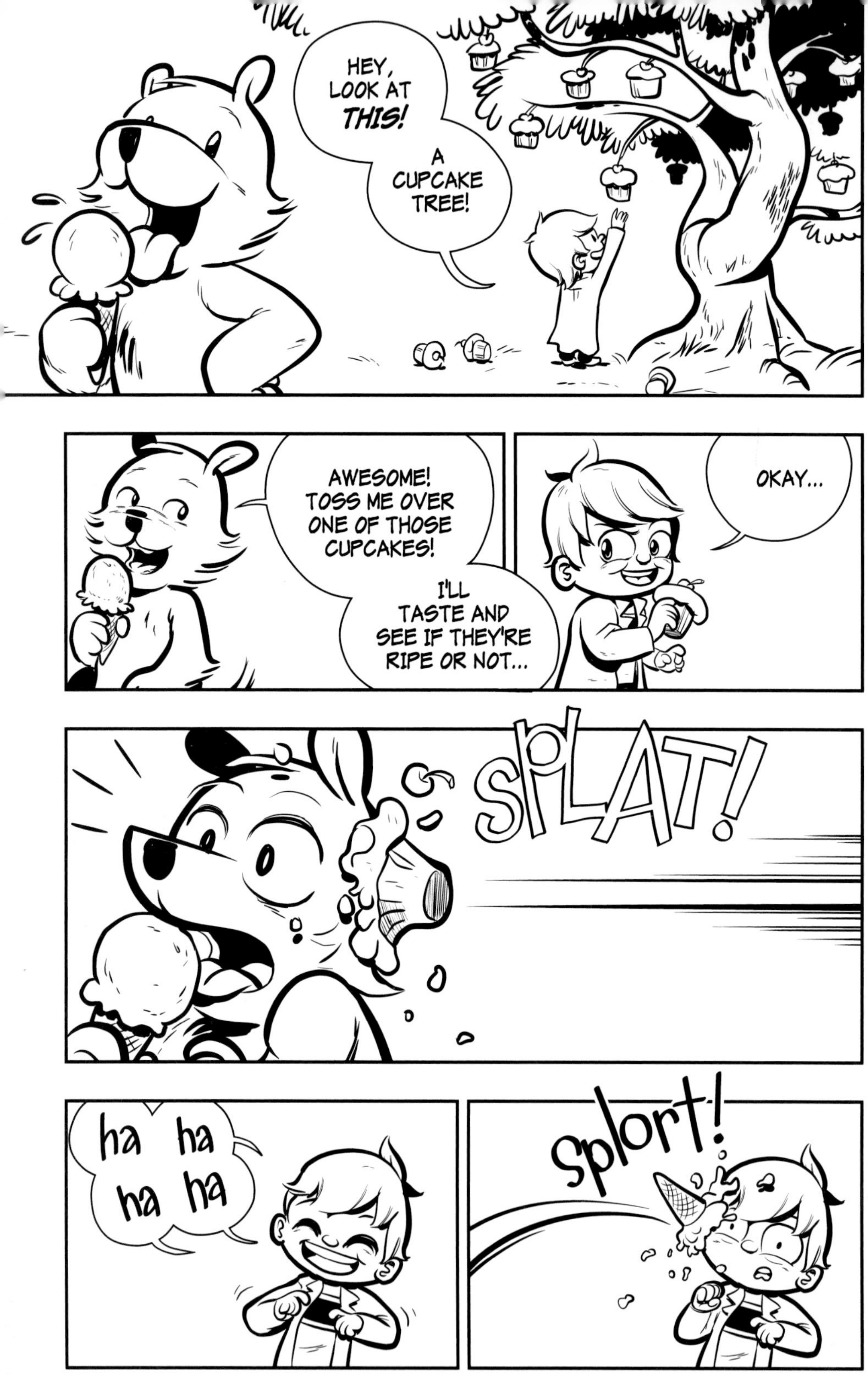
HEY, LOOK AT THIS!
A CUPCAKE TREE!
AWESOME! TOSS ME OVER ONE OF THOSE CUPCAKES!
I'LL TASTE AND SEE IF THEY'RE RIPE OR NOT...
OKAY...
SPLAT!
ha ha ha ha
splort!

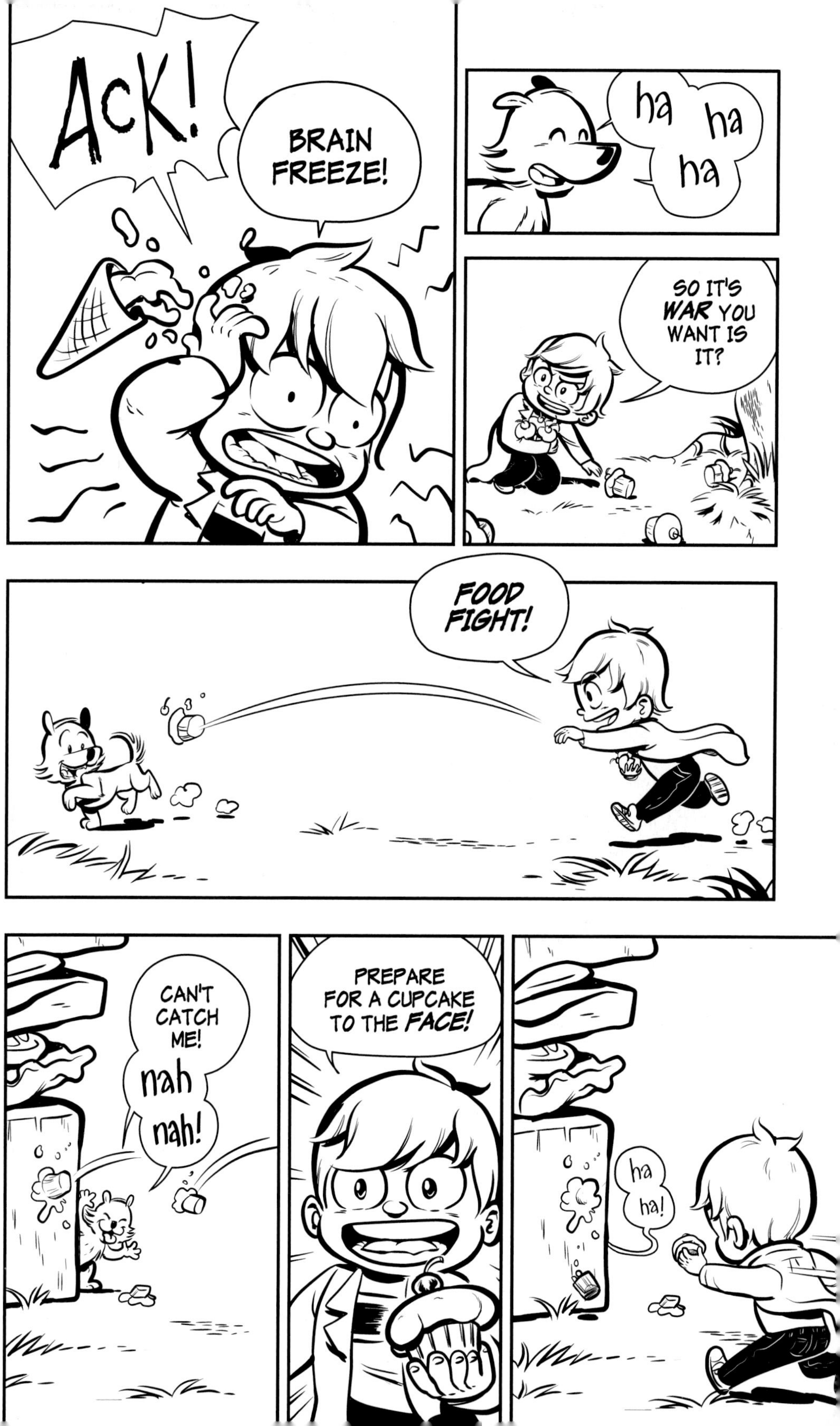
ACK!
BRAIN FREEZE!
ha ha ha
SO IT'S WAR YOU WANT IS IT?
FOOD FIGHT!
CAN'T CATCH ME!
nah nah!
PREPARE FOR A CUPCAKE TO THE FACE!
ha ha!

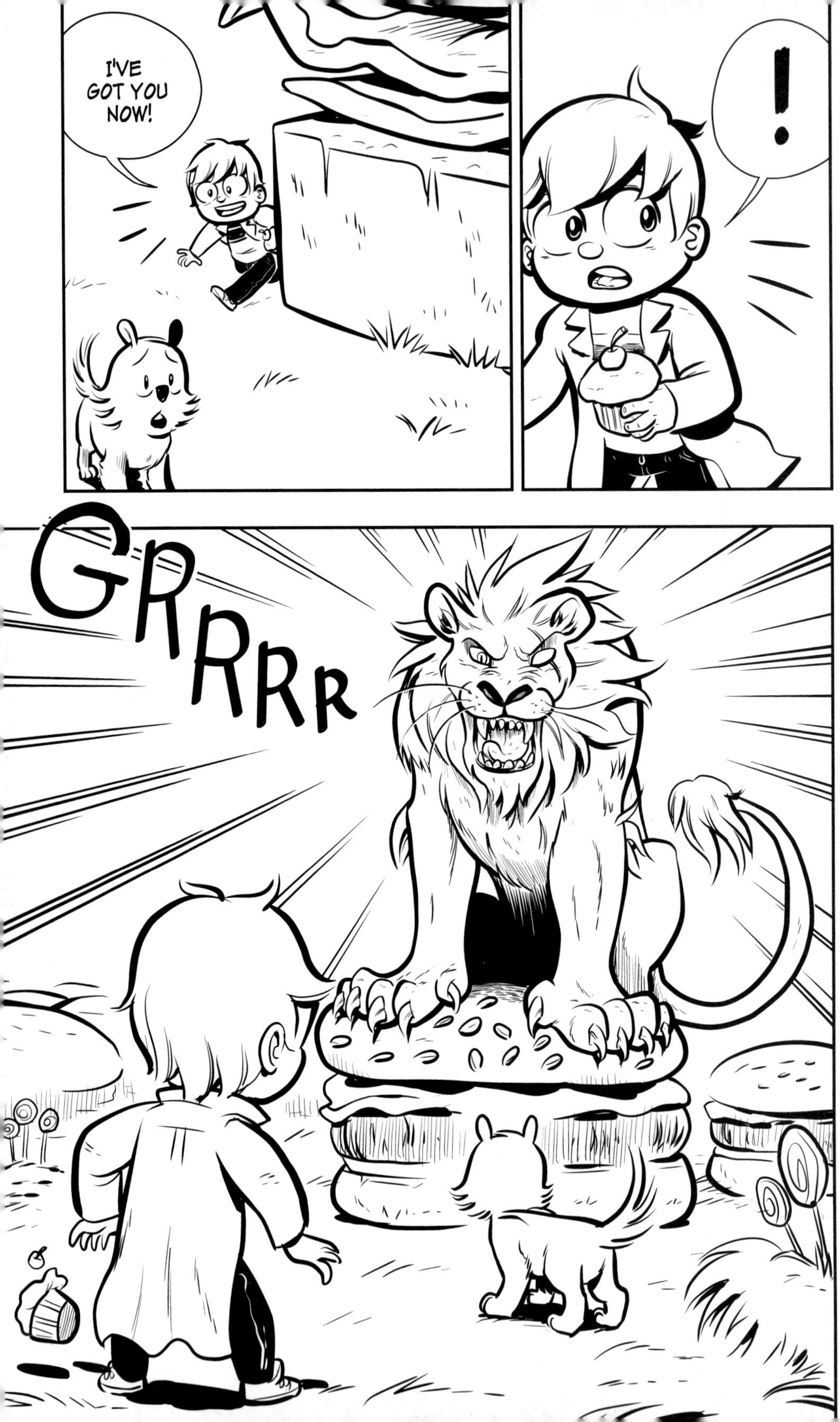
I'VE GOT YOU NOW!
!
GRRRR

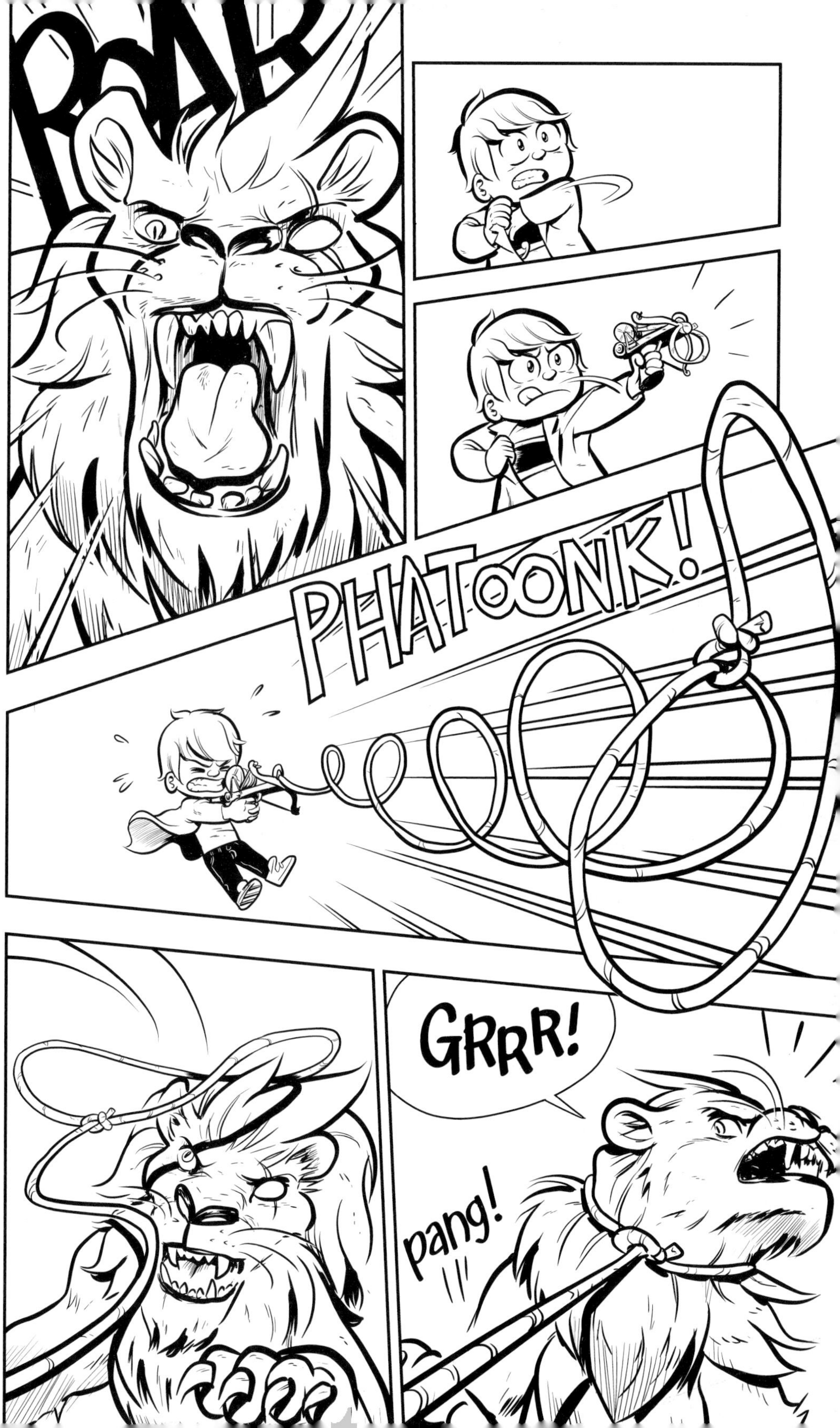
ROAR
PHATOONK!
GRRR!
pang!

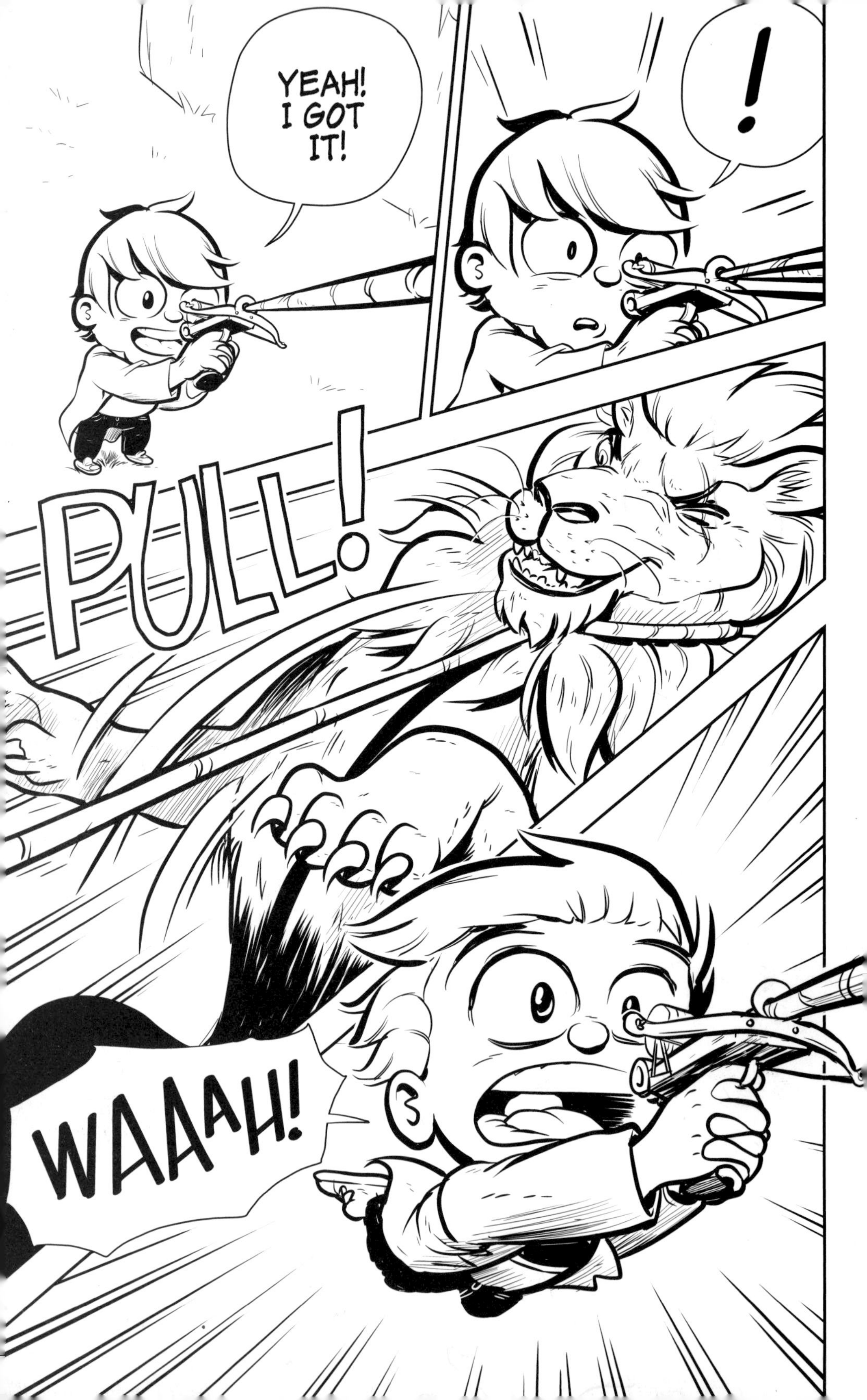
YEAH! I GOT IT!
!
PULL!
WAAAH!

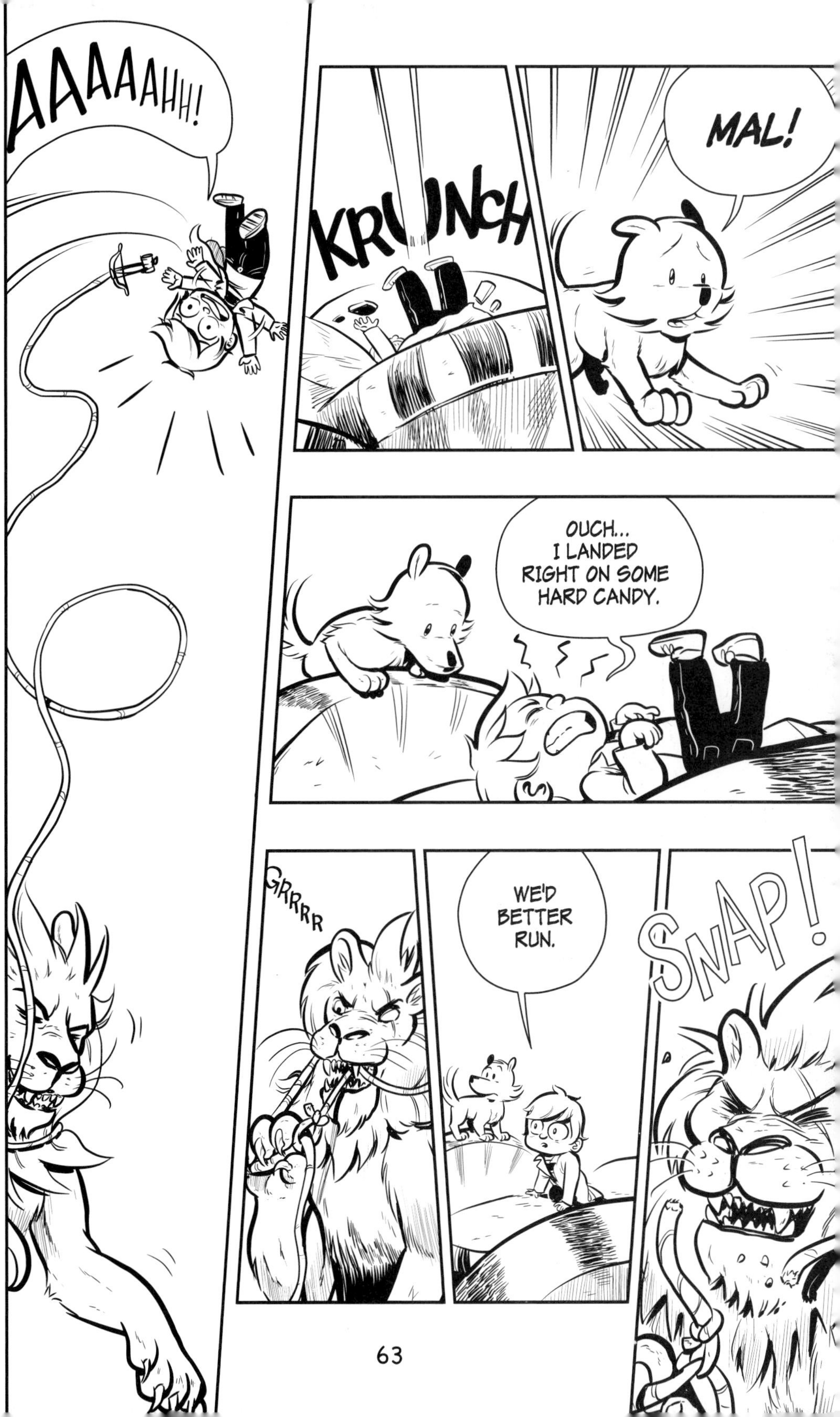
AAAAAHH!
KRUNCH
MAL!
OUCH... I LANDED RIGHT ON SOME HARD CANDY.
GRRRR
WE'D BETTER RUN.
SNAP!

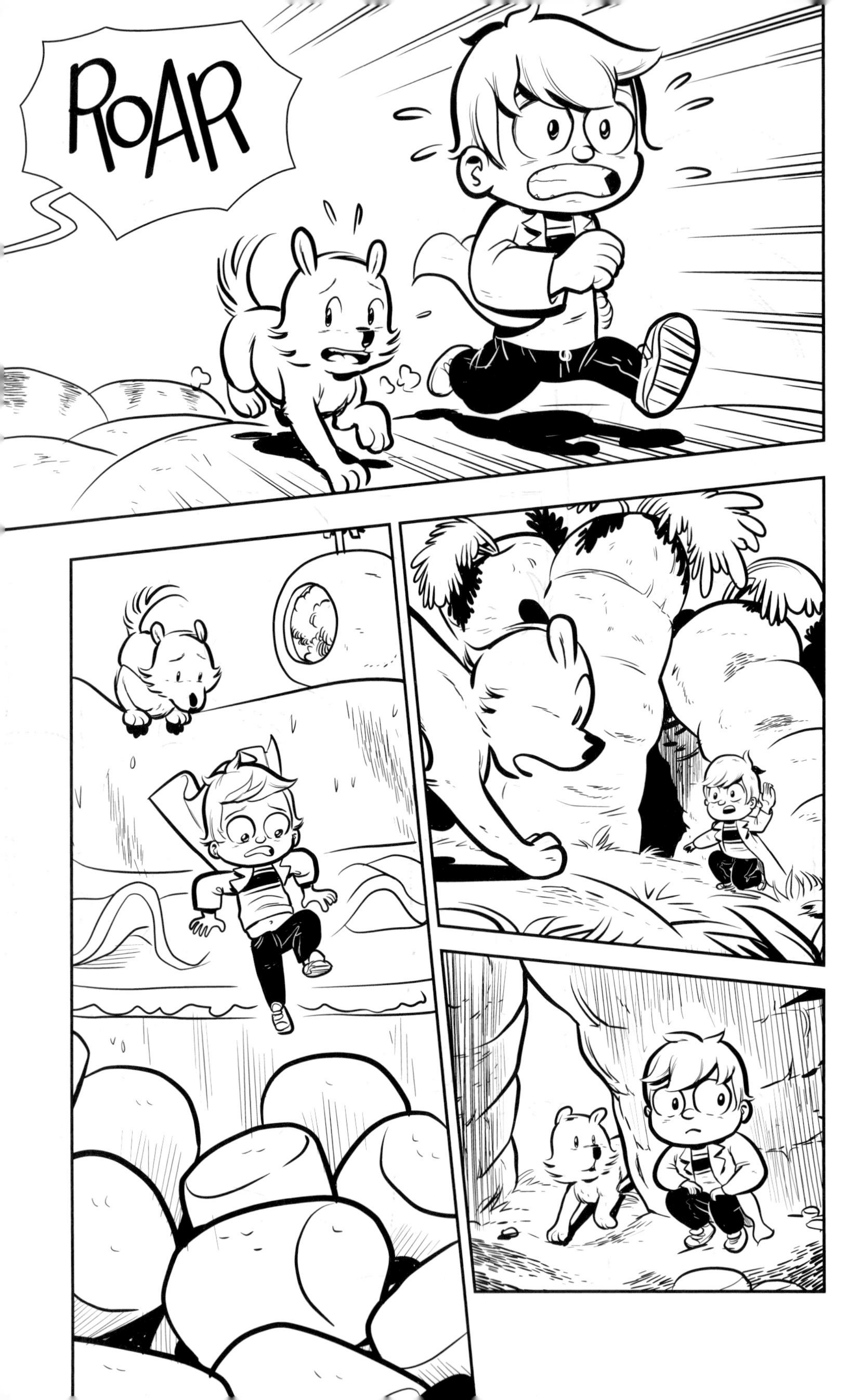
ROAR

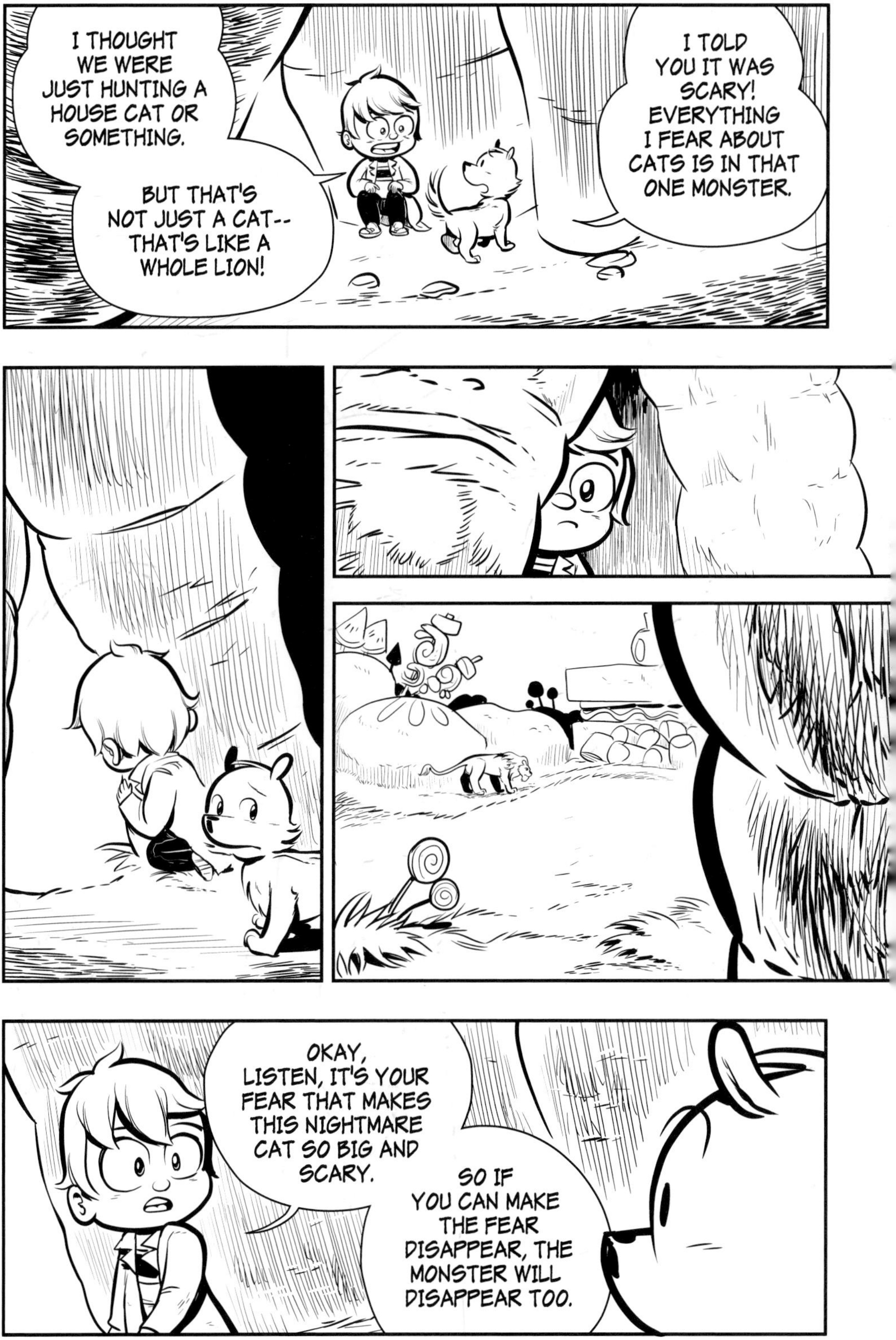
I THOUGHT WE WERE JUST HUNTING A HOUSE CAT OR SOMETHING.
BUT THAT'S NOT JUST A CAT-- THAT'S LIKE A WHOLE LION!
I TOLD YOU IT WAS SCARY! EVERYTHING I FEAR ABOUT CATS IS IN THAT ONE MONSTER.
OKAY, LISTEN, IT'S YOUR FEAR THAT MAKES THIS NIGHTMARE CAT SO BIG AND SCARY.
SO IF YOU CAN MAKE THE FEAR DISAPPEAR, THE MONSTER WILL DISAPPEAR TOO.

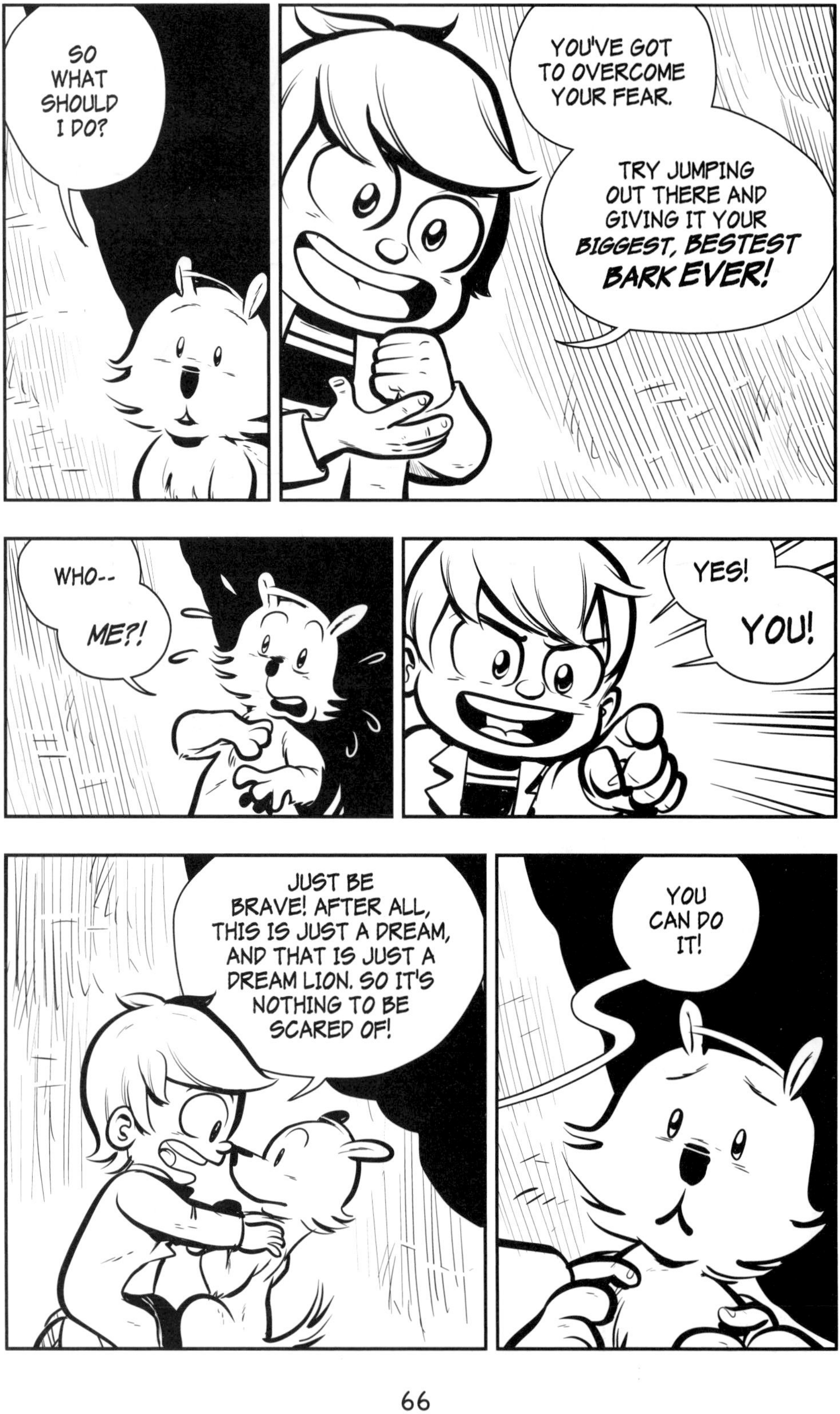
SO WHAT SHOULD I DO?
YOU'VE GOT TO OVERCOME YOUR FEAR.
TRY JUMPING OUT THERE AND GIVING IT YOUR BIGGEST, BESTEST BARK EVER!
WHO-- ME?!
YES! YOU!
JUST BE BRAVE! AFTER ALL, THIS IS JUST A DREAM, AND THAT IS JUST A DREAM LION. SO IT'S NOTHING TO BE SCARED OF!
YOU CAN DO IT!

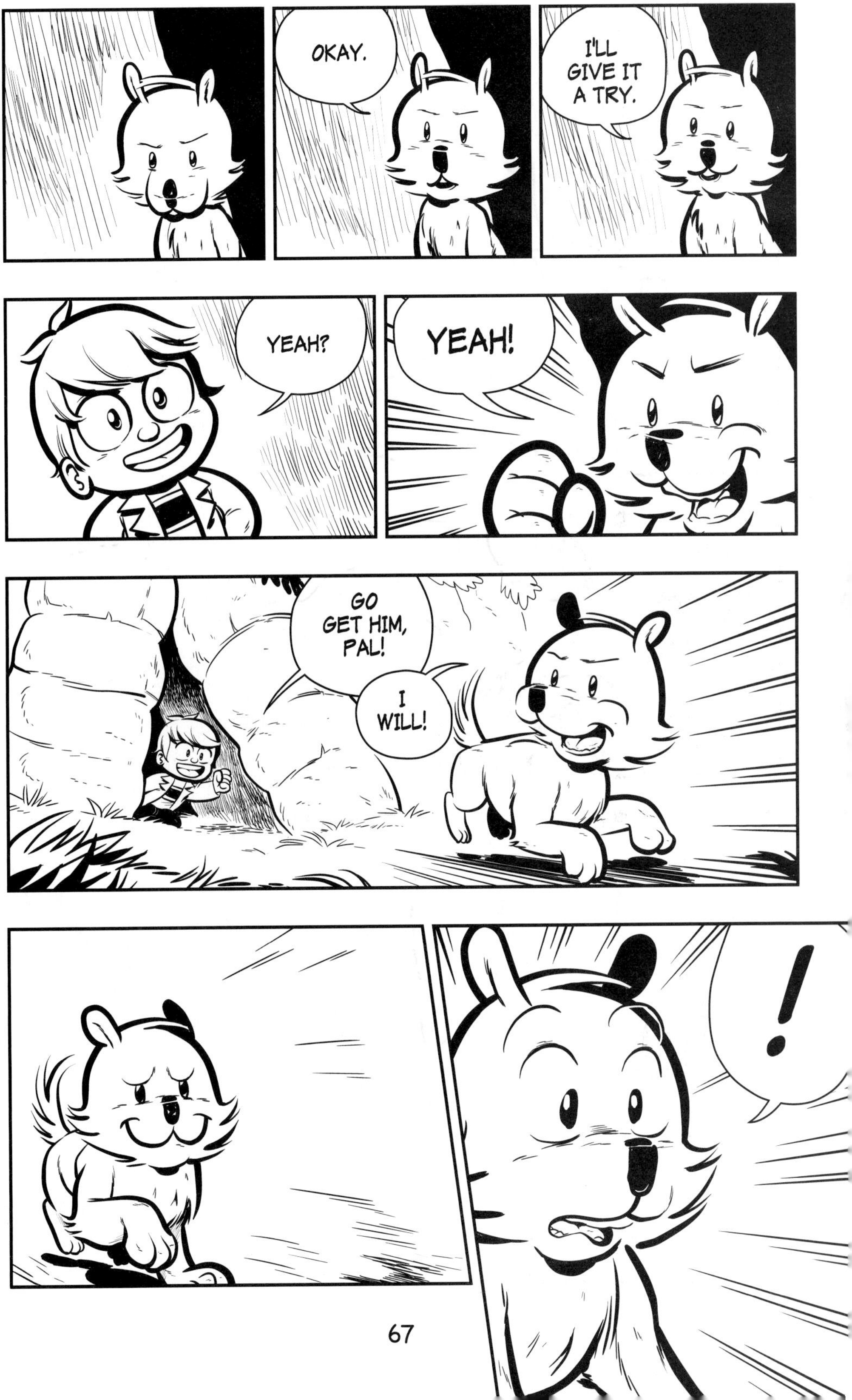
OKAY.
I'LL GIVE IT A TRY.
YEAH?
YEAH!
GO GET HIM, PAL!
I WILL!
!

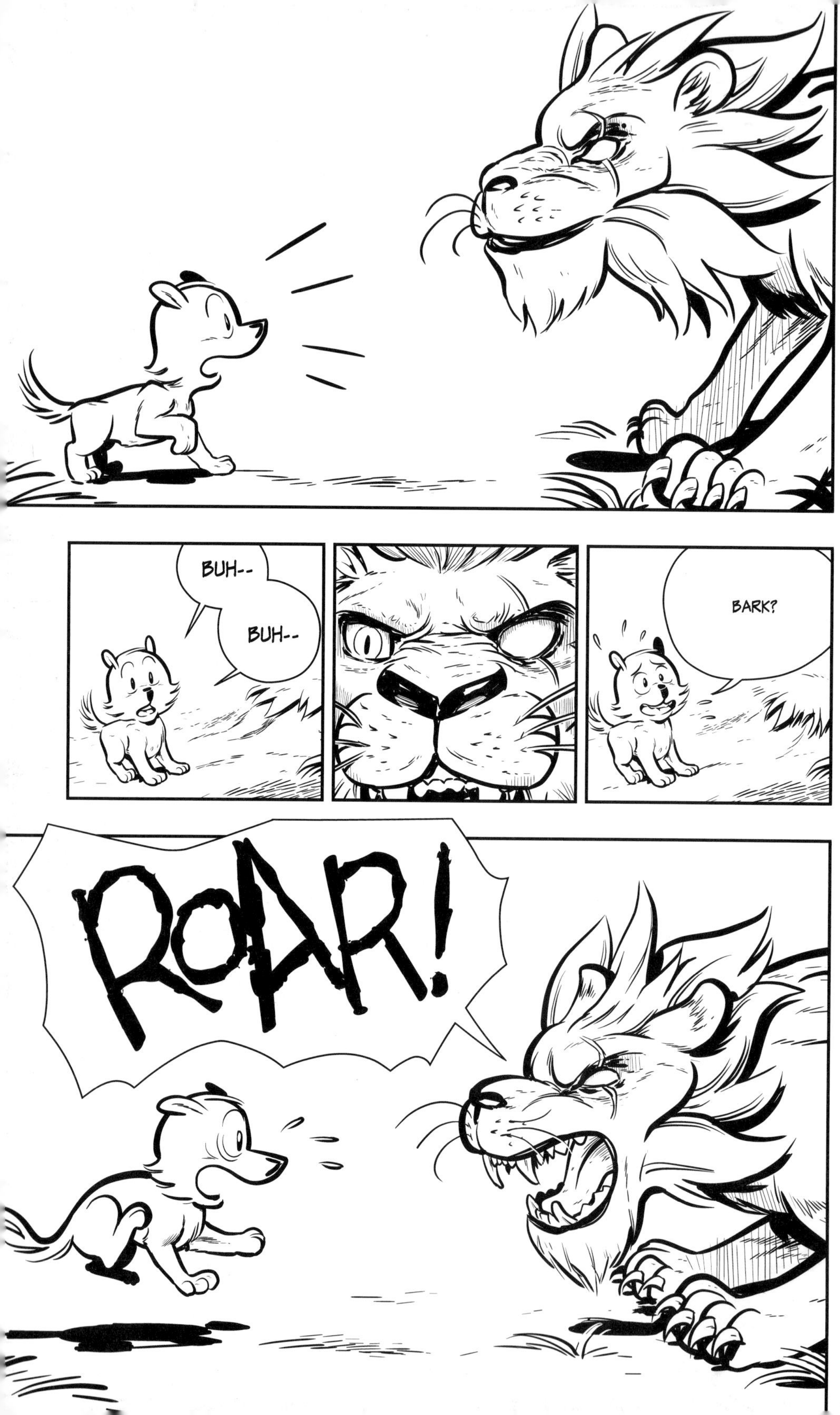
BUH--
BUH--
BARK?
ROAR!

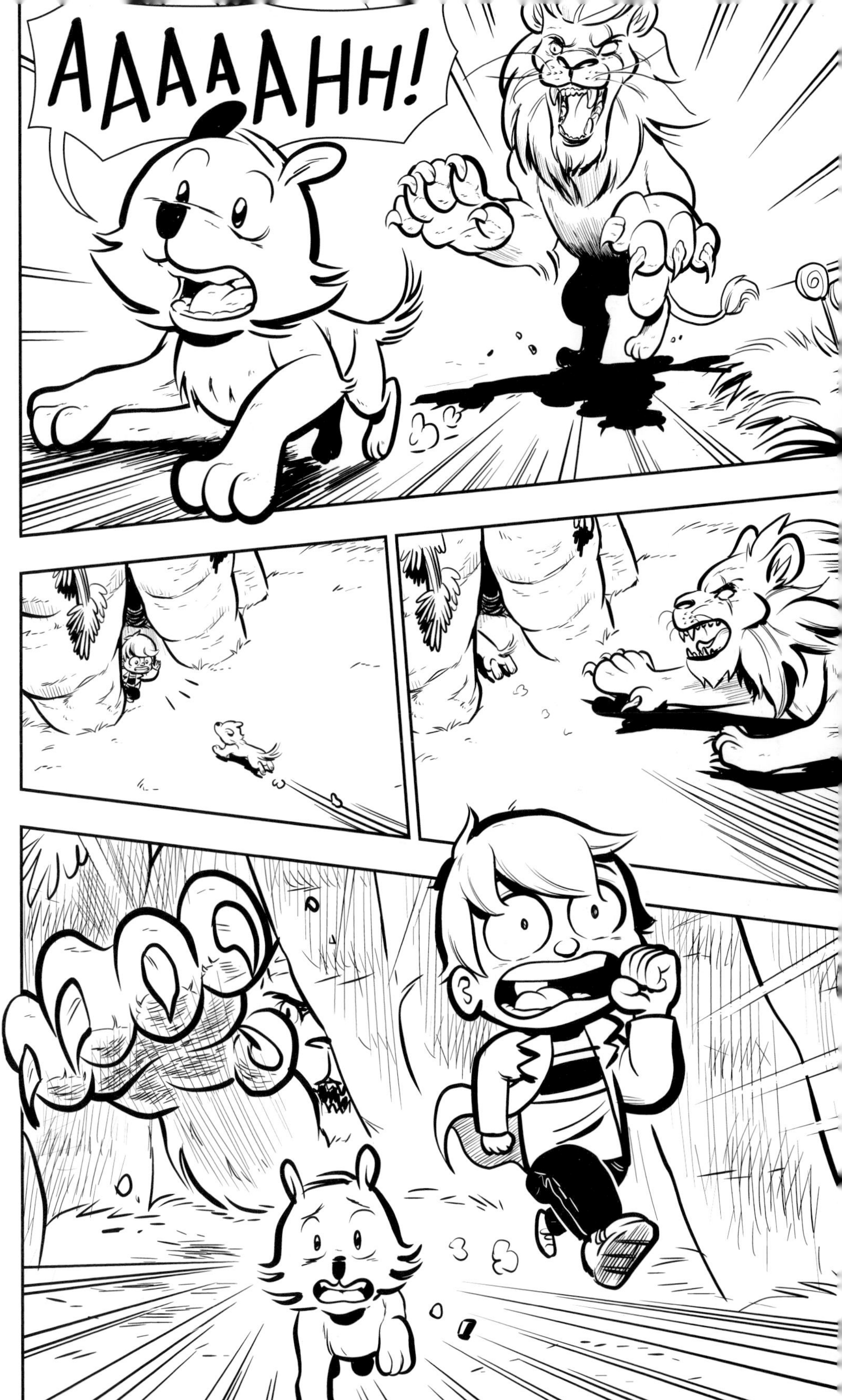
AAAAAHH!

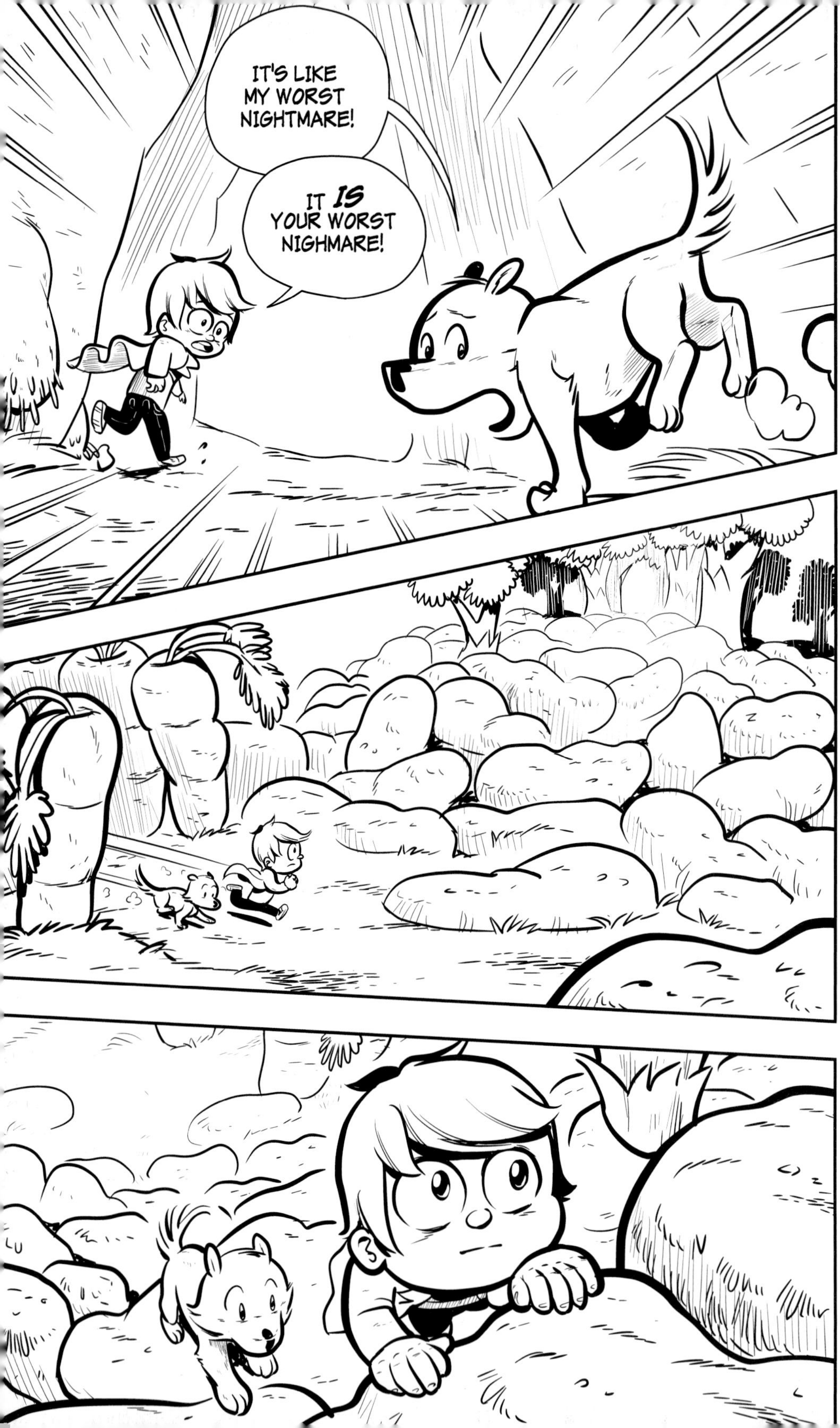
IT'S LIKE MY WORST NIGHTMARE!
IT IS YOUR WORST NIGHMARE!

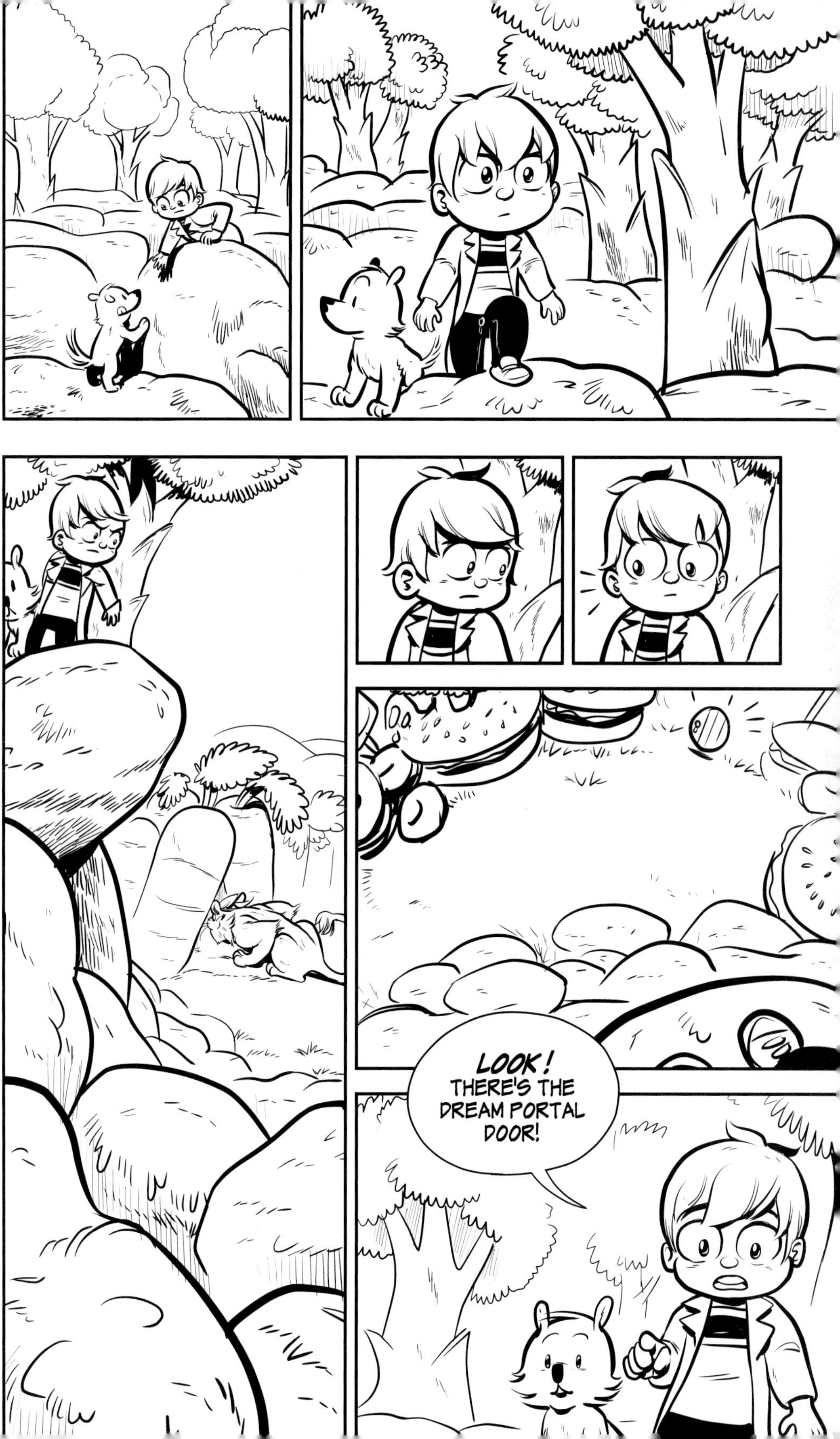
LOOK! THERE'S THE DREAM PORTAL DOOR!

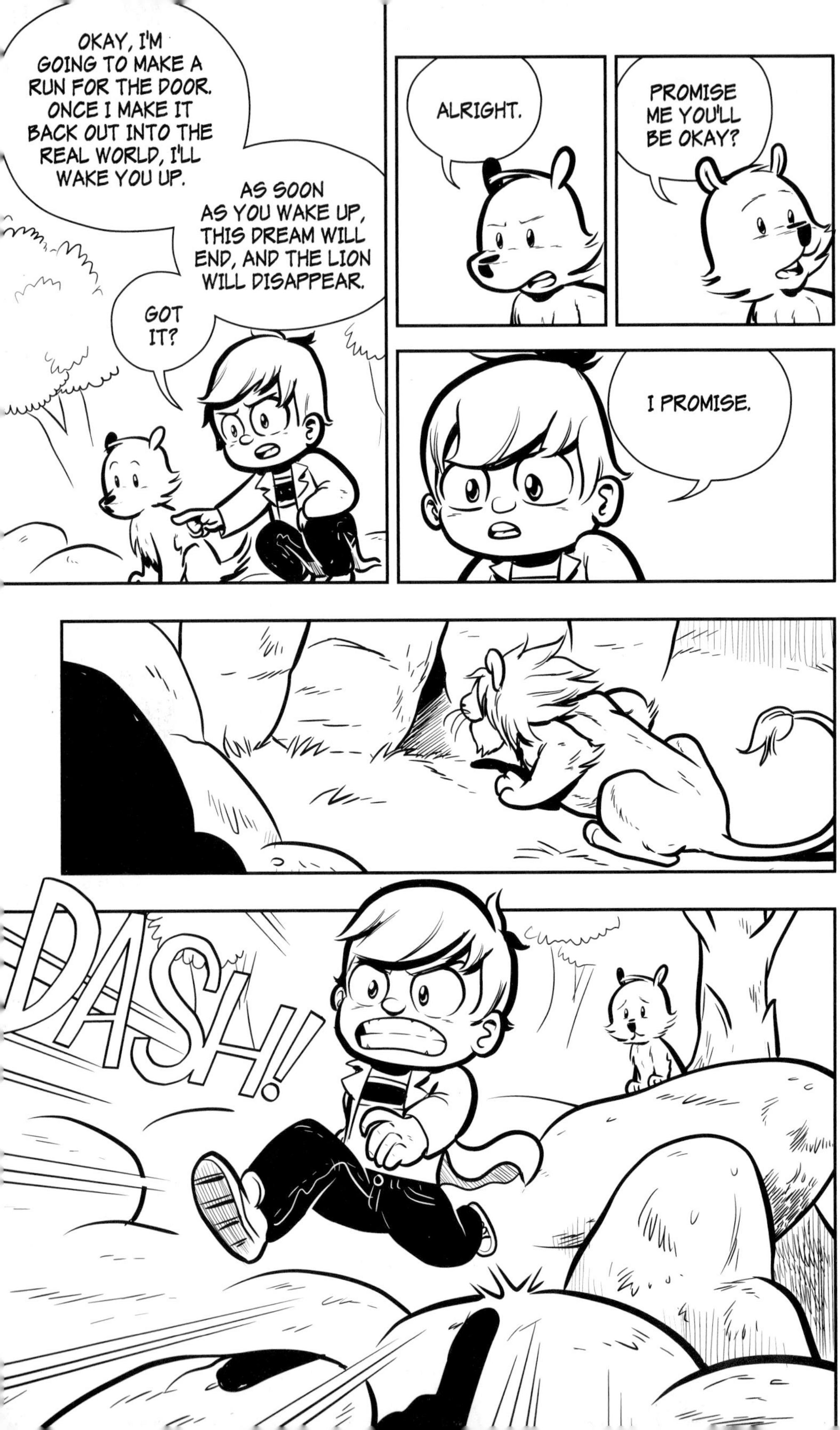
OKAY, I'M GOING TO MAKE A RUN FOR THE DOOR. ONCE I MAKE IT BACK OUT INTO THE REAL WORLD, I'LL WAKE YOU UP.
AS SOON AS YOU WAKE UP, THIS DREAM WILL END, AND THE LION WILL DISAPPEAR.
GOT IT?
ALRIGHT.
PROMISE ME YOU'LL BE OKAY?
I PROMISE.
DASH!!

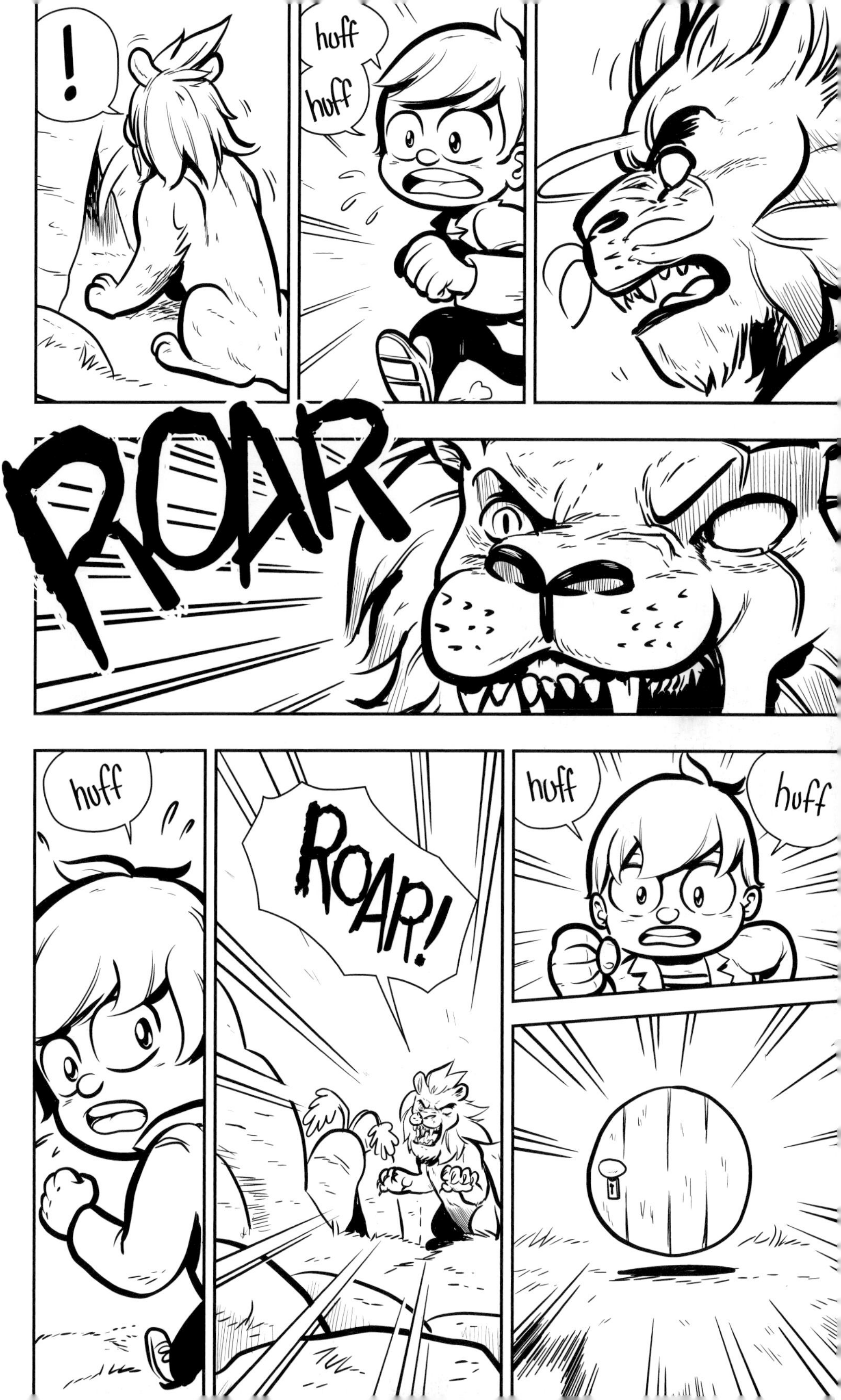
!
huff
huff
ROAR
huff
ROAR!
huff
huff

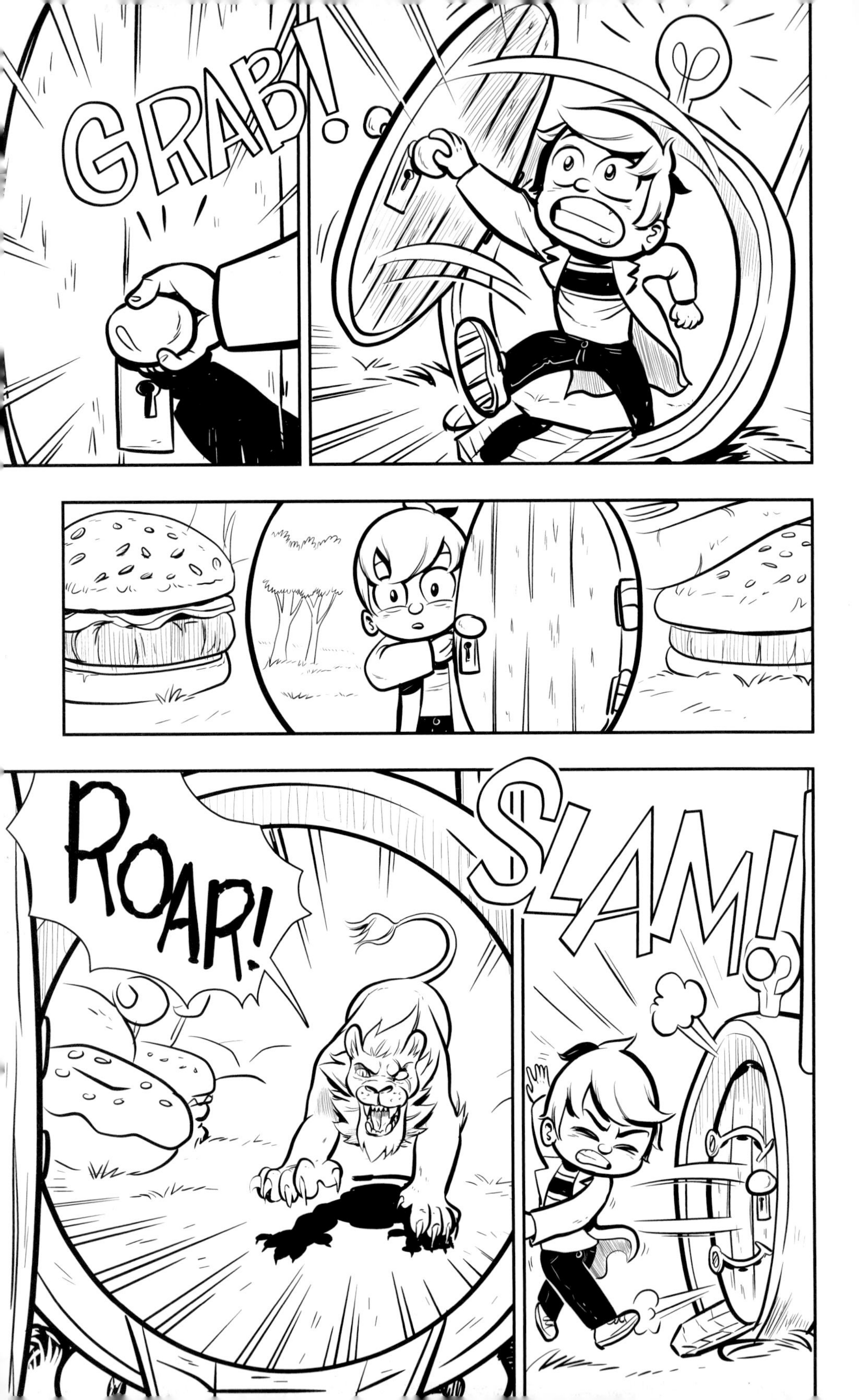
GRAB!
ROAR!
SLAM!

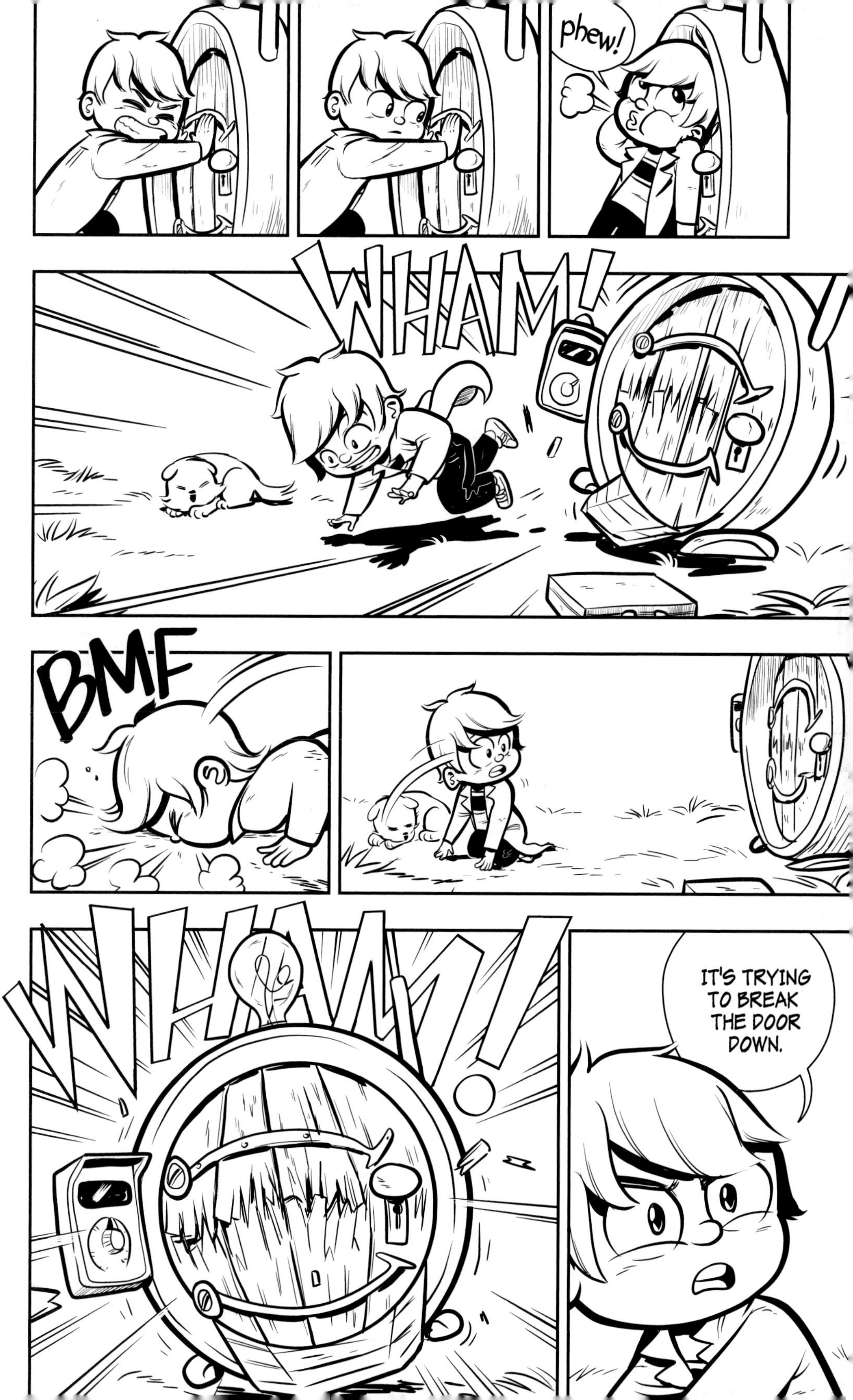
phew!
WHAM!
BMF
WHAM!
IT'S TRYING TO BREAK THE DOOR DOWN.

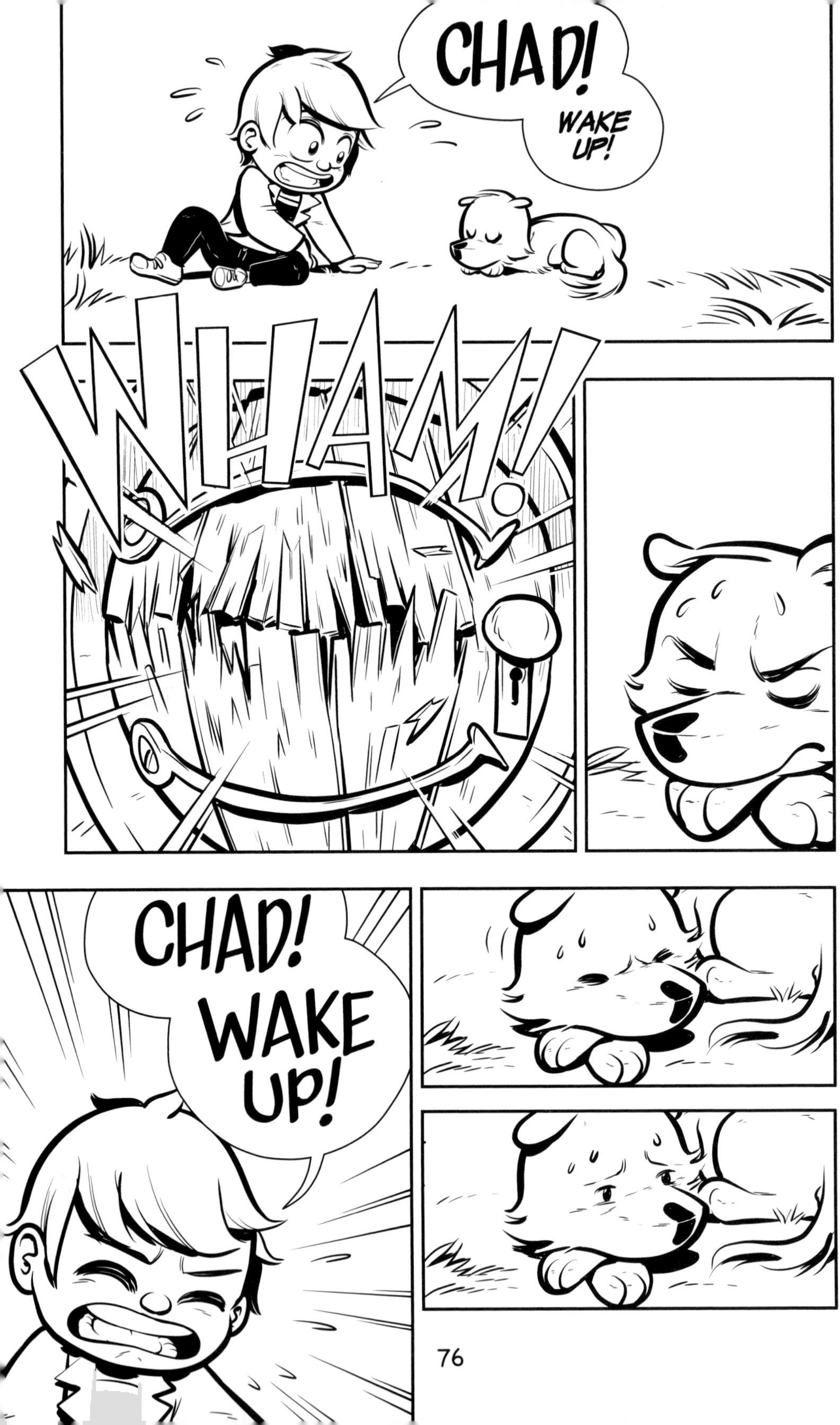
CHAD! WAKE UP!
WHAM!
CHAD! WAKE UP!

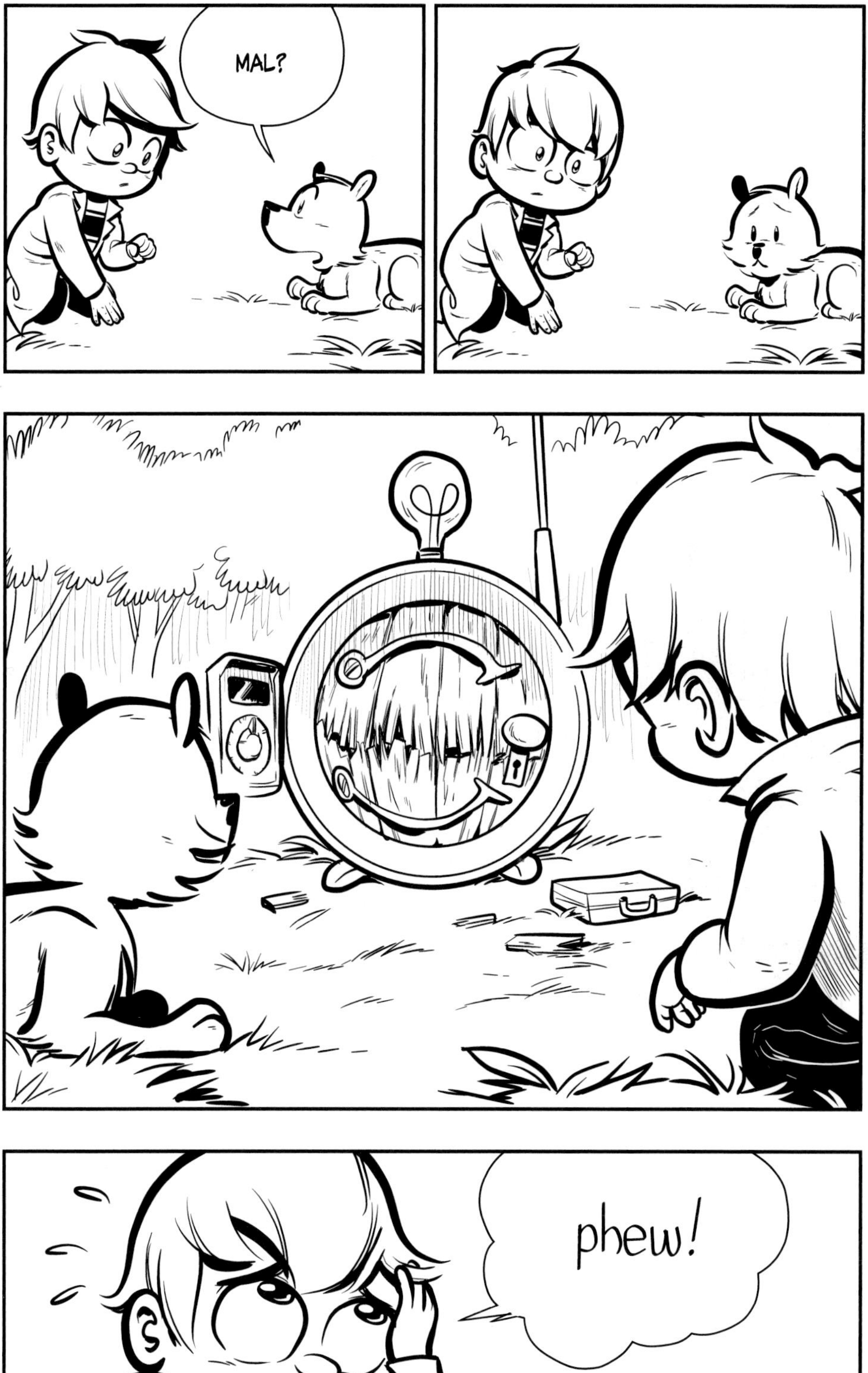
MAL?
phew!

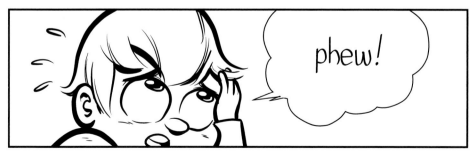

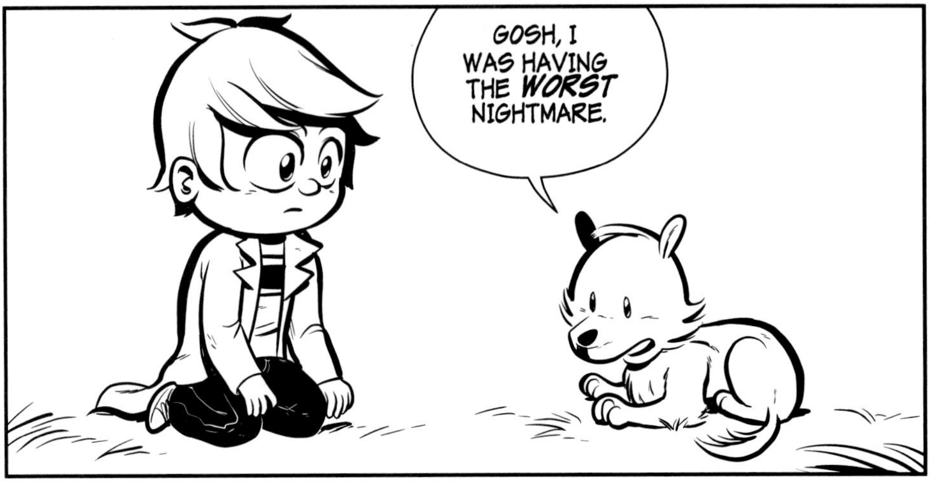
GOSH, I WAS HAVING THE WORST NIGHTMARE.

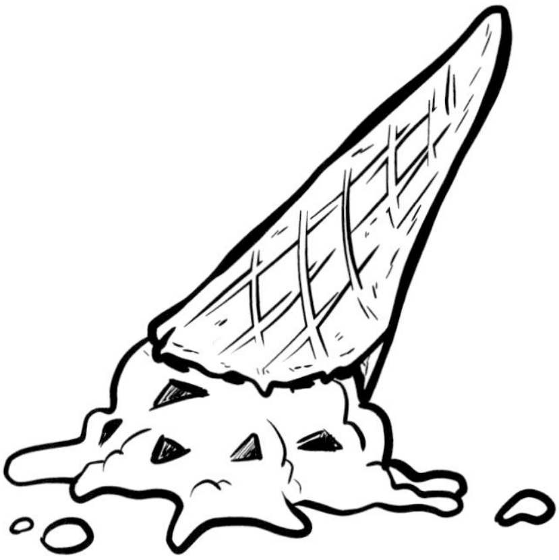

CHAPTER 4

Grounded

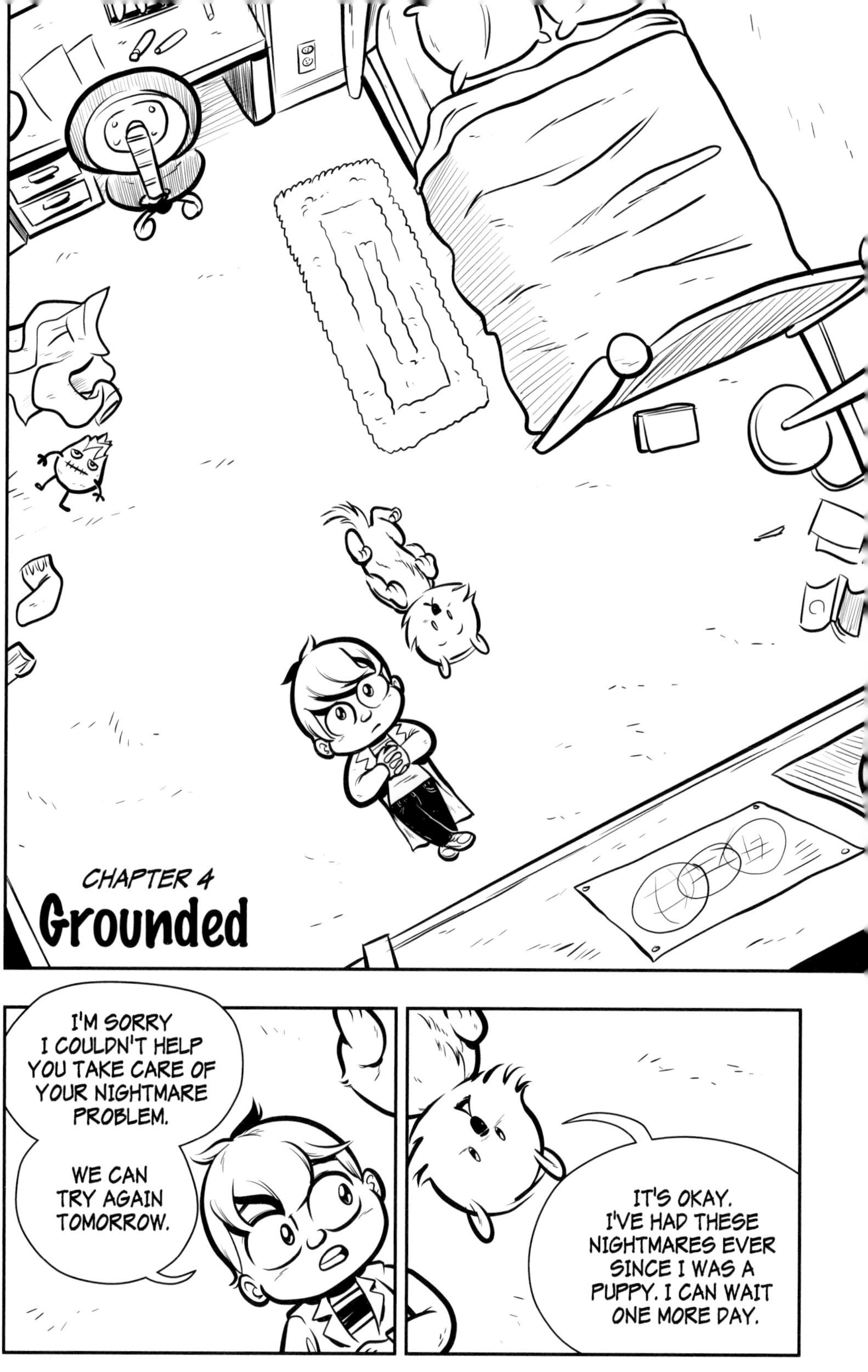
I'M SORRY I COULDN'T HELP YOU TAKE CARE OF YOUR NIGHTMARE PROBLEM.
WE CAN TRY AGAIN TOMORROW.
IT'S OKAY. I'VE HAD THESE NIGHTMARES EVER SINCE I WAS A PUPPY. I CAN WAIT ONE MORE DAY.

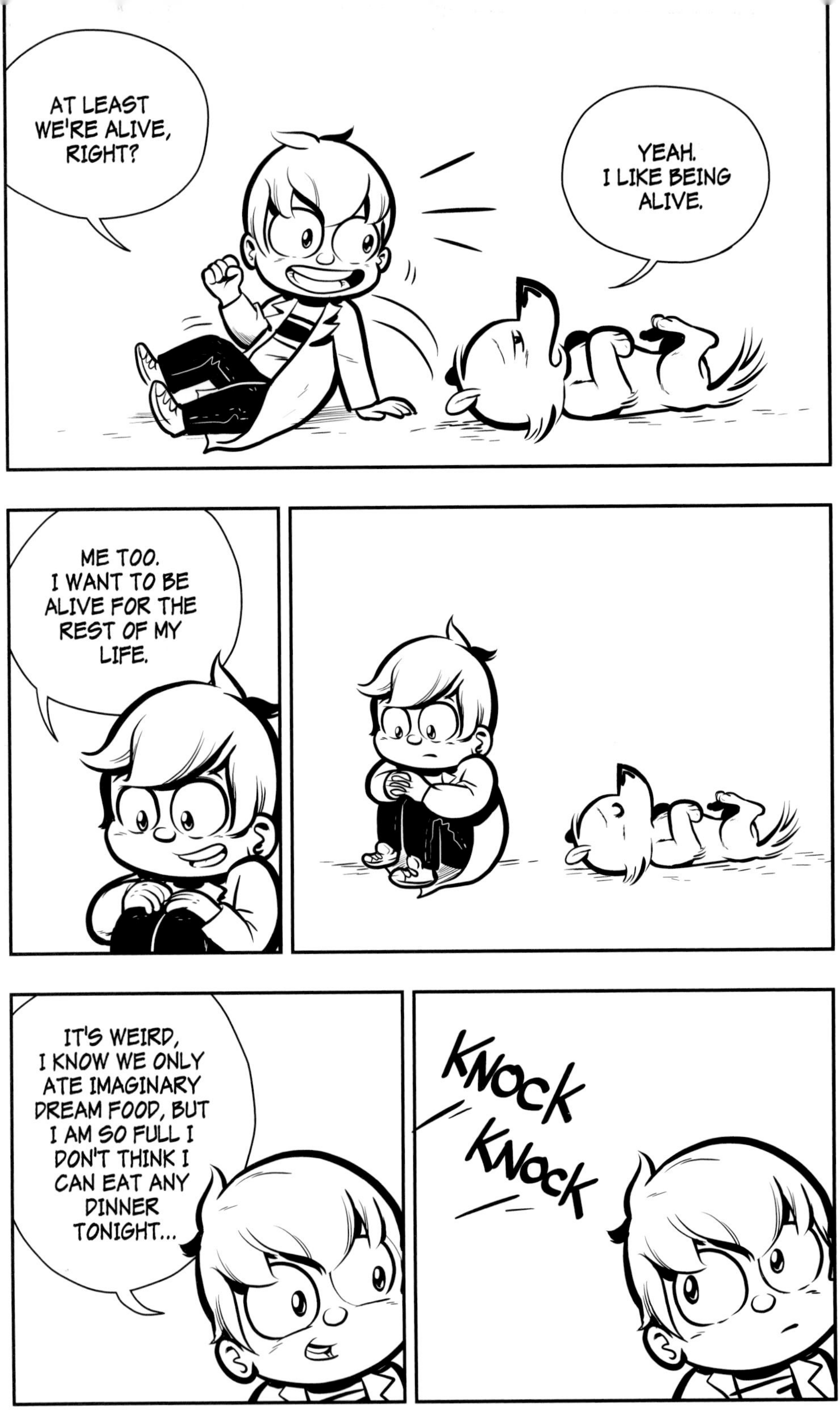
AT LEAST WE'RE ALIVE, RIGHT?
YEAH. I LIKE BEING ALIVE.
ME TOO. I WANT TO BE ALIVE FOR THE REST OF MY LIFE.
IT'S WEIRD, I KNOW WE ONLY ATE IMAGINARY DREAM FOOD, BUT I AM SO FULL I DON'T THINK I CAN EAT ANY DINNER TONIGHT...
KNOCK KNOCK

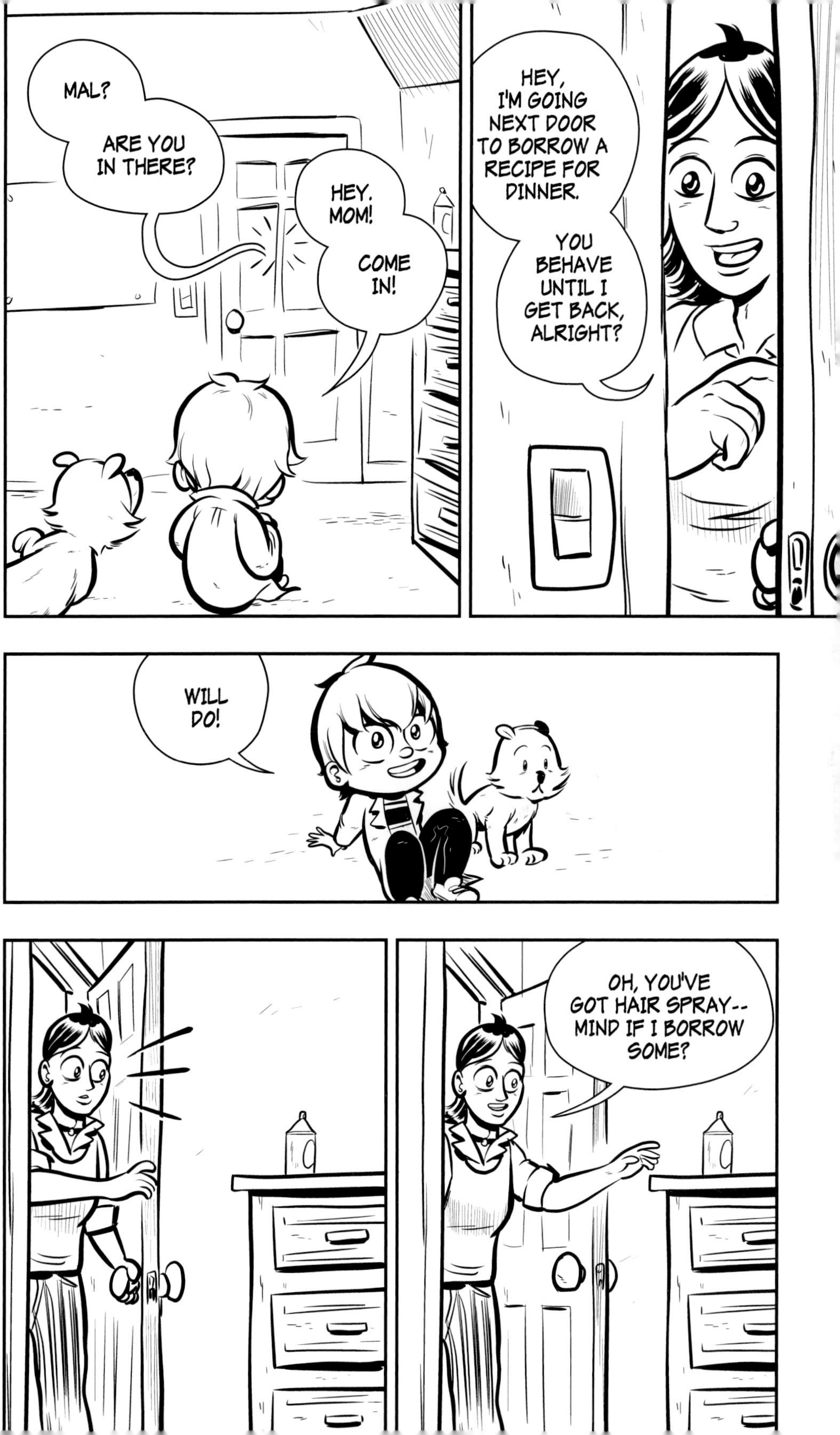
MAL?
ARE YOU IN THERE?
HEY. MOM!
COME IN!
HEY, I'M GOING NEXT DOOR TO BORROW A RECIPE FOR DINNER.
YOU BEHAVE UNTIL I GET BACK, ALRIGHT?
WILL DO!
OH, YOU'VE GOT HAIR SPRAY-- MIND IF I BORROW SOME?

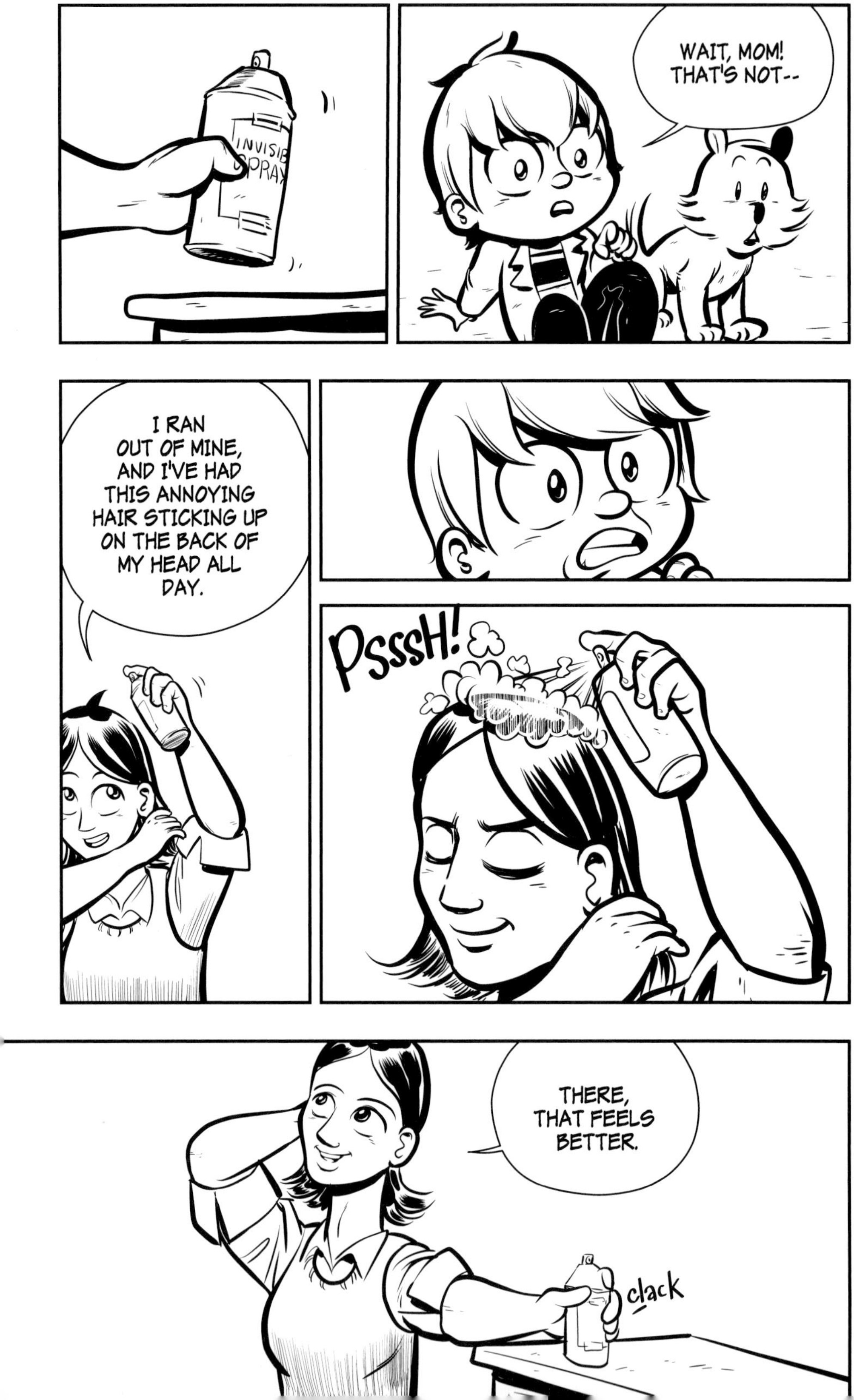
WAIT, MOM! THAT'S NOT--
I RAN OUT OF MINE, AND I'VE HAD THIS ANNOYING HAIR STICKING UP ON THE BACK OF MY HEAD ALL DAY.
PSSSH!
THERE, THAT FEELS BETTER.
clack

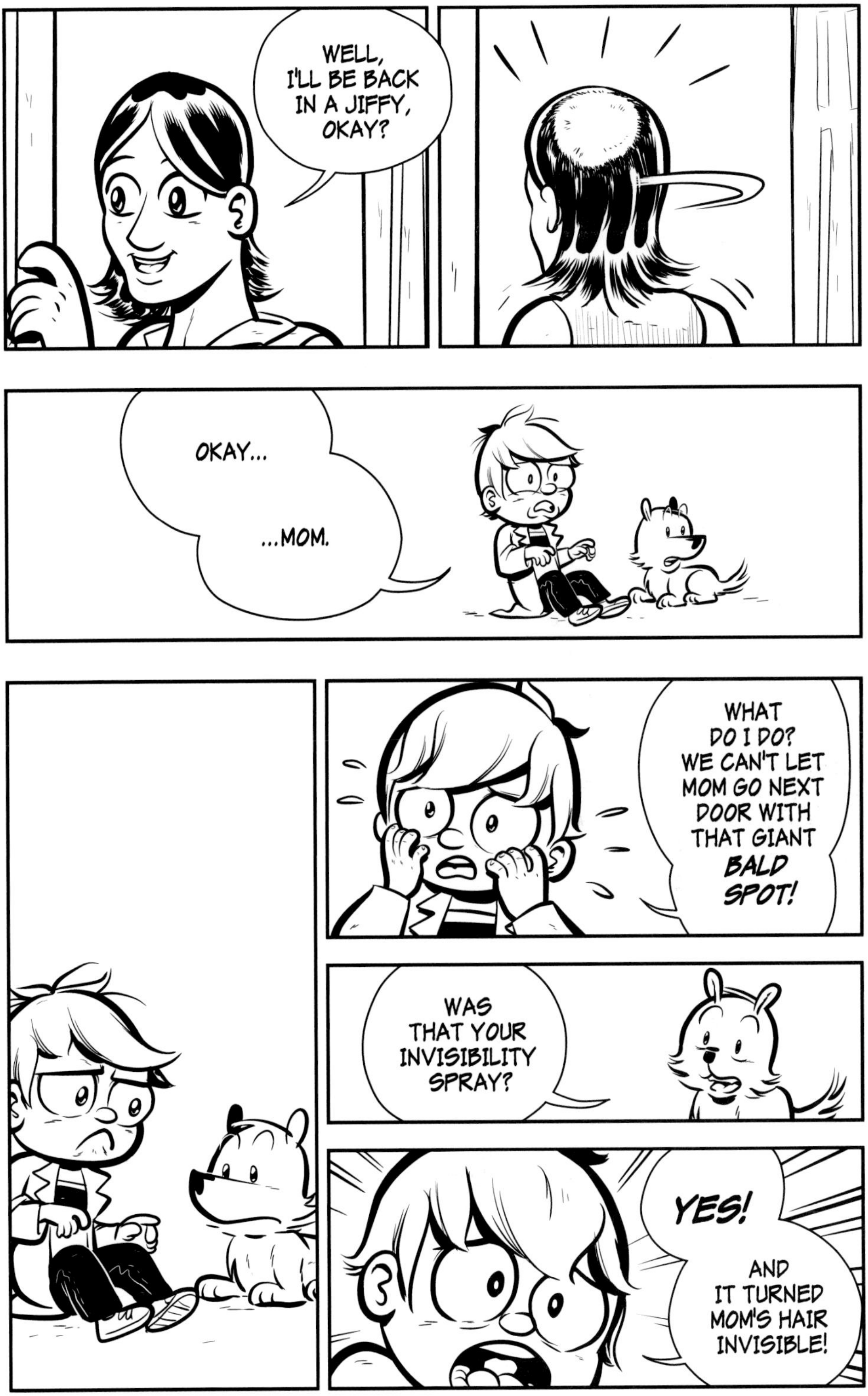
WELL, I'LL BE BACK IN A JIFFY, OKAY?
OKAY...
...MOM.
WHAT DO I DO? WE CAN'T LET MOM GO NEXT DOOR WITH THAT GIANT BALD SPOT!
WAS THAT YOUR INVISIBILITY SPRAY?
YES!
AND IT TURNED MOM'S HAIR INVISIBLE!

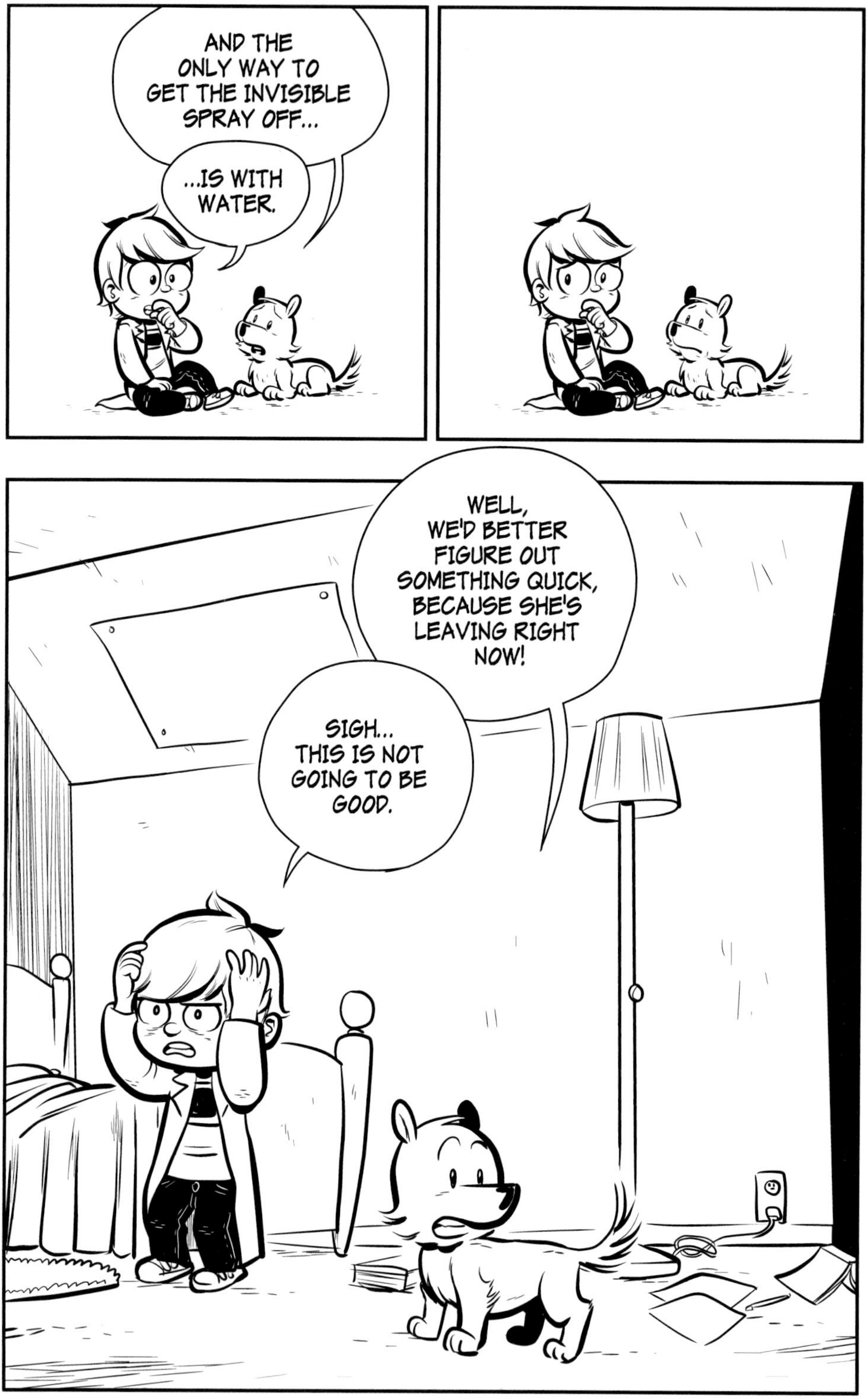
AND THE ONLY WAY TO GET THE INVISIBLE SPRAY OFF...
...IS WITH WATER.
WELL, WE'D BETTER FIGURE OUT SOMETHING QUICK, BECAUSE SHE'S LEAVING RIGHT NOW!
SIGH... THIS IS NOT GOING TO BE GOOD.

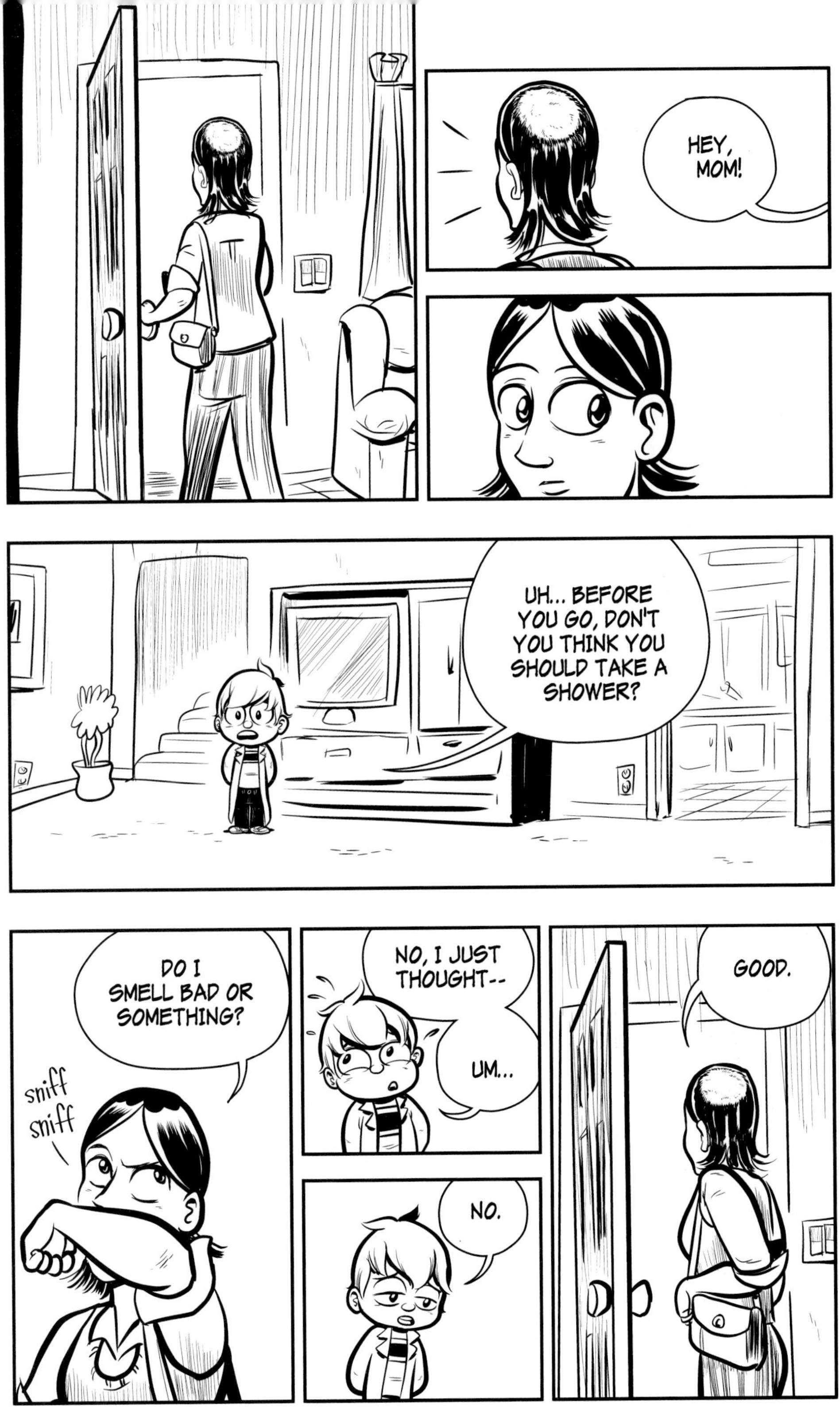
HEY, MOM!
UH... BEFORE YOU GO, DON'T YOU THINK YOU SHOULD TAKE A SHOWER?
DO I SMELL BAD OR SOMETHING?
sniff sniff
NO, I JUST THOUGHT--
UM...
NO.
GOOD.

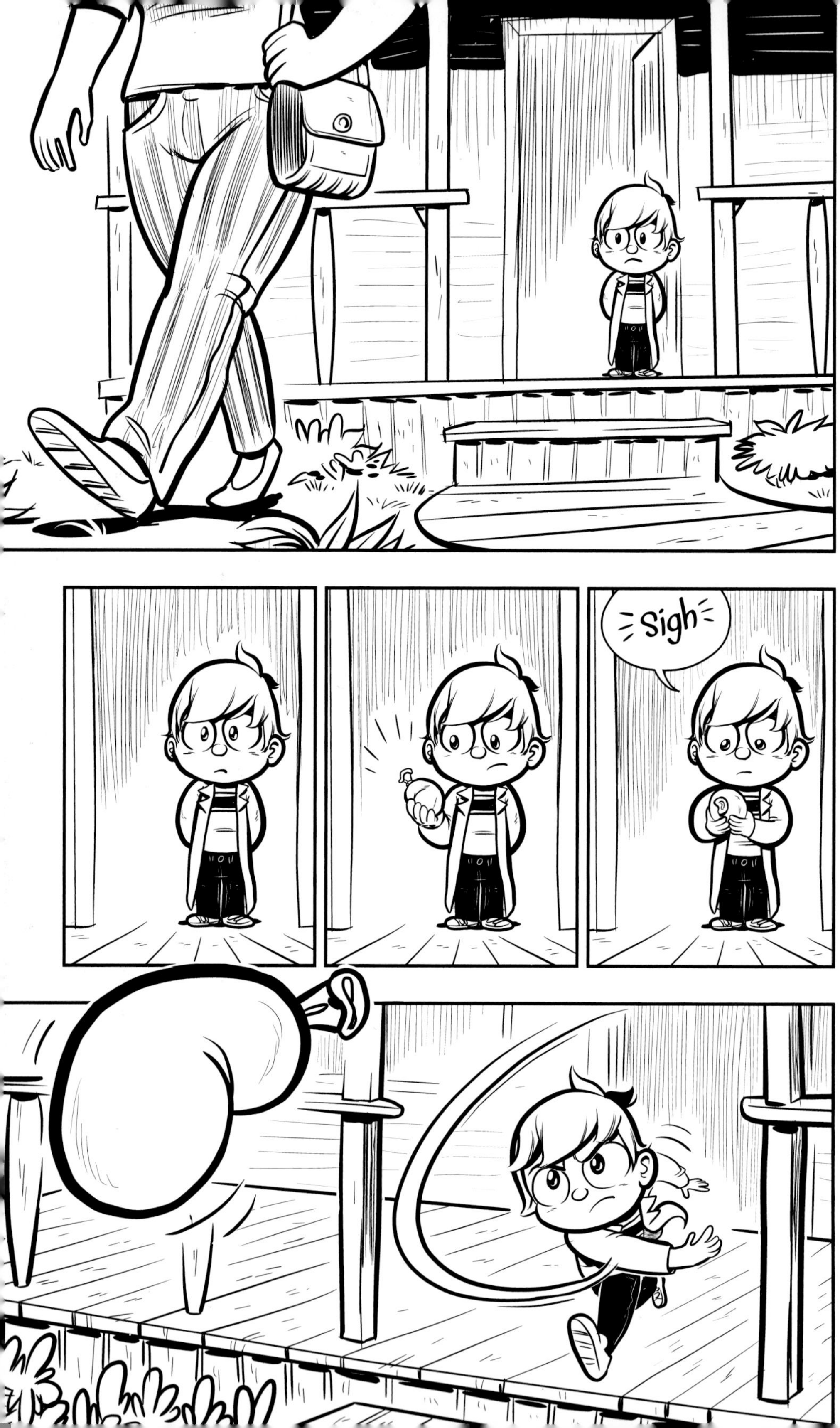
Sigh

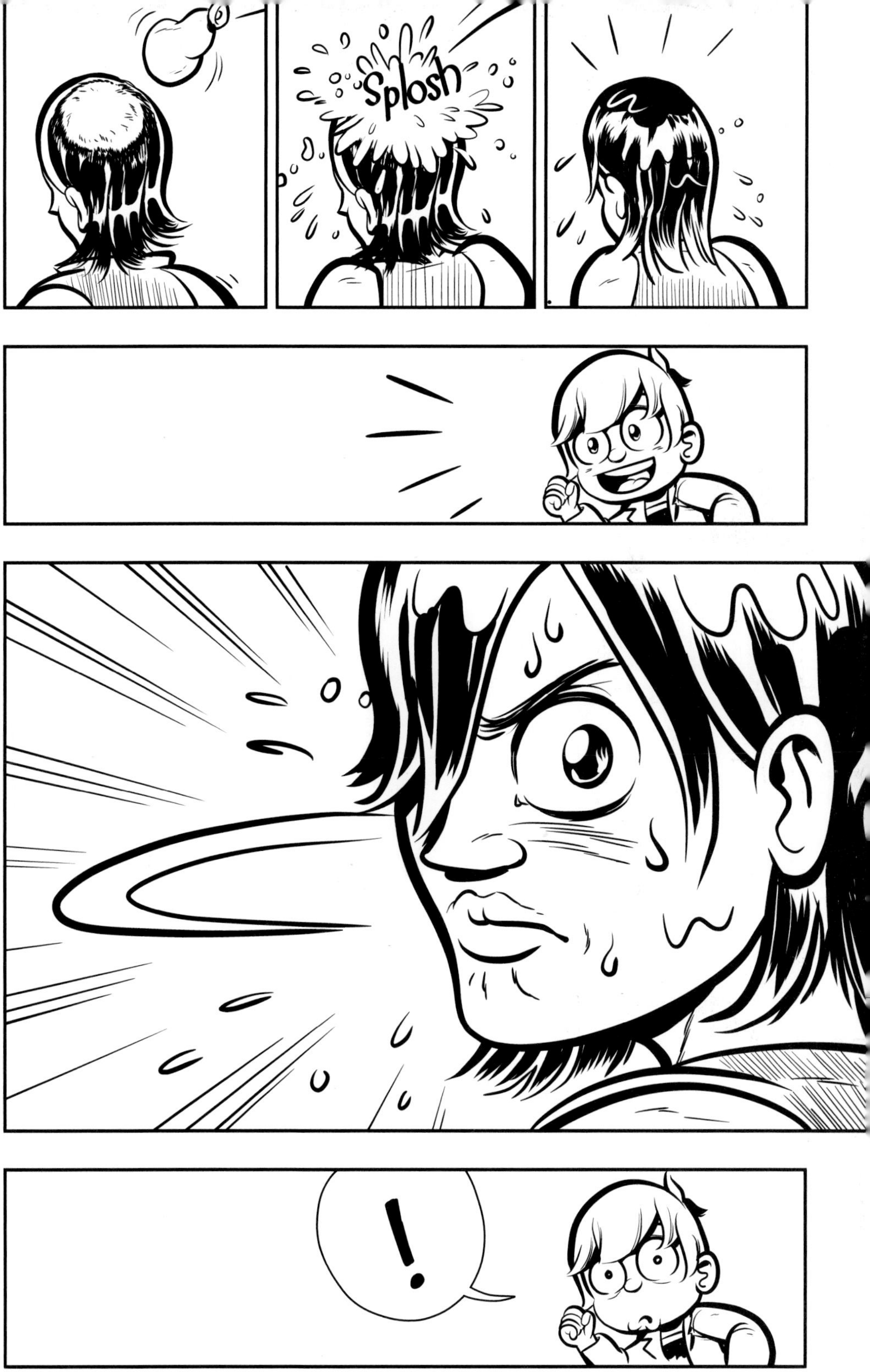
Splosh
!

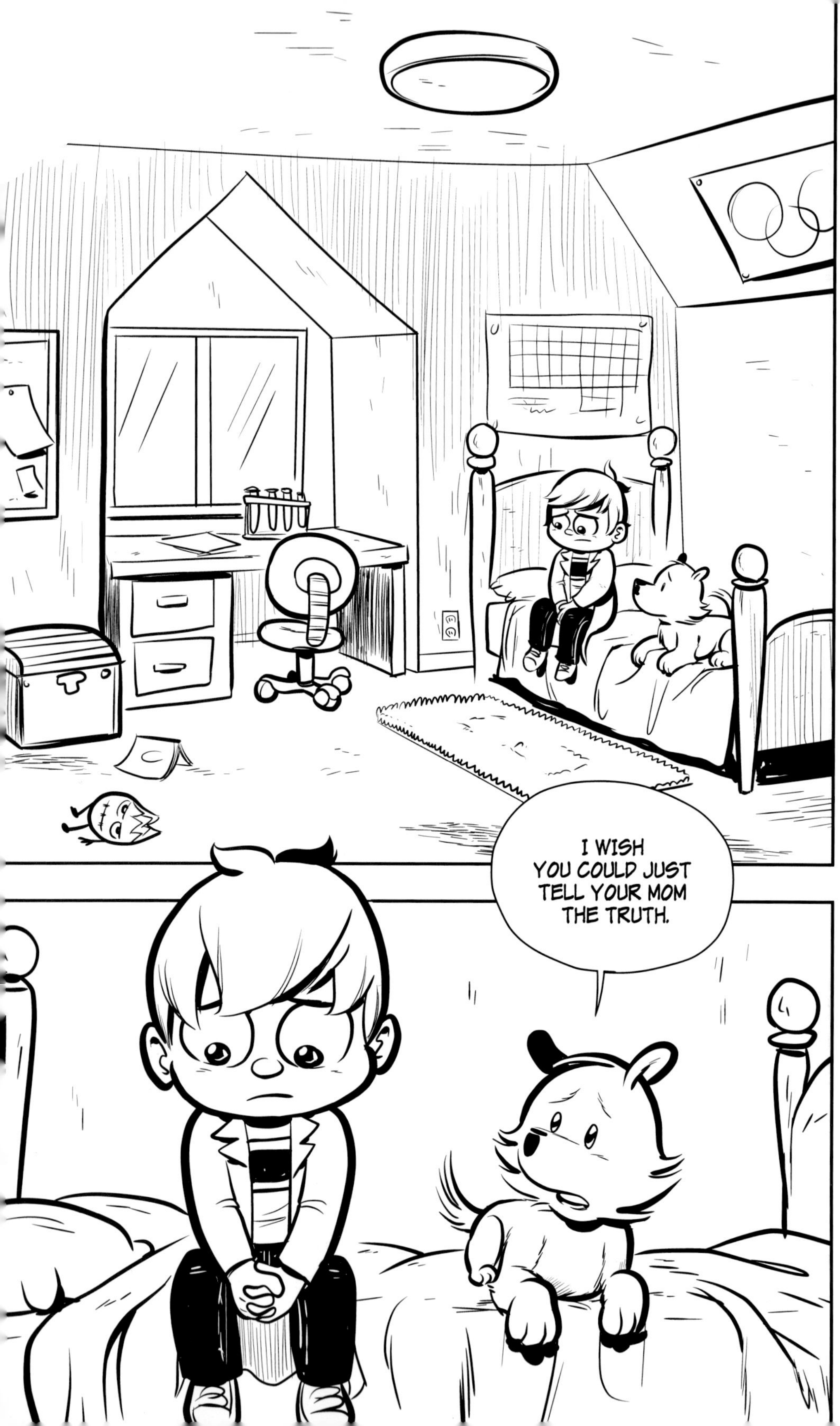
I WISH YOU COULD JUST TELL YOUR MOM THE TRUTH.

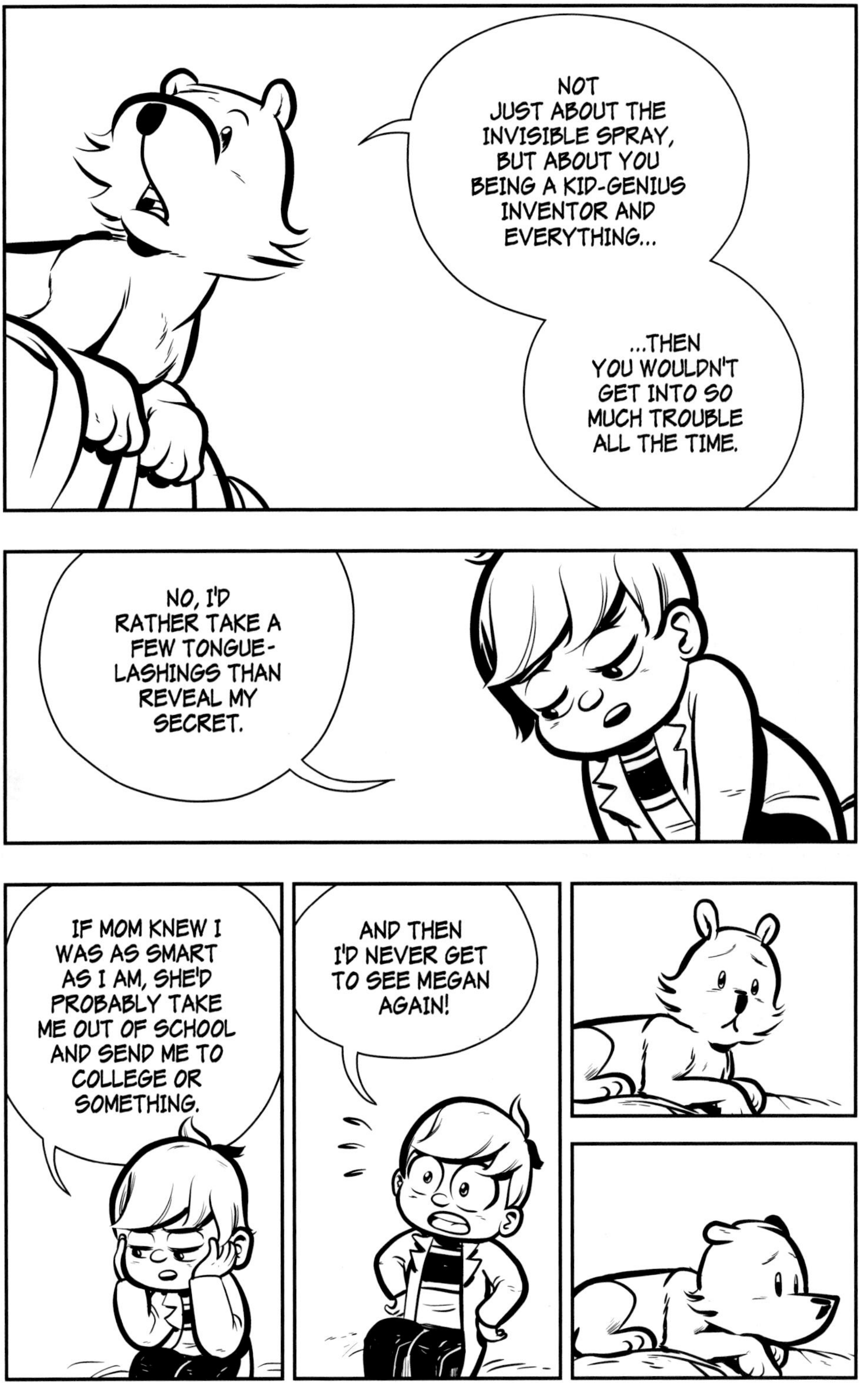
NOT JUST ABOUT THE INVISIBLE SPRAY, BUT ABOUT YOU BEING A KID-GENIUS INVENTOR AND EVERYTHING...
...THEN YOU WOULDN'T GET INTO SO MUCH TROUBLE ALL THE TIME.
NO, I'D RATHER TAKE A FEW TONGUE-LASHINGS THAN REVEAL MY SECRET.
IF MOM KNEW I WAS AS SMART AS I AM, SHE'D PROBABLY TAKE ME OUT OF SCHOOL AND SEND ME TO COLLEGE OR SOMETHING.
AND THEN I'D NEVER GET TO SEE MEGAN AGAIN!

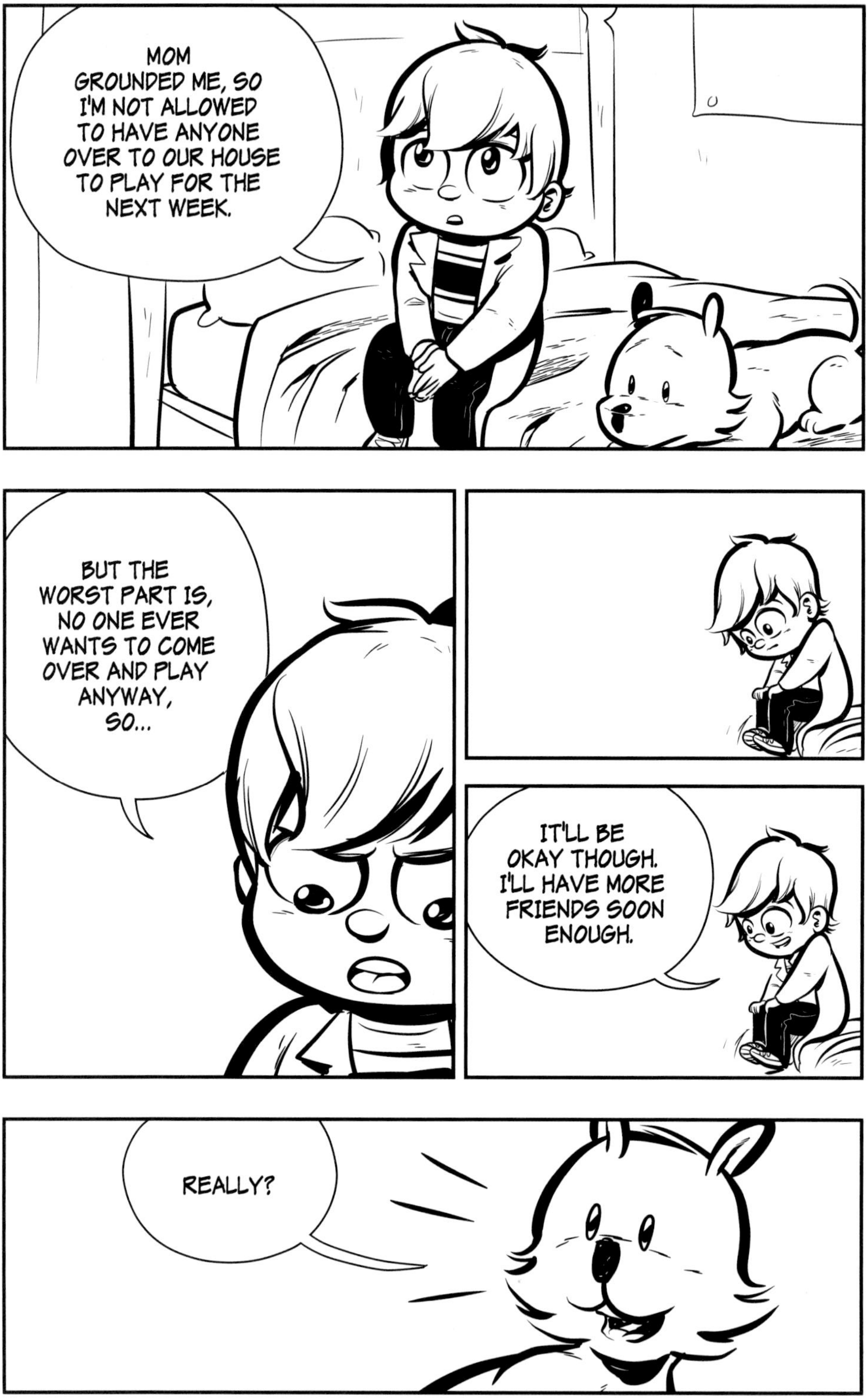
MOM GROUNDED ME, SO I'M NOT ALLOWED TO HAVE ANYONE OVER TO OUR HOUSE TO PLAY FOR THE NEXT WEEK.
BUT THE WORST PART IS, NO ONE EVER WANTS TO COME OVER AND PLAY ANYWAY, SO...
IT'LL BE OKAY THOUGH. I'LL HAVE MORE FRIENDS SOON ENOUGH.
REALLY?

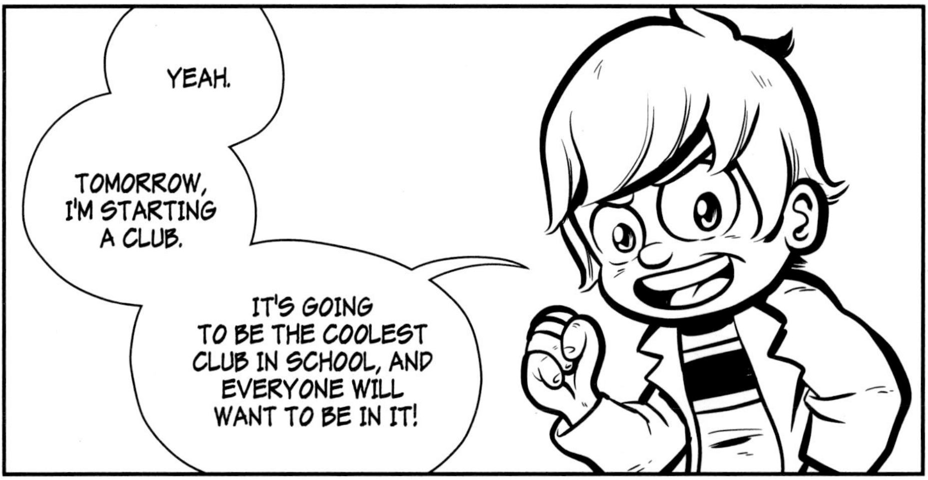
YEAH.
TOMORROW, I'M STARTING A CLUB.
IT'S GOING TO BE THE COOLEST CLUB IN SCHOOL, AND EVERYONE WILL WANT TO BE IN IT!

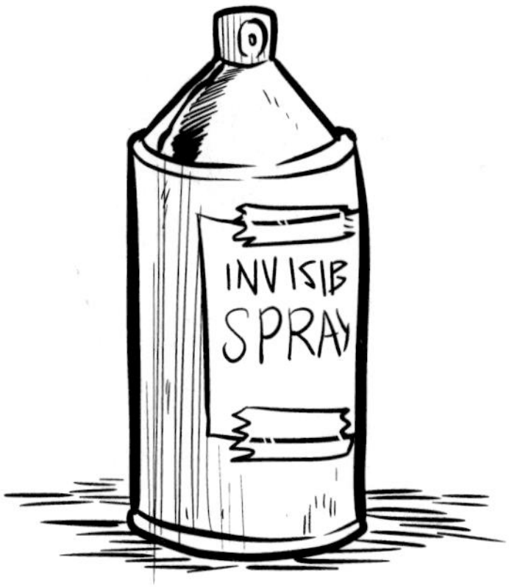
INVISIB
SPRAY

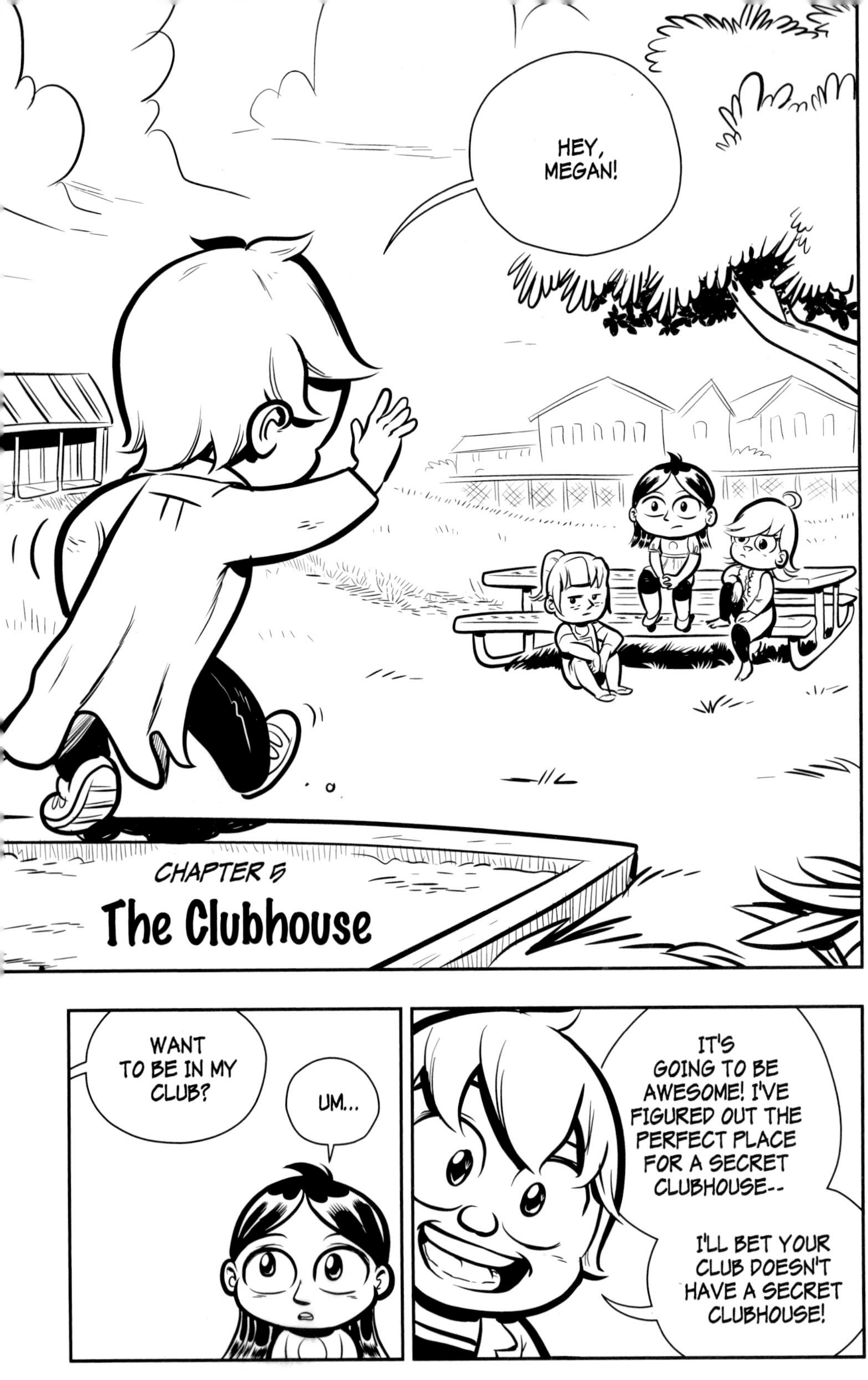
HEY, MEGAN!
CHAPTER 5
The Clubhouse
WANT TO BE IN MY CLUB?
UM...
IT'S GOING TO BE AWESOME! I'VE FIGURED OUT THE PERFECT PLACE FOR A SECRET CLUBHOUSE--
I'LL BET YOUR CLUB DOESN'T HAVE A SECRET CLUBHOUSE!

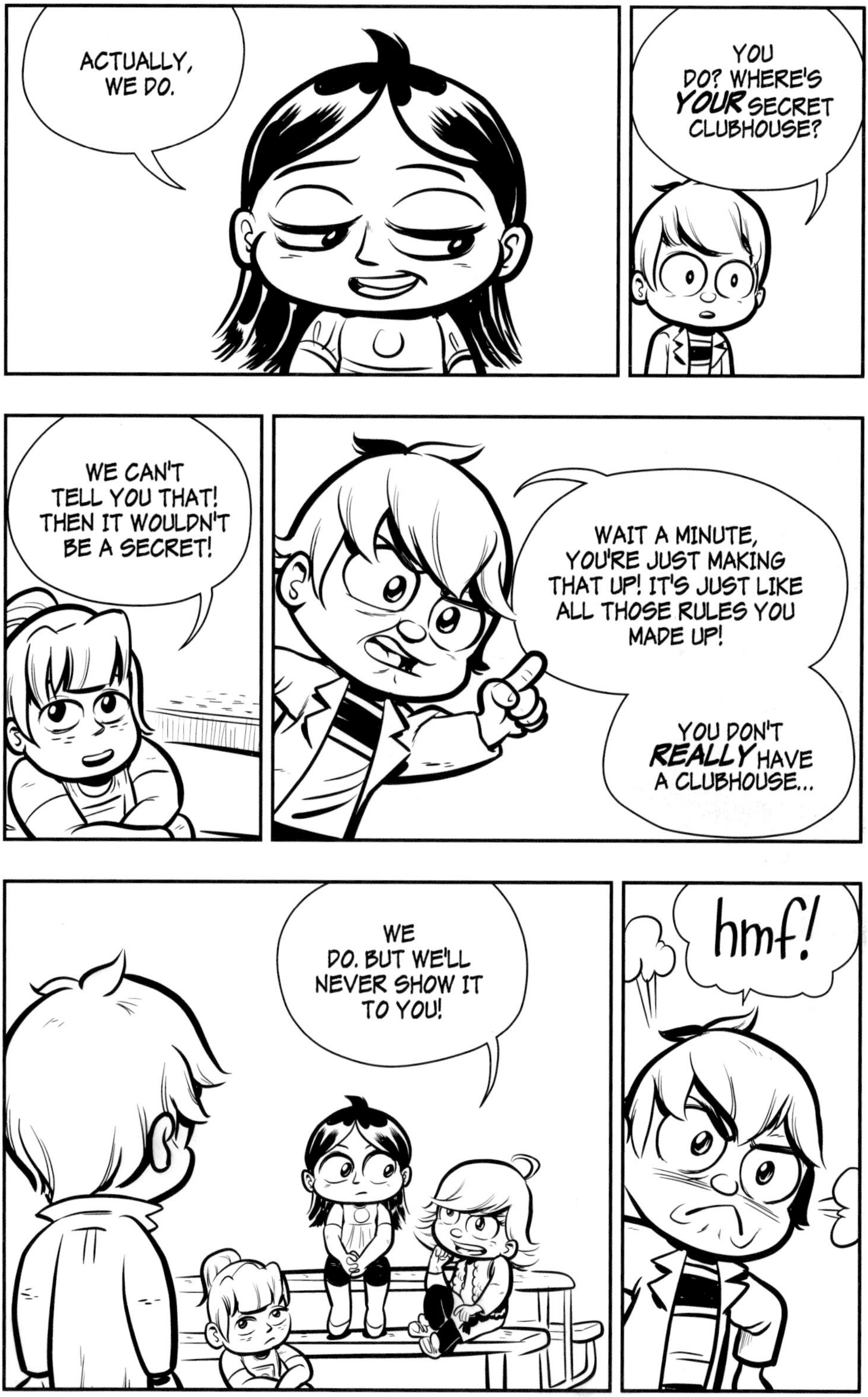
ACTUALLY, WE DO.
YOU DO? WHERE'S YOUR SECRET CLUBHOUSE?
WE CAN'T TELL YOU THAT! THEN IT WOULDN'T BE A SECRET!
WAIT A MINUTE, YOU'RE JUST MAKING THAT UP! IT'S JUST LIKE ALL THOSE RULES YOU MADE UP!
YOU DON'T REALLY HAVE A CLUBHOUSE...
WE DO. BUT WE'LL NEVER SHOW IT TO YOU!
hmf!

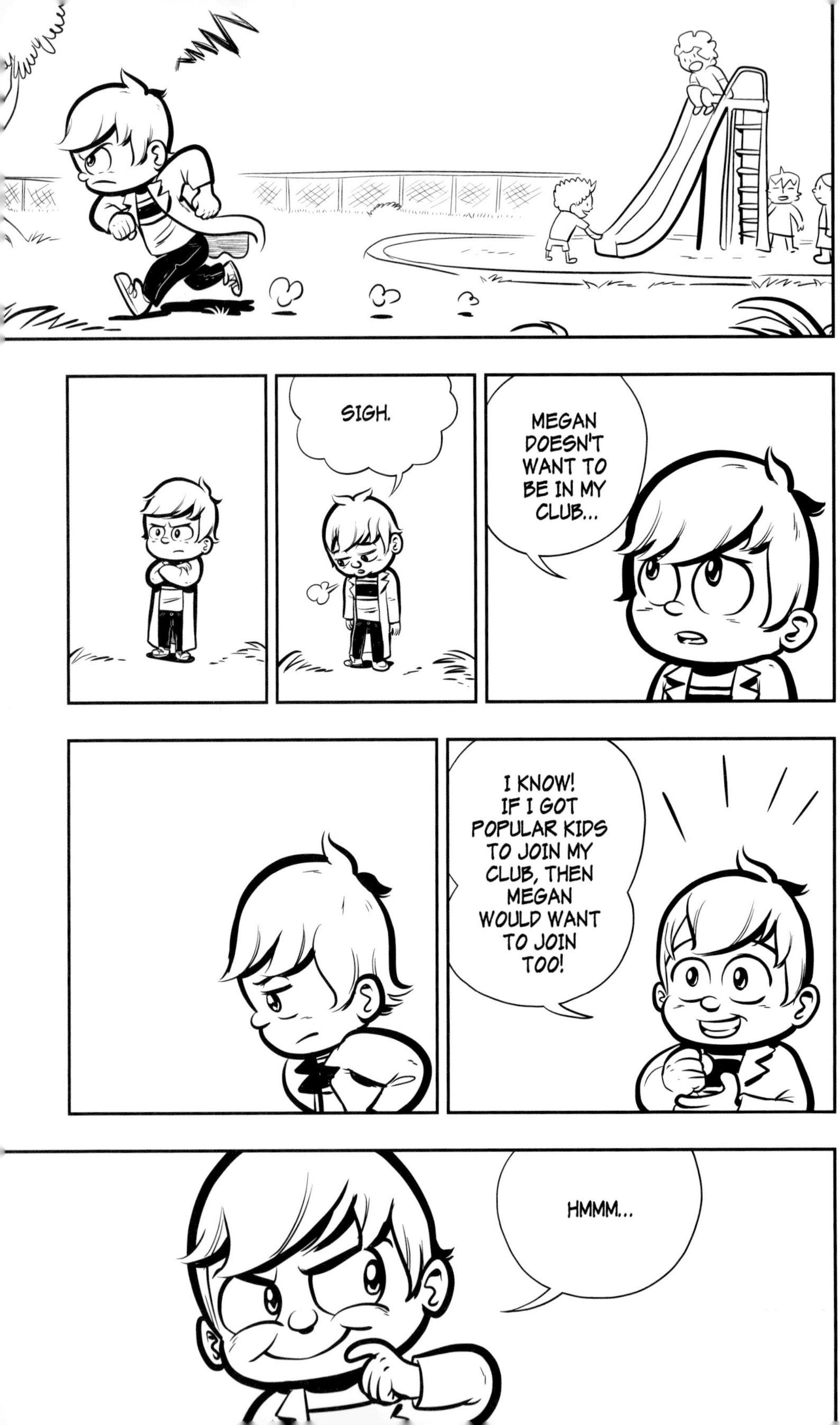
SIGH.
MEGAN DOESN'T WANT TO BE IN MY CLUB...
I KNOW! IF I GOT POPULAR KIDS TO JOIN MY CLUB, THEN MEGAN WOULD WANT TO JOIN TOO!
HMMM...

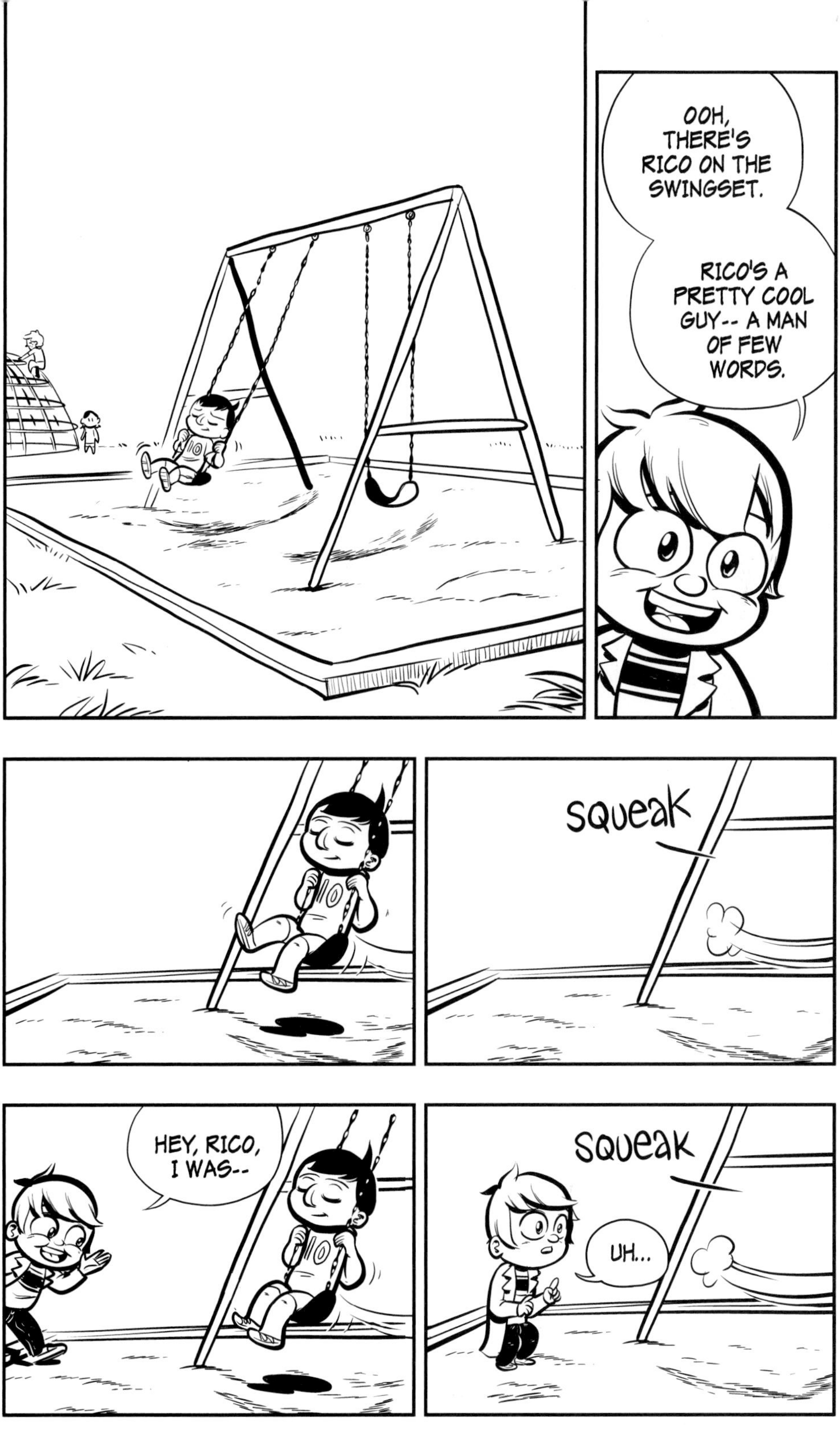
OOH, THERE'S RICO ON THE SWINGSET.
RICO'S A PRETTY COOL GUY-- A MAN OF FEW WORDS.
SQUEAK
HEY, RICO, I WAS--
SQUEAK
UH...

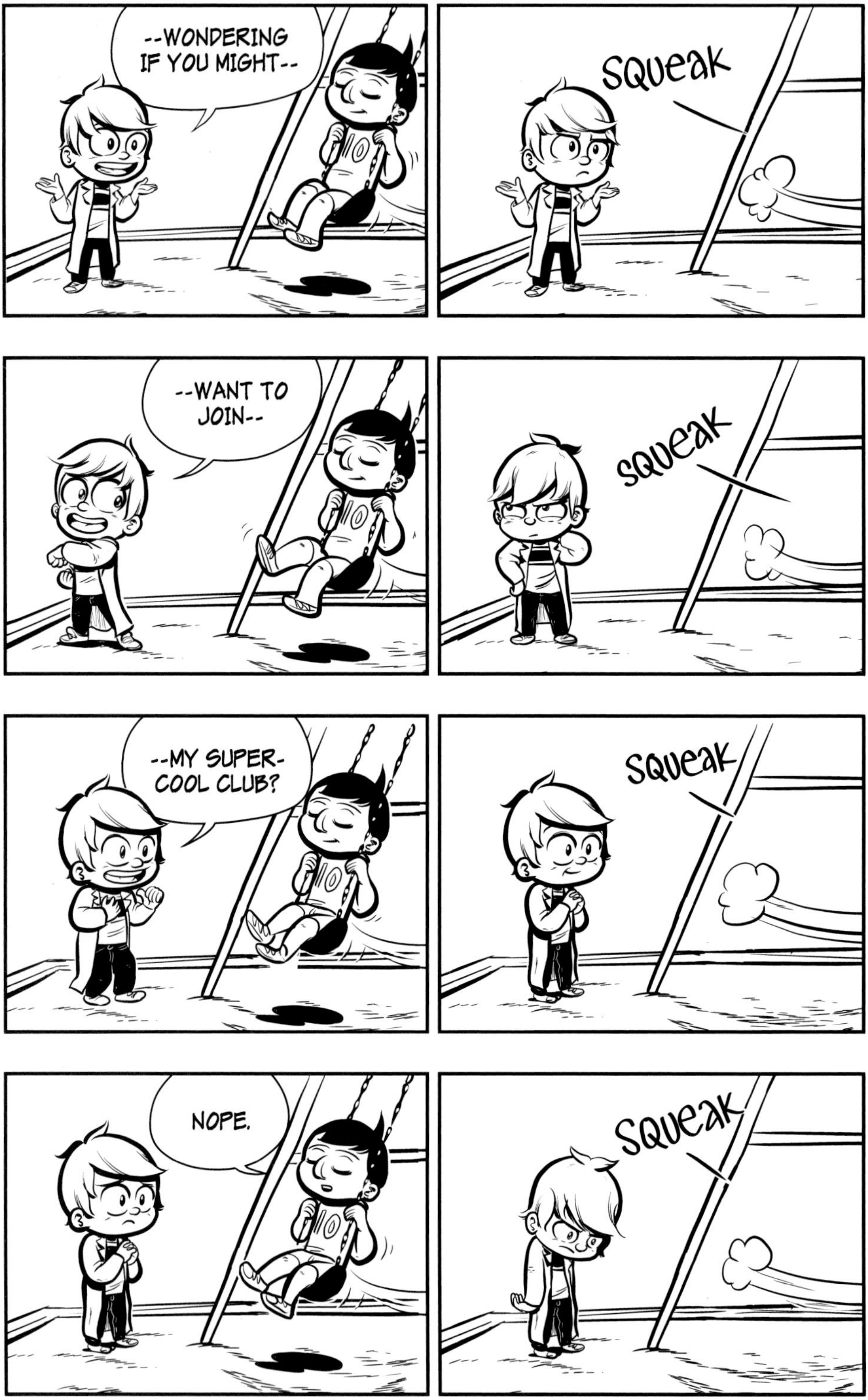
--WONDERING IF YOU MIGHT--
SQUEAK
--WANT TO JOIN--
SQUEAK
--MY SUPER-COOL CLUB?
SQUEAK
NOPE.
SQUEAK

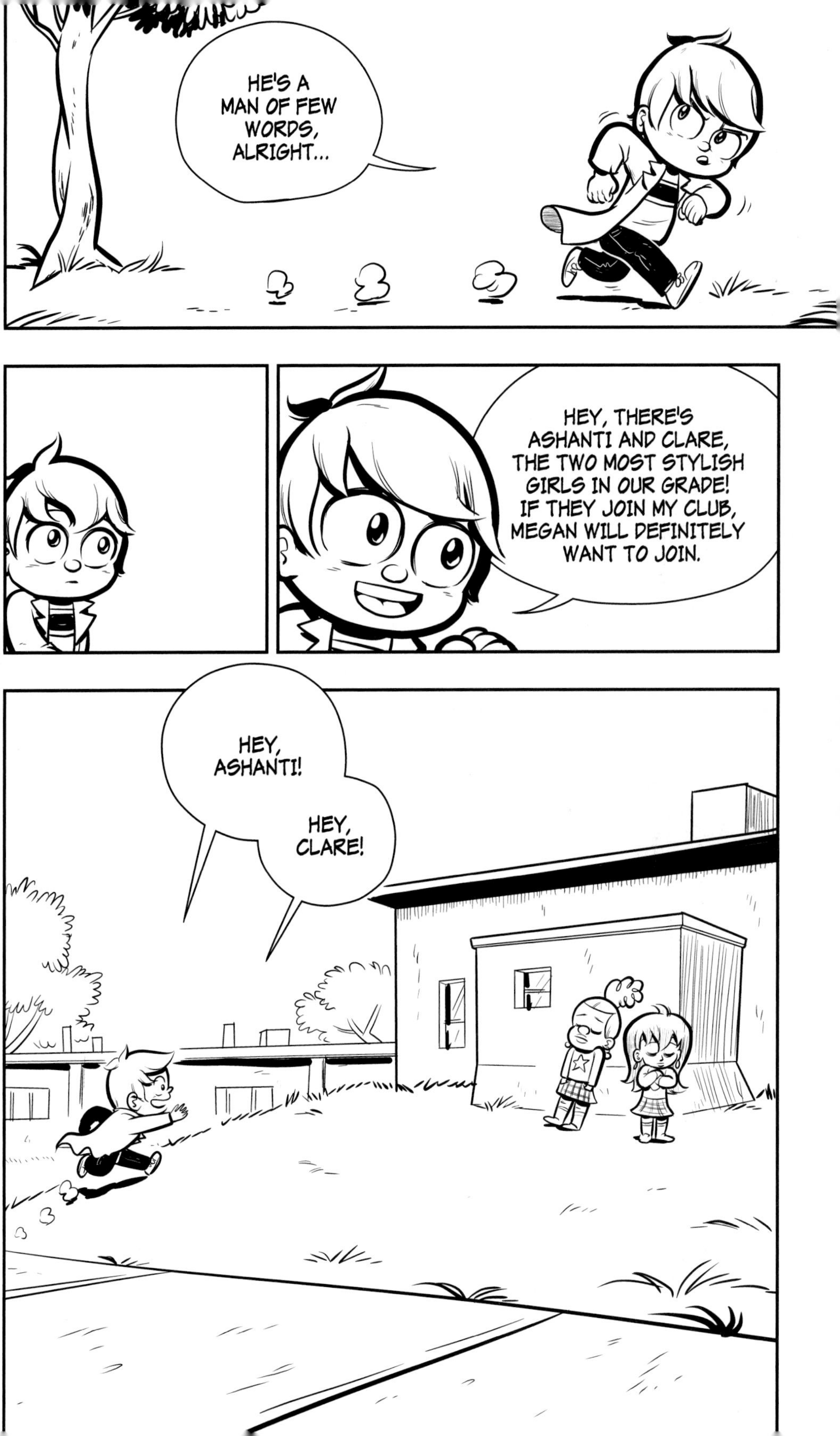
HE'S A MAN OF FEW WORDS, ALRIGHT...
HEY, THERE'S ASHANTI AND CLARE, THE TWO MOST STYLISH GIRLS IN OUR GRADE! IF THEY JOIN MY CLUB, MEGAN WILL DEFINITELY WANT TO JOIN.
HEY, ASHANTI!
HEY, CLARE!

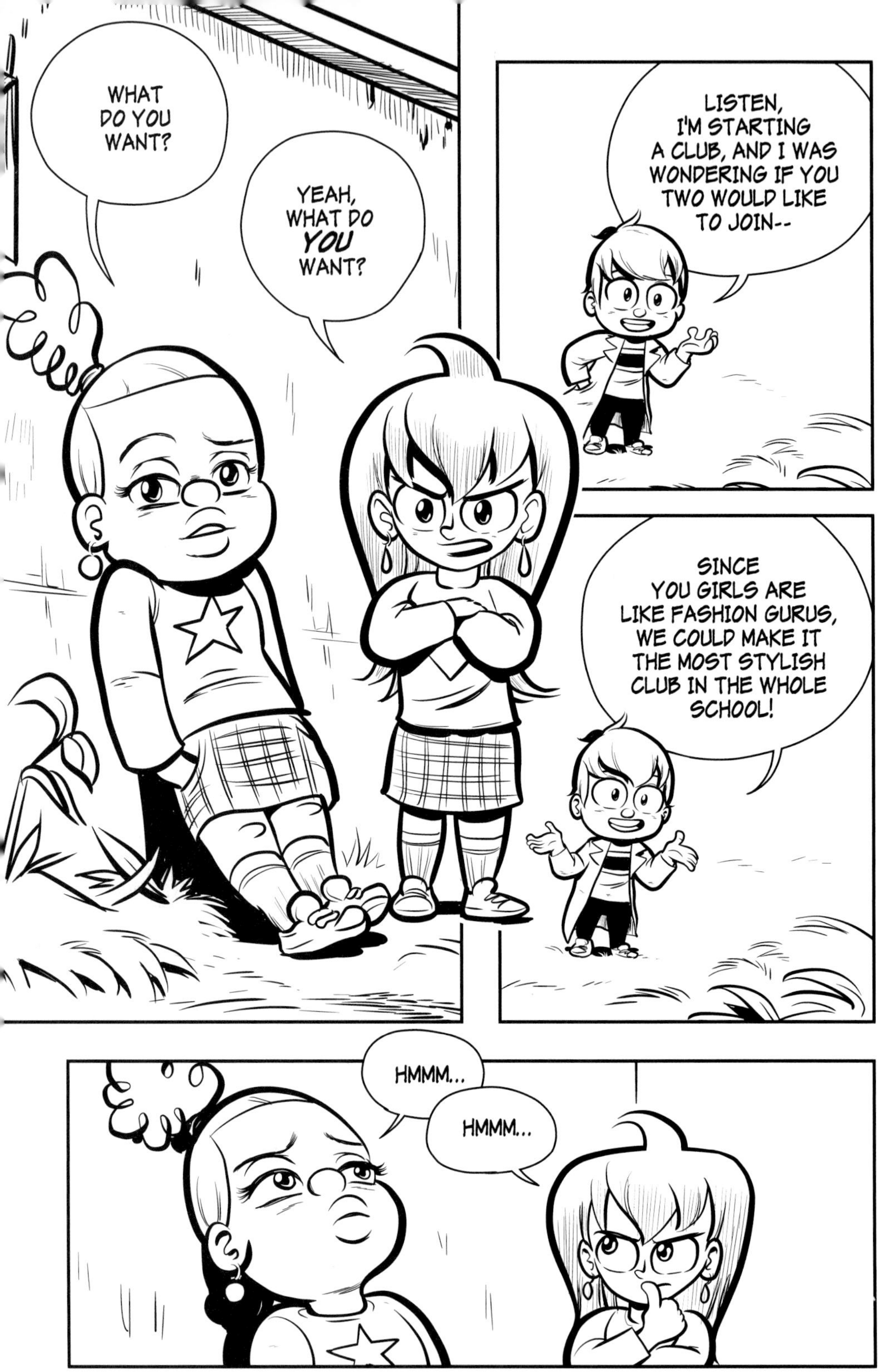
WHAT DO YOU WANT?
YEAH, WHAT DO *YOU* WANT?
LISTEN, I'M STARTING A CLUB, AND I WAS WONDERING IF YOU TWO WOULD LIKE TO JOIN--
SINCE YOU GIRLS ARE LIKE FASHION GURUS, WE COULD MAKE IT THE MOST STYLISH CLUB IN THE WHOLE SCHOOL!
HMMM...
HMMM...

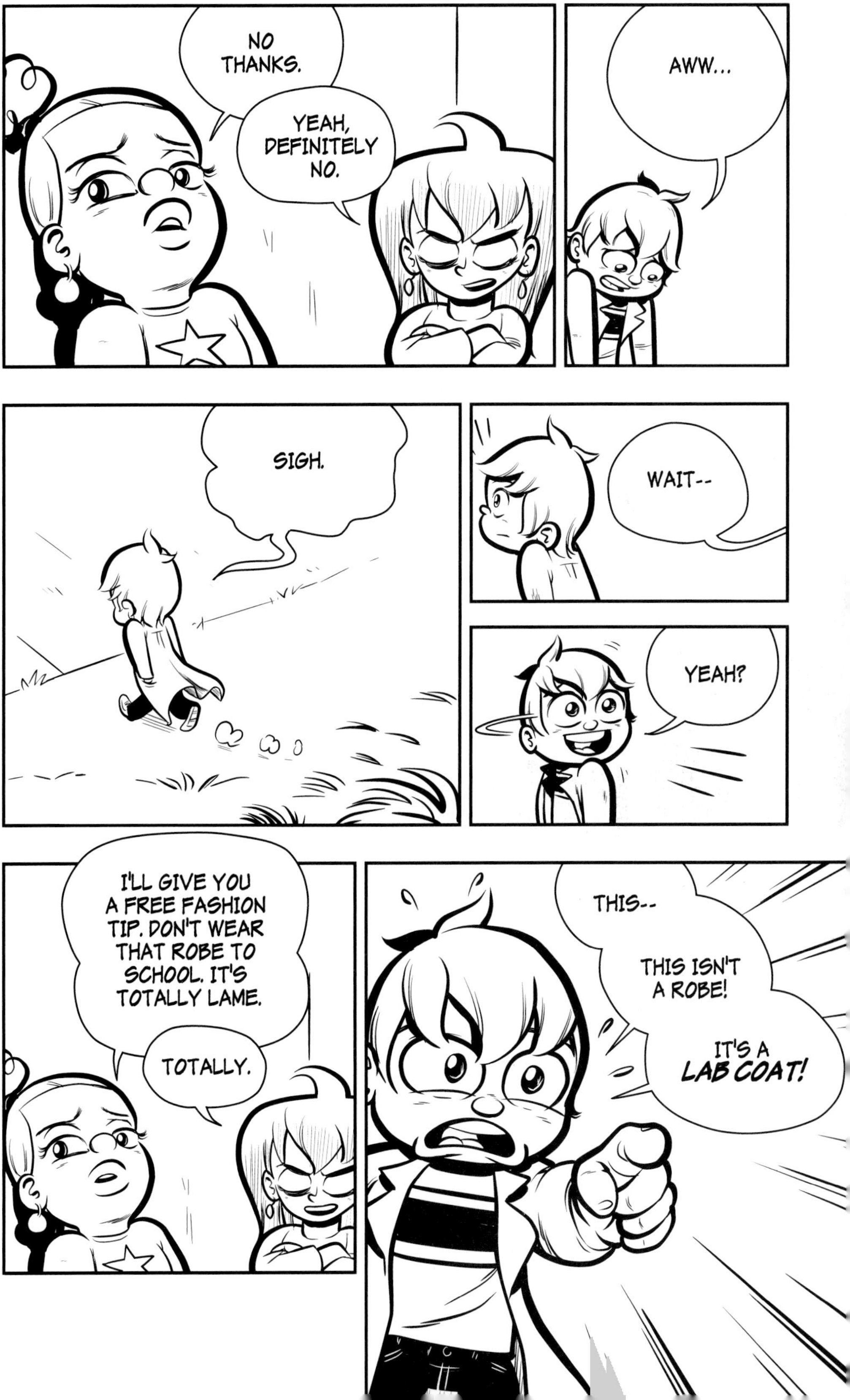
NO THANKS.
YEAH, DEFINITELY NO.
AWW...
SIGH.
WAIT--
YEAH?
I'LL GIVE YOU A FREE FASHION TIP. DON'T WEAR THAT ROBE TO SCHOOL. IT'S TOTALLY LAME.
TOTALLY.
THIS--
THIS ISN'T A ROBE!
IT'S A *LAB COAT!*

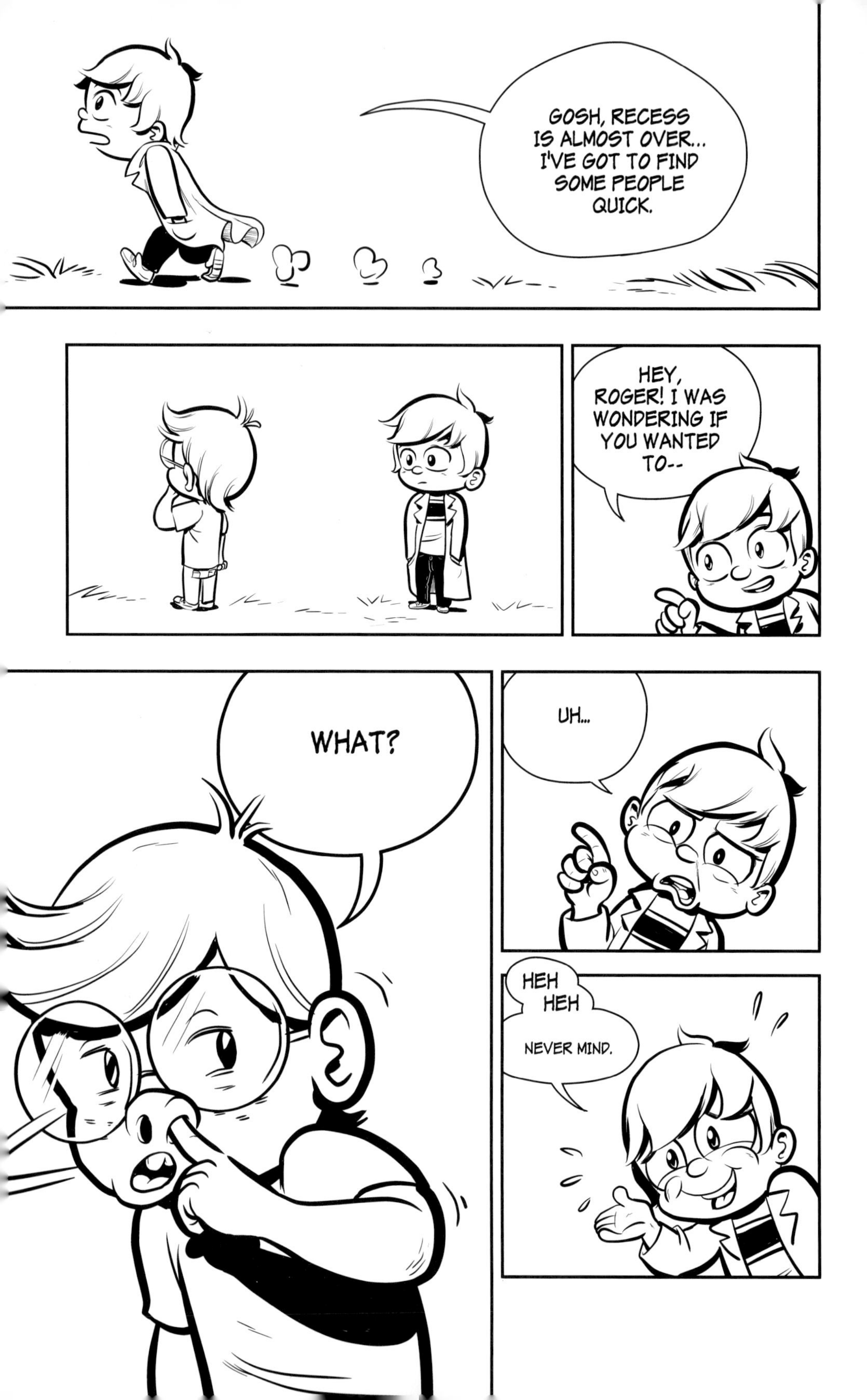
GOSH, RECESS IS ALMOST OVER... I'VE GOT TO FIND SOME PEOPLE QUICK.
HEY, ROGER! I WAS WONDERING IF YOU WANTED TO--
WHAT?
UH...
HEH HEH
NEVER MIND.

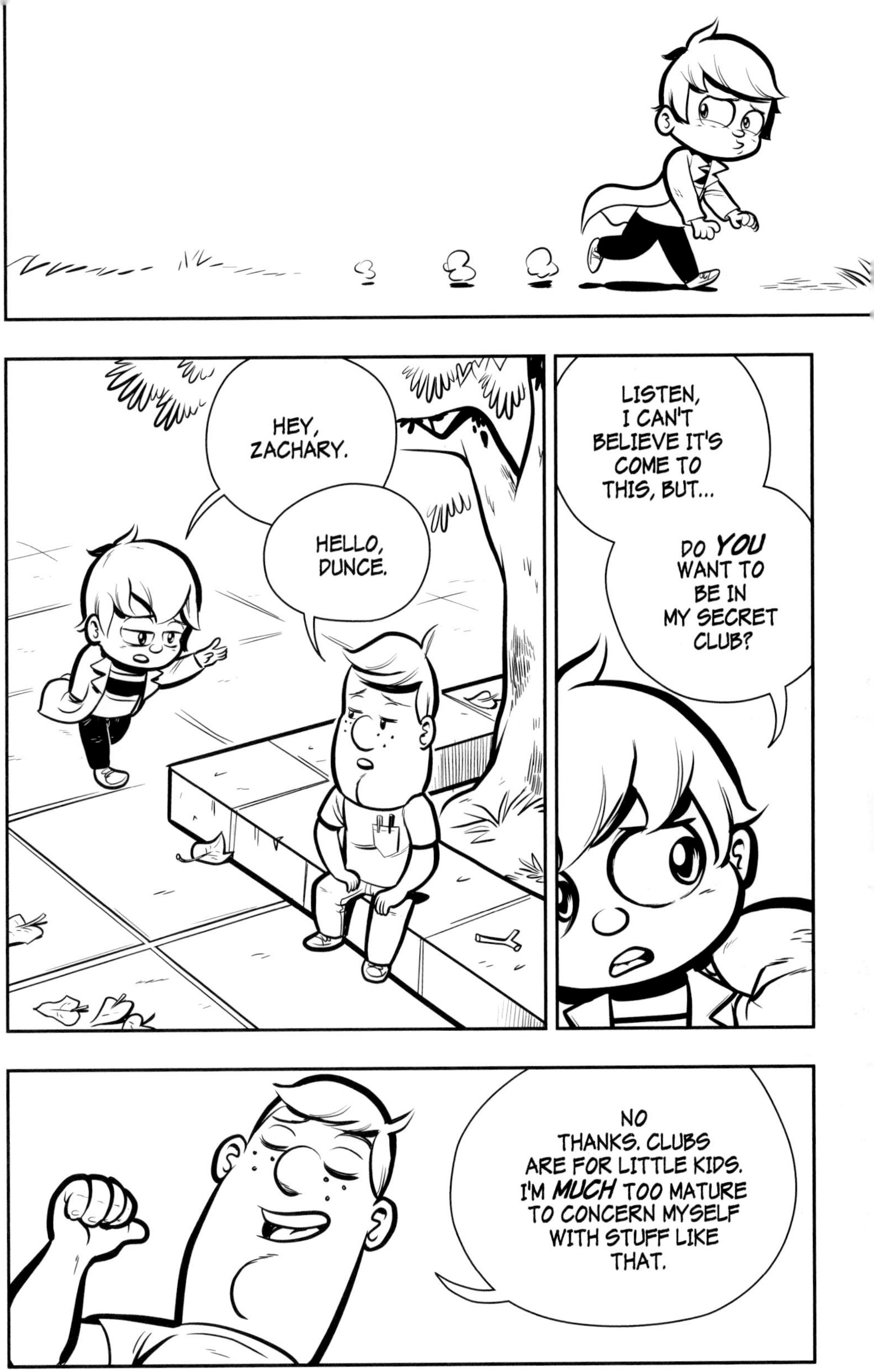
HEY, ZACHARY.
HELLO, DUNCE.
LISTEN, I CAN'T BELIEVE IT'S COME TO THIS, BUT...
DO *YOU* WANT TO BE IN MY SECRET CLUB?
NO THANKS. CLUBS ARE FOR LITTLE KIDS. I'M *MUCH* TOO MATURE TO CONCERN MYSELF WITH STUFF LIKE THAT.

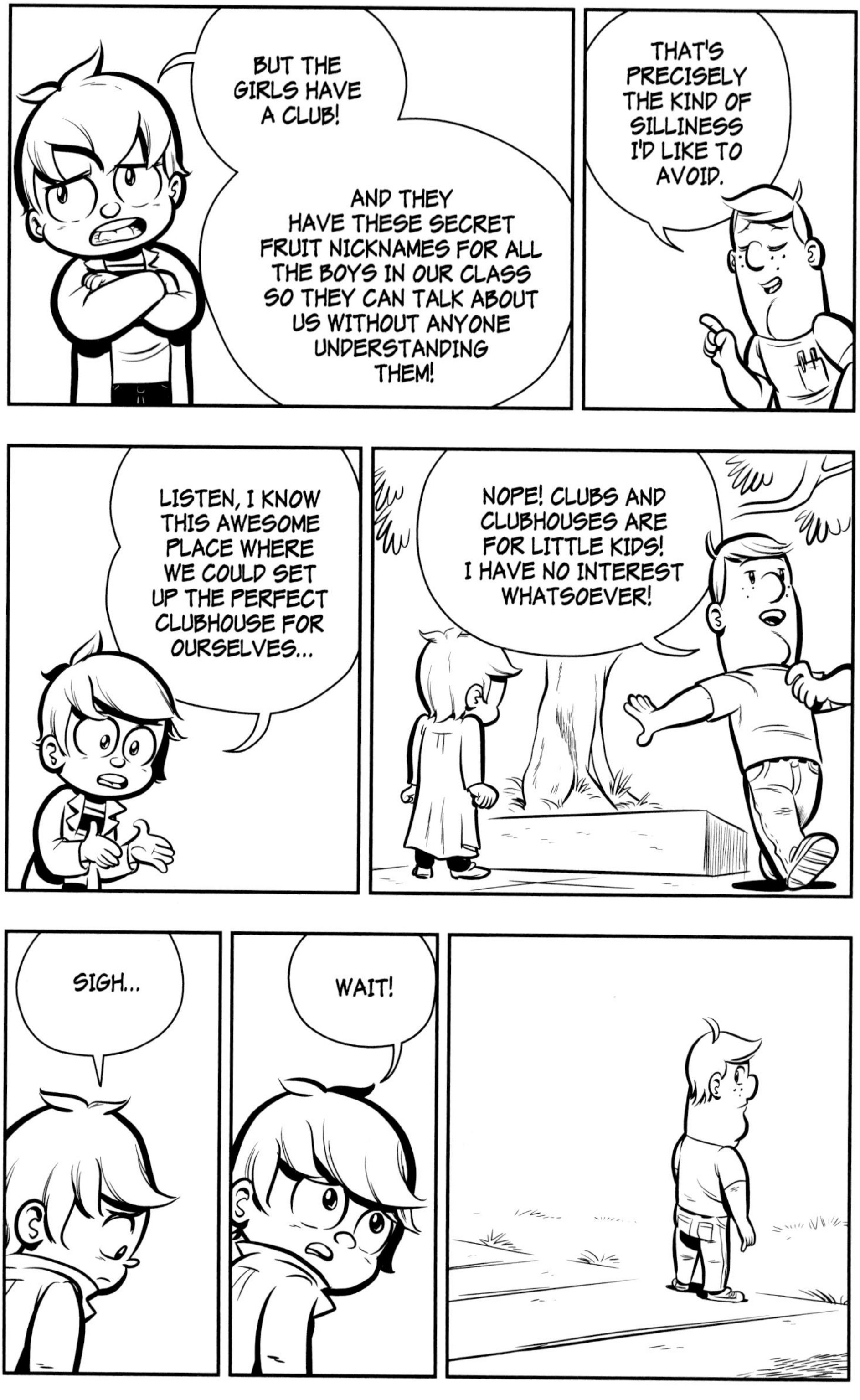
BUT THE GIRLS HAVE A CLUB!
AND THEY HAVE THESE SECRET FRUIT NICKNAMES FOR ALL THE BOYS IN OUR CLASS SO THEY CAN TALK ABOUT US WITHOUT ANYONE UNDERSTANDING THEM!
THAT'S PRECISELY THE KIND OF SILLINESS I'D LIKE TO AVOID.
LISTEN, I KNOW THIS AWESOME PLACE WHERE WE COULD SET UP THE PERFECT CLUBHOUSE FOR OURSELVES...
NOPE! CLUBS AND CLUBHOUSES ARE FOR LITTLE KIDS! I HAVE NO INTEREST WHATSOEVER!
SIGH...
WAIT!

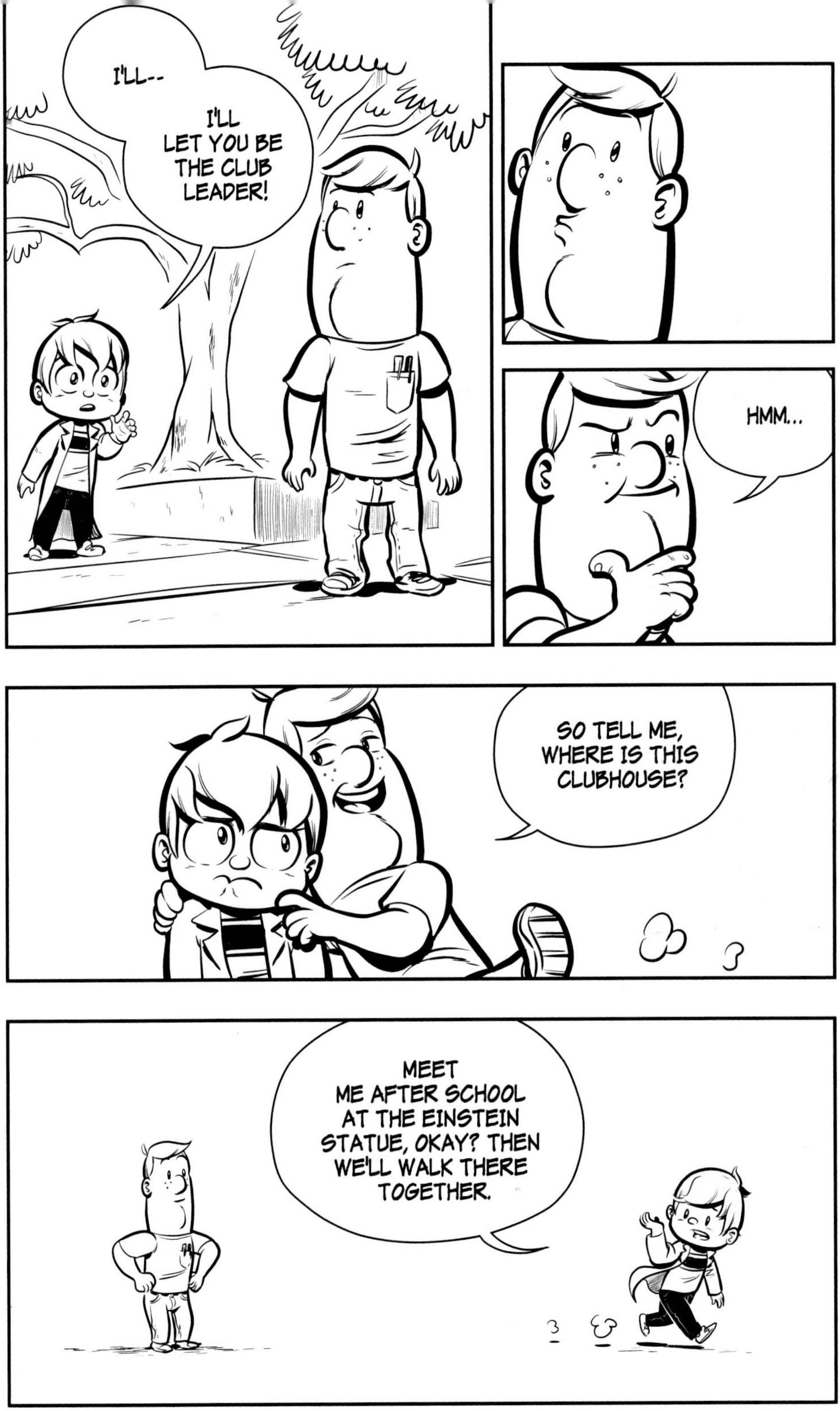
I'LL--
I'LL LET YOU BE THE CLUB LEADER!
HMM...
SO TELL ME, WHERE IS THIS CLUBHOUSE?
MEET ME AFTER SCHOOL AT THE EINSTEIN STATUE, OKAY? THEN WE'LL WALK THERE TOGETHER.

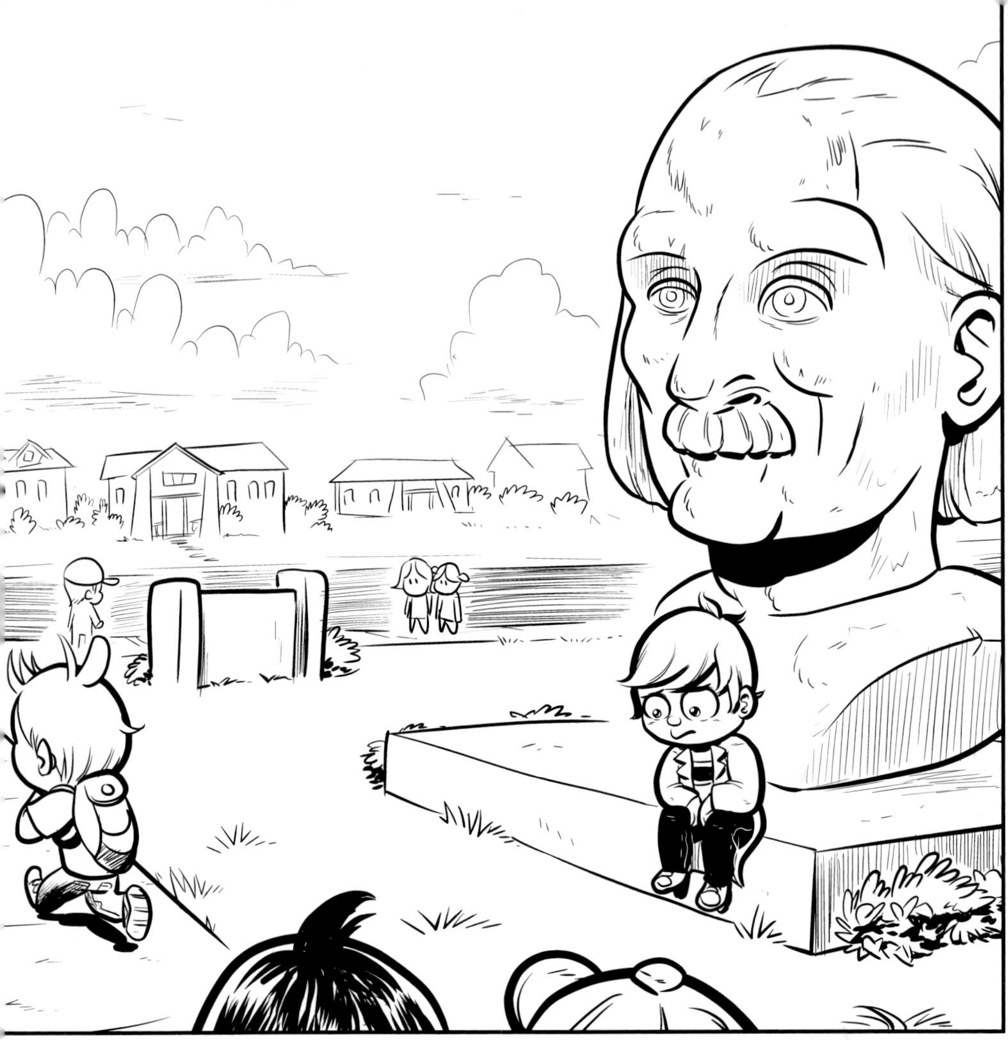

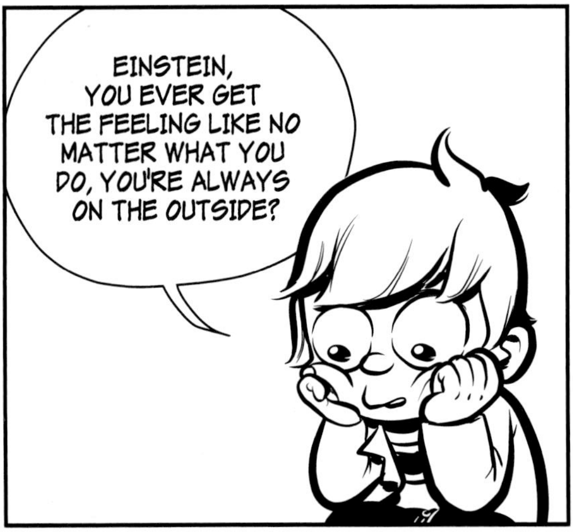
EINSTEIN, YOU EVER GET THE FEELING LIKE NO MATTER WHAT YOU DO, YOU'RE ALWAYS ON THE OUTSIDE?

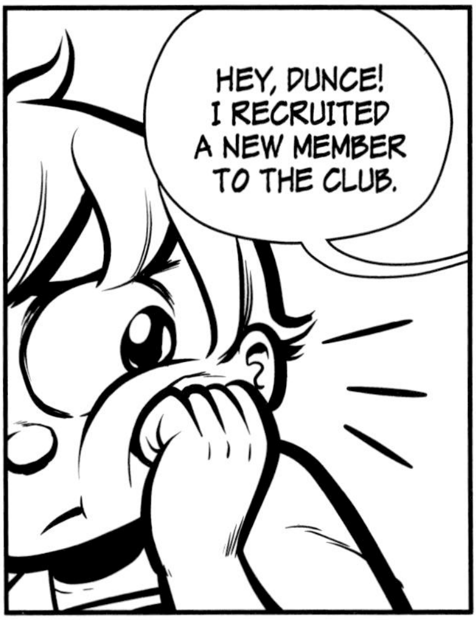
HEY, DUNCE! I RECRUITED A NEW MEMBER TO THE CLUB.

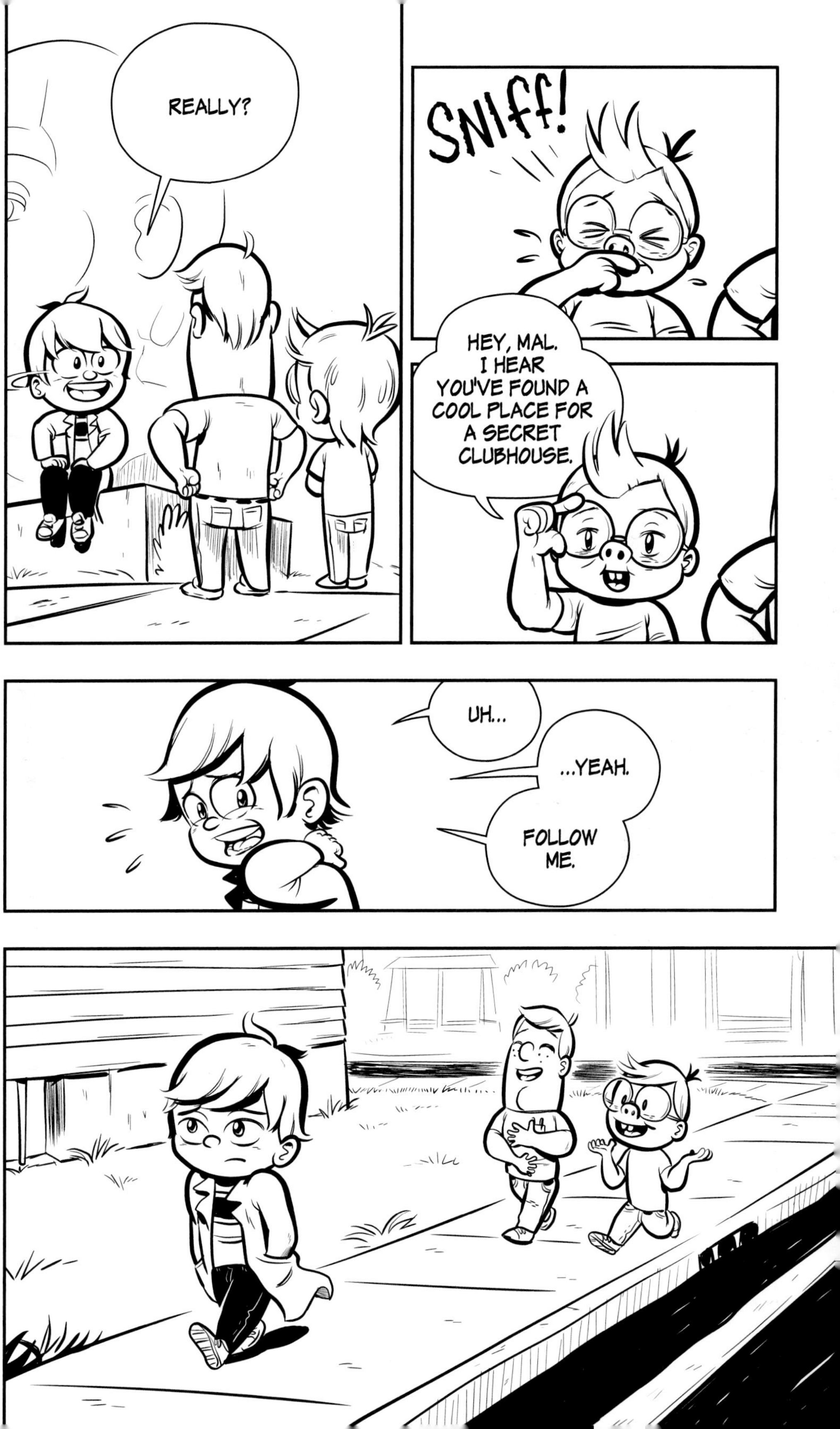
REALLY?
SNIFF!
HEY, MAL. I HEAR YOU'VE FOUND A COOL PLACE FOR A SECRET CLUBHOUSE.
UH...
...YEAH.
FOLLOW ME.

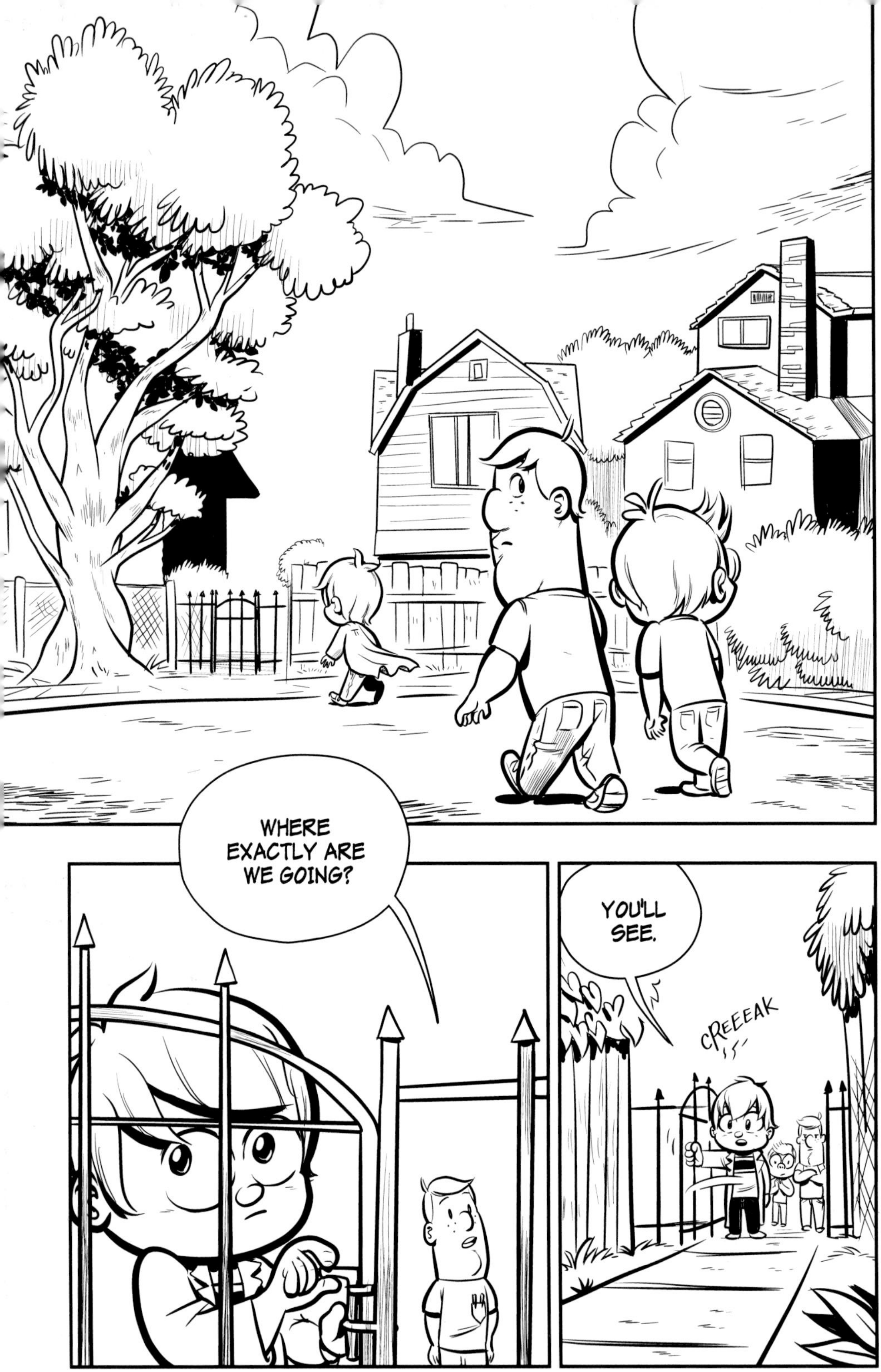
WHERE EXACTLY ARE WE GOING?
YOU'LL SEE.
CREEEAK

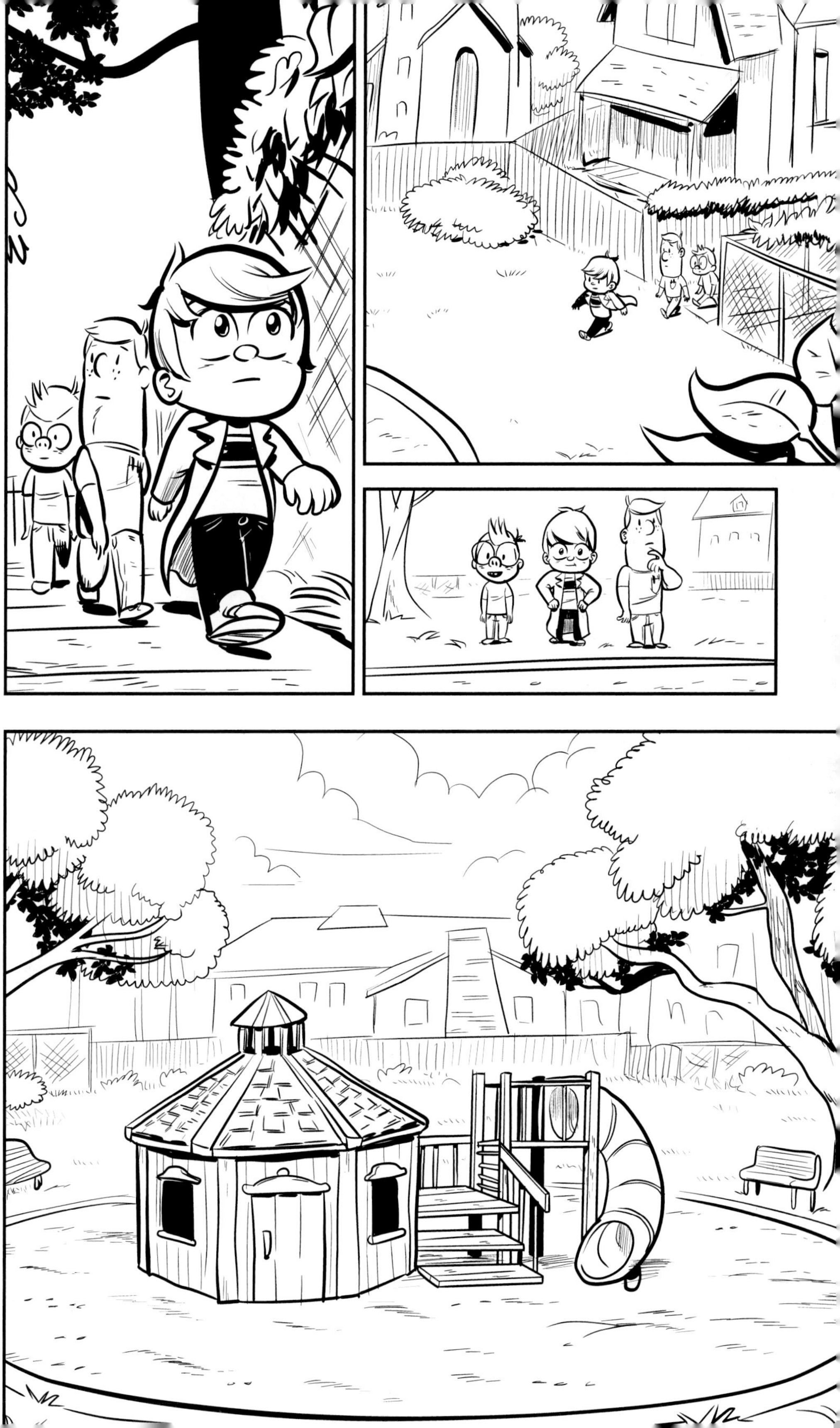

HEY, COOL! I NEVER KNEW THERE WAS A PLAYGROUND BACK HERE.

MY MOM SHOWED ME THIS PLACE. SHE USED TO PLAY HERE WHEN SHE WAS A LITTLE GIRL.

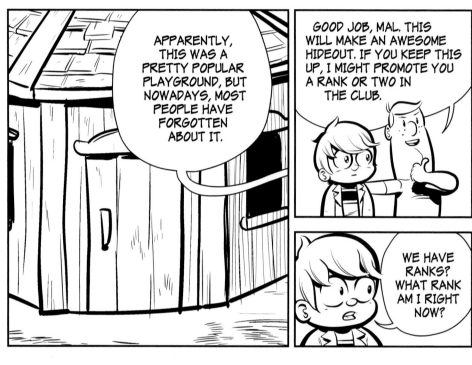

APPARENTLY, THIS WAS A PRETTY POPULAR PLAYGROUND, BUT NOWADAYS, MOST PEOPLE HAVE FORGOTTEN ABOUT IT.

GOOD JOB, MAL. THIS WILL MAKE AN AWESOME HIDEOUT. IF YOU KEEP THIS UP, I MIGHT PROMOTE YOU A RANK OR TWO IN THE CLUB.

WE HAVE RANKS? WHAT RANK AM I RIGHT NOW?

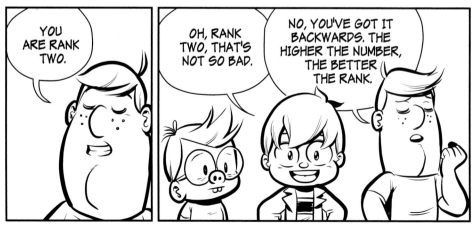

YOU ARE RANK TWO.

OH, RANK TWO, THAT'S NOT SO BAD.

NO, YOU'VE GOT IT BACKWARDS. THE HIGHER THE NUMBER, THE BETTER THE RANK.

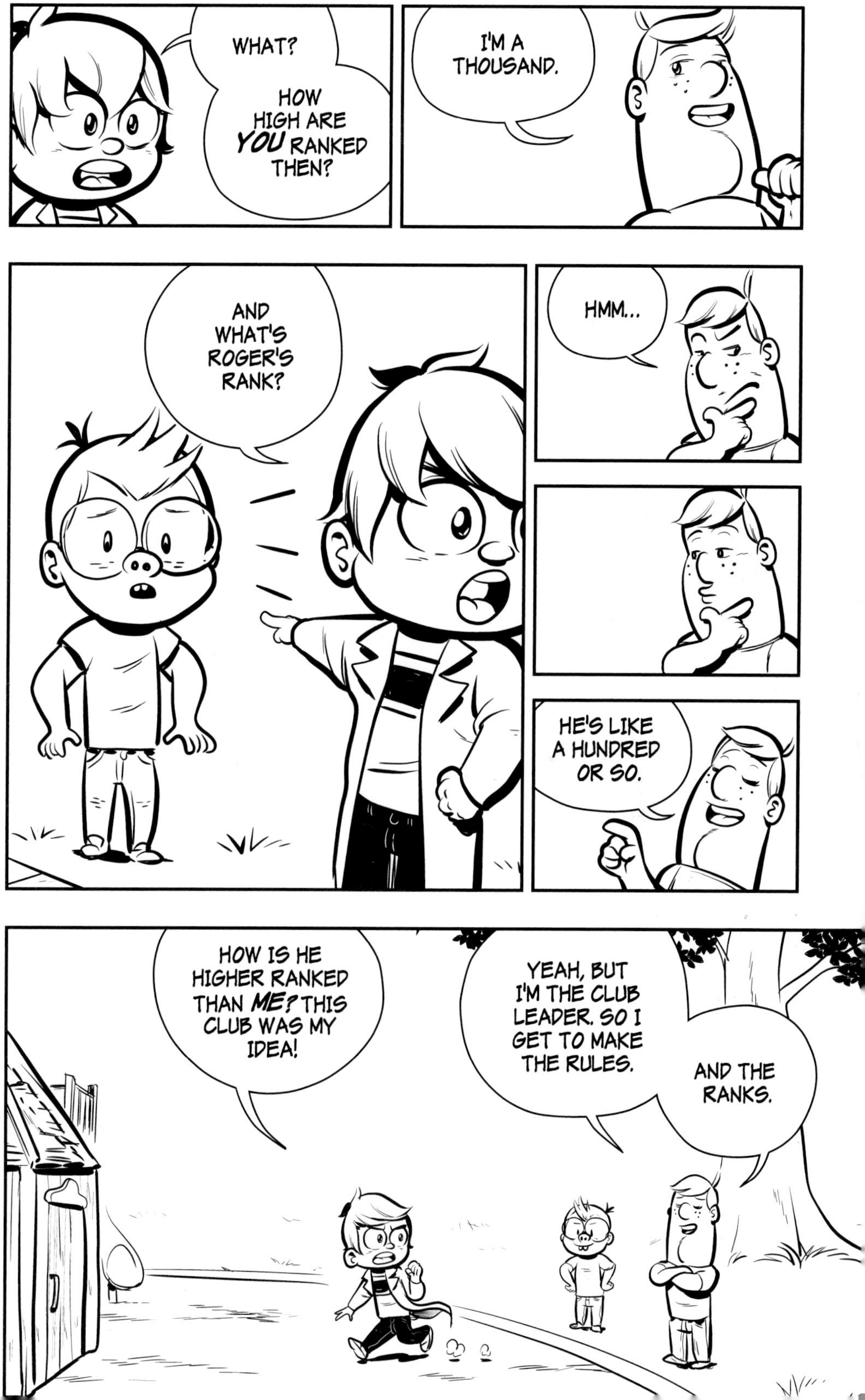
WHAT?
HOW HIGH ARE YOU RANKED THEN?
I'M A THOUSAND.
AND WHAT'S ROGER'S RANK?
HMM...
HE'S LIKE A HUNDRED OR SO.
HOW IS HE HIGHER RANKED THAN ME? THIS CLUB WAS MY IDEA!
YEAH, BUT I'M THE CLUB LEADER. SO I GET TO MAKE THE RULES.
AND THE RANKS.

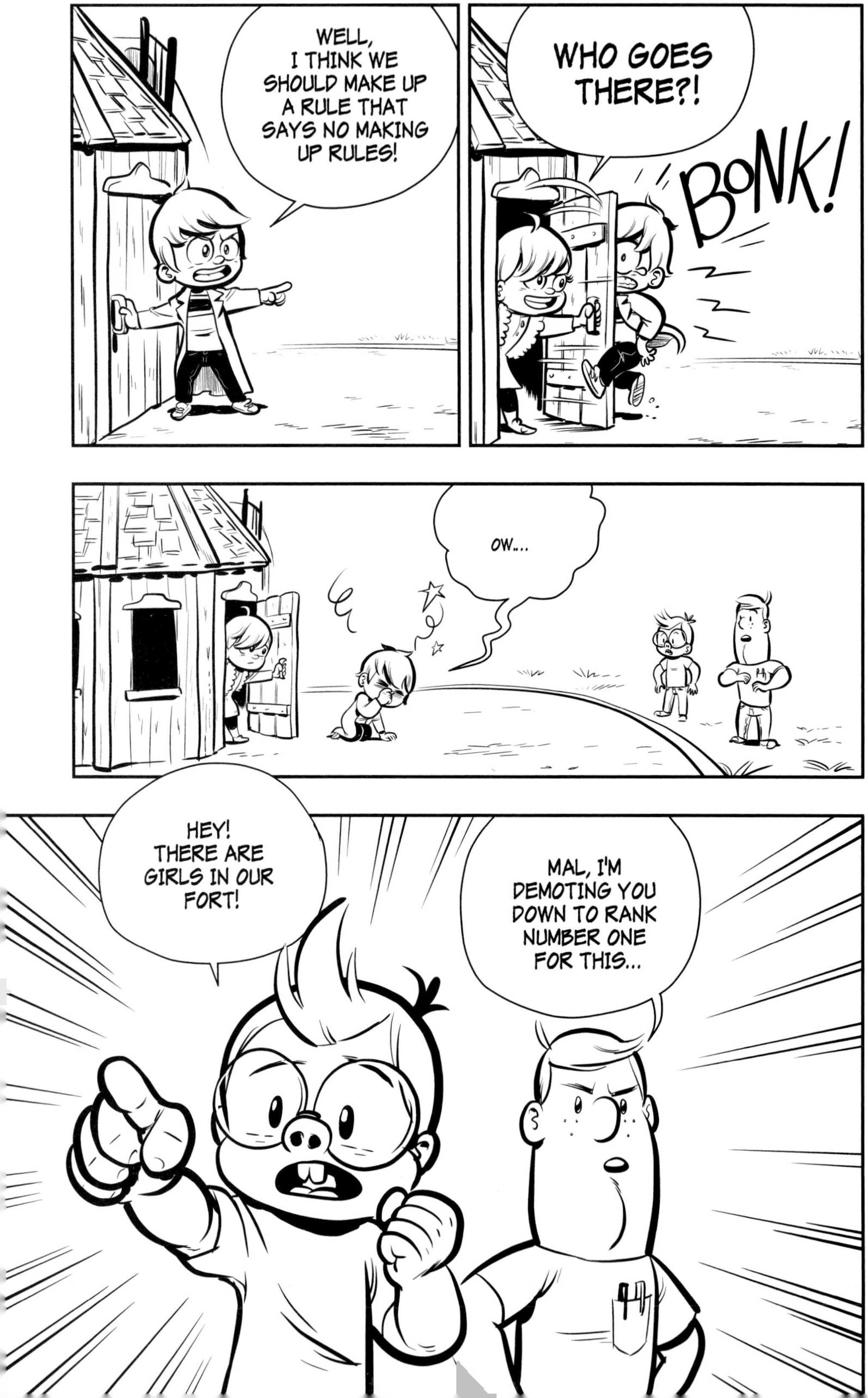
WELL, I THINK WE SHOULD MAKE UP A RULE THAT SAYS NO MAKING UP RULES!
WHO GOES THERE?!
BONK!
OW...
HEY! THERE ARE GIRLS IN OUR FORT!
MAL, I'M DEMOTING YOU DOWN TO RANK NUMBER ONE FOR THIS...

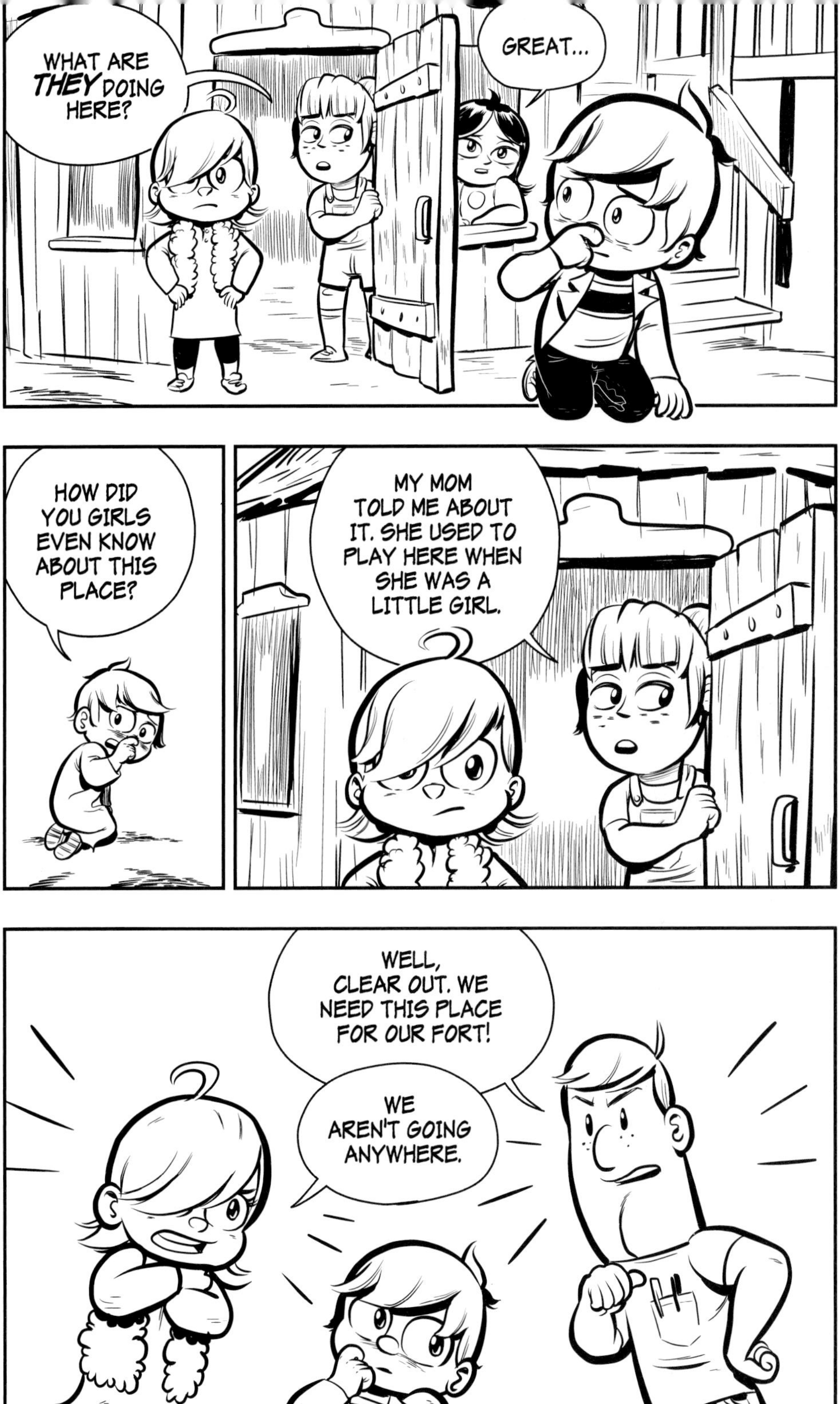
WHAT ARE THEY DOING HERE?
GREAT...
HOW DID YOU GIRLS EVEN KNOW ABOUT THIS PLACE?
MY MOM TOLD ME ABOUT IT. SHE USED TO PLAY HERE WHEN SHE WAS A LITTLE GIRL.
WELL, CLEAR OUT. WE NEED THIS PLACE FOR OUR FORT!
WE AREN'T GOING ANYWHERE.

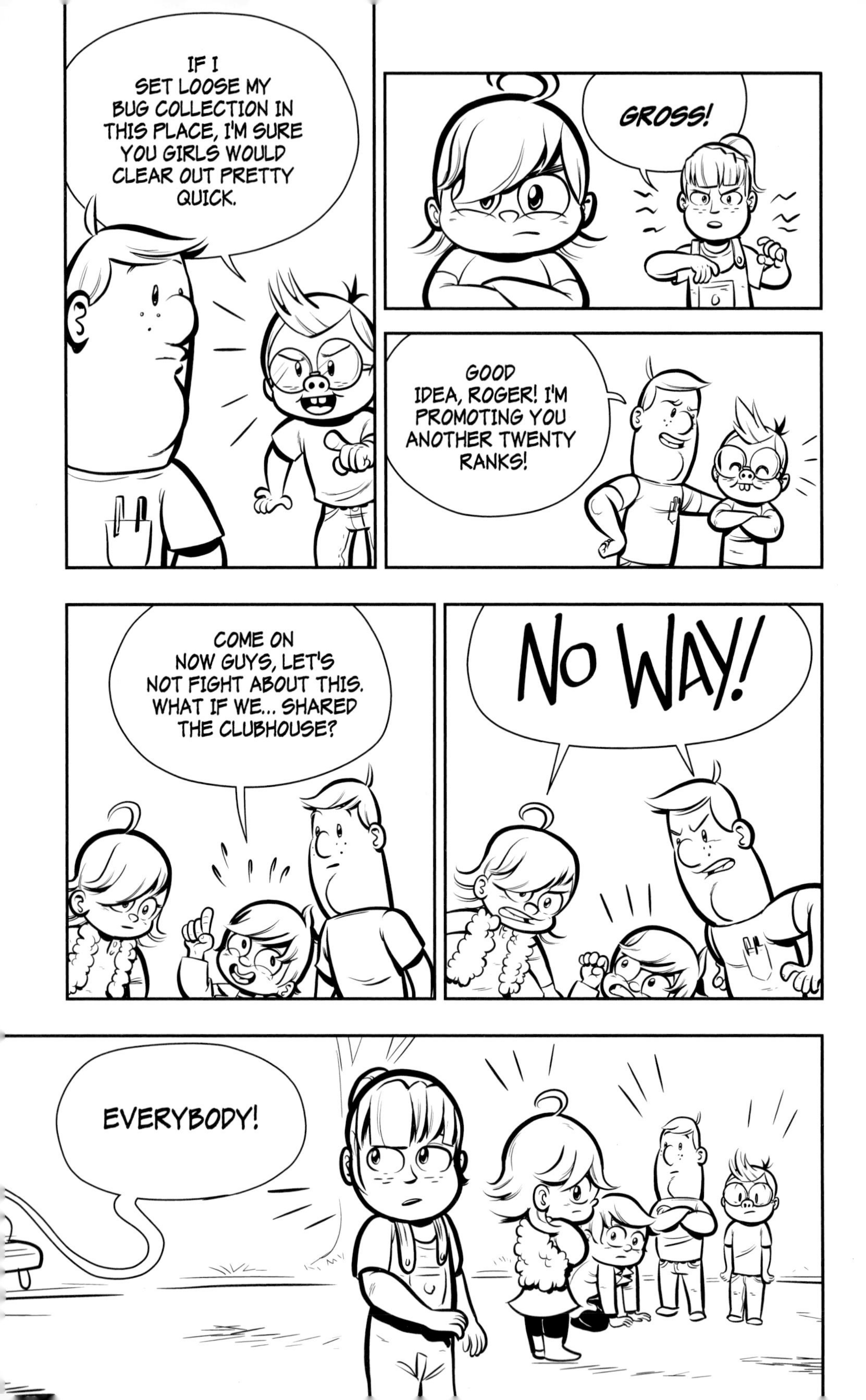
IF I SET LOOSE MY BUG COLLECTION IN THIS PLACE, I'M SURE YOU GIRLS WOULD CLEAR OUT PRETTY QUICK.
GROSS!
GOOD IDEA, ROGER! I'M PROMOTING YOU ANOTHER TWENTY RANKS!
COME ON NOW GUYS, LET'S NOT FIGHT ABOUT THIS. WHAT IF WE... SHARED THE CLUBHOUSE?
NO WAY!
EVERYBODY!

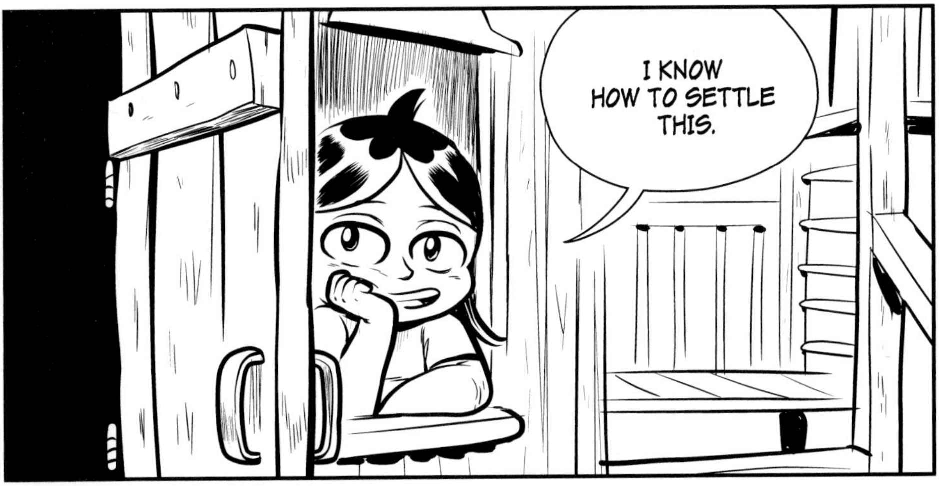
I KNOW HOW TO SETTLE THIS.

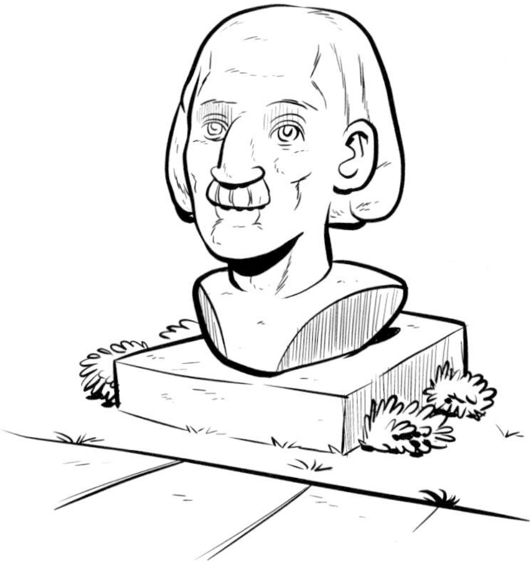

CHAPTER 6
The Game

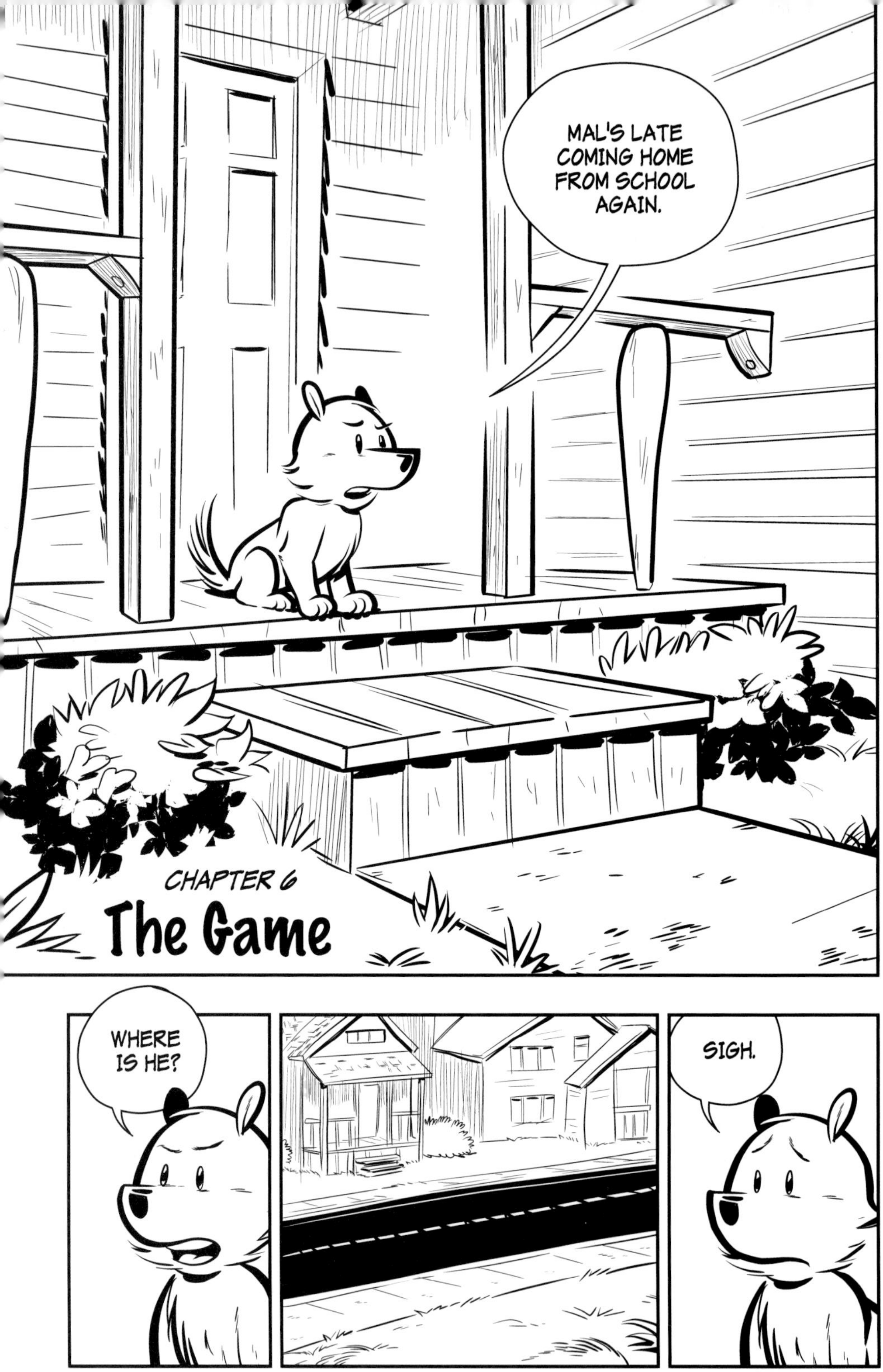
MAL'S LATE COMING HOME FROM SCHOOL AGAIN.
WHERE IS HE?
SIGH.

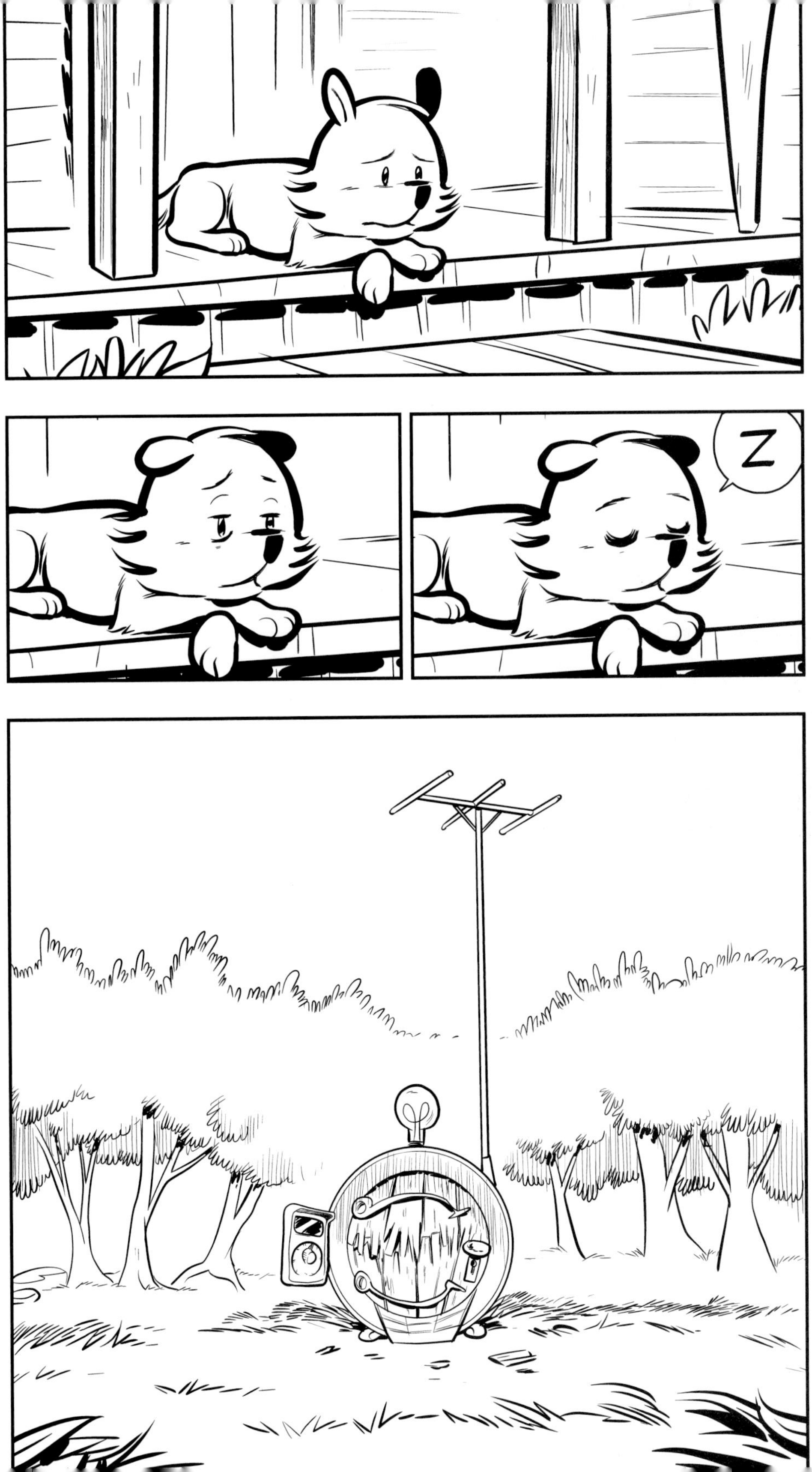
Z

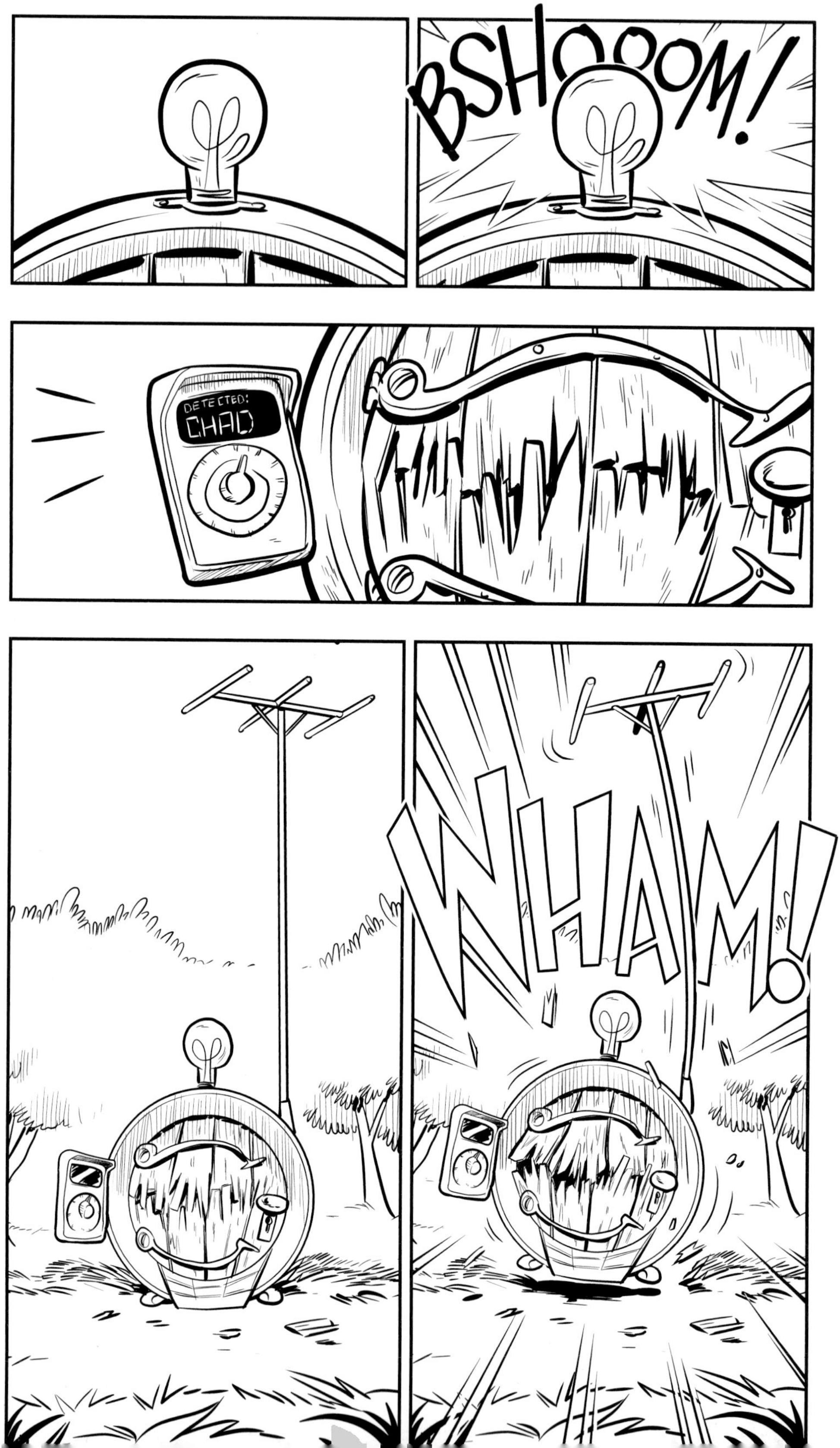
BSHOOOM!
DETECTED:
CHAD
WHAM!

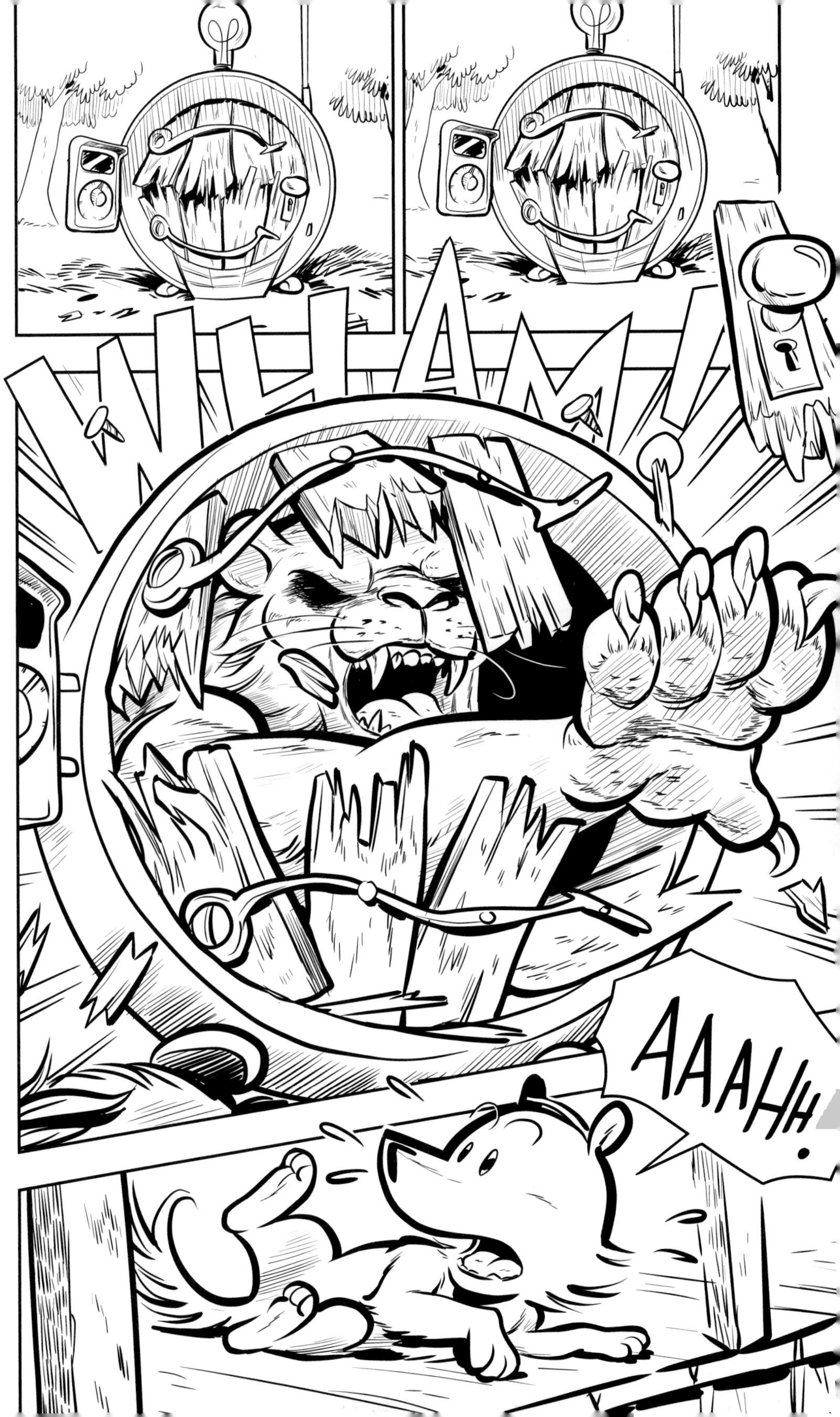
WHAM!
AAAHH!

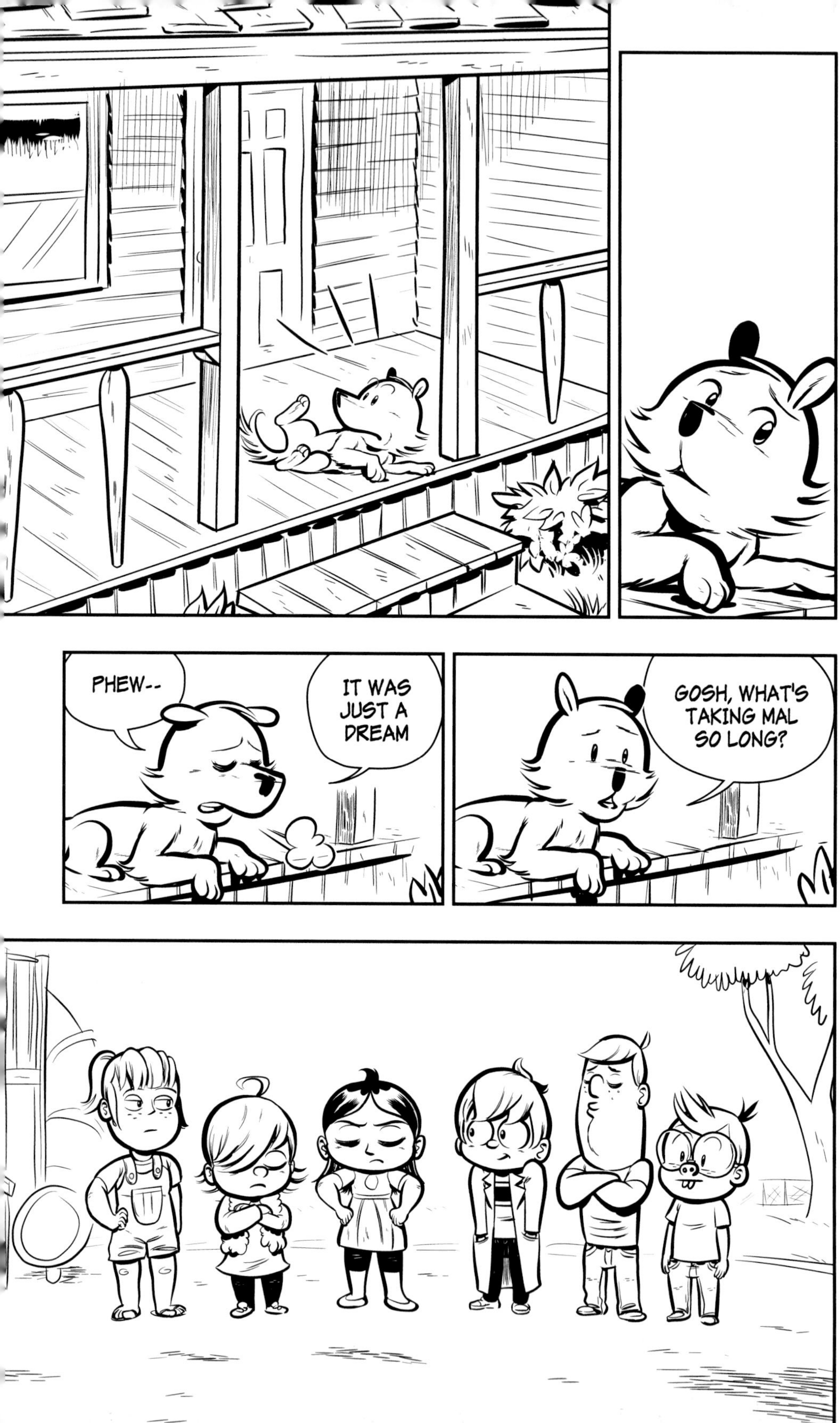
PHEW--
IT WAS JUST A DREAM
GOSH, WHAT'S TAKING MAL SO LONG?

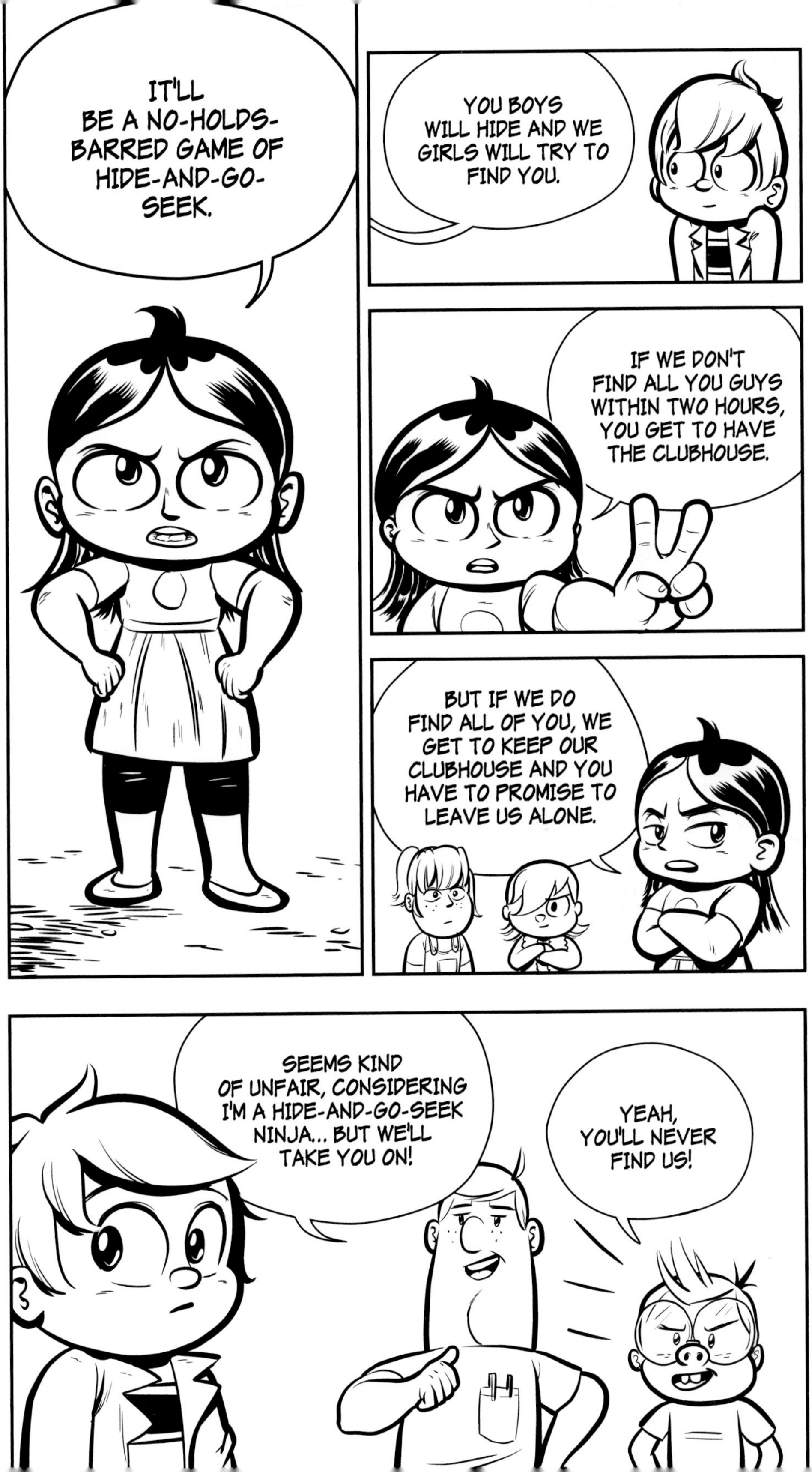
IT'LL BE A NO-HOLDS-BARRED GAME OF HIDE-AND-GO-SEEK.
YOU BOYS WILL HIDE AND WE GIRLS WILL TRY TO FIND YOU.
IF WE DON'T FIND ALL YOU GUYS WITHIN TWO HOURS, YOU GET TO HAVE THE CLUBHOUSE.
BUT IF WE DO FIND ALL OF YOU, WE GET TO KEEP OUR CLUBHOUSE AND YOU HAVE TO PROMISE TO LEAVE US ALONE.
SEEMS KIND OF UNFAIR, CONSIDERING I'M A HIDE-AND-GO-SEEK NINJA... BUT WE'LL TAKE YOU ON!
YEAH, YOU'LL NEVER FIND US!

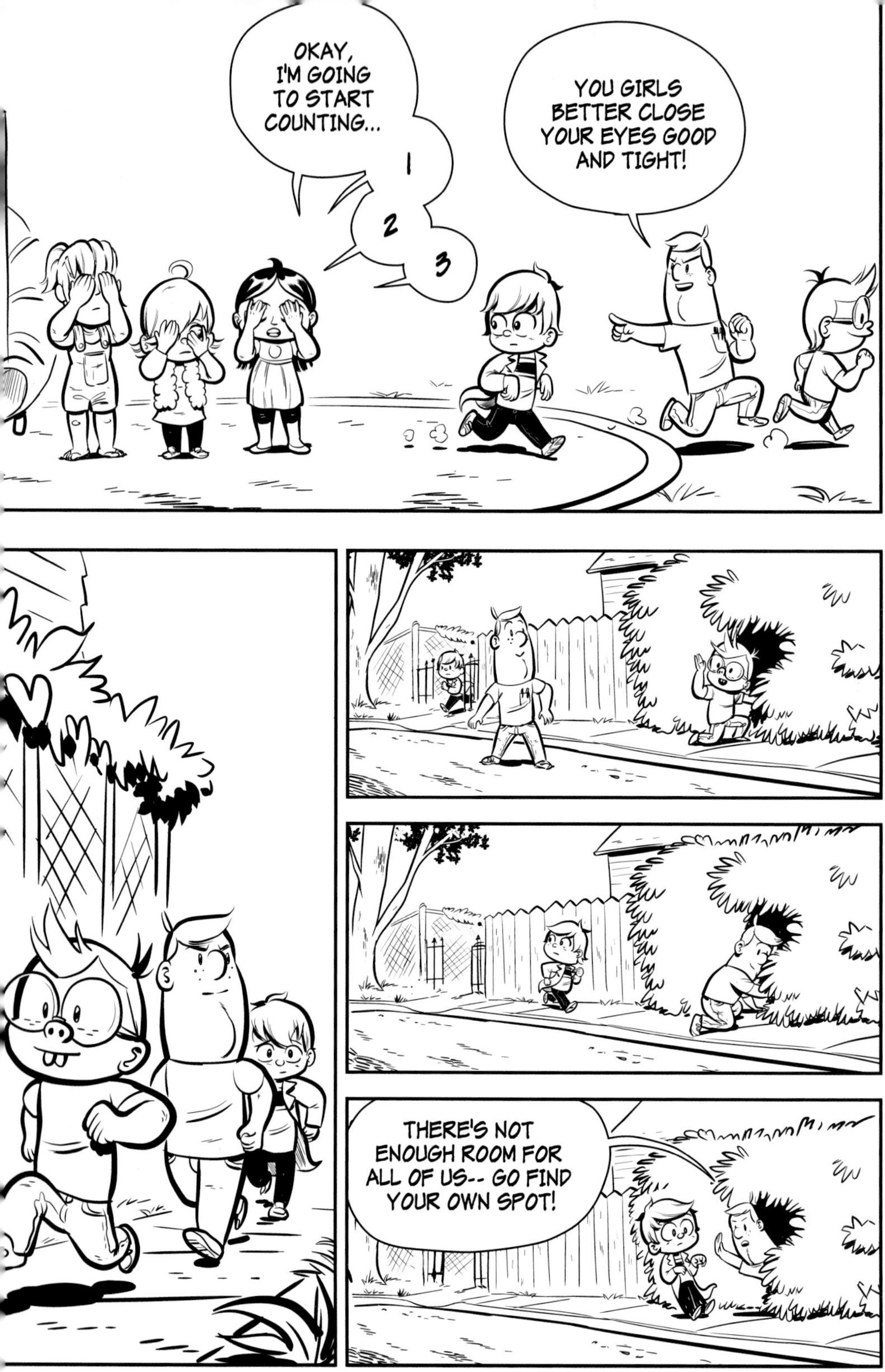
OKAY, I'M GOING TO START COUNTING...
1
2
3
YOU GIRLS BETTER CLOSE YOUR EYES GOOD AND TIGHT!
THERE'S NOT ENOUGH ROOM FOR ALL OF US-- GO FIND YOUR OWN SPOT!

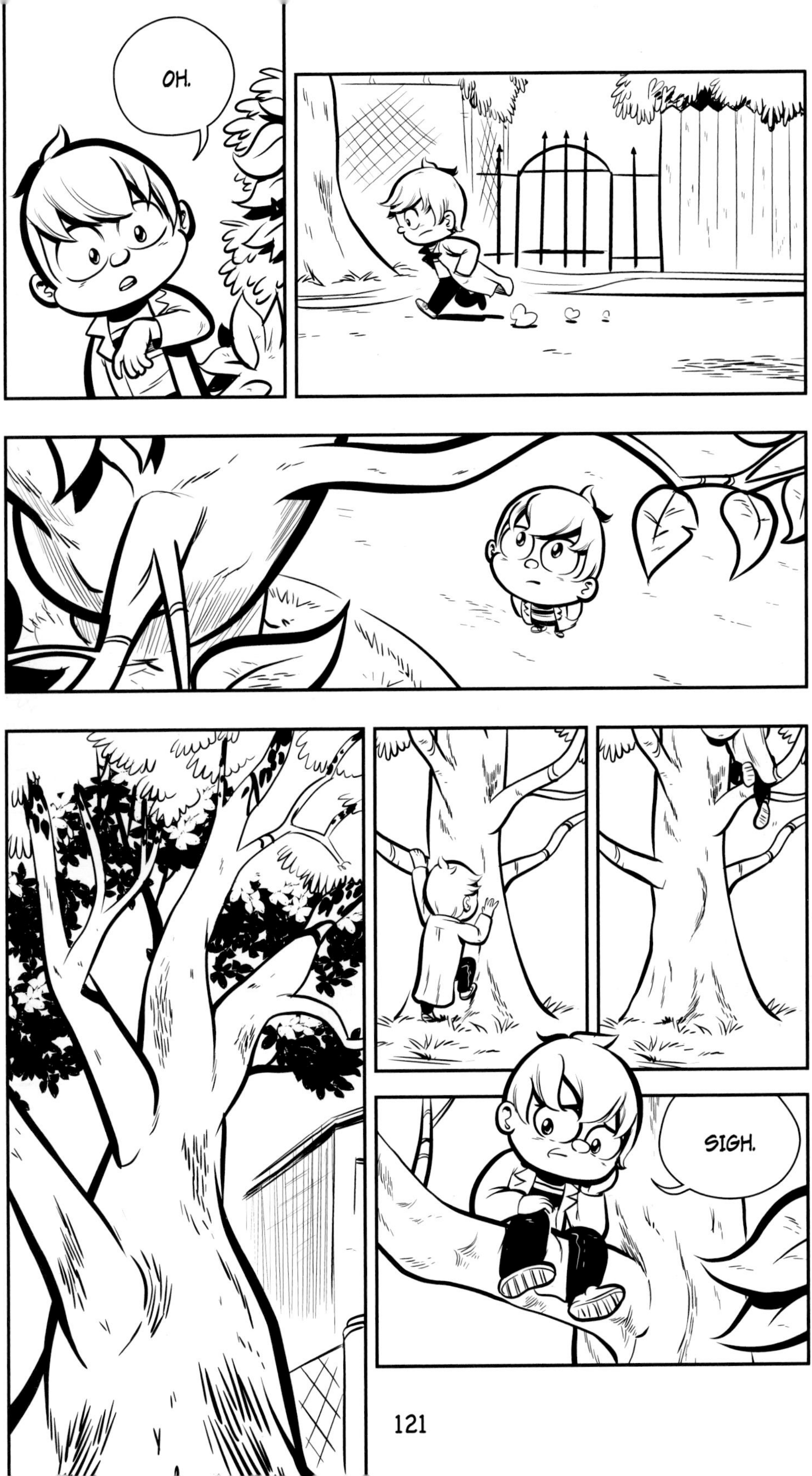
OH.
SIGH.

I DIDN'T WANT THINGS TO TURN OUT THIS WAY...
NOW I'M ON A TEAM FIGHTING AGAINST MEGAN.
!
THAT'S STRANGE... THE GIRLS ARE GOING BACK INTO THE CLUBHOUSE. THEY'RE SUPPOSED TO BE LOOKING FOR US!
HMMM...

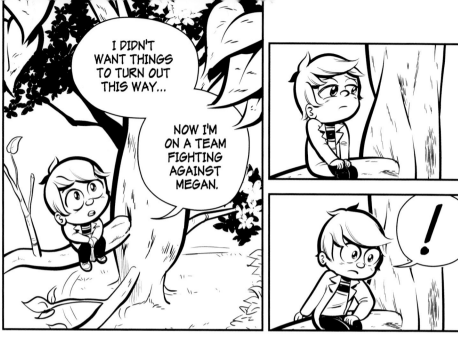

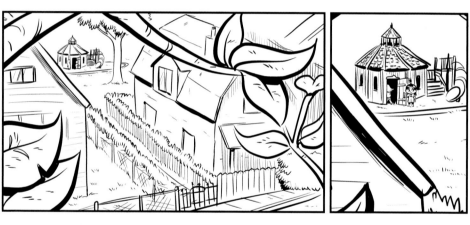

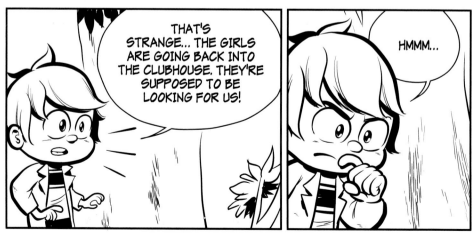

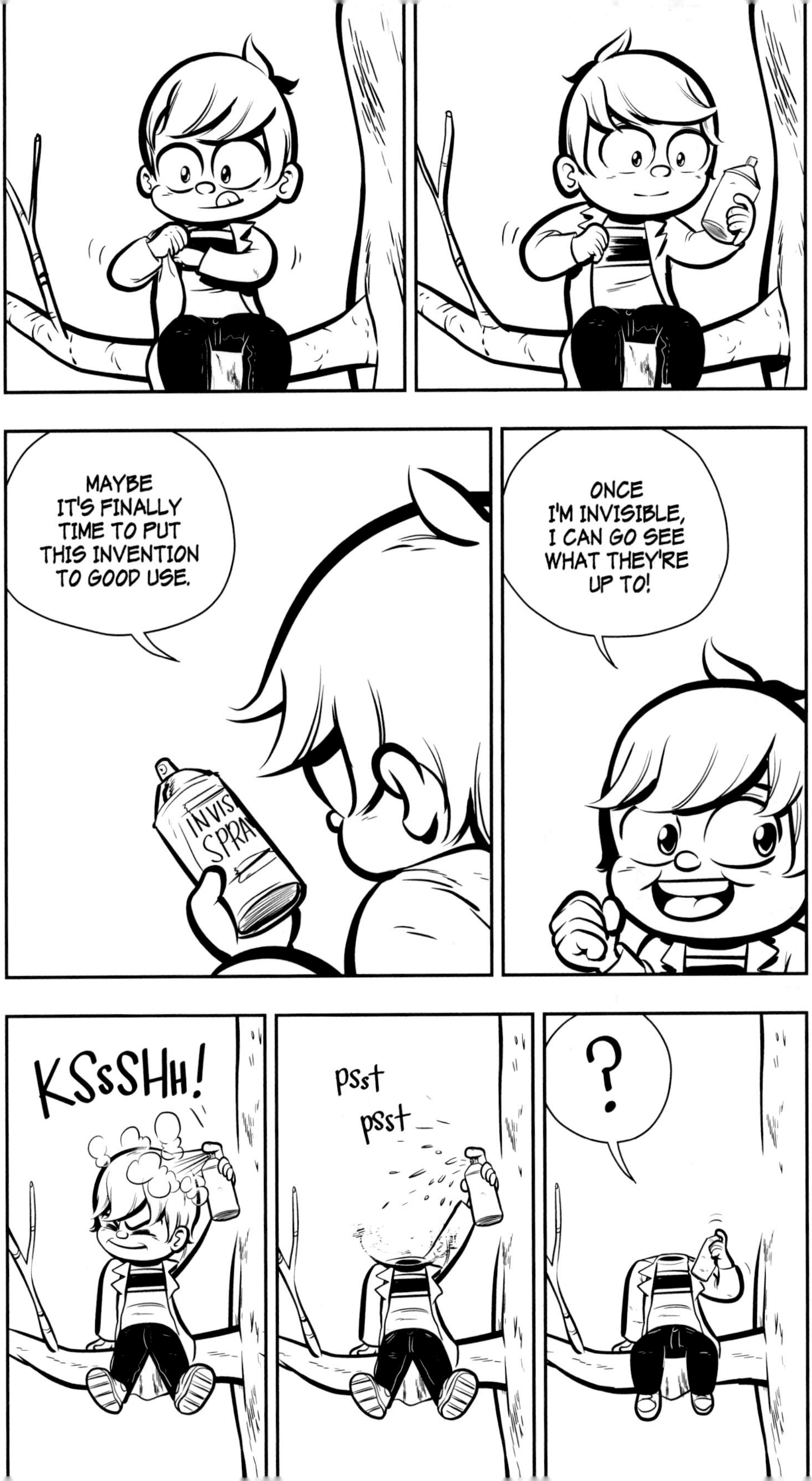
MAYBE IT'S FINALLY TIME TO PUT THIS INVENTION TO GOOD USE.
INVIS SPRA
ONCE I'M INVISIBLE, I CAN GO SEE WHAT THEY'RE UP TO!
KSsSHH!
psst
psst
?

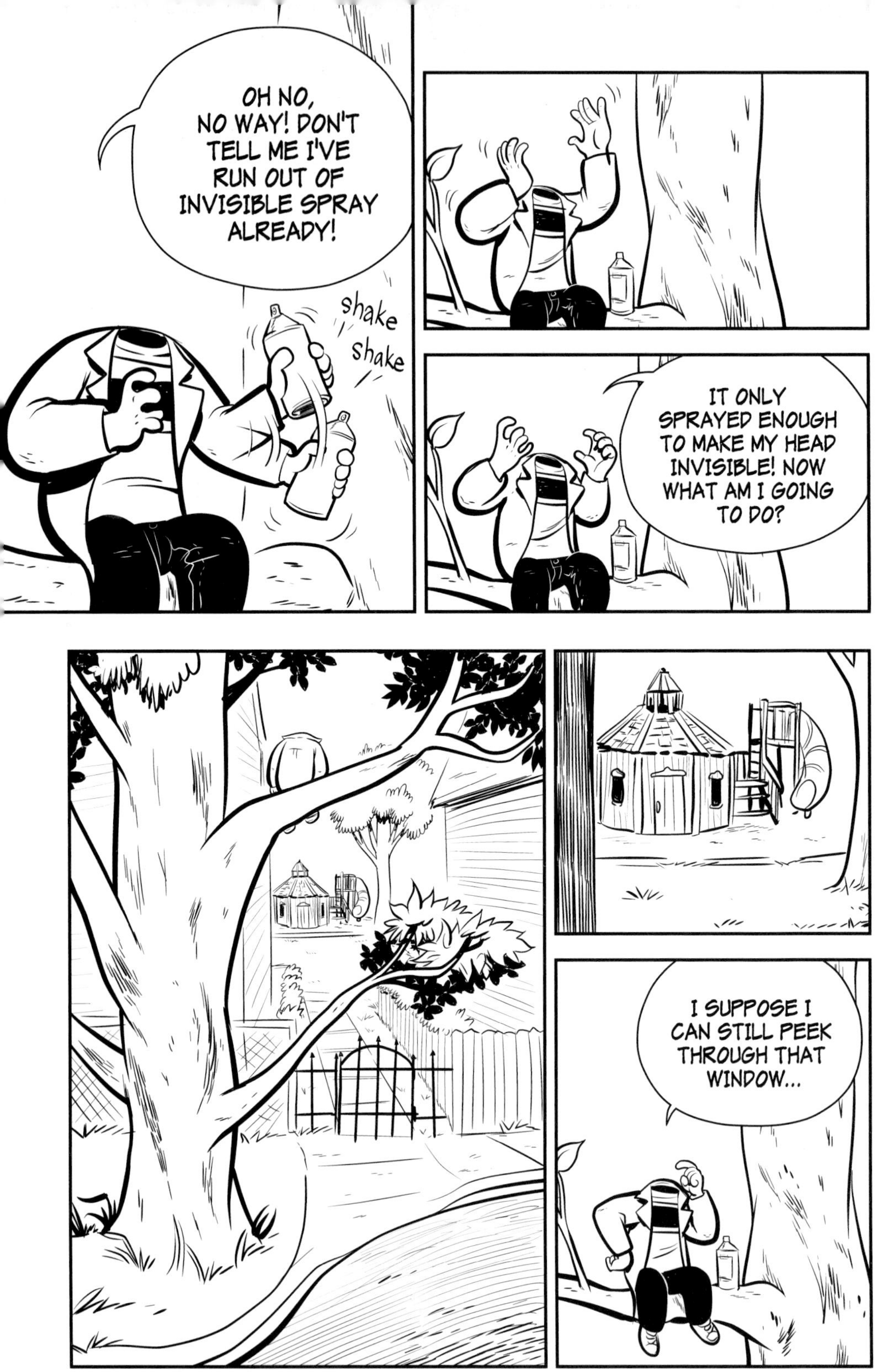
OH NO, NO WAY! DON'T TELL ME I'VE RUN OUT OF INVISIBLE SPRAY ALREADY!
shake
shake
IT ONLY SPRAYED ENOUGH TO MAKE MY HEAD INVISIBLE! NOW WHAT AM I GOING TO DO?
I SUPPOSE I CAN STILL PEEK THROUGH THAT WINDOW...

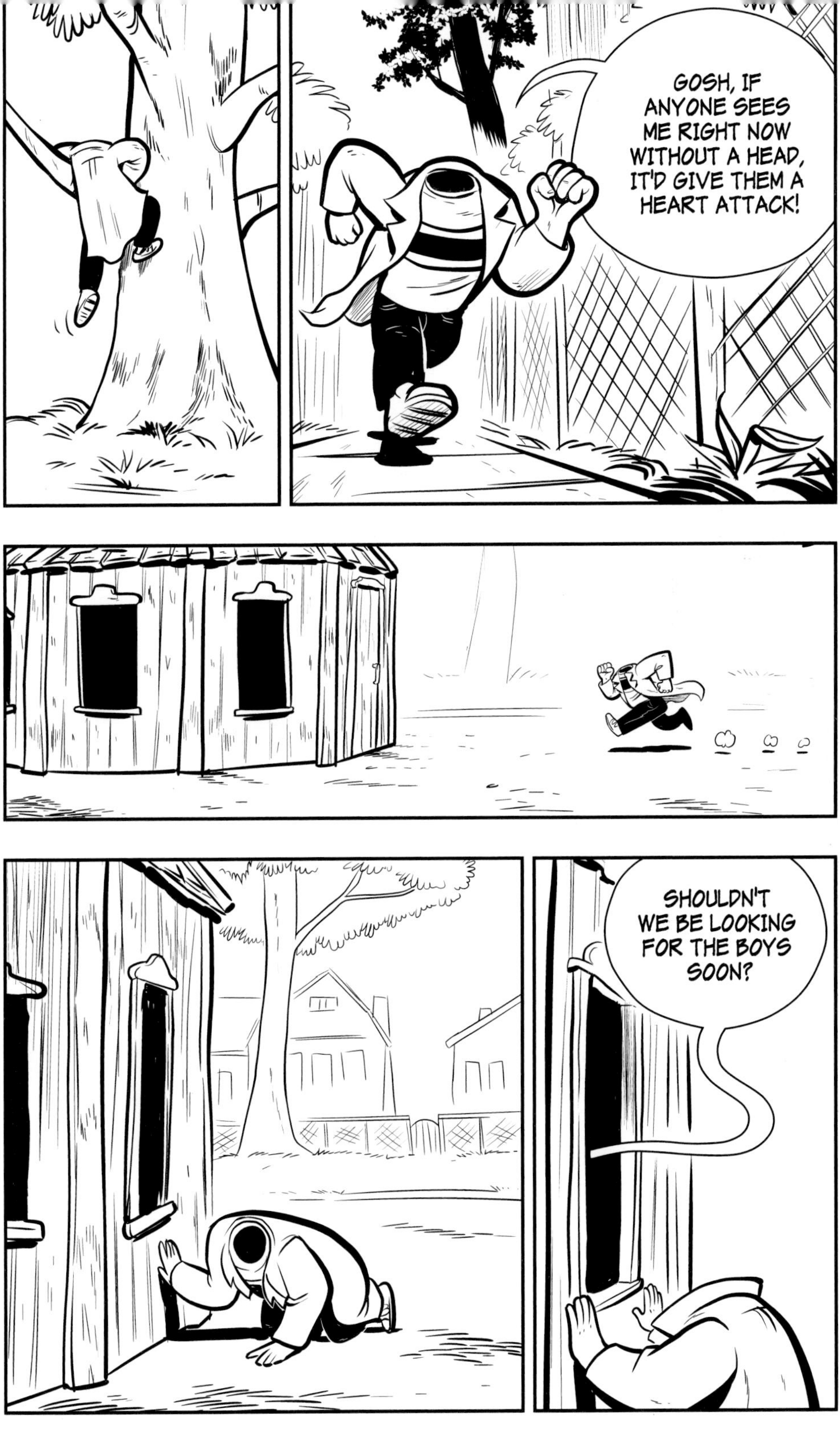
GOSH, IF ANYONE SEES ME RIGHT NOW WITHOUT A HEAD, IT'D GIVE THEM A HEART ATTACK!
SHOULDN'T WE BE LOOKING FOR THE BOYS SOON?

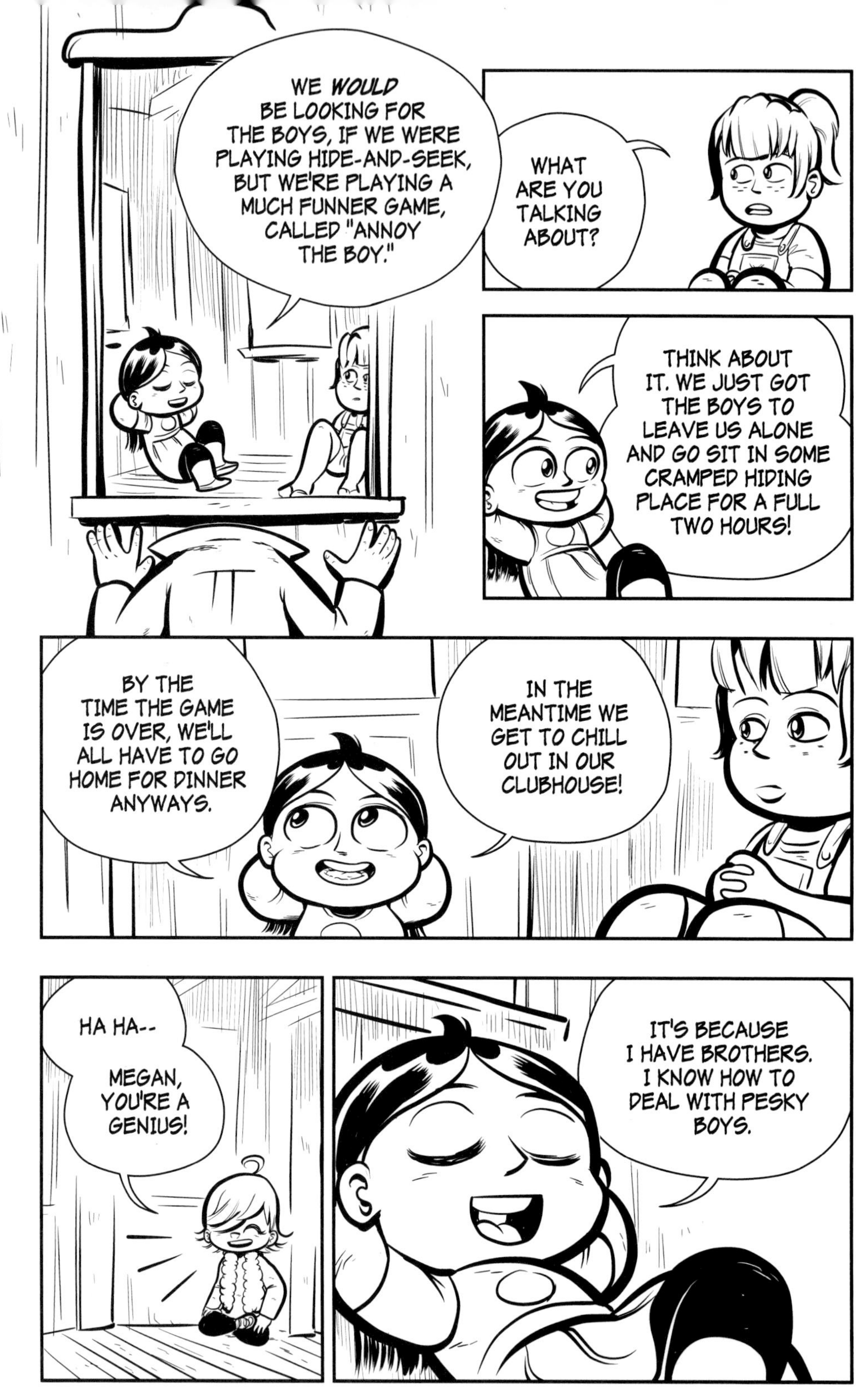
WE *WOULD* BE LOOKING FOR THE BOYS, IF WE WERE PLAYING HIDE-AND-SEEK, BUT WE'RE PLAYING A MUCH FUNNER GAME, CALLED "ANNOY THE BOY."
WHAT ARE YOU TALKING ABOUT?
THINK ABOUT IT. WE JUST GOT THE BOYS TO LEAVE US ALONE AND GO SIT IN SOME CRAMPED HIDING PLACE FOR A FULL TWO HOURS!
BY THE TIME THE GAME IS OVER, WE'LL ALL HAVE TO GO HOME FOR DINNER ANYWAYS.
IN THE MEANTIME WE GET TO CHILL OUT IN OUR CLUBHOUSE!
HA HA--
MEGAN, YOU'RE A GENIUS!
IT'S BECAUSE I HAVE BROTHERS. I KNOW HOW TO DEAL WITH PESKY BOYS.

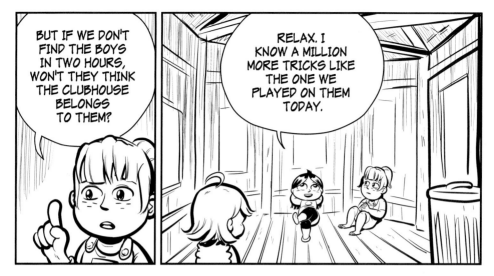

BUT IF WE DON'T FIND THE BOYS IN TWO HOURS, WON'T THEY THINK THE CLUBHOUSE BELONGS TO THEM?

RELAX. I KNOW A MILLION MORE TRICKS LIKE THE ONE WE PLAYED ON THEM TODAY.

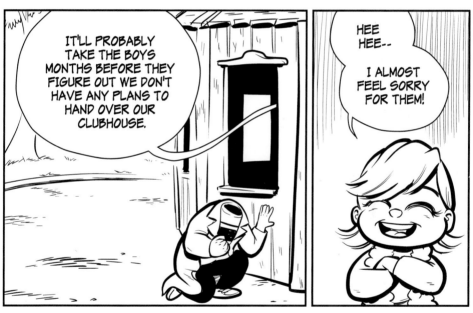

IT'LL PROBABLY TAKE THE BOYS MONTHS BEFORE THEY FIGURE OUT WE DON'T HAVE ANY PLANS TO HAND OVER OUR CLUBHOUSE.

HEE HEE--

I ALMOST FEEL SORRY FOR THEM!

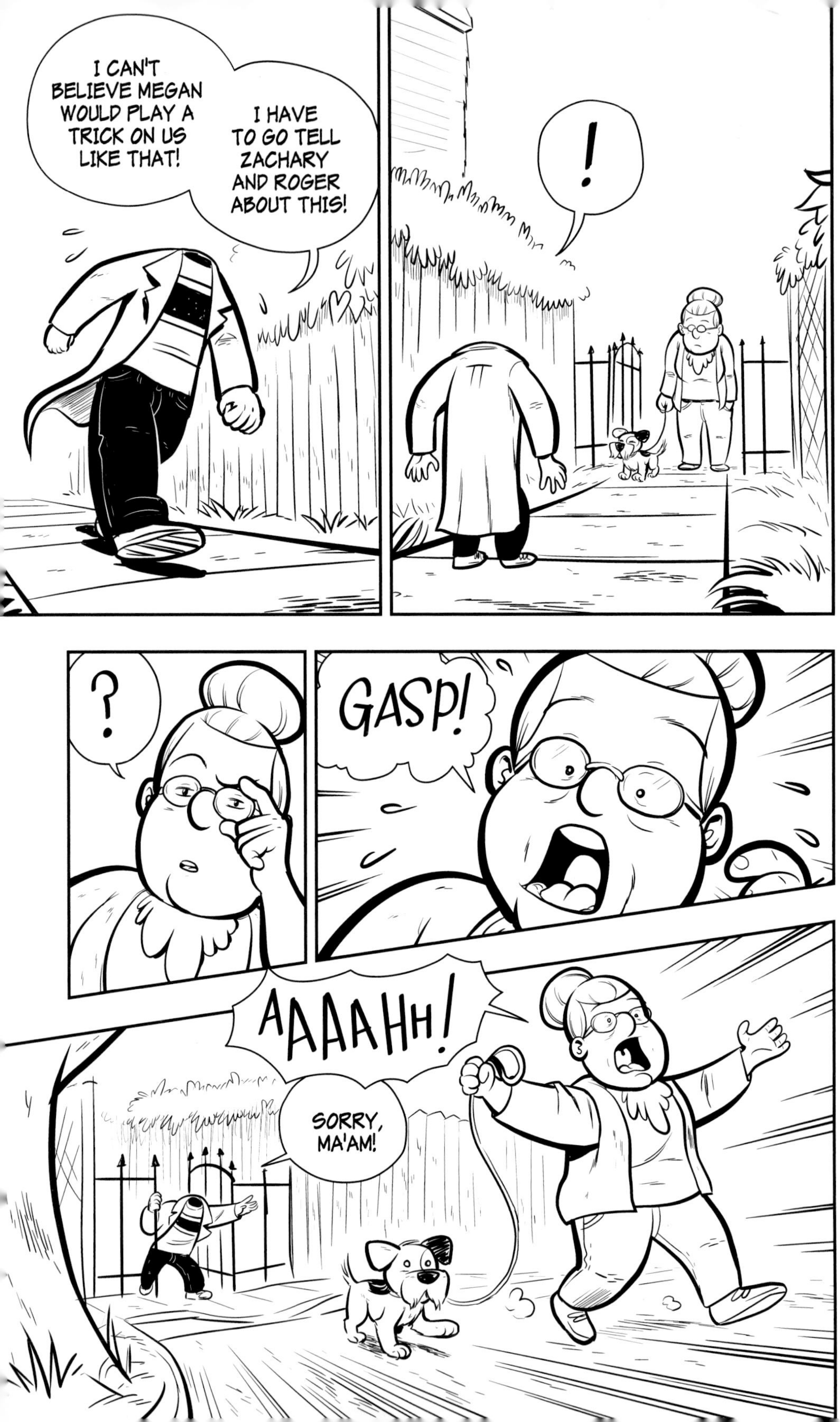
I CAN'T BELIEVE MEGAN WOULD PLAY A TRICK ON US LIKE THAT!
I HAVE TO GO TELL ZACHARY AND ROGER ABOUT THIS!
!
?
GASP!
AAAAHH!
SORRY, MA'AM!

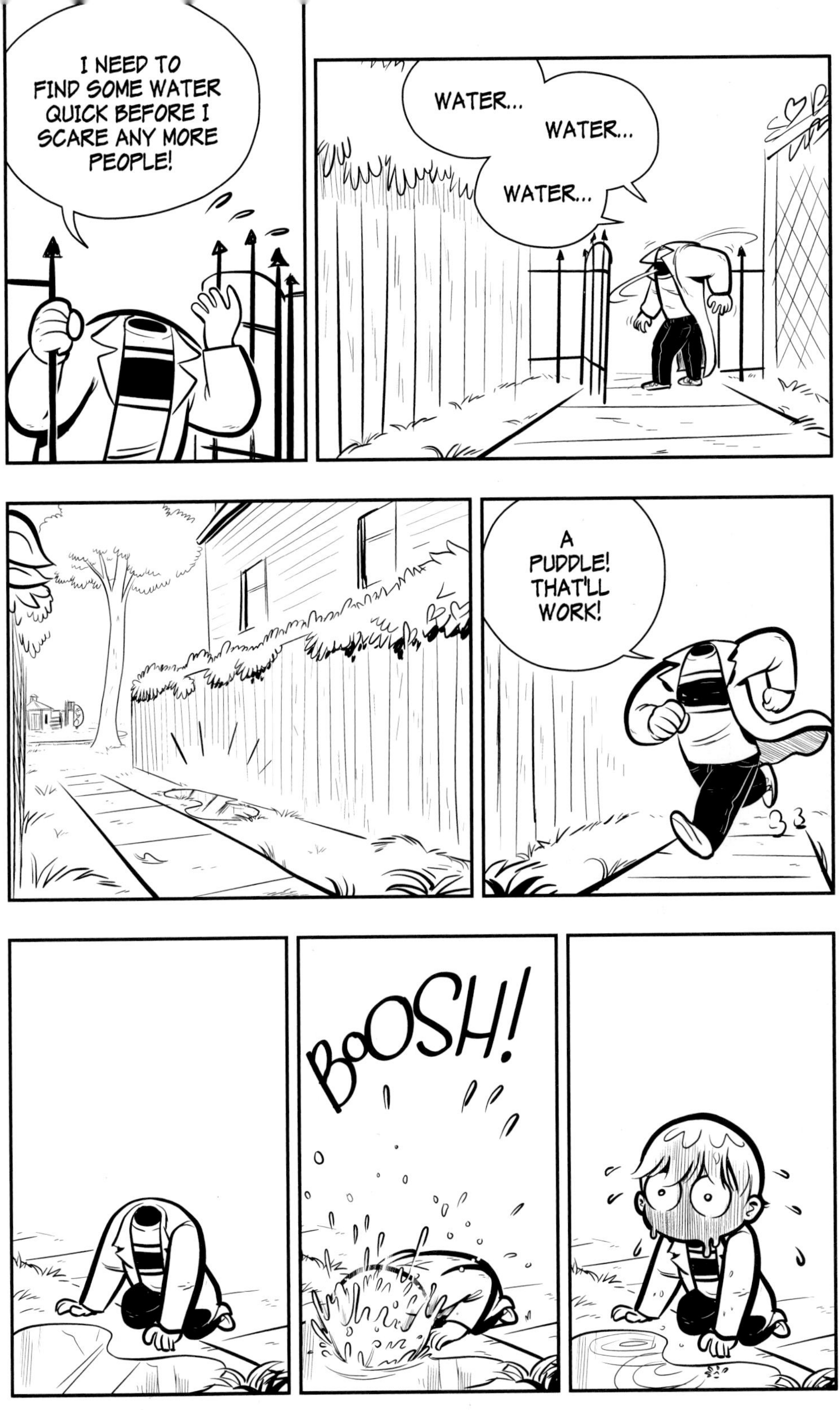
I NEED TO FIND SOME WATER QUICK BEFORE I SCARE ANY MORE PEOPLE!
WATER... WATER... WATER...
A PUDDLE! THAT'LL WORK!
BOOSH!

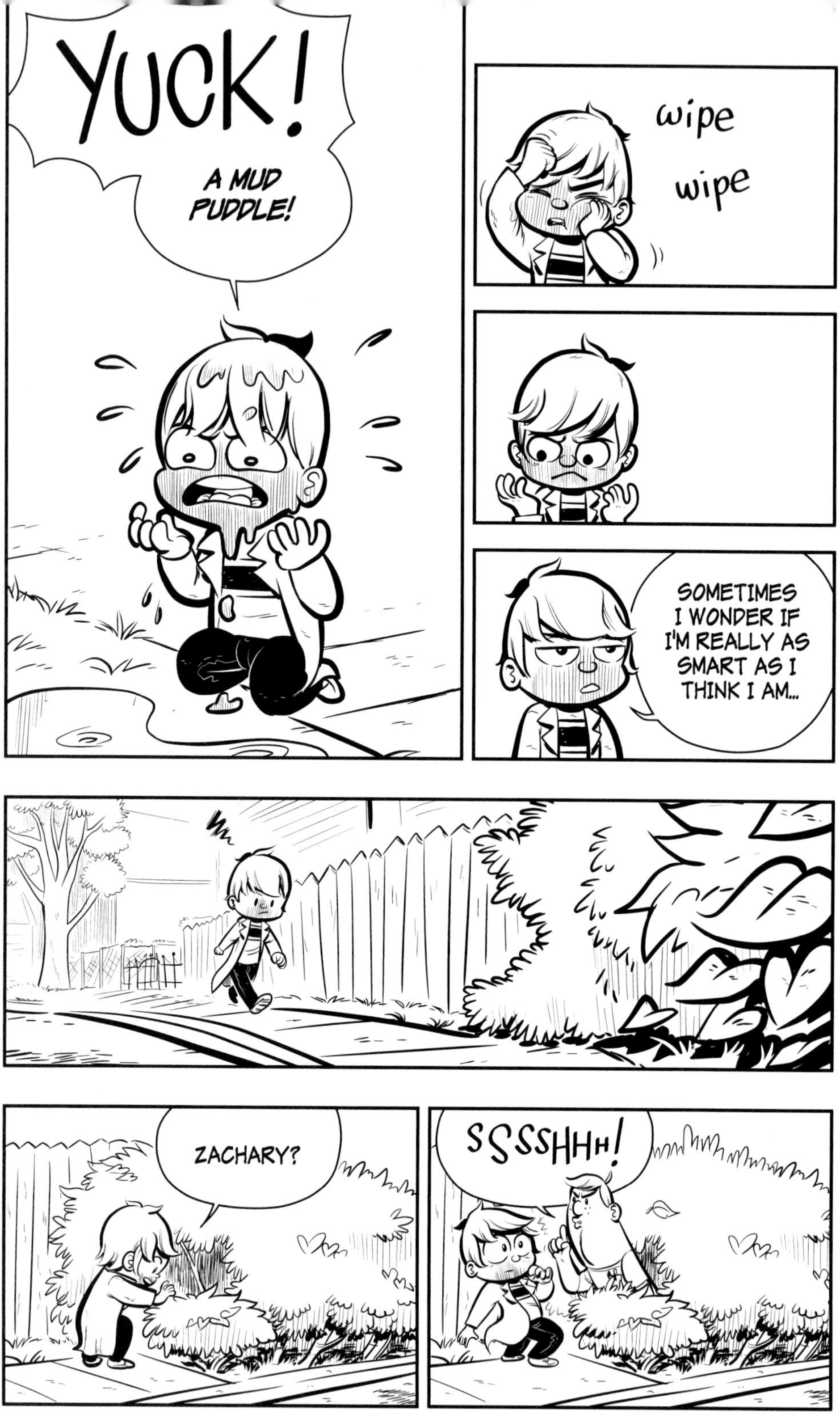
YUCK!
A MUD PUDDLE!
wipe
wipe
SOMETIMES I WONDER IF I'M REALLY AS SMART AS I THINK I AM...
ZACHARY?
SSSSHHH!

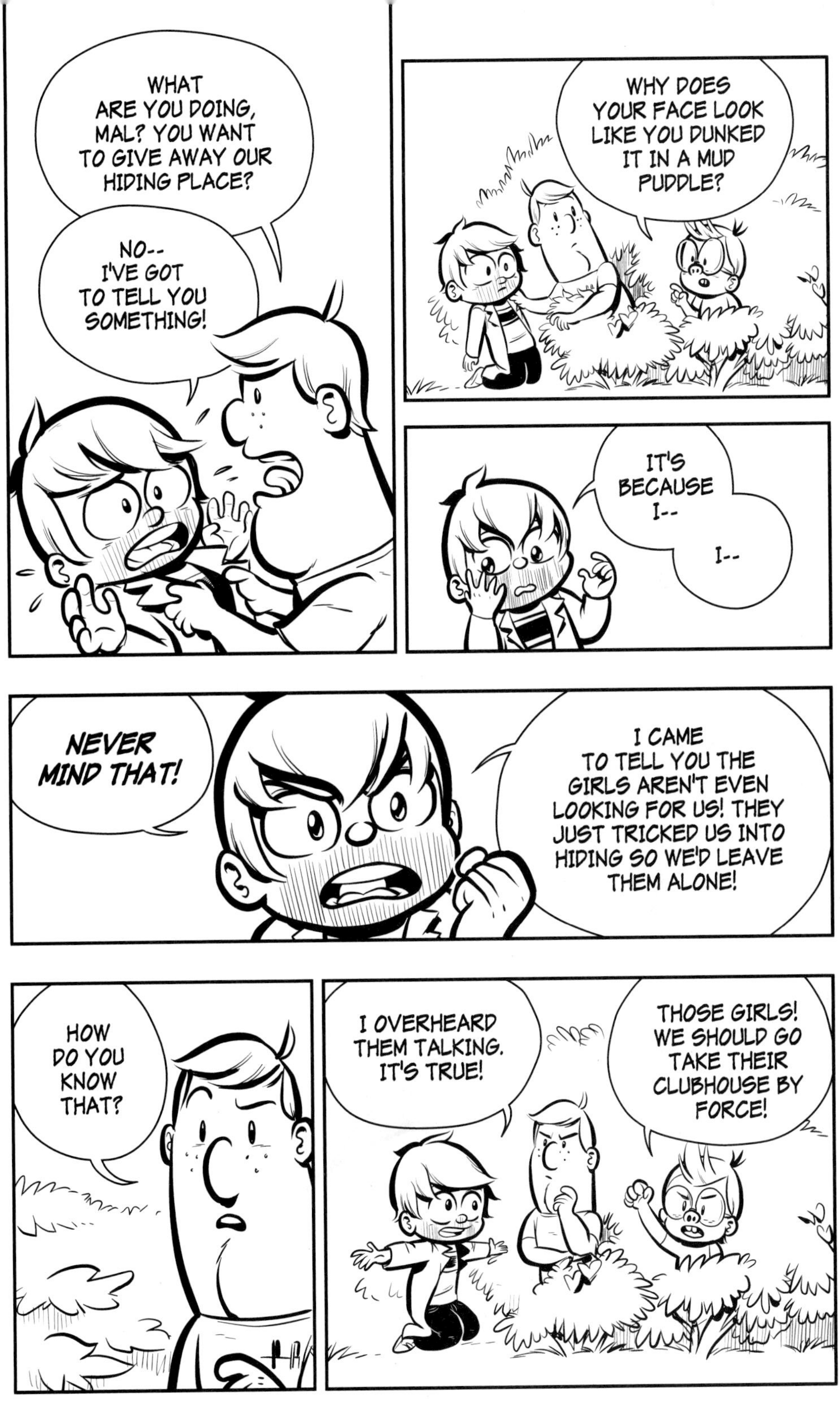
WHAT ARE YOU DOING, MAL? YOU WANT TO GIVE AWAY OUR HIDING PLACE?
NO-- I'VE GOT TO TELL YOU SOMETHING!
WHY DOES YOUR FACE LOOK LIKE YOU DUNKED IT IN A MUD PUDDLE?
IT'S BECAUSE I--
I--
NEVER MIND THAT!
I CAME TO TELL YOU THE GIRLS AREN'T EVEN LOOKING FOR US! THEY JUST TRICKED US INTO HIDING SO WE'D LEAVE THEM ALONE!
HOW DO YOU KNOW THAT?
I OVERHEARD THEM TALKING. IT'S TRUE!
THOSE GIRLS! WE SHOULD GO TAKE THEIR CLUBHOUSE BY FORCE!

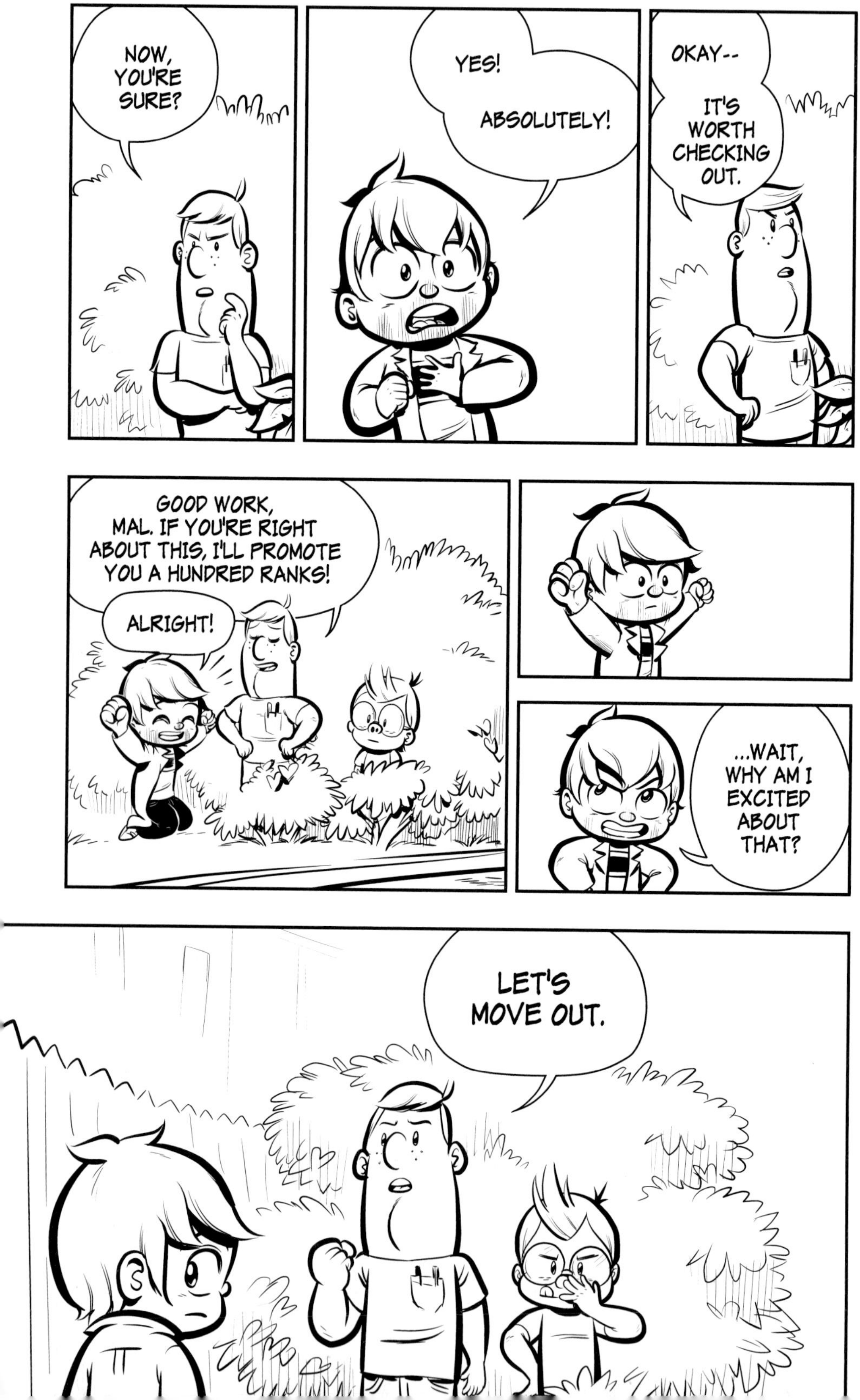
NOW, YOU'RE SURE?
YES!
ABSOLUTELY!
OKAY--
IT'S WORTH CHECKING OUT.
GOOD WORK, MAL. IF YOU'RE RIGHT ABOUT THIS, I'LL PROMOTE YOU A HUNDRED RANKS!
ALRIGHT!
...WAIT, WHY AM I EXCITED ABOUT THAT?
LET'S MOVE OUT.

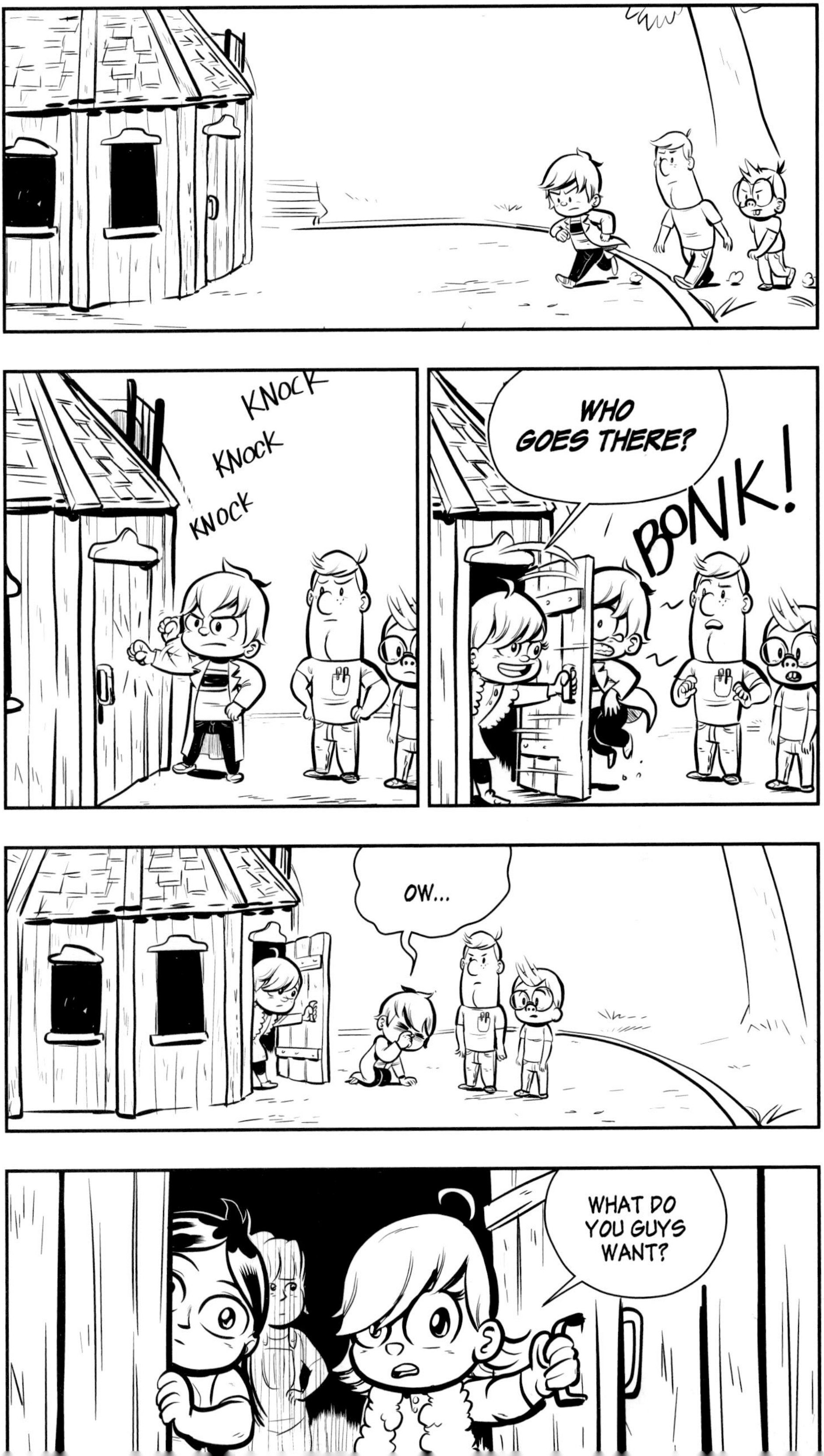
KNOCK
KNOCK
KNOCK
WHO GOES THERE?
BONK!
OW...
WHAT DO YOU GUYS WANT?

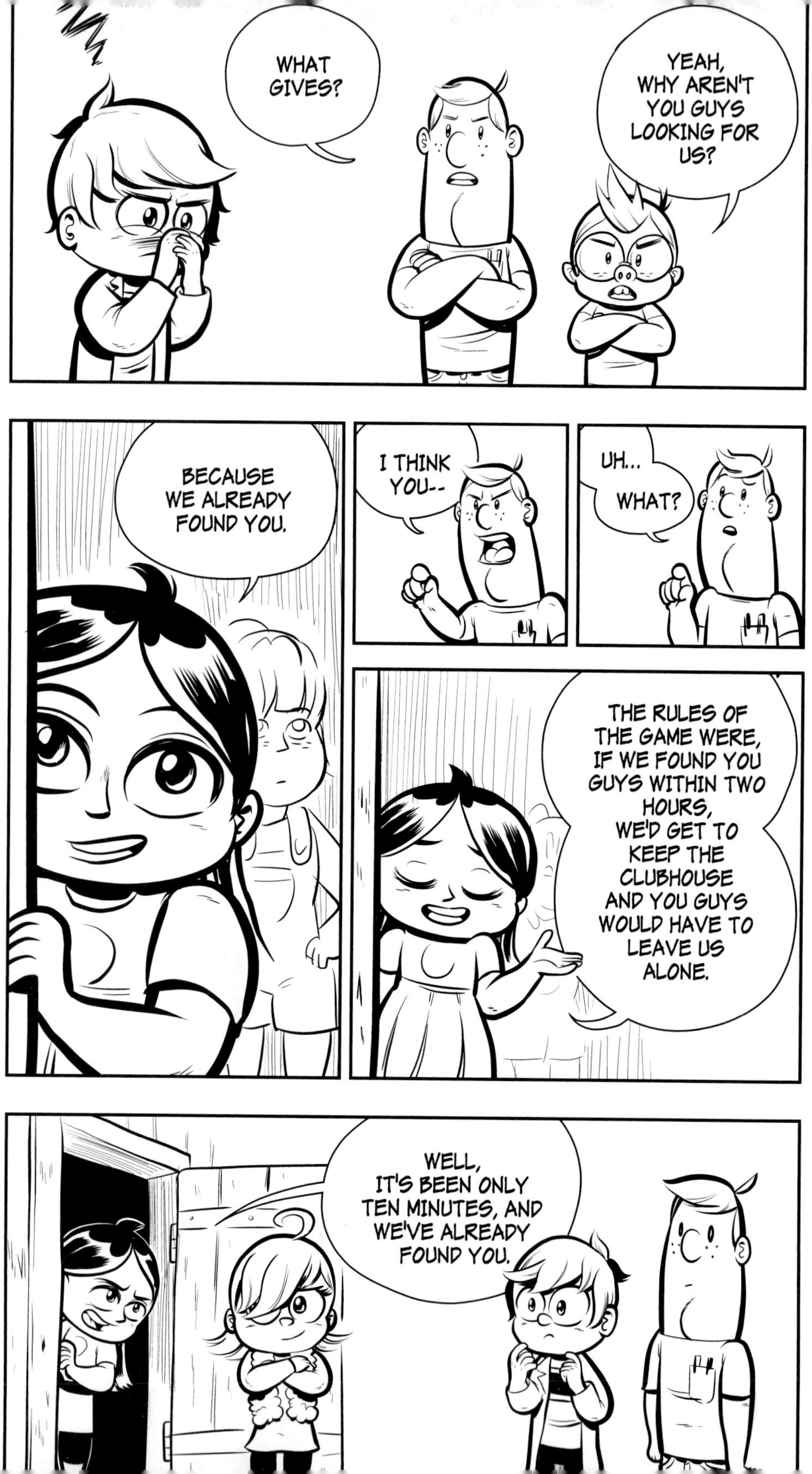
WHAT GIVES?
YEAH, WHY AREN'T YOU GUYS LOOKING FOR US?
BECAUSE WE ALREADY FOUND YOU.
I THINK YOU--
UH...
WHAT?
THE RULES OF THE GAME WERE, IF WE FOUND YOU GUYS WITHIN TWO HOURS, WE'D GET TO KEEP THE CLUBHOUSE AND YOU GUYS WOULD HAVE TO LEAVE US ALONE.
WELL, IT'S BEEN ONLY TEN MINUTES, AND WE'VE ALREADY FOUND YOU.

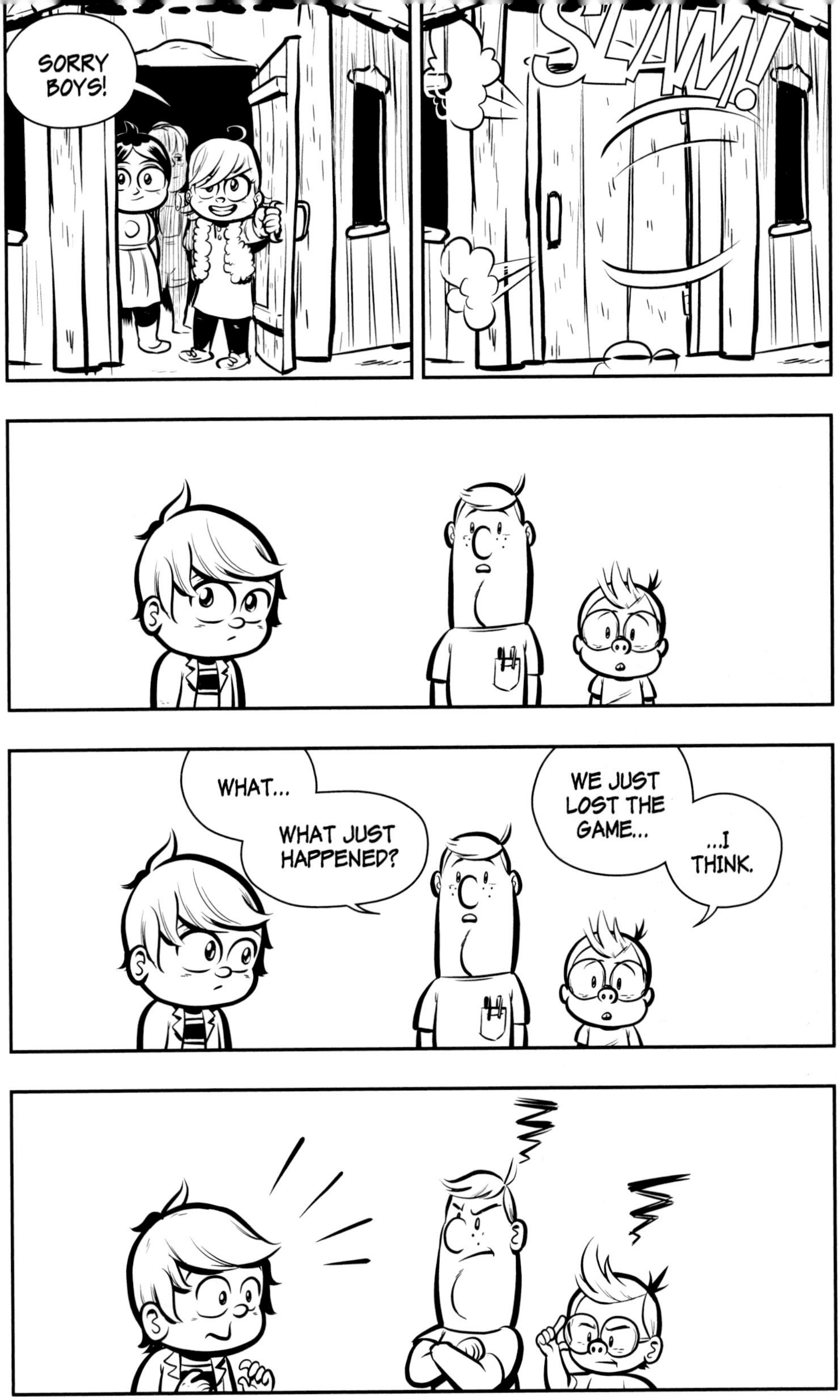
SORRY BOYS!
SLAM!
WHAT...
WHAT JUST HAPPENED?
WE JUST LOST THE GAME...
...I THINK.

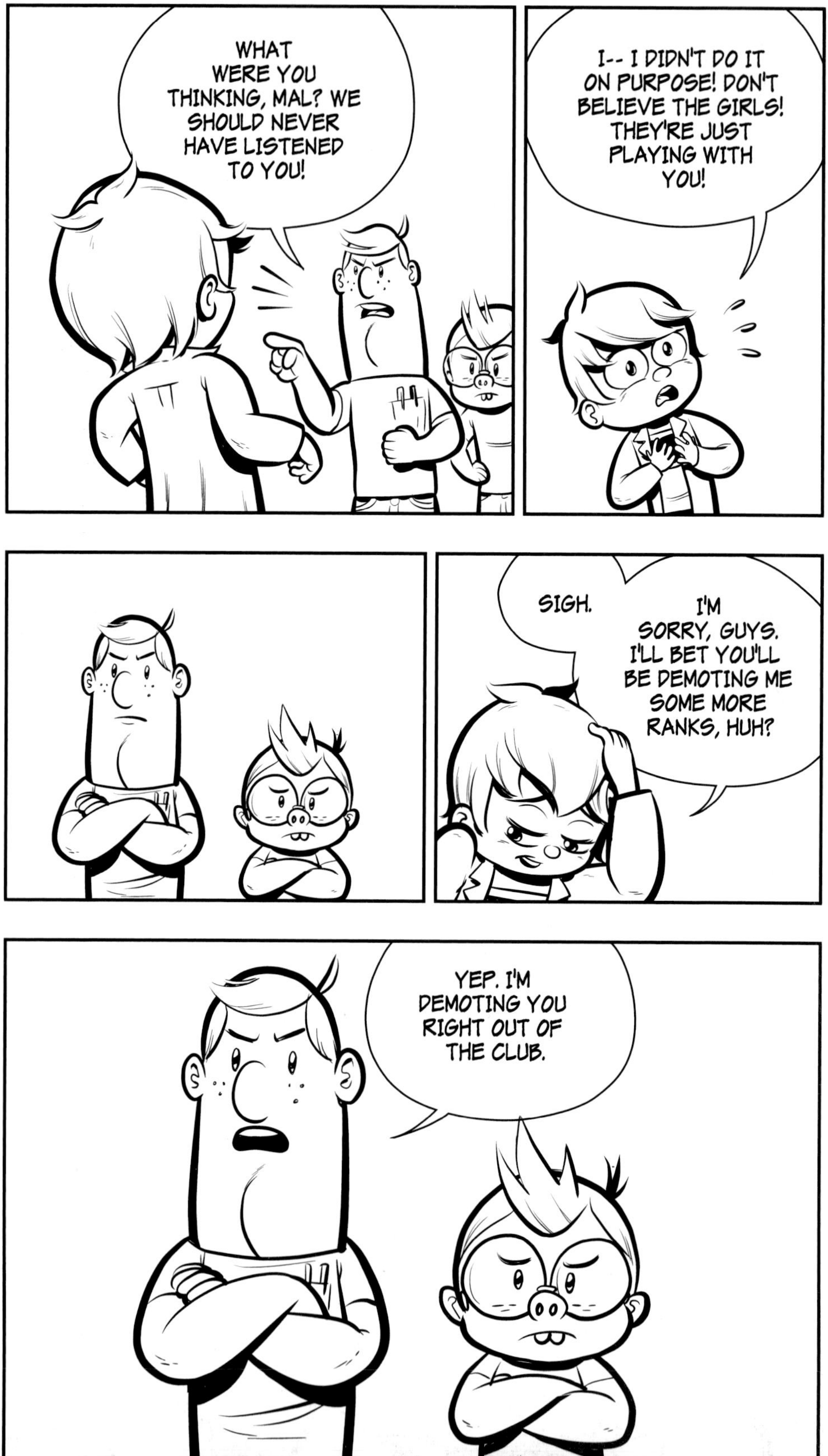
WHAT WERE YOU THINKING, MAL? WE SHOULD NEVER HAVE LISTENED TO YOU!
I-- I DIDN'T DO IT ON PURPOSE! DON'T BELIEVE THE GIRLS! THEY'RE JUST PLAYING WITH YOU!
SIGH.
I'M SORRY, GUYS. I'LL BET YOU'LL BE DEMOTING ME SOME MORE RANKS, HUH?
YEP. I'M DEMOTING YOU RIGHT OUT OF THE CLUB.

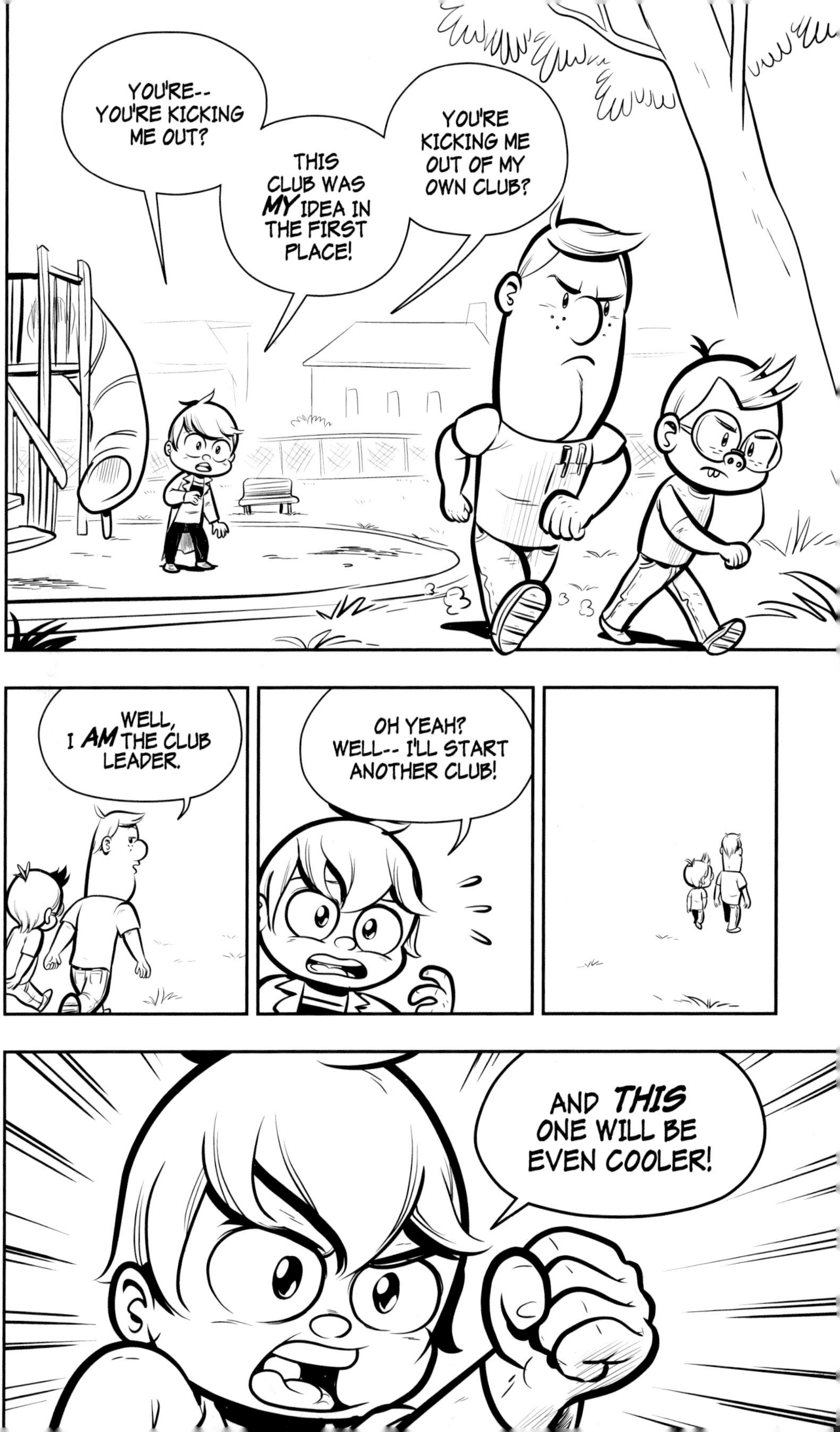
YOU'RE-- YOU'RE KICKING ME OUT?
THIS CLUB WAS MY IDEA IN THE FIRST PLACE!
YOU'RE KICKING ME OUT OF MY OWN CLUB?
WELL, I AM THE CLUB LEADER.
OH YEAH? WELL-- I'LL START ANOTHER CLUB!
AND THIS ONE WILL BE EVEN COOLER!

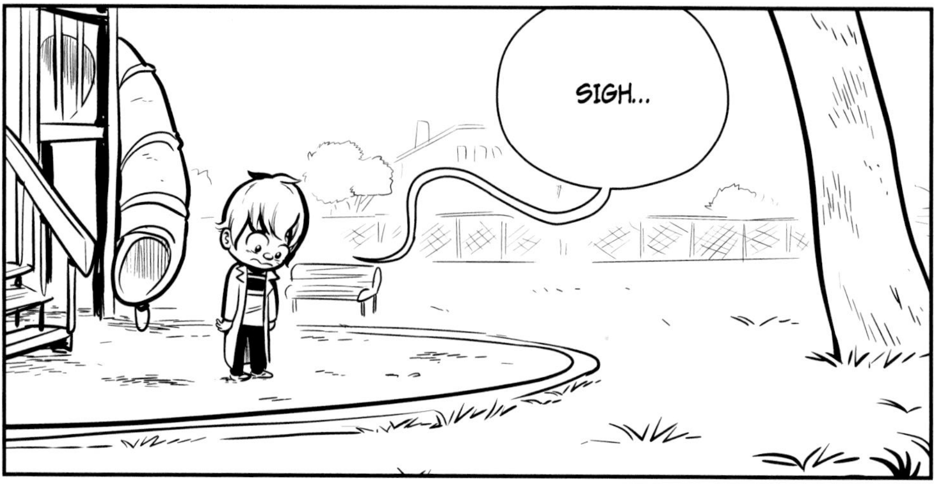
SIGH...

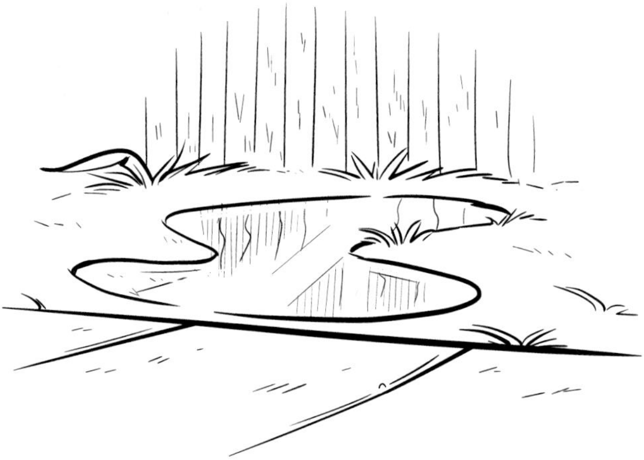

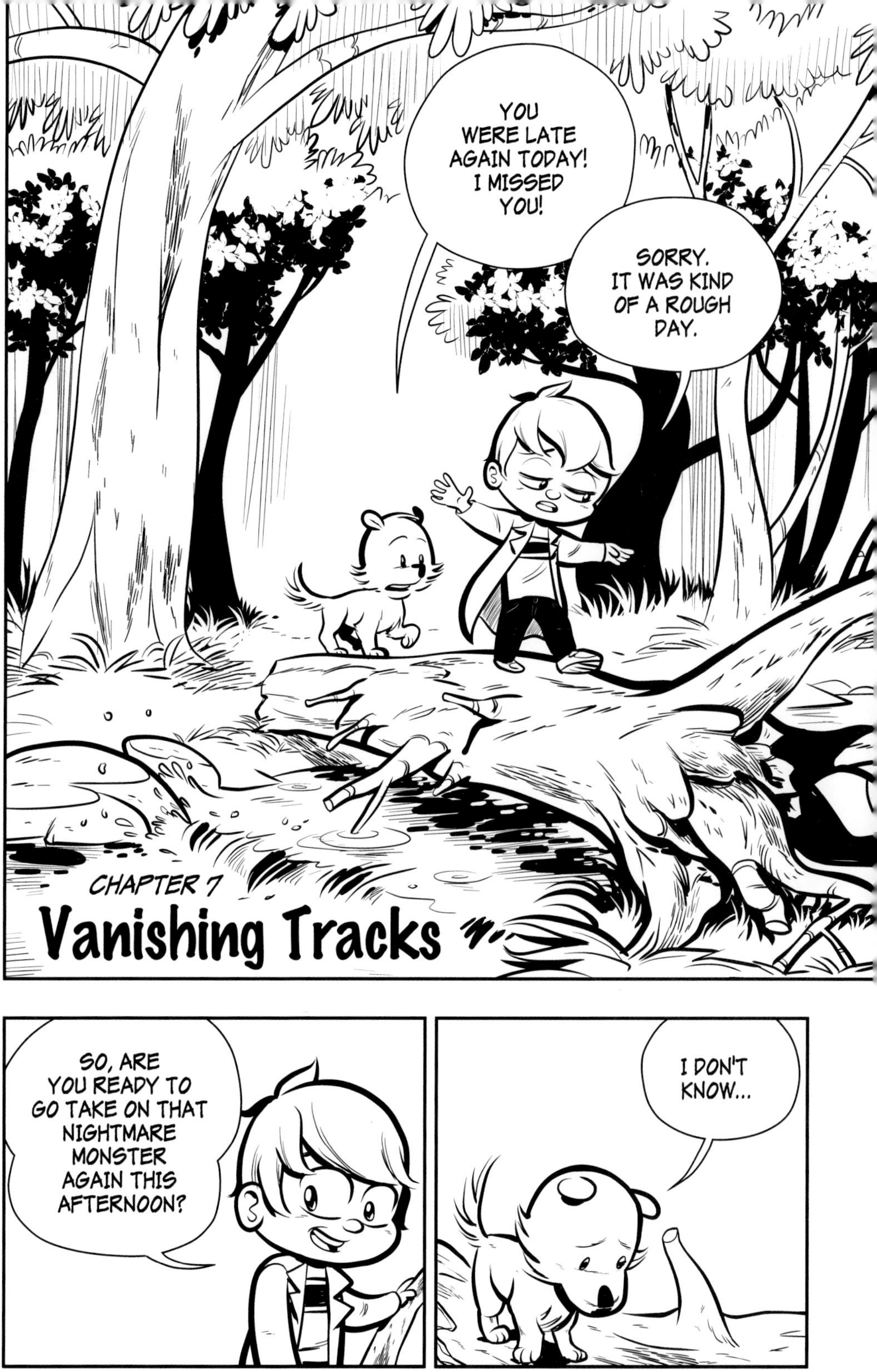
YOU WERE LATE AGAIN TODAY! I MISSED YOU!
SORRY. IT WAS KIND OF A ROUGH DAY.
CHAPTER 7
Vanishing Tracks
SO, ARE YOU READY TO GO TAKE ON THAT NIGHTMARE MONSTER AGAIN THIS AFTERNOON?
I DON'T KNOW...

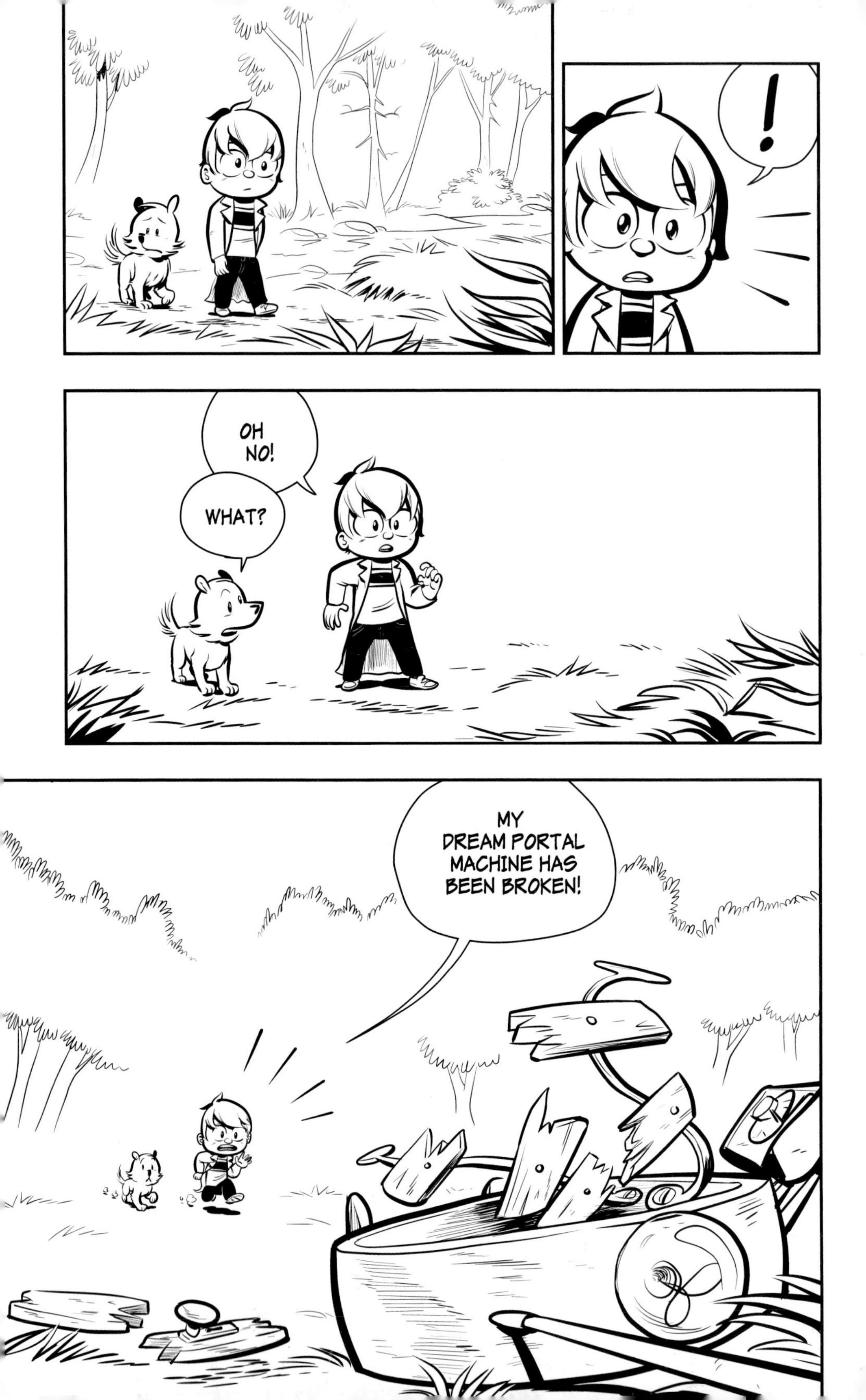
!
OH NO!
WHAT?
MY DREAM PORTAL MACHINE HAS BEEN BROKEN!

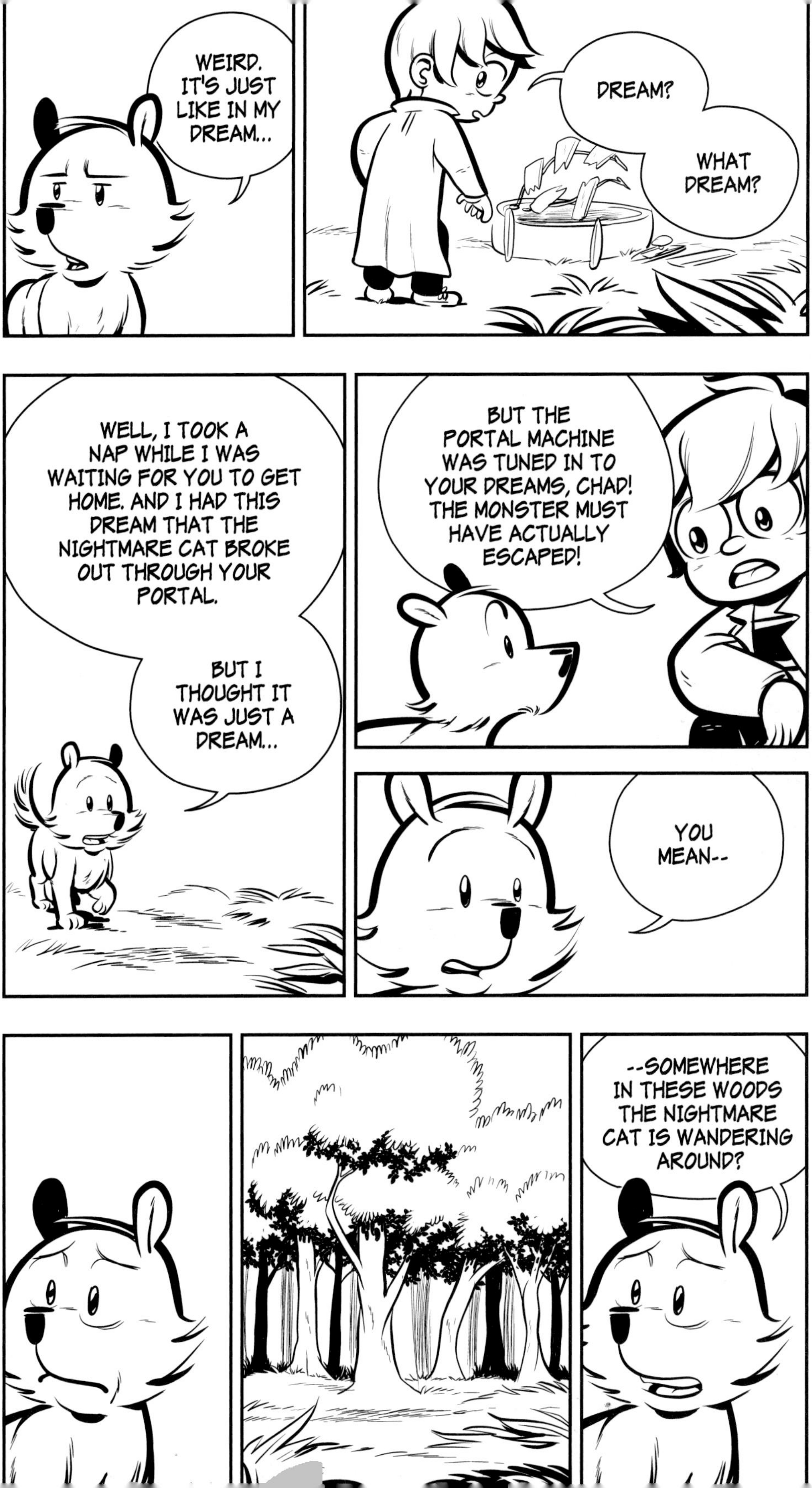
WEIRD. IT'S JUST LIKE IN MY DREAM...
DREAM?
WHAT DREAM?
WELL, I TOOK A NAP WHILE I WAS WAITING FOR YOU TO GET HOME. AND I HAD THIS DREAM THAT THE NIGHTMARE CAT BROKE OUT THROUGH YOUR PORTAL.
BUT I THOUGHT IT WAS JUST A DREAM...
BUT THE PORTAL MACHINE WAS TUNED IN TO YOUR DREAMS, CHAD! THE MONSTER MUST HAVE ACTUALLY ESCAPED!
YOU MEAN--
--SOMEWHERE IN THESE WOODS THE NIGHTMARE CAT IS WANDERING AROUND?

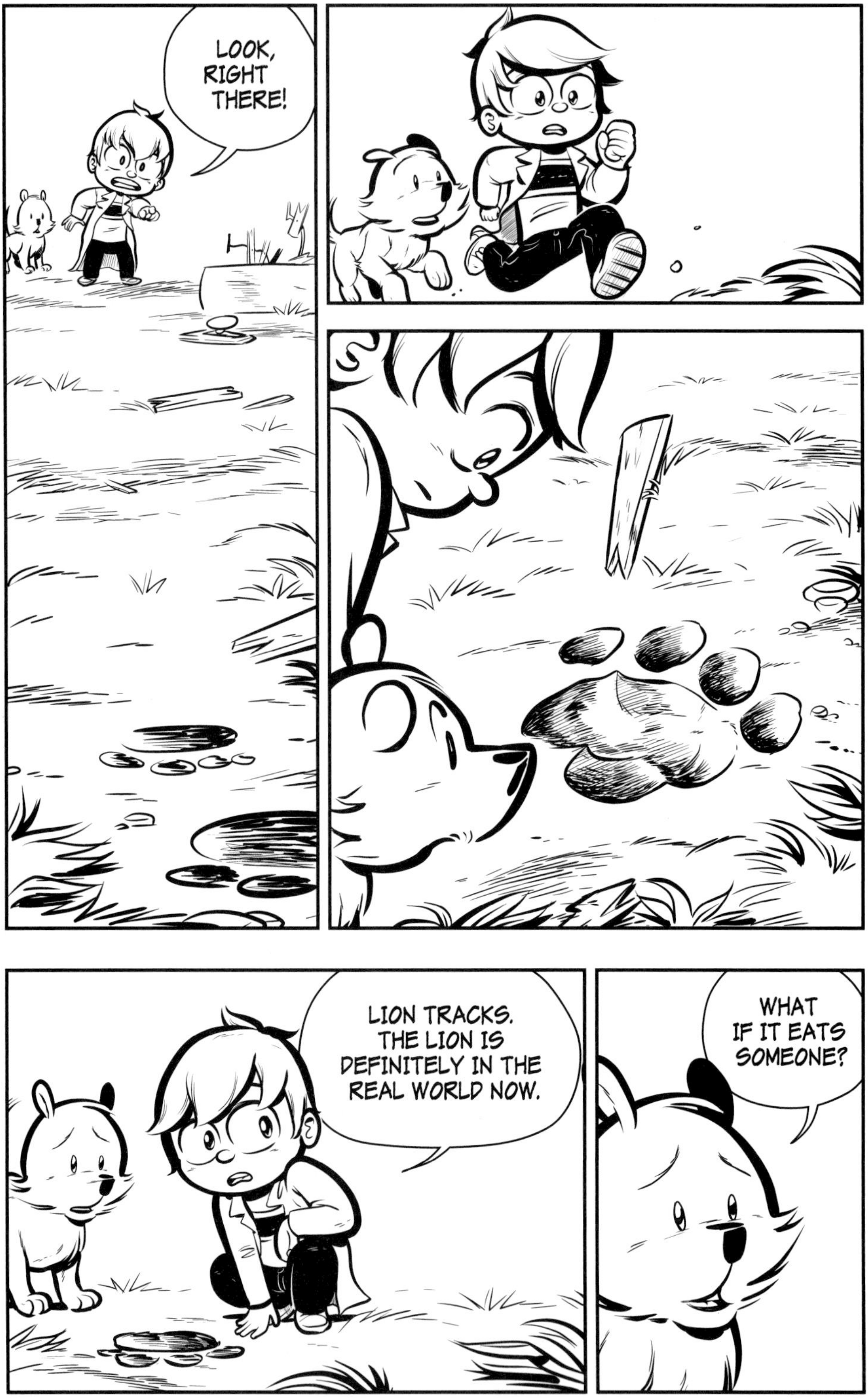
LOOK, RIGHT THERE!
LION TRACKS. THE LION IS DEFINITELY IN THE REAL WORLD NOW.
WHAT IF IT EATS SOMEONE?

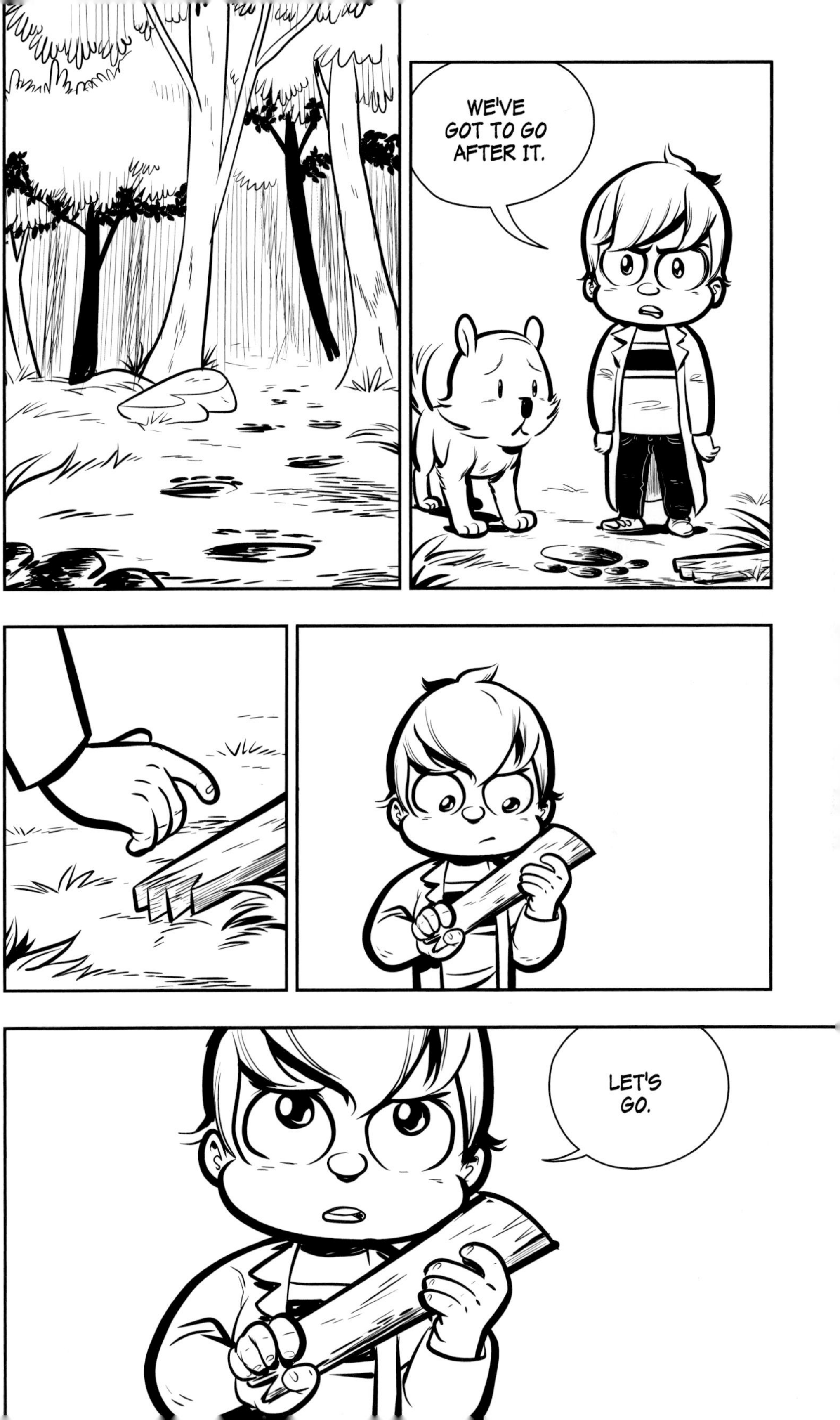
WE'VE GOT TO GO AFTER IT.
LET'S GO.

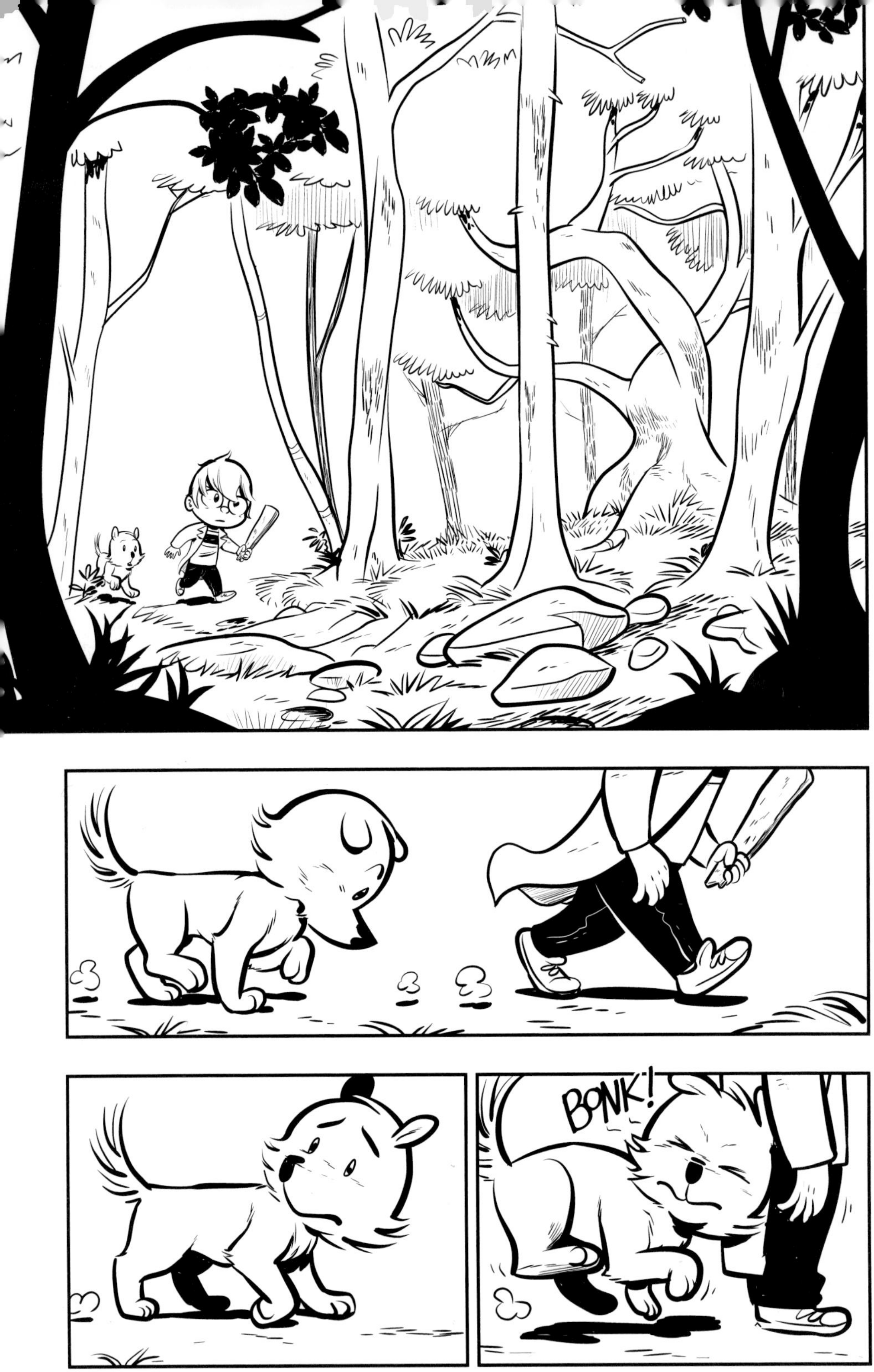
BONK!

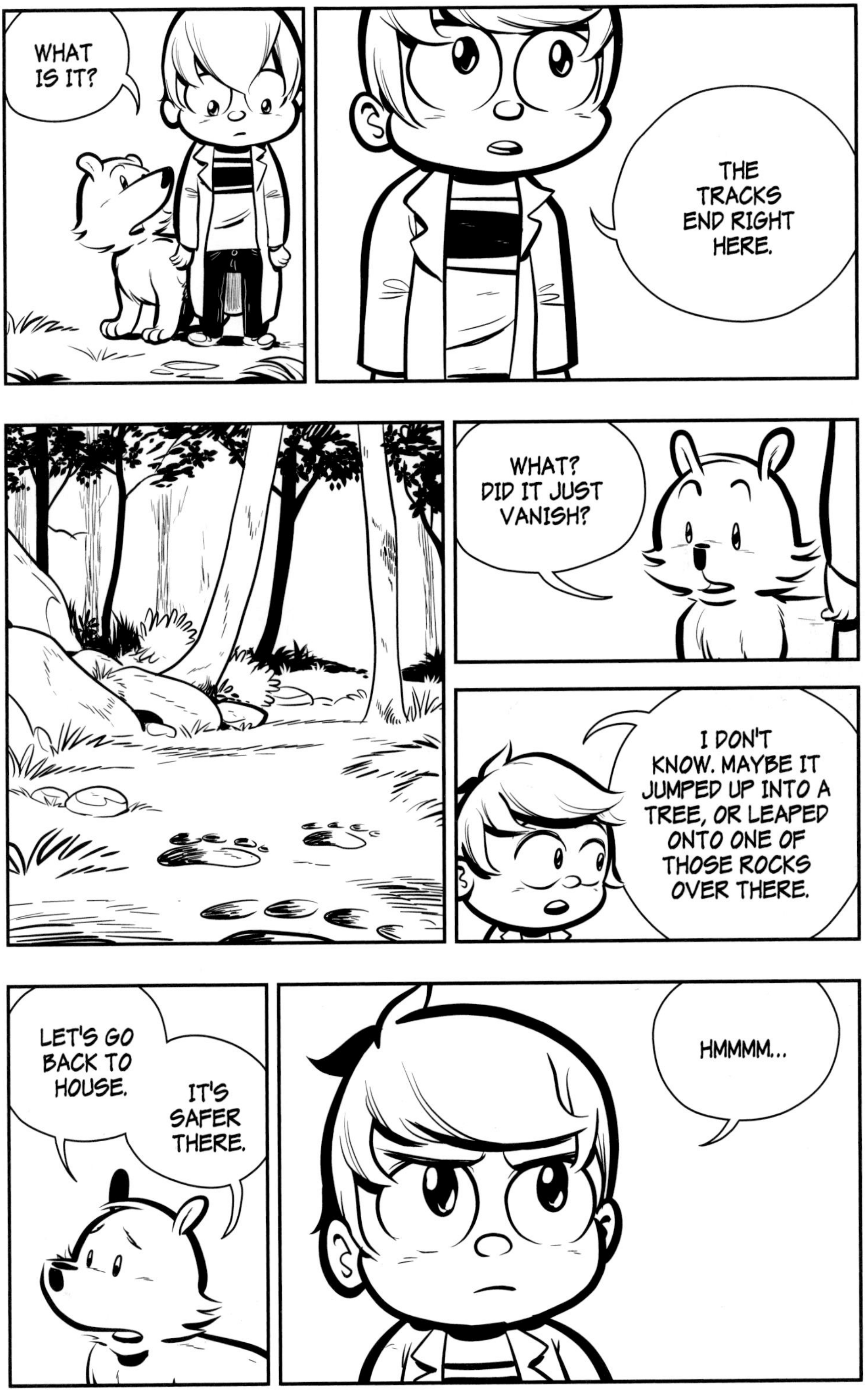
WHAT IS IT?
THE TRACKS END RIGHT HERE.
WHAT? DID IT JUST VANISH?
I DON'T KNOW. MAYBE IT JUMPED UP INTO A TREE, OR LEAPED ONTO ONE OF THOSE ROCKS OVER THERE.
LET'S GO BACK TO HOUSE.
IT'S SAFER THERE.
HMMMM...

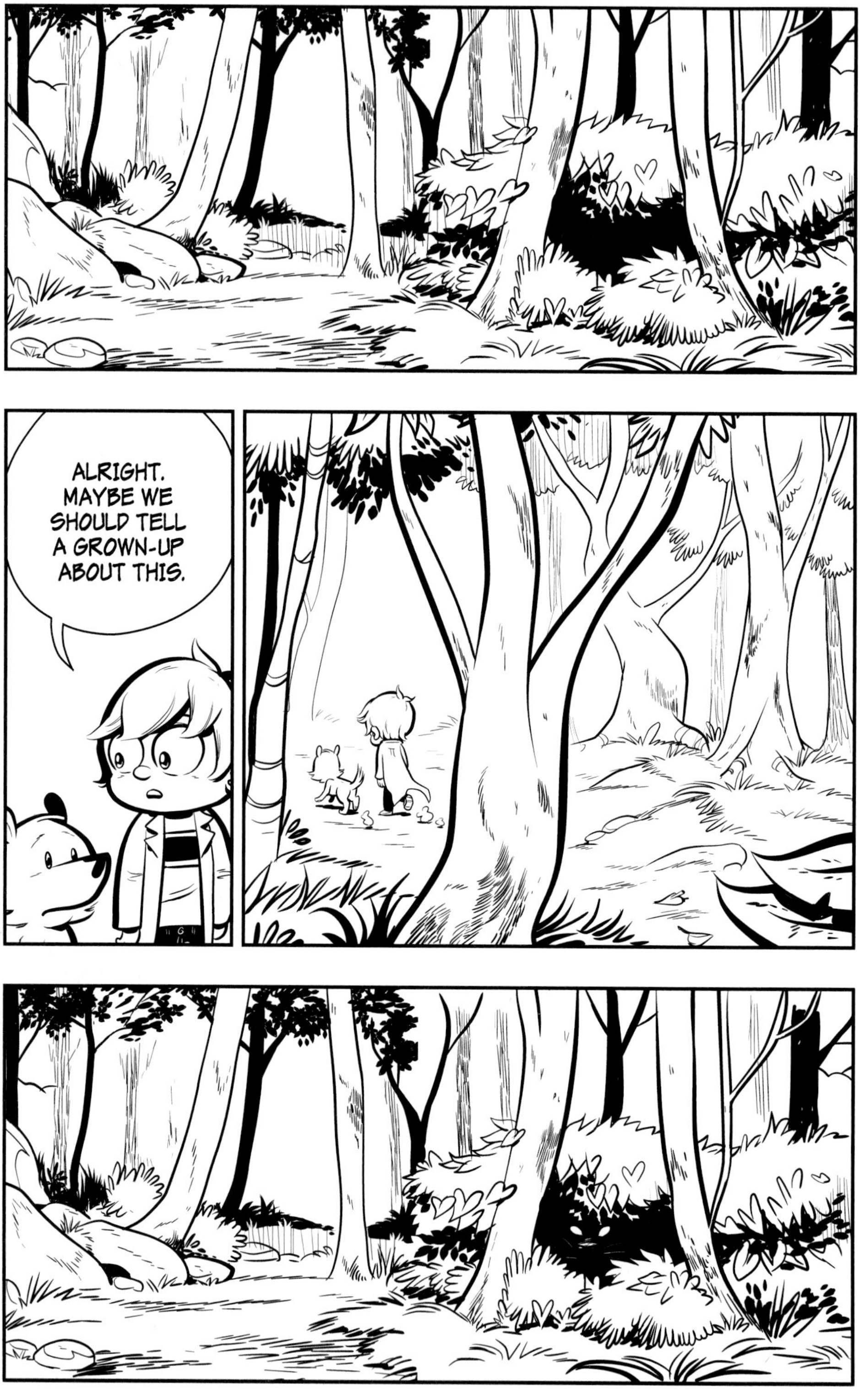
ALRIGHT. MAYBE WE SHOULD TELL A GROWN-UP ABOUT THIS.

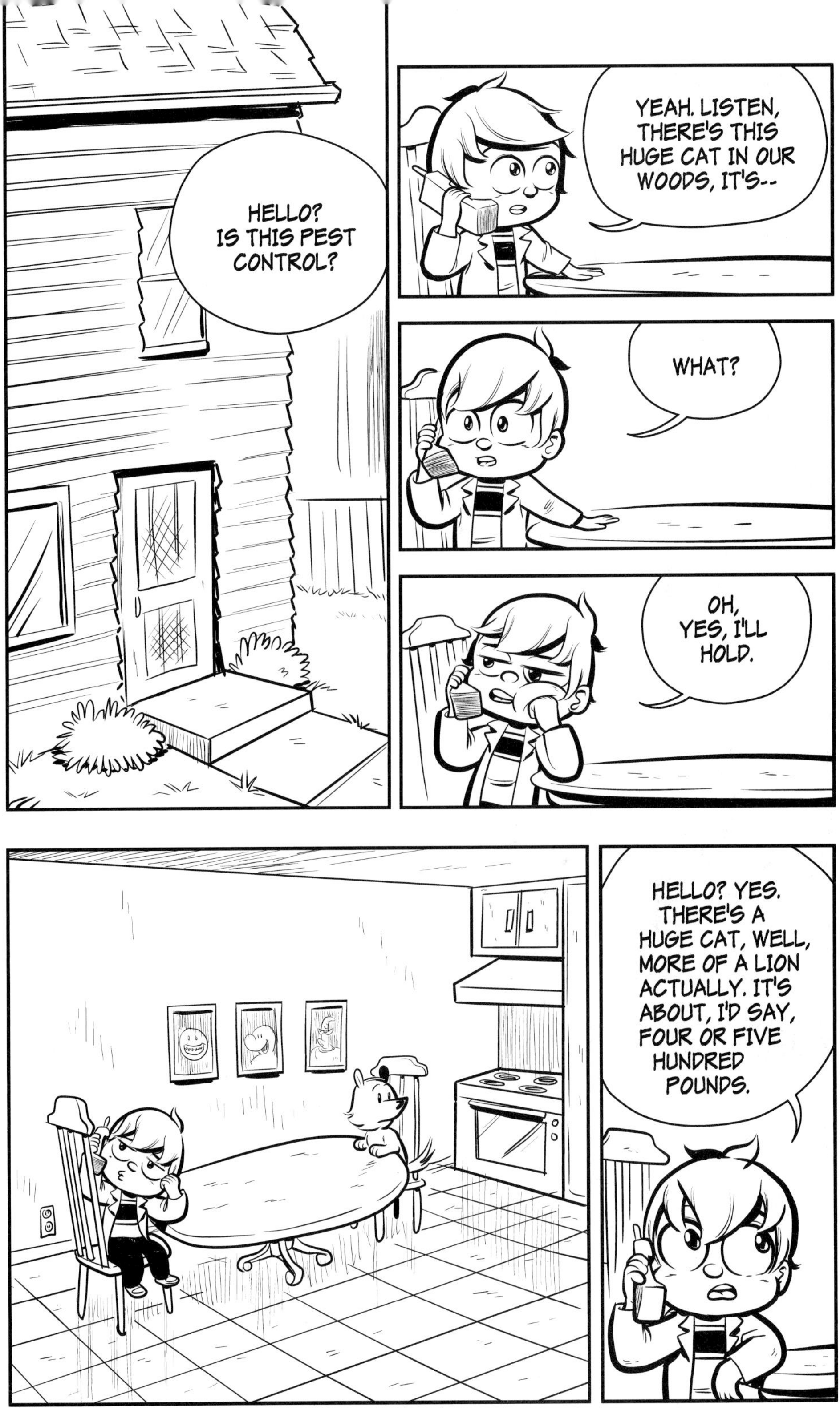
HELLO? IS THIS PEST CONTROL?
YEAH. LISTEN, THERE'S THIS HUGE CAT IN OUR WOODS, IT'S--
WHAT?
OH, YES, I'LL HOLD.
HELLO? YES. THERE'S A HUGE CAT, WELL, MORE OF A LION ACTUALLY. IT'S ABOUT, I'D SAY, FOUR OR FIVE HUNDRED POUNDS.

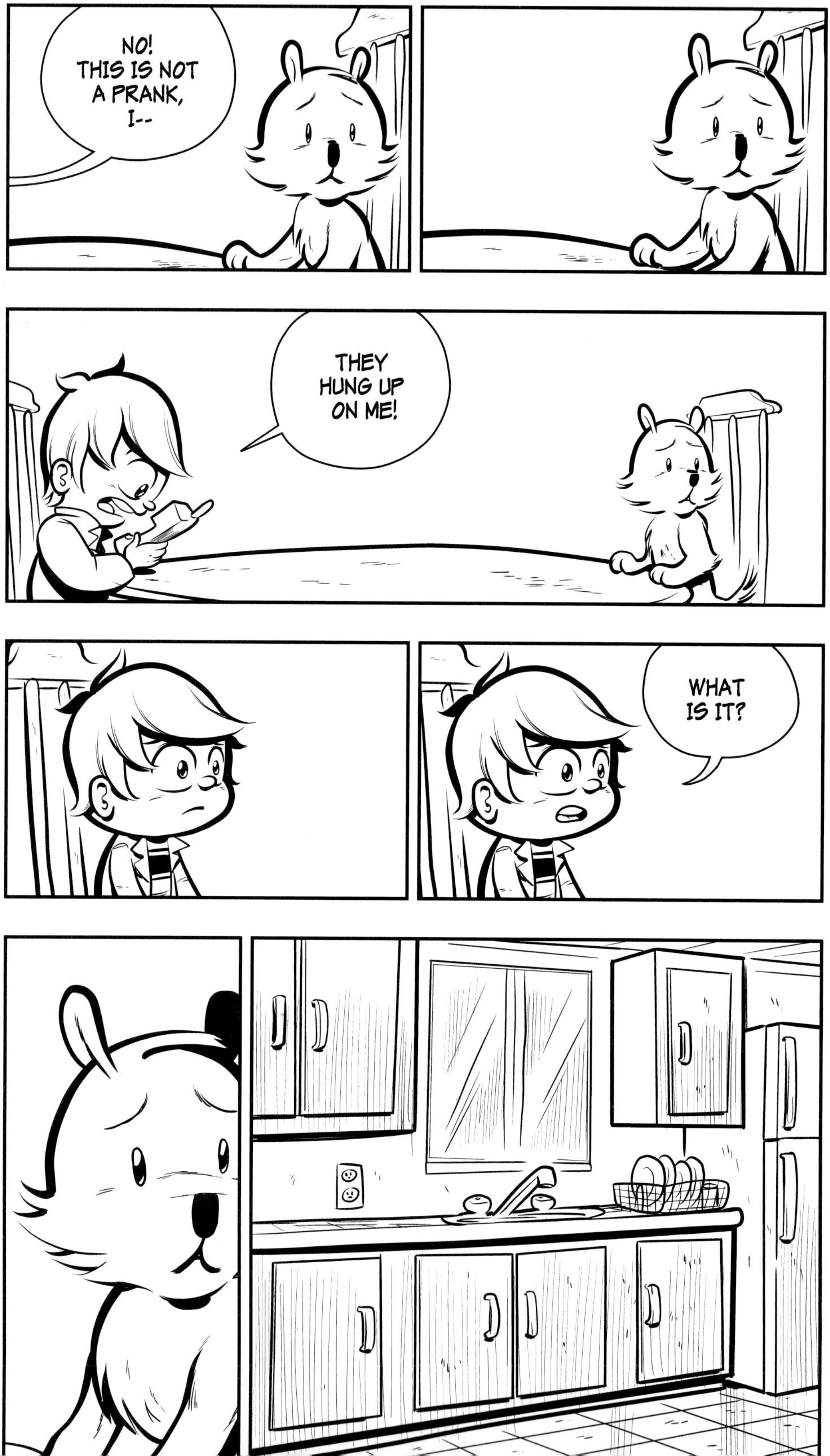
NO! THIS IS NOT A PRANK, I--
THEY HUNG UP ON ME!
WHAT IS IT?

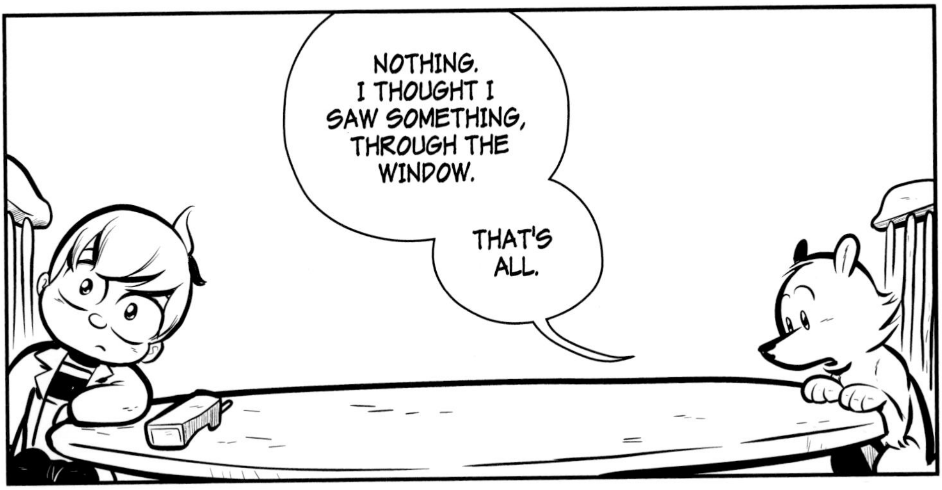
NOTHING. I THOUGHT I SAW SOMETHING, THROUGH THE WINDOW.
THAT'S ALL.

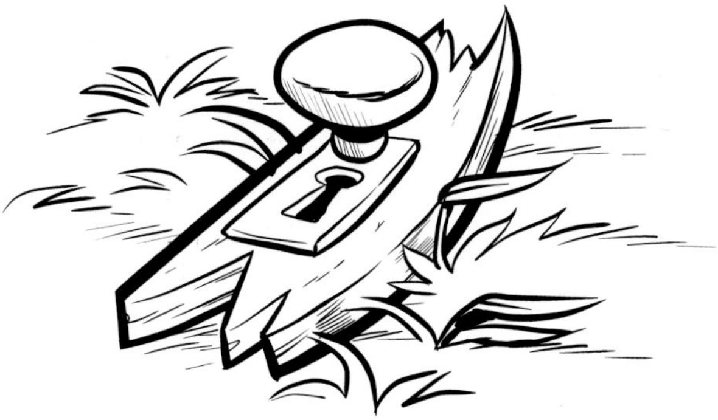

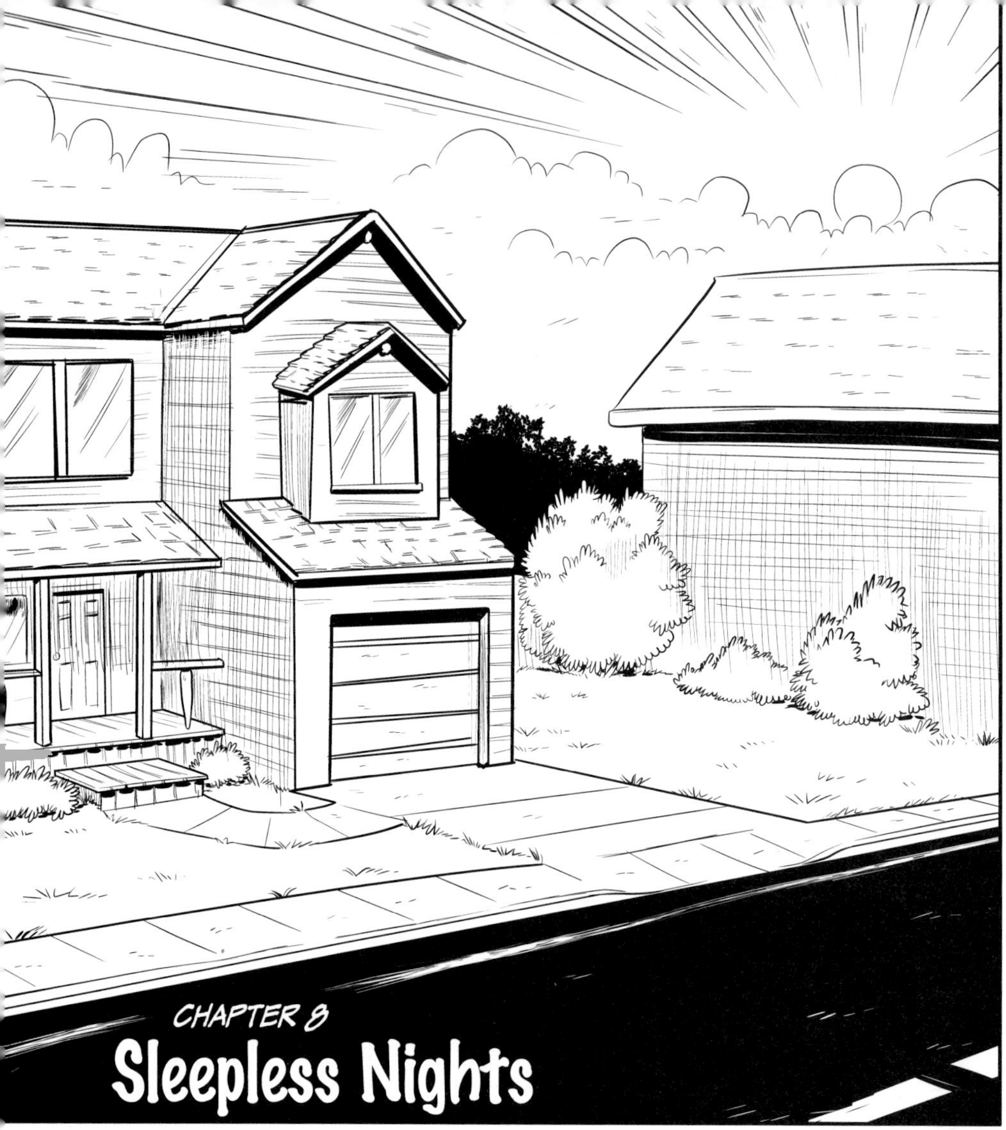

CHAPTER 8
Sleepless Nights

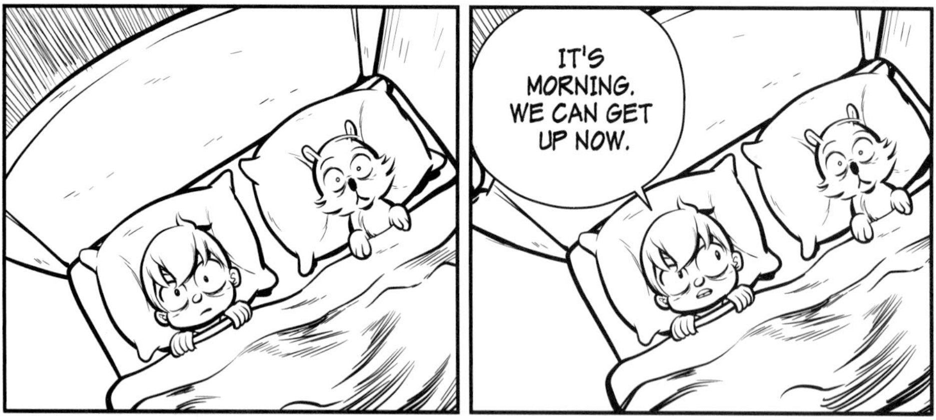
IT'S MORNING. WE CAN GET UP NOW.

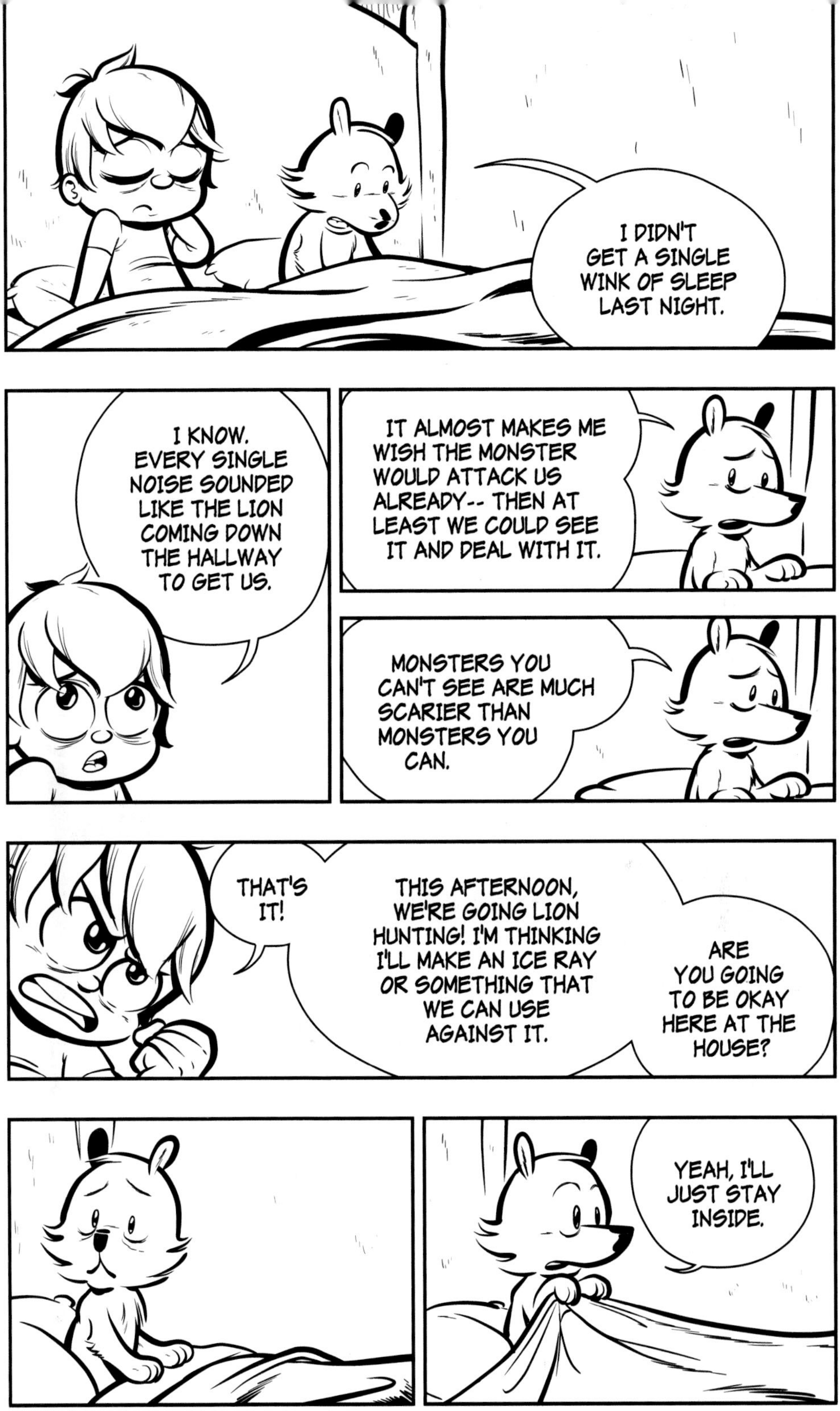
I DIDN'T GET A SINGLE WINK OF SLEEP LAST NIGHT.
I KNOW. EVERY SINGLE NOISE SOUNDED LIKE THE LION COMING DOWN THE HALLWAY TO GET US.
IT ALMOST MAKES ME WISH THE MONSTER WOULD ATTACK US ALREADY-- THEN AT LEAST WE COULD SEE IT AND DEAL WITH IT.
MONSTERS YOU CAN'T SEE ARE MUCH SCARIER THAN MONSTERS YOU CAN.
THAT'S IT!
THIS AFTERNOON, WE'RE GOING LION HUNTING! I'M THINKING I'LL MAKE AN ICE RAY OR SOMETHING THAT WE CAN USE AGAINST IT.
ARE YOU GOING TO BE OKAY HERE AT THE HOUSE?
YEAH, I'LL JUST STAY INSIDE.

EINSTEIN
ELEMENTARY

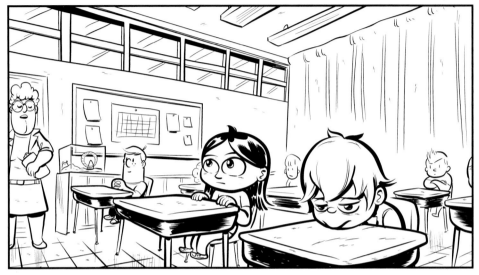

TICK

TOCK

TICK

TOCK

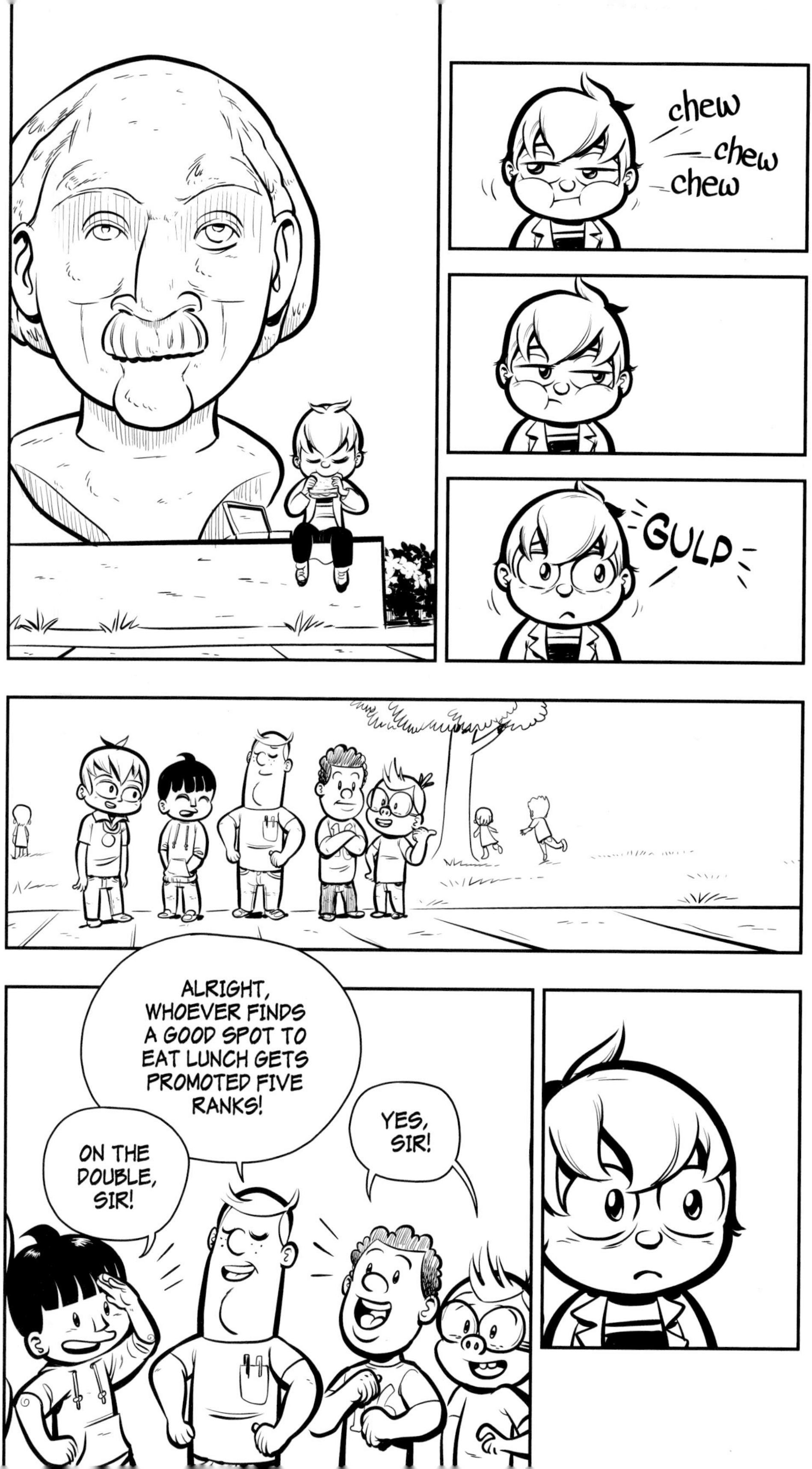
chew
chew
chew
GULP
ALRIGHT, WHOEVER FINDS A GOOD SPOT TO EAT LUNCH GETS PROMOTED FIVE RANKS!
ON THE DOUBLE, SIR!
YES, SIR!

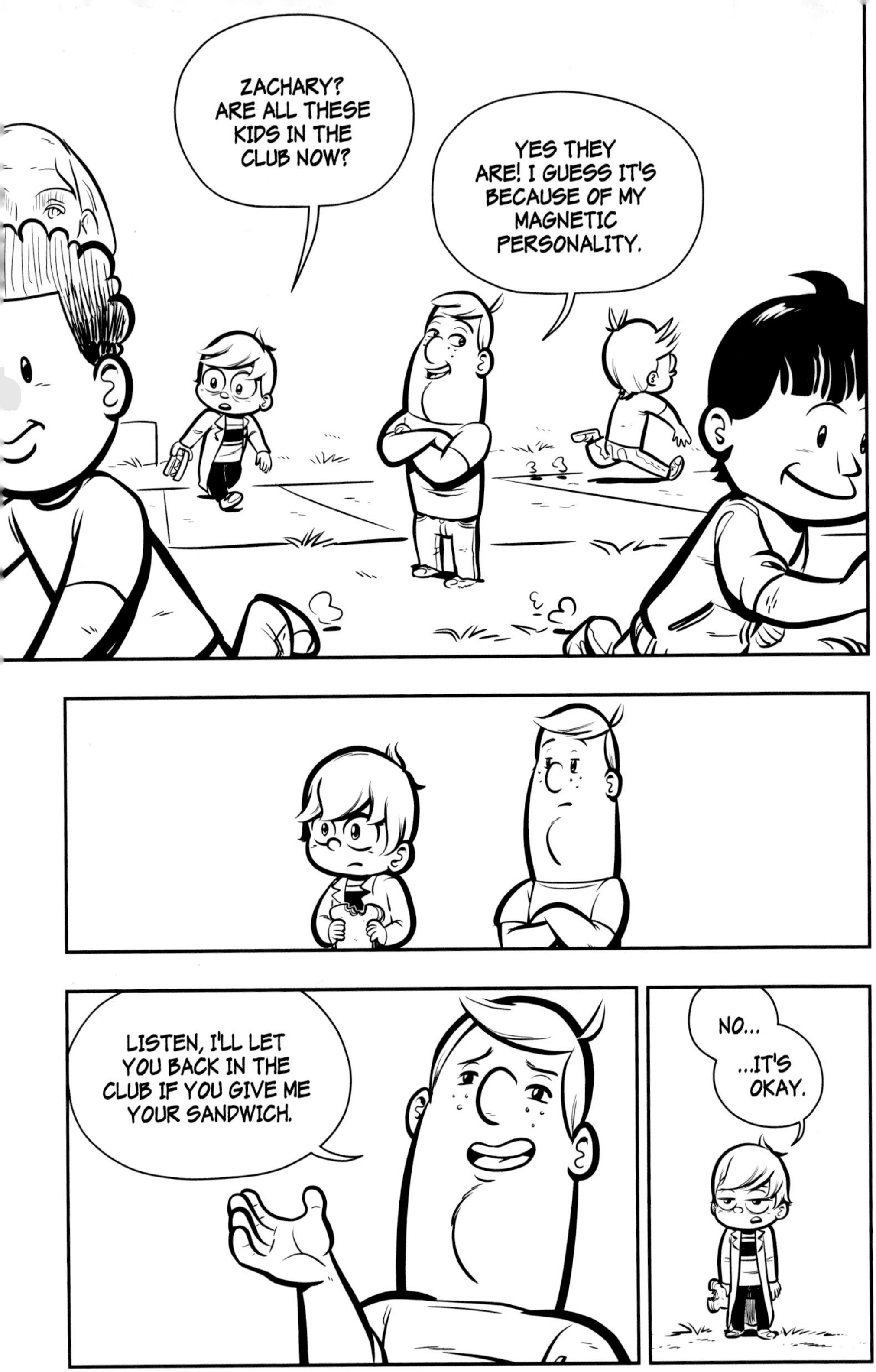
ZACHARY? ARE ALL THESE KIDS IN THE CLUB NOW?
YES THEY ARE! I GUESS IT'S BECAUSE OF MY MAGNETIC PERSONALITY.
LISTEN, I'LL LET YOU BACK IN THE CLUB IF YOU GIVE ME YOUR SANDWICH.
NO...
...IT'S OKAY.

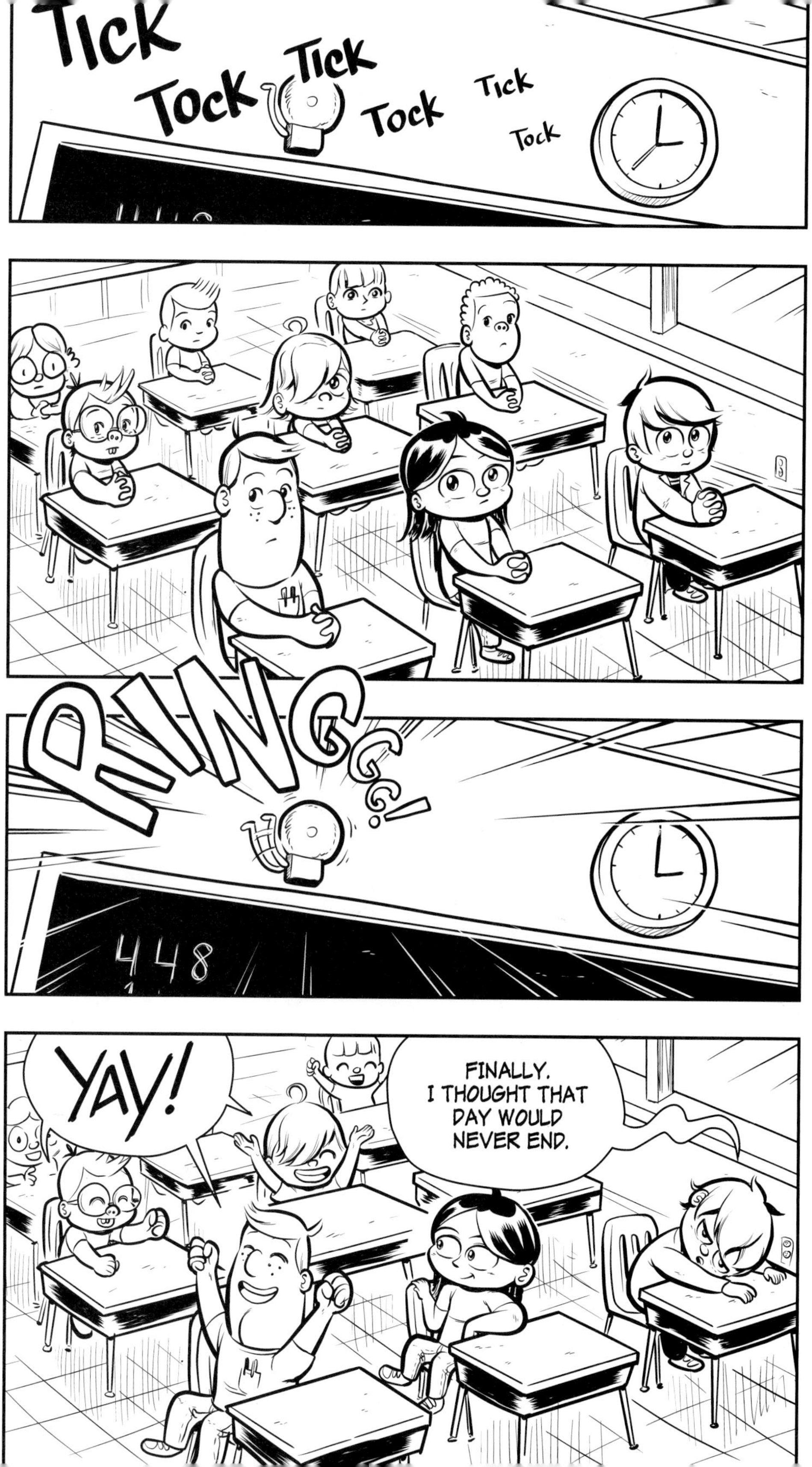
TICK
TOCK
TICK
TOCK
TICK
TOCK
RINGGG!
YAY!
FINALLY.
I THOUGHT THAT
DAY WOULD
NEVER END.

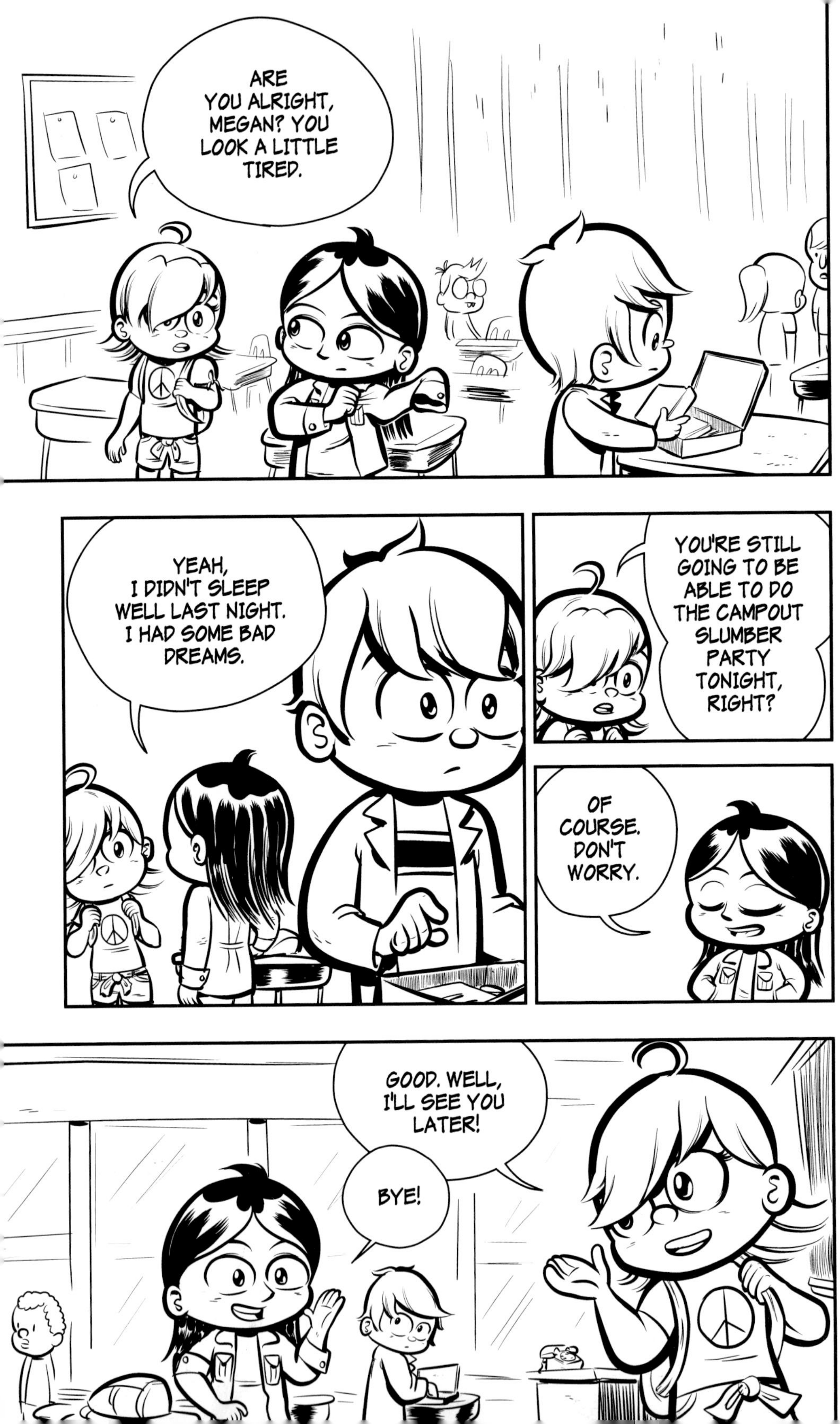
ARE YOU ALRIGHT, MEGAN? YOU LOOK A LITTLE TIRED.
YEAH, I DIDN'T SLEEP WELL LAST NIGHT. I HAD SOME BAD DREAMS.
YOU'RE STILL GOING TO BE ABLE TO DO THE CAMPOUT SLUMBER PARTY TONIGHT, RIGHT?
OF COURSE. DON'T WORRY.
GOOD. WELL, I'LL SEE YOU LATER!
BYE!

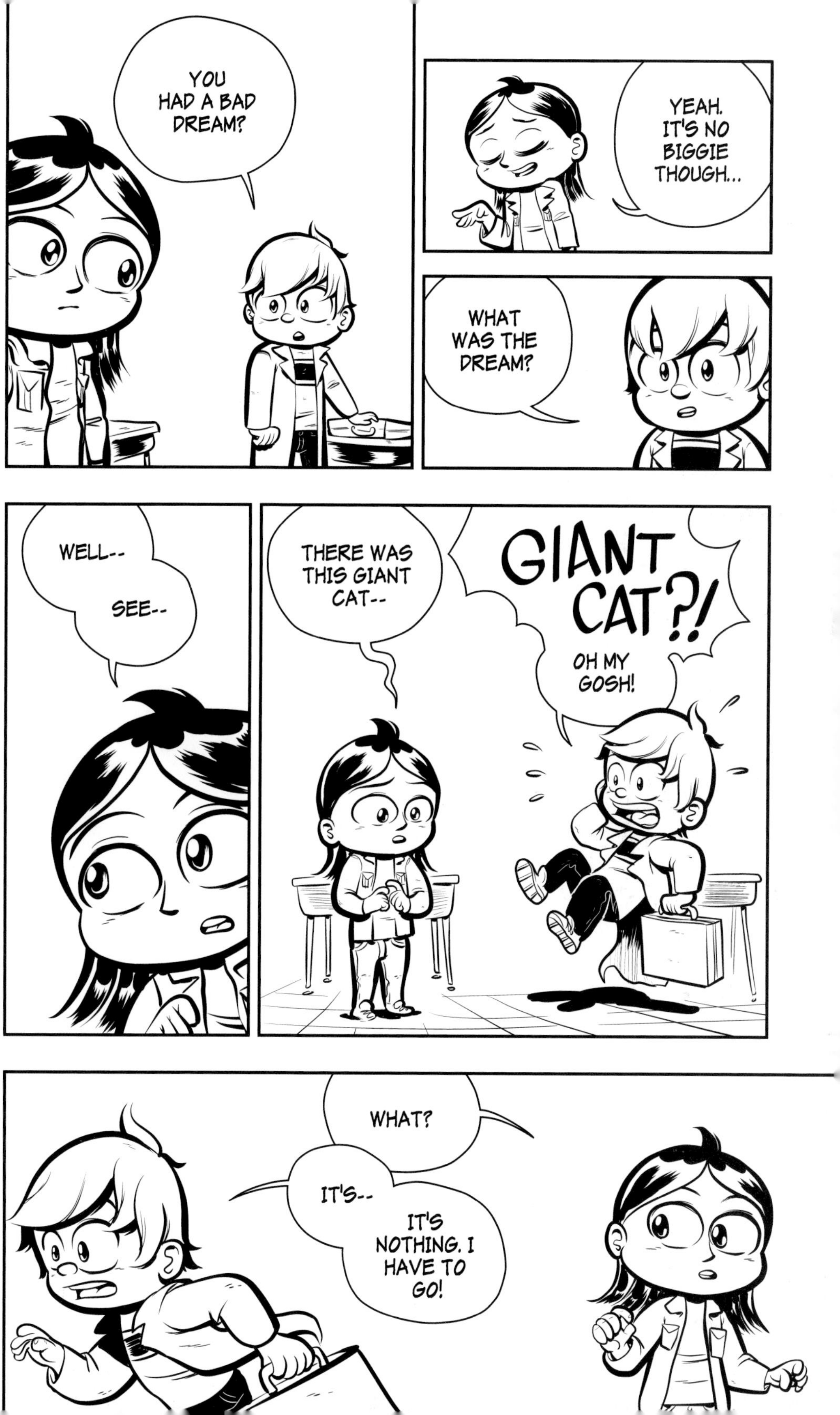
YOU HAD A BAD DREAM?
YEAH. IT'S NO BIGGIE THOUGH...
WHAT WAS THE DREAM?
WELL--
SEE--
THERE WAS THIS GIANT CAT--
GIANT CAT?!
OH MY GOSH!
WHAT?
IT'S--
IT'S NOTHING. I HAVE TO GO!

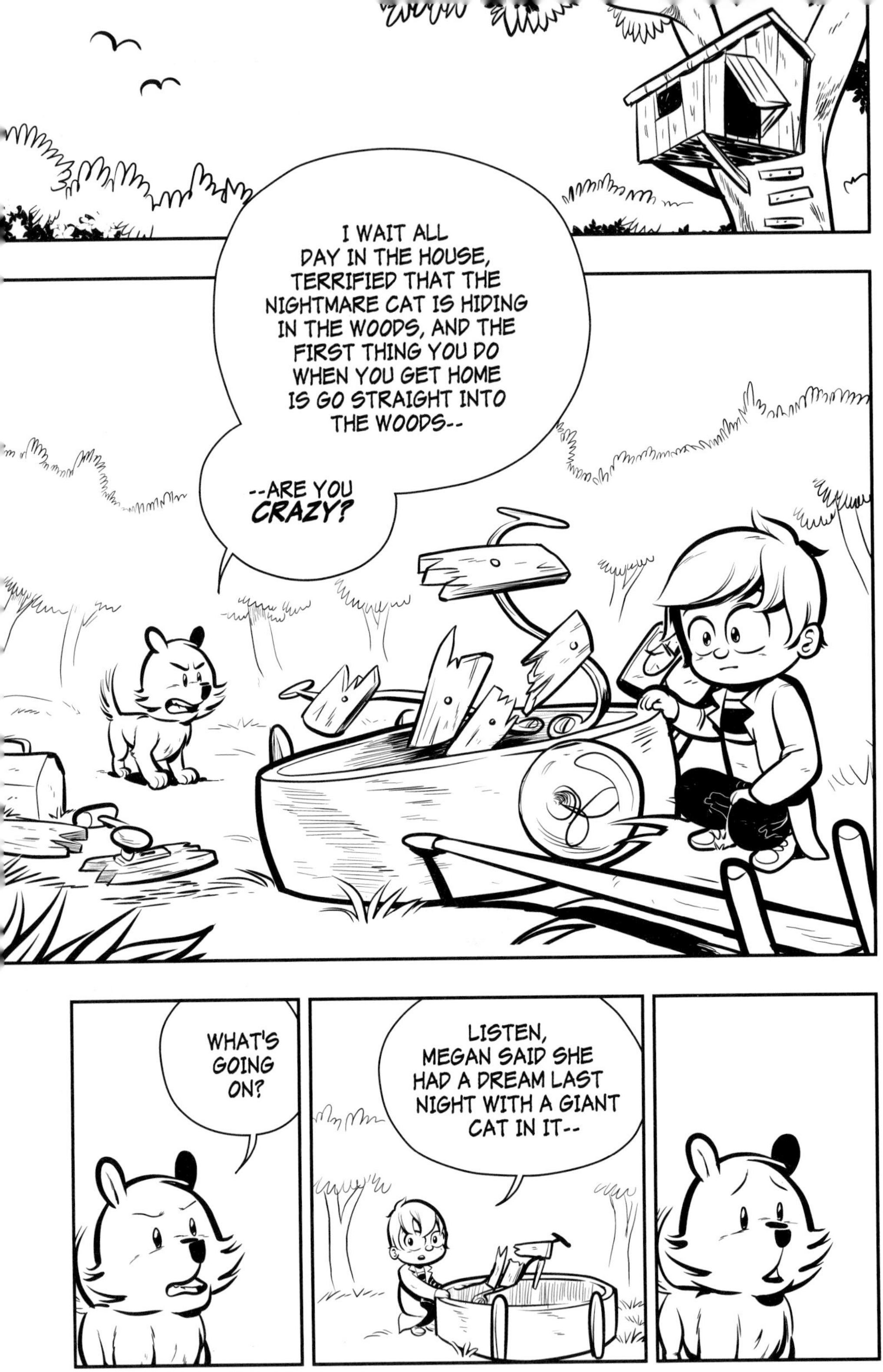
I WAIT ALL DAY IN THE HOUSE, TERRIFIED THAT THE NIGHTMARE CAT IS HIDING IN THE WOODS, AND THE FIRST THING YOU DO WHEN YOU GET HOME IS GO STRAIGHT INTO THE WOODS--
--ARE YOU *CRAZY?*
WHAT'S GOING ON?
LISTEN, MEGAN SAID SHE HAD A DREAM LAST NIGHT WITH A GIANT CAT IN IT--

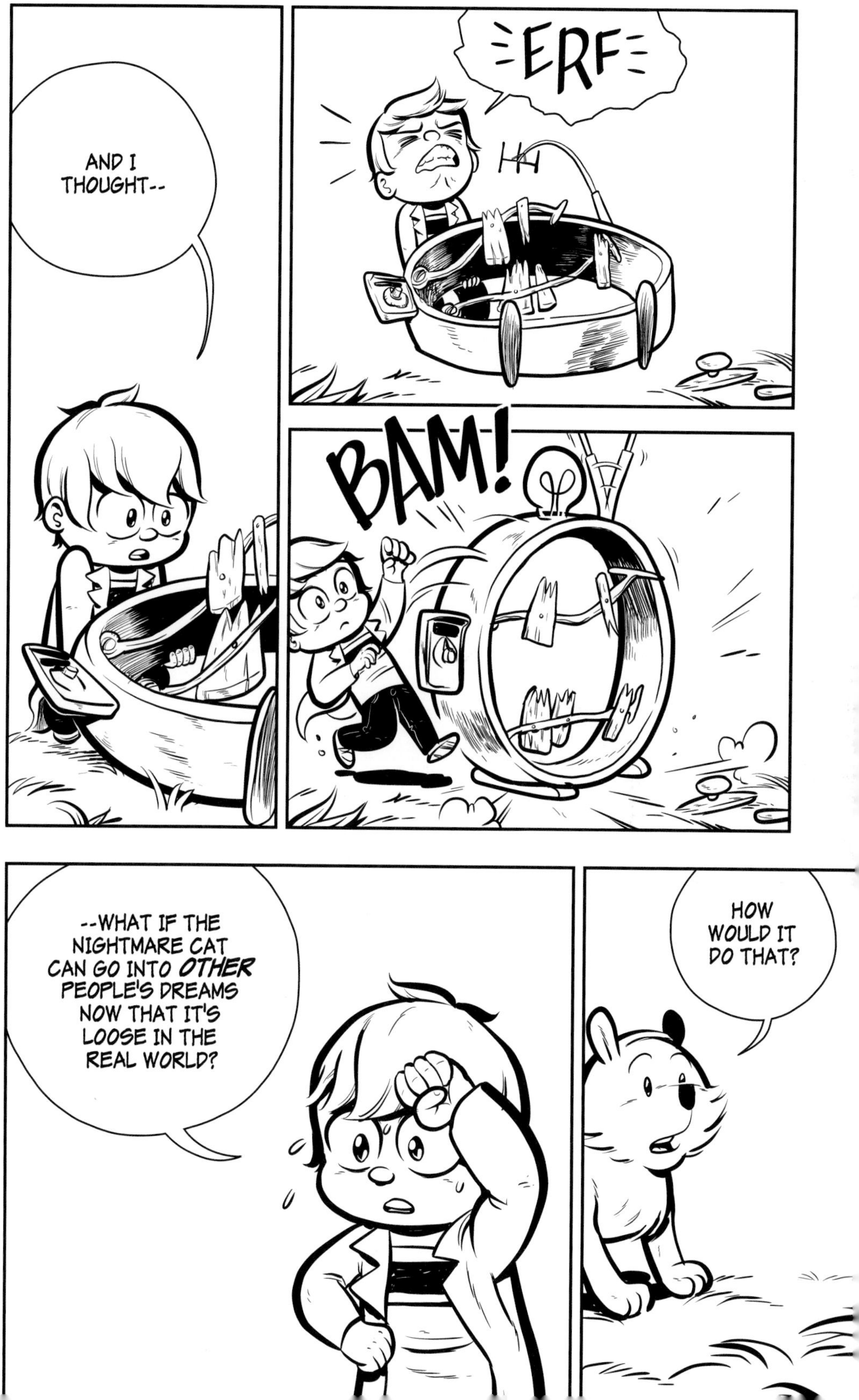
AND I THOUGHT--
ERF
BAM!
--WHAT IF THE NIGHTMARE CAT CAN GO INTO *OTHER* PEOPLE'S DREAMS NOW THAT IT'S LOOSE IN THE REAL WORLD?
HOW WOULD IT DO THAT?

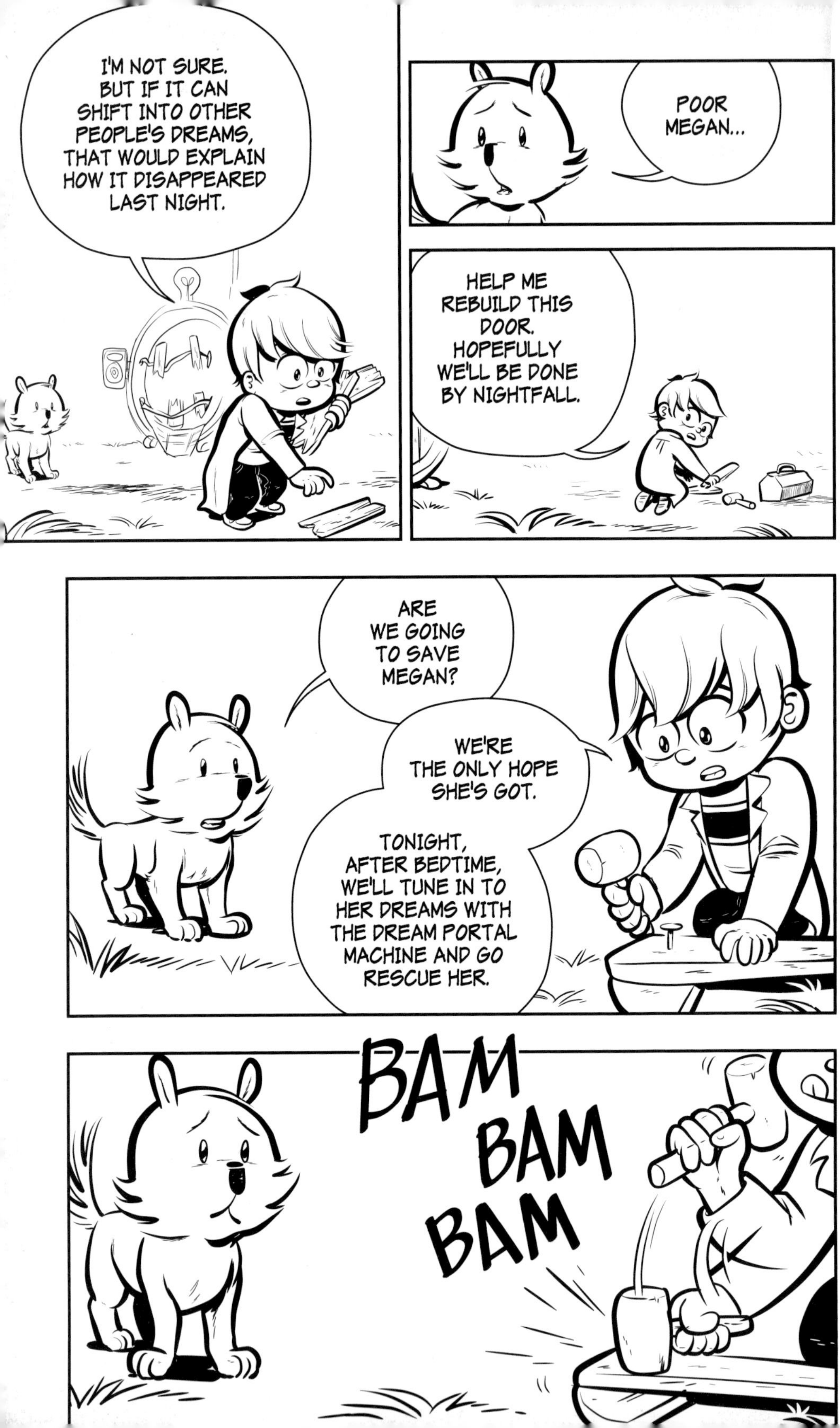
I'M NOT SURE. BUT IF IT CAN SHIFT INTO OTHER PEOPLE'S DREAMS, THAT WOULD EXPLAIN HOW IT DISAPPEARED LAST NIGHT.
POOR MEGAN...
HELP ME REBUILD THIS DOOR. HOPEFULLY WE'LL BE DONE BY NIGHTFALL.
ARE WE GOING TO SAVE MEGAN?
WE'RE THE ONLY HOPE SHE'S GOT.
TONIGHT, AFTER BEDTIME, WE'LL TUNE IN TO HER DREAMS WITH THE DREAM PORTAL MACHINE AND GO RESCUE HER.
BAM
BAM
BAM

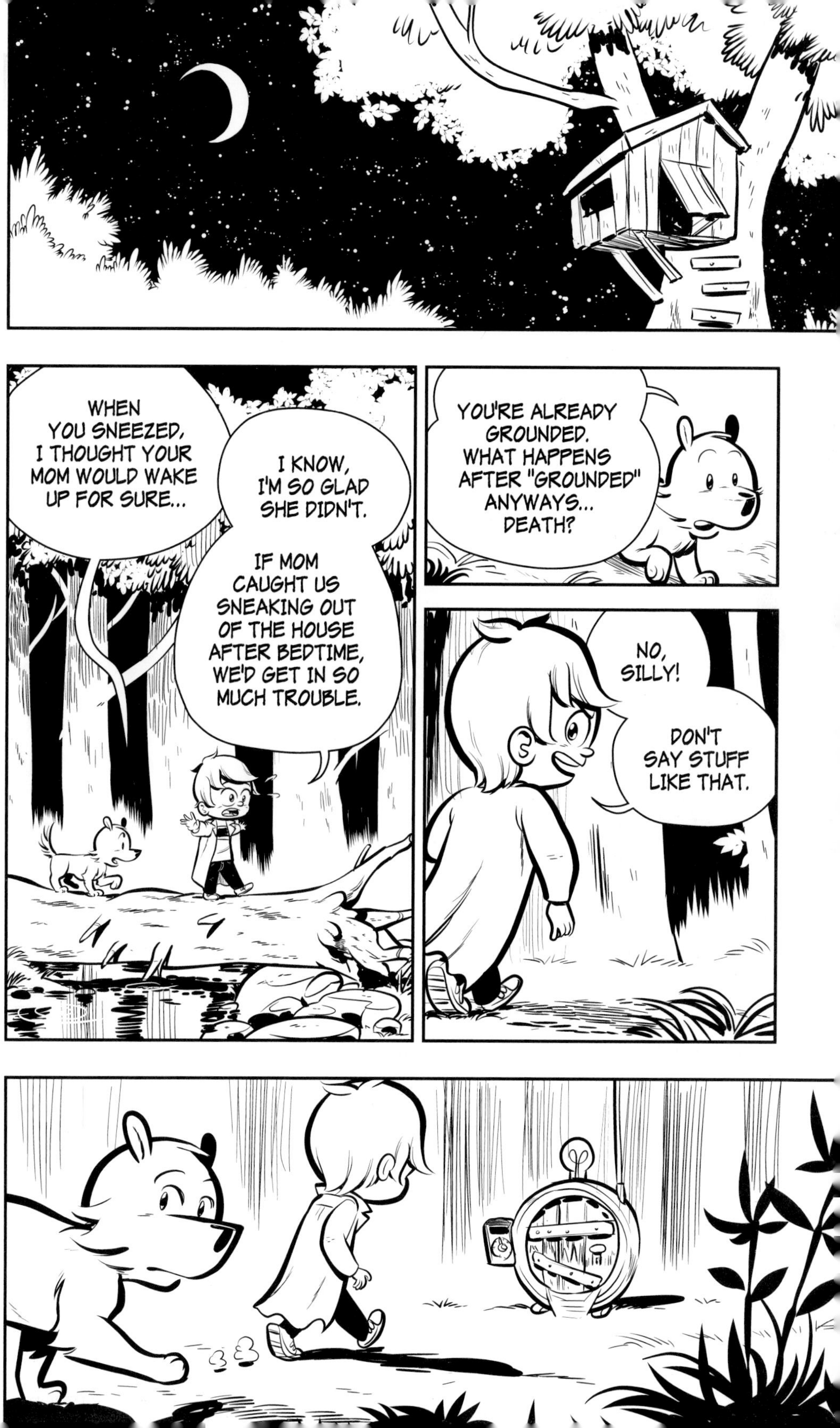

WHEN YOU SNEEZED, I THOUGHT YOUR MOM WOULD WAKE UP FOR SURE...
I KNOW, I'M SO GLAD SHE DIDN'T.
IF MOM CAUGHT US SNEAKING OUT OF THE HOUSE AFTER BEDTIME, WE'D GET IN SO MUCH TROUBLE.
YOU'RE ALREADY GROUNDED. WHAT HAPPENS AFTER "GROUNDED" ANYWAYS... DEATH?
NO, SILLY!
DON'T SAY STUFF LIKE THAT.

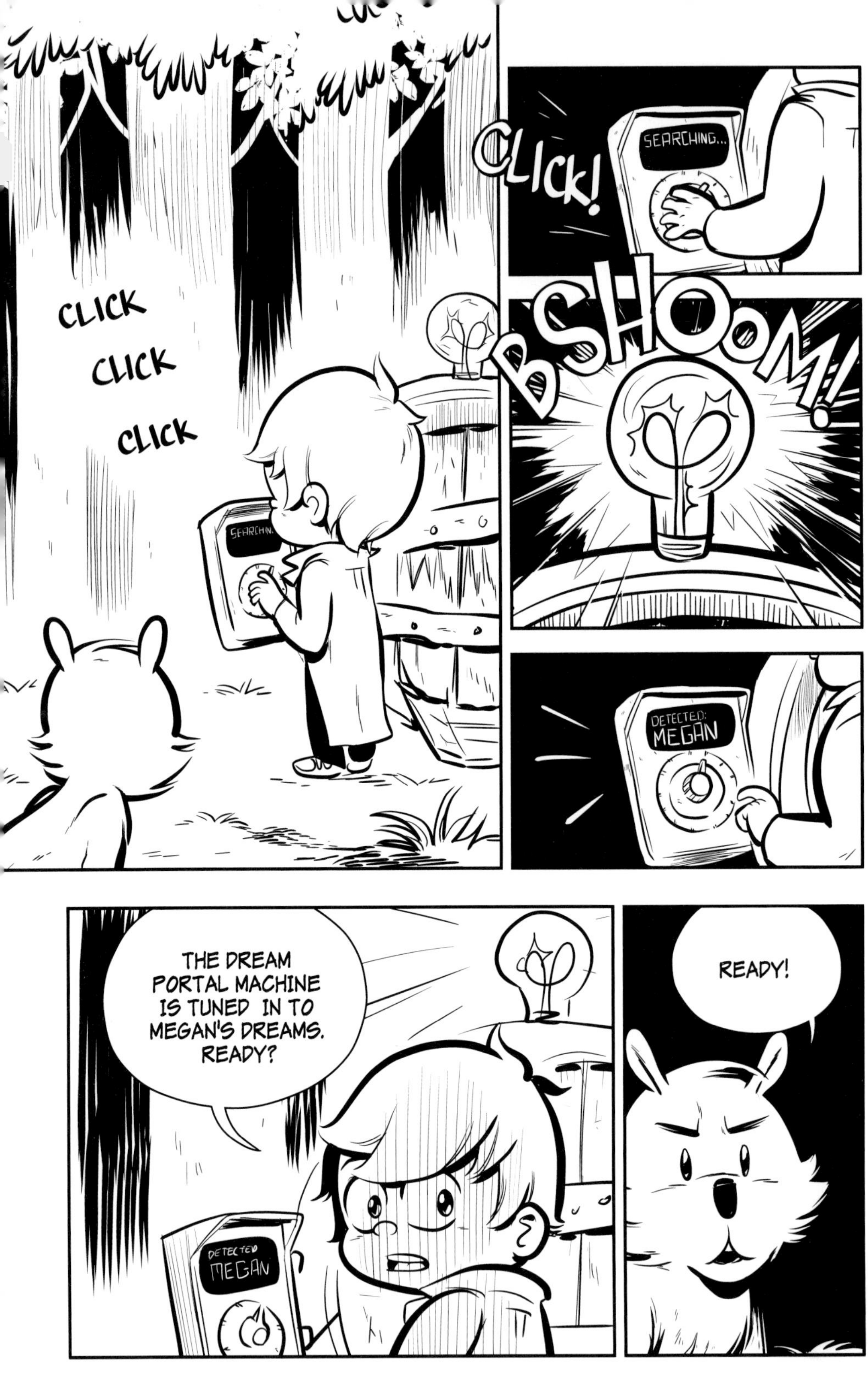
CLICK
CLICK
CLICK
SEARCHING...
CLICK!
SEARCHING...
BSHOOM!
DETECTED: MEGAN
THE DREAM PORTAL MACHINE IS TUNED IN TO MEGAN'S DREAMS. READY?
DETECTED MEGAN
READY!

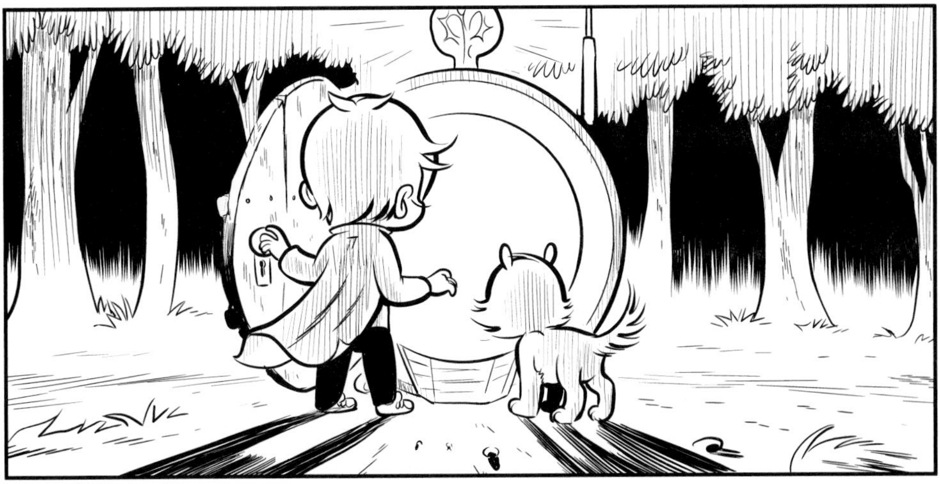

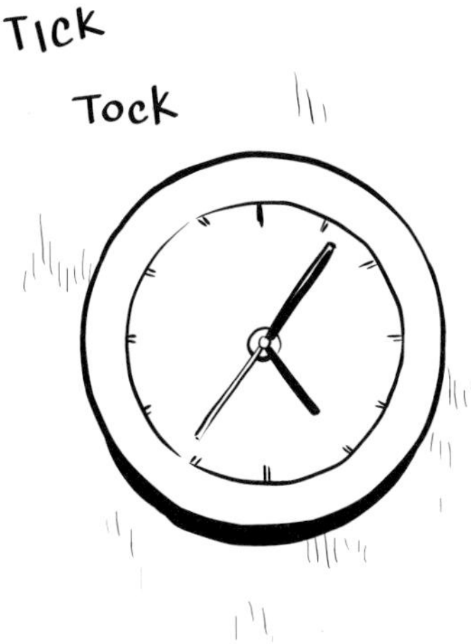
TICK
TOCK

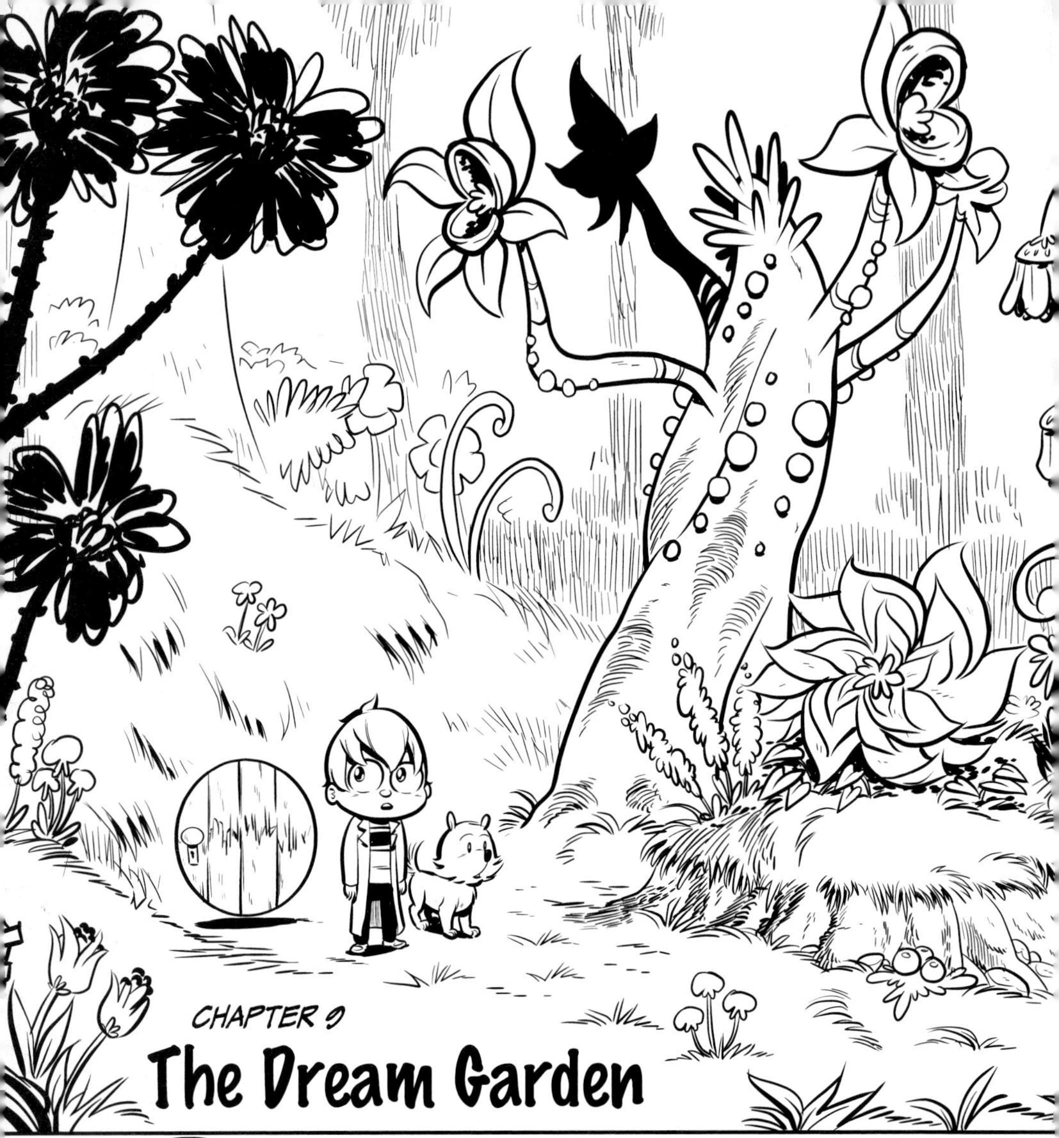
CHAPTER 9
The Dream Garden

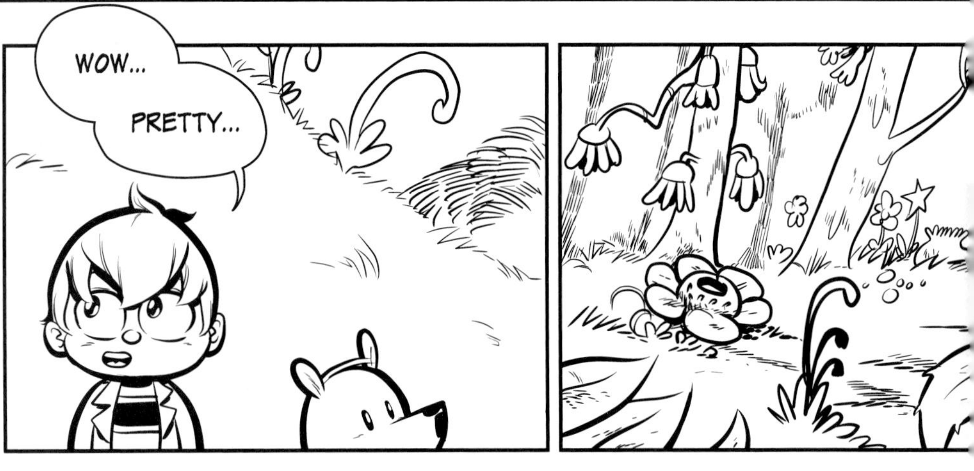
WOW...
PRETTY...

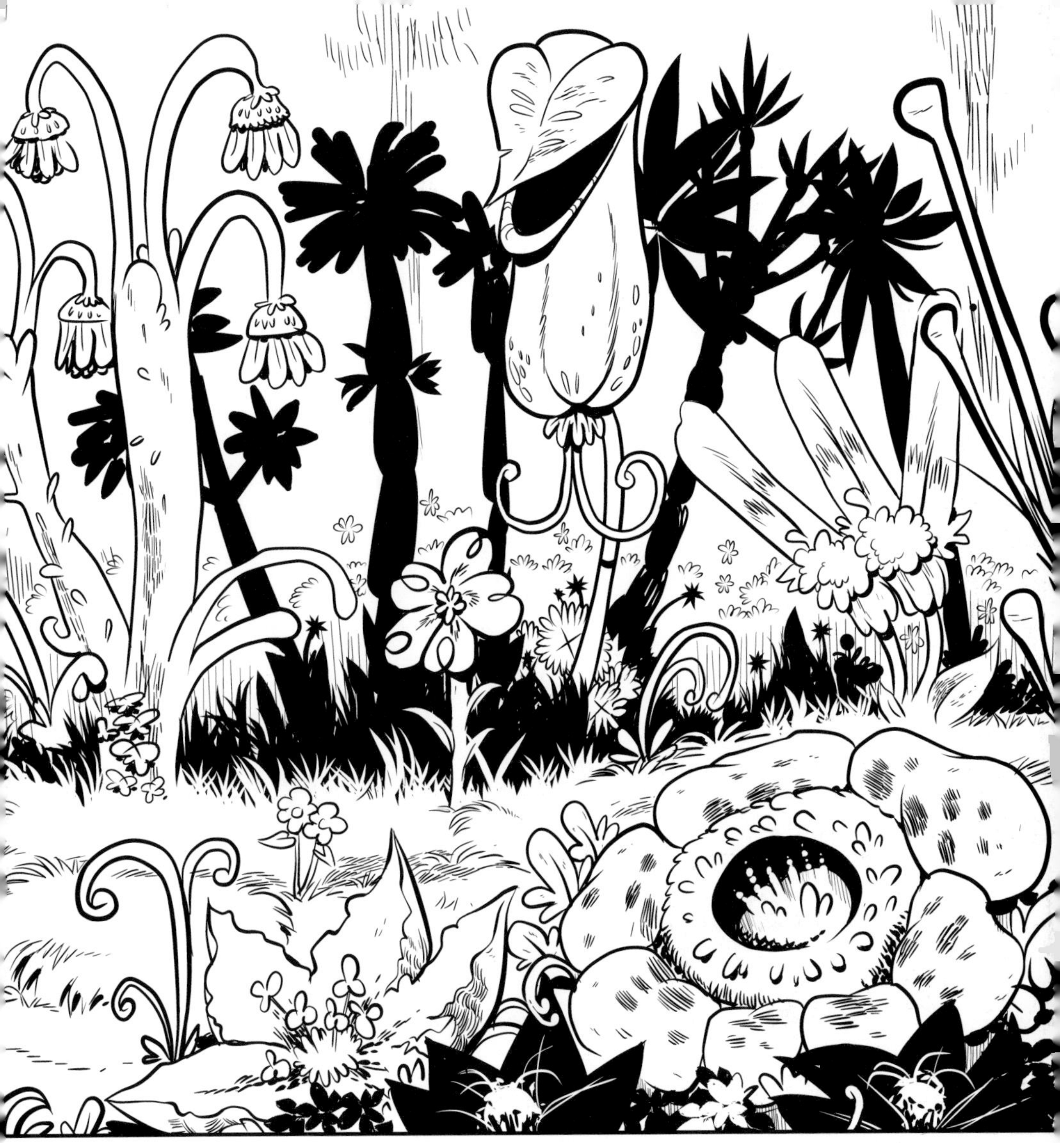

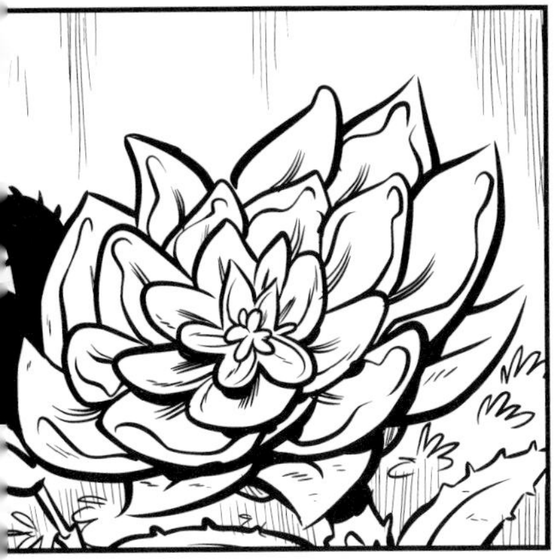

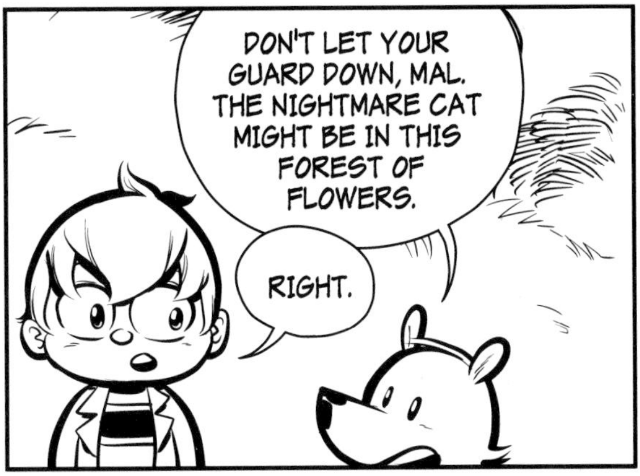
DON'T LET YOUR GUARD DOWN, MAL. THE NIGHTMARE CAT MIGHT BE IN THIS FOREST OF FLOWERS.
RIGHT.

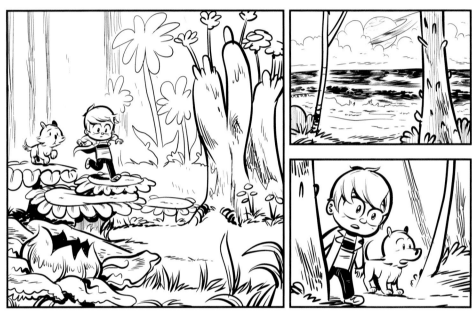

SSSHHH

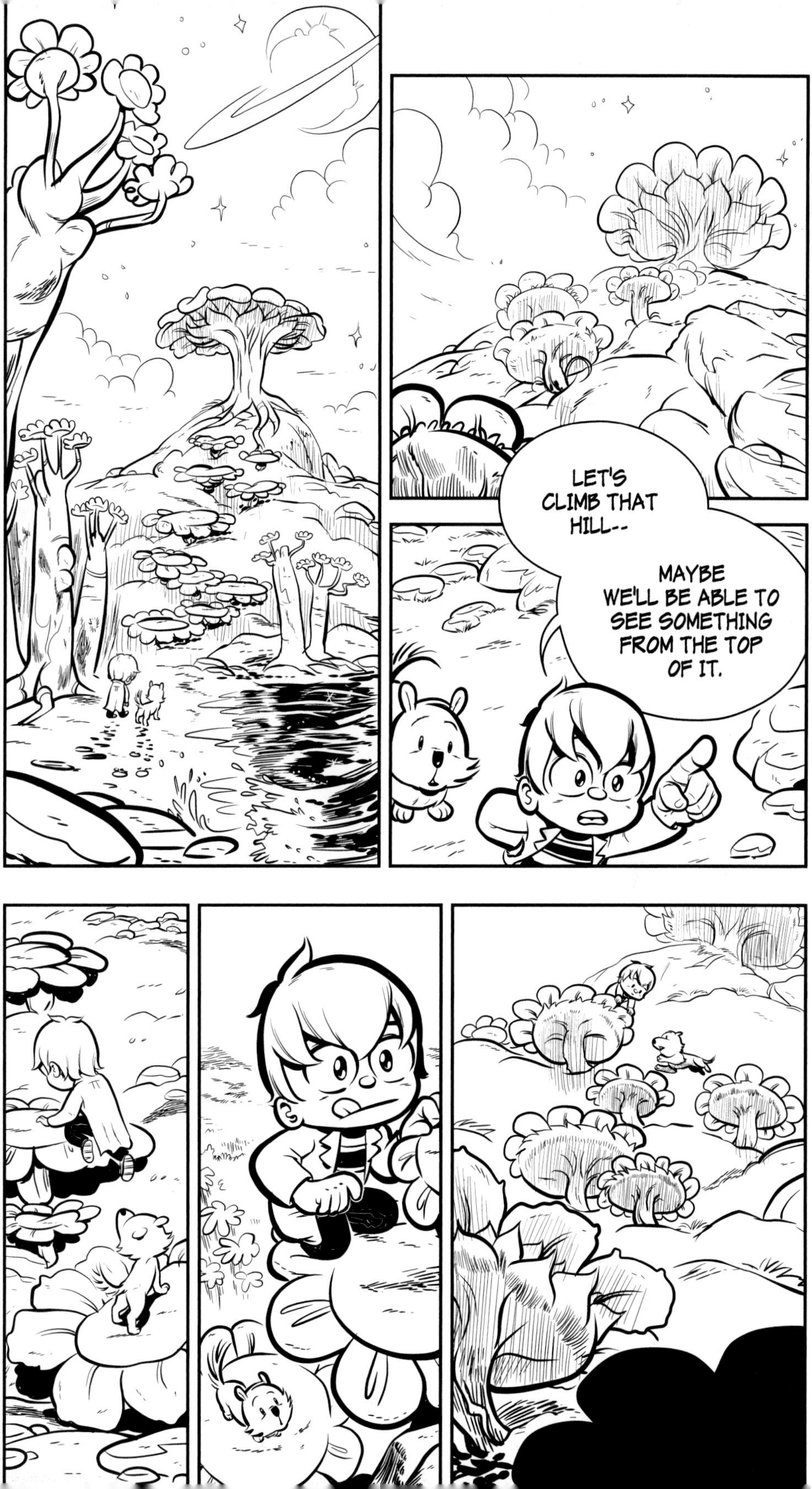
LET'S CLIMB THAT HILL--
MAYBE WE'LL BE ABLE TO SEE SOMETHING FROM THE TOP OF IT.

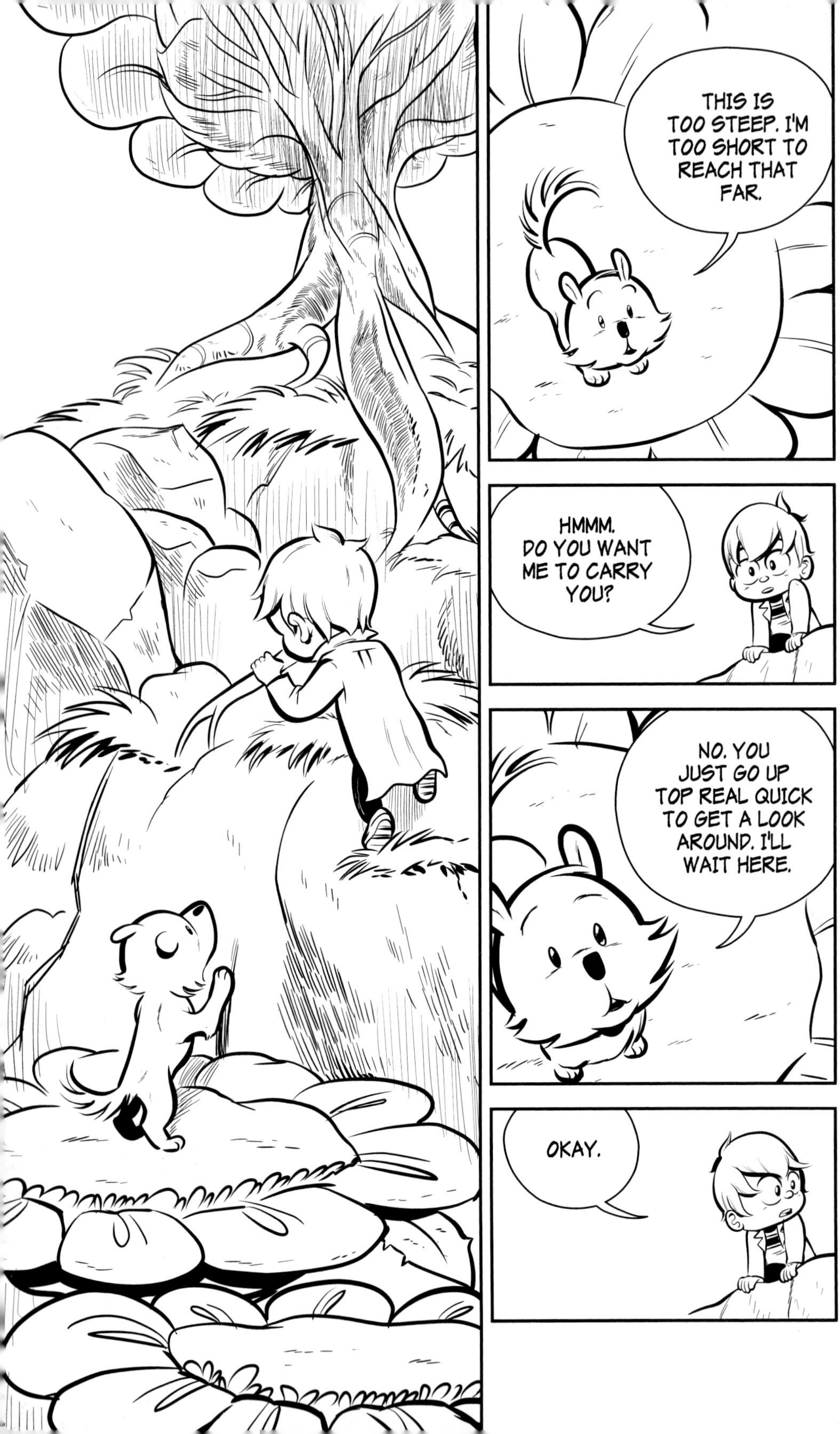
THIS IS TOO STEEP. I'M TOO SHORT TO REACH THAT FAR.
HMMM. DO YOU WANT ME TO CARRY YOU?
NO. YOU JUST GO UP TOP REAL QUICK TO GET A LOOK AROUND. I'LL WAIT HERE.
OKAY.

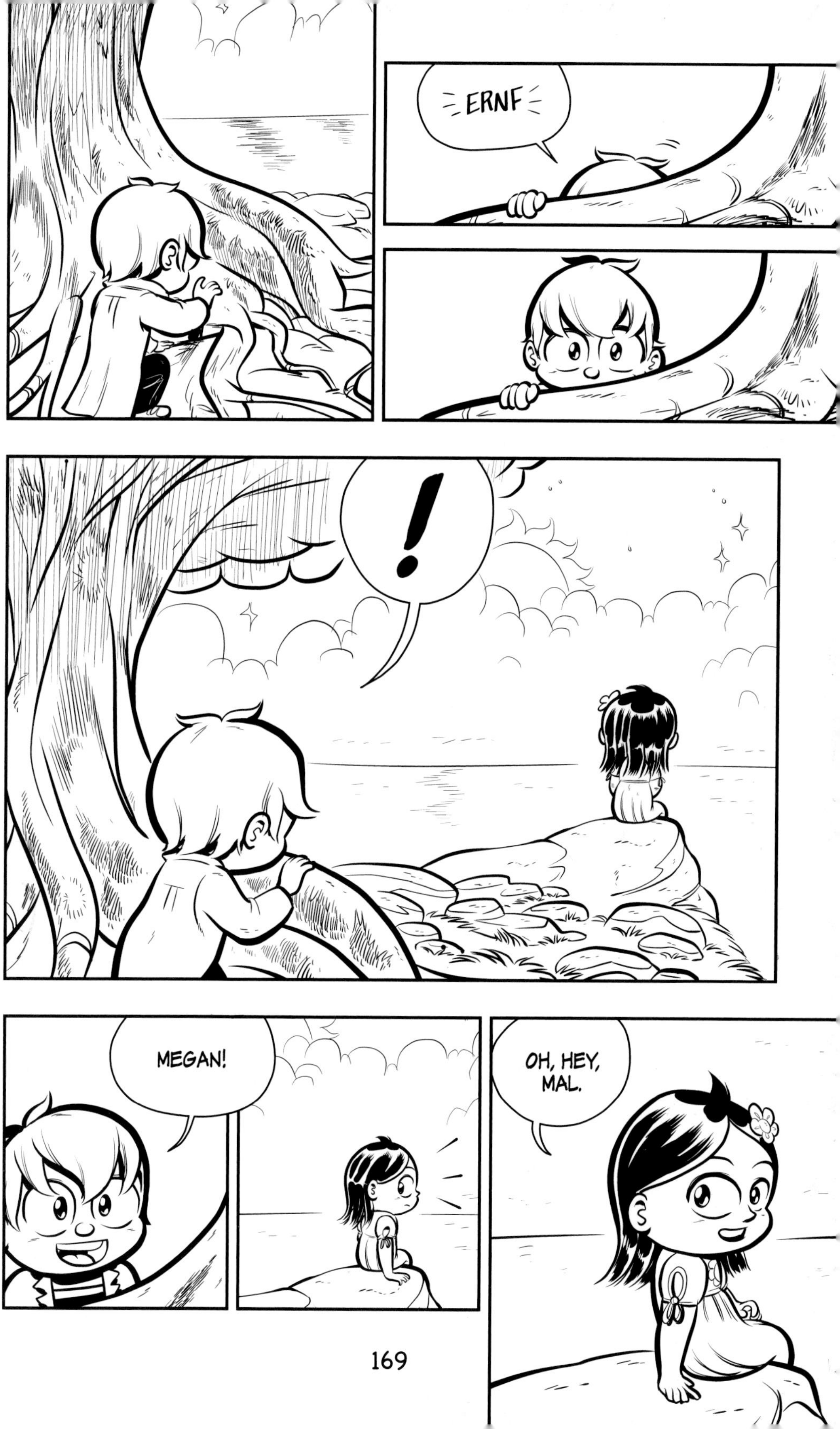
ERNF
!
MEGAN!
OH, HEY, MAL.

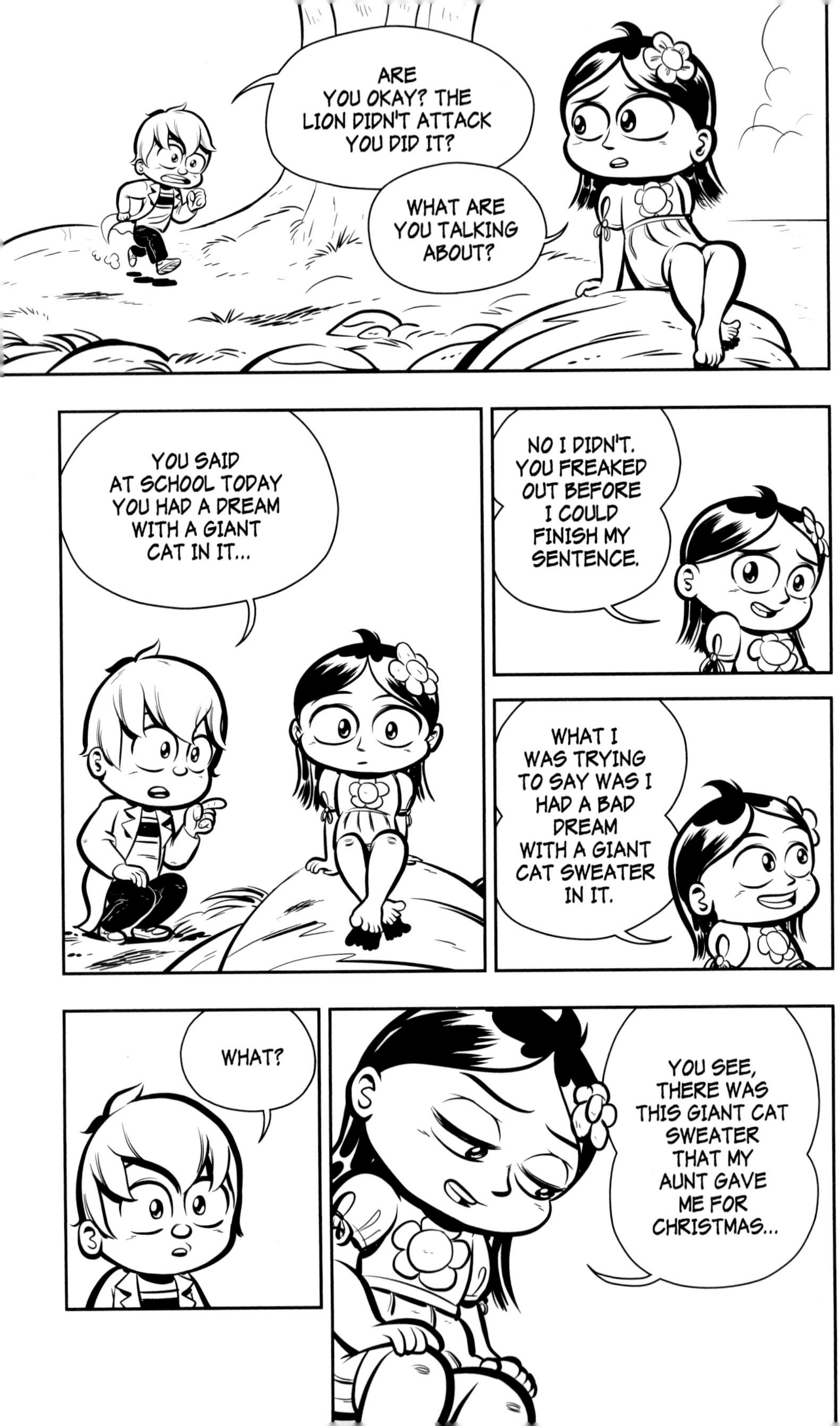
ARE YOU OKAY? THE LION DIDN'T ATTACK YOU DID IT?
WHAT ARE YOU TALKING ABOUT?
YOU SAID AT SCHOOL TODAY YOU HAD A DREAM WITH A GIANT CAT IN IT...
NO I DIDN'T. YOU FREAKED OUT BEFORE I COULD FINISH MY SENTENCE.
WHAT I WAS TRYING TO SAY WAS I HAD A BAD DREAM WITH A GIANT CAT SWEATER IN IT.
WHAT?
YOU SEE, THERE WAS THIS GIANT CAT SWEATER THAT MY AUNT GAVE ME FOR CHRISTMAS...

I DREAMED THAT MY MOM FORCED ME TO TRY ON THAT SWEATER, EVEN THOUGH IT WAS TOO BIG FOR ME.

THEN I TRIED TO TAKE IT OFF, BUT NO MATTER WHAT I DID IT WOULDN'T COME OFF!

MY MOM TOOK ME TO THE DOCTOR, AND HE SAID THE SWEATER WAS ATTACHED TO ME, AND I'D BE STUCK WEARING IT FOR THE REST OF MY LIFE!

AND THEN I DREAMED I HAD TO GO TO SCHOOL, AND EVERYONE SAW ME IN THAT HORRIBLE CAT SWEATER, AND EVERYONE LAUGHED AT ME, EVEN ASHLEY AND CARLY.

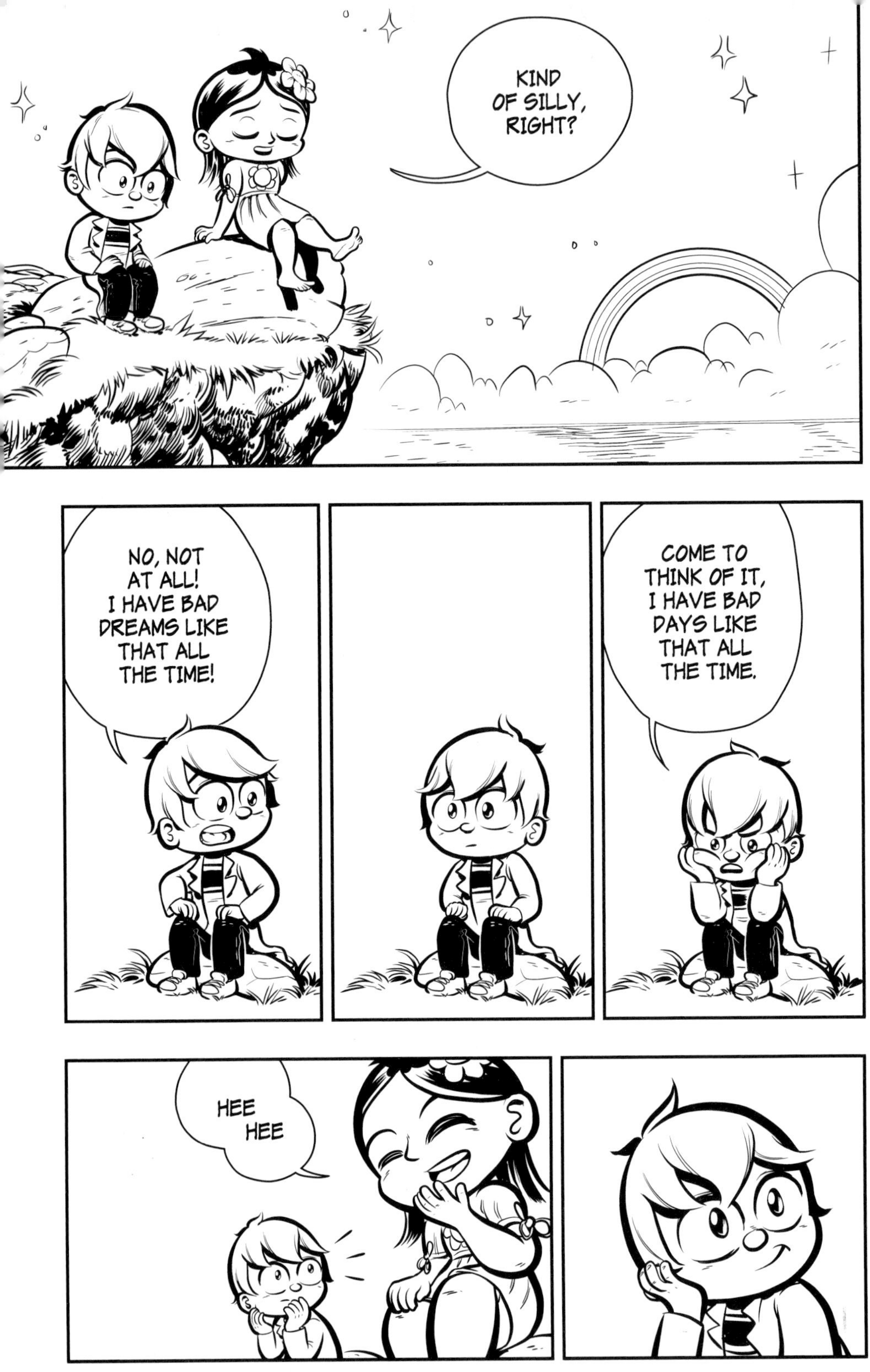
KIND OF SILLY, RIGHT?
NO, NOT AT ALL! I HAVE BAD DREAMS LIKE THAT ALL THE TIME!
COME TO THINK OF IT, I HAVE BAD DAYS LIKE THAT ALL THE TIME.
HEE HEE

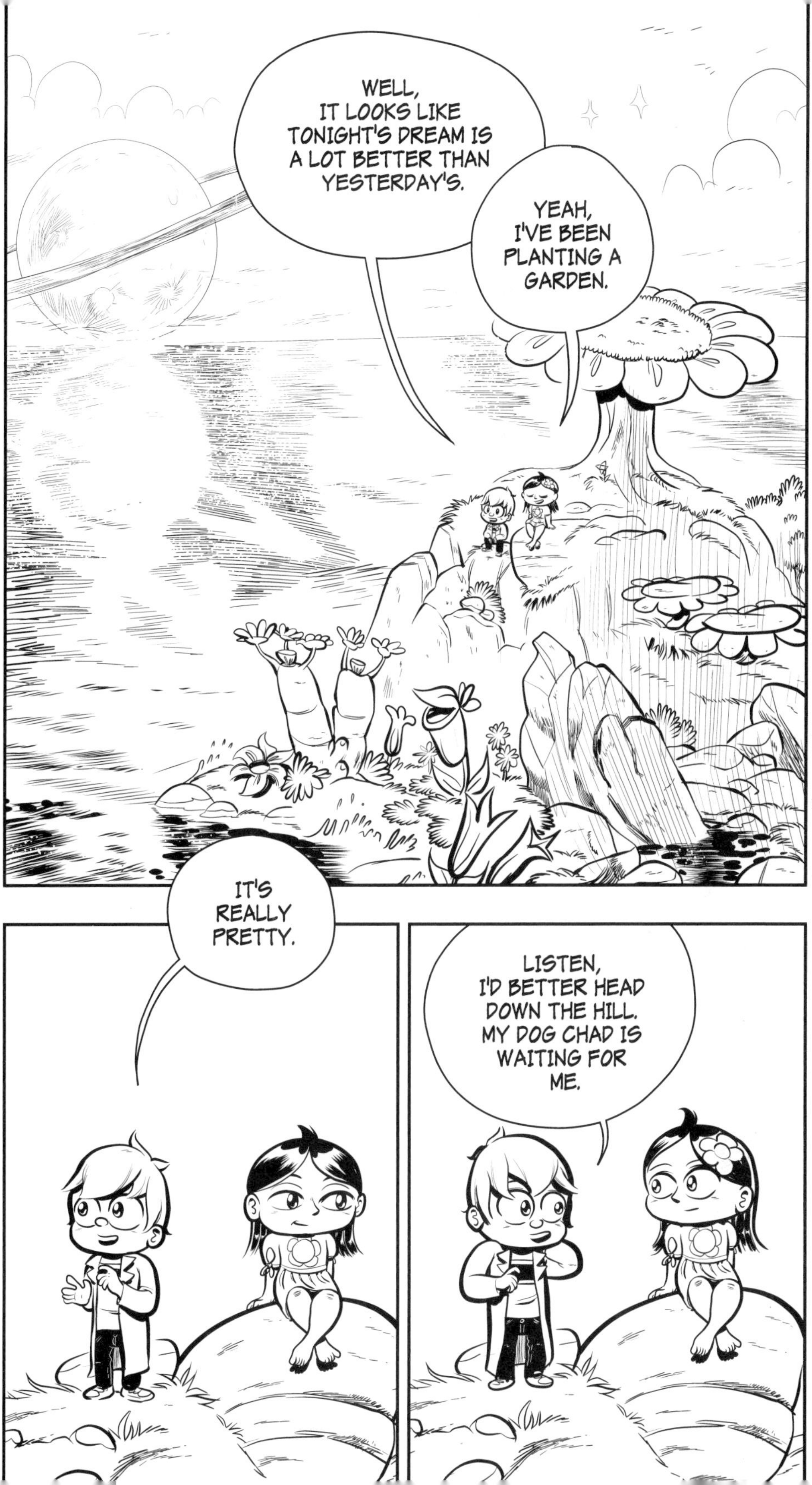
WELL, IT LOOKS LIKE TONIGHT'S DREAM IS A LOT BETTER THAN YESTERDAY'S.
YEAH, I'VE BEEN PLANTING A GARDEN.
IT'S REALLY PRETTY.
LISTEN, I'D BETTER HEAD DOWN THE HILL. MY DOG CHAD IS WAITING FOR ME.

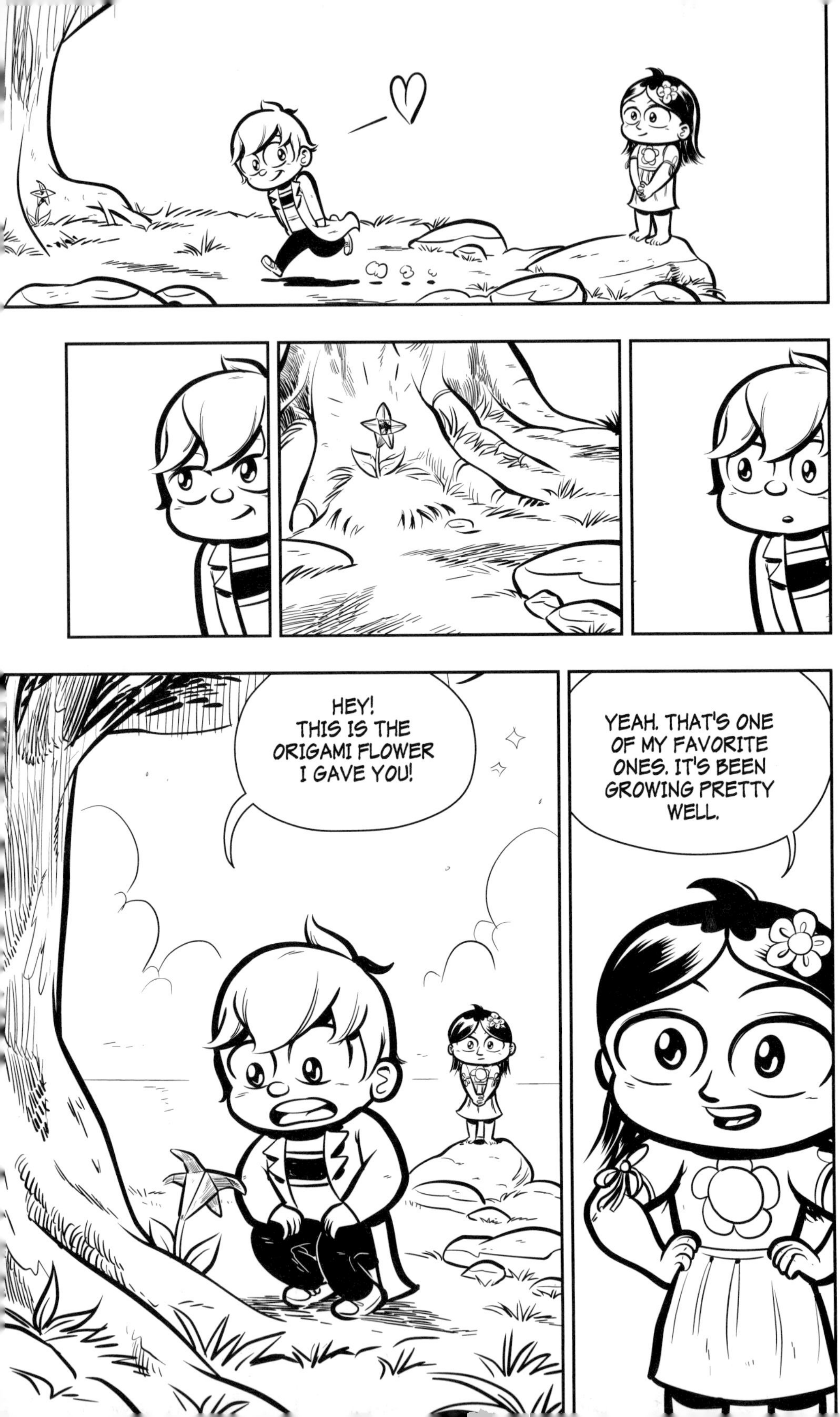
HEY!
THIS IS THE
ORIGAMI FLOWER
I GAVE YOU!
YEAH. THAT'S ONE
OF MY FAVORITE
ONES. IT'S BEEN
GROWING PRETTY
WELL.

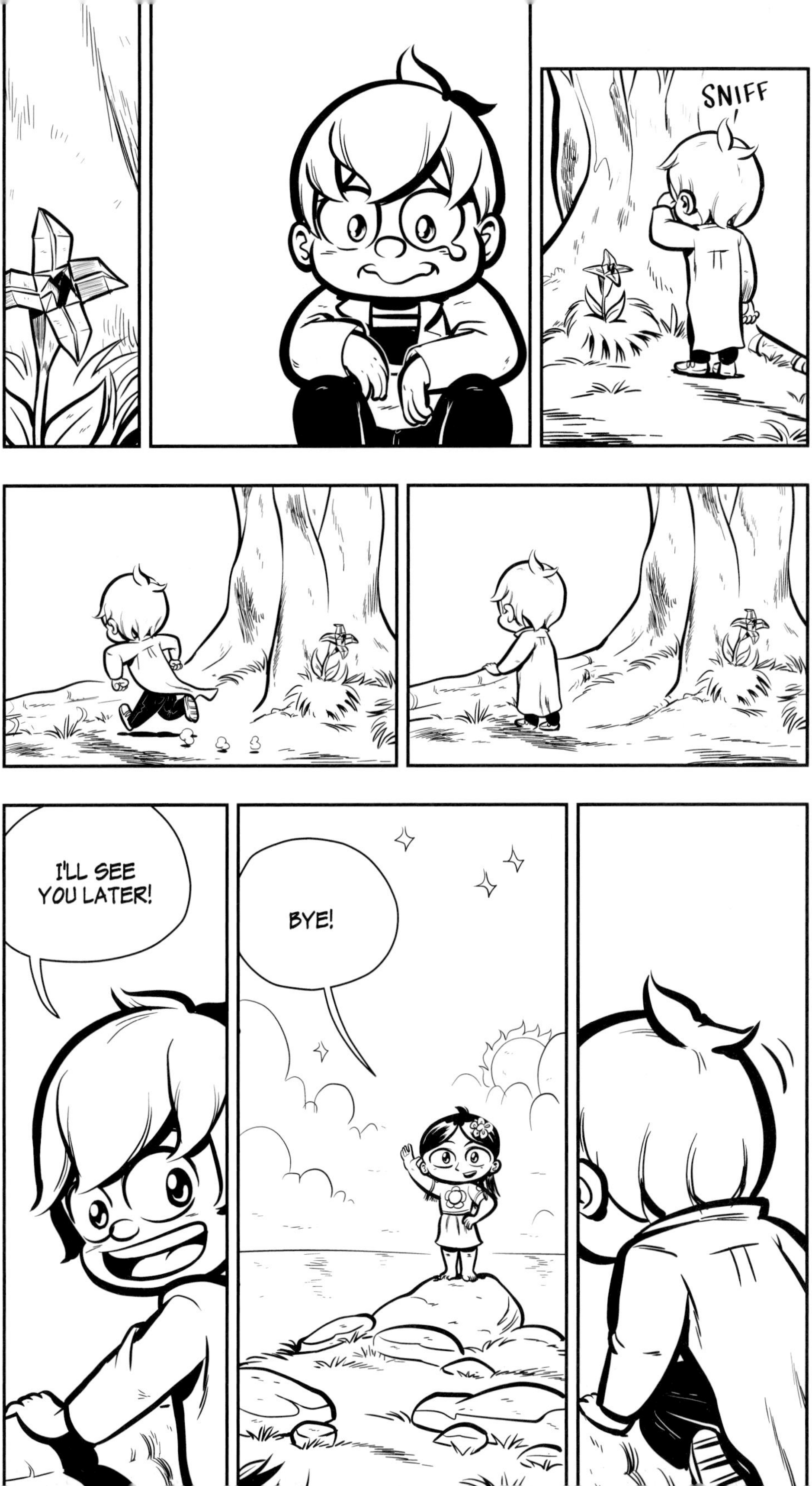
SNIFF
I'LL SEE YOU LATER!
BYE!

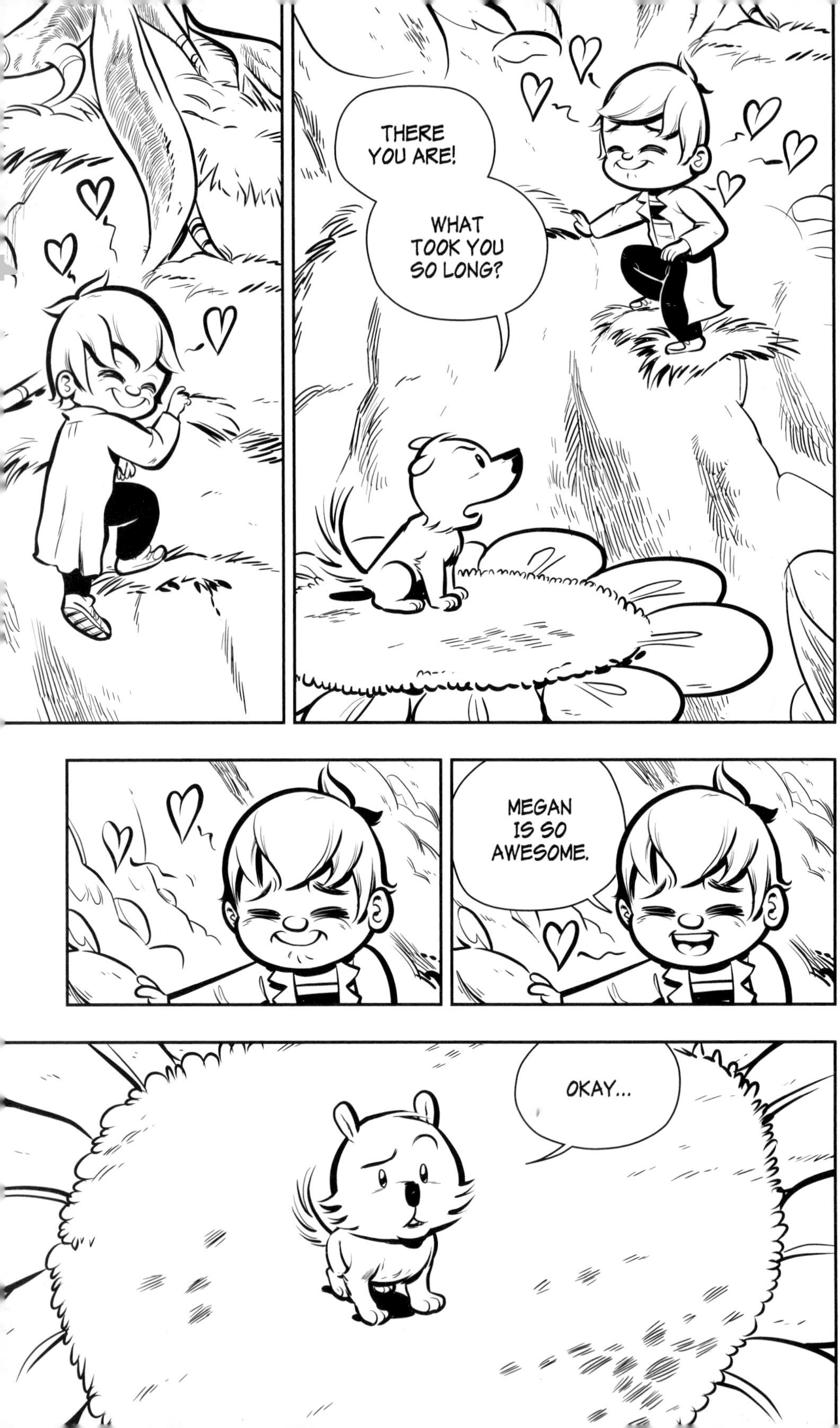
THERE YOU ARE!
WHAT TOOK YOU SO LONG?
MEGAN IS SO AWESOME.
OKAY...

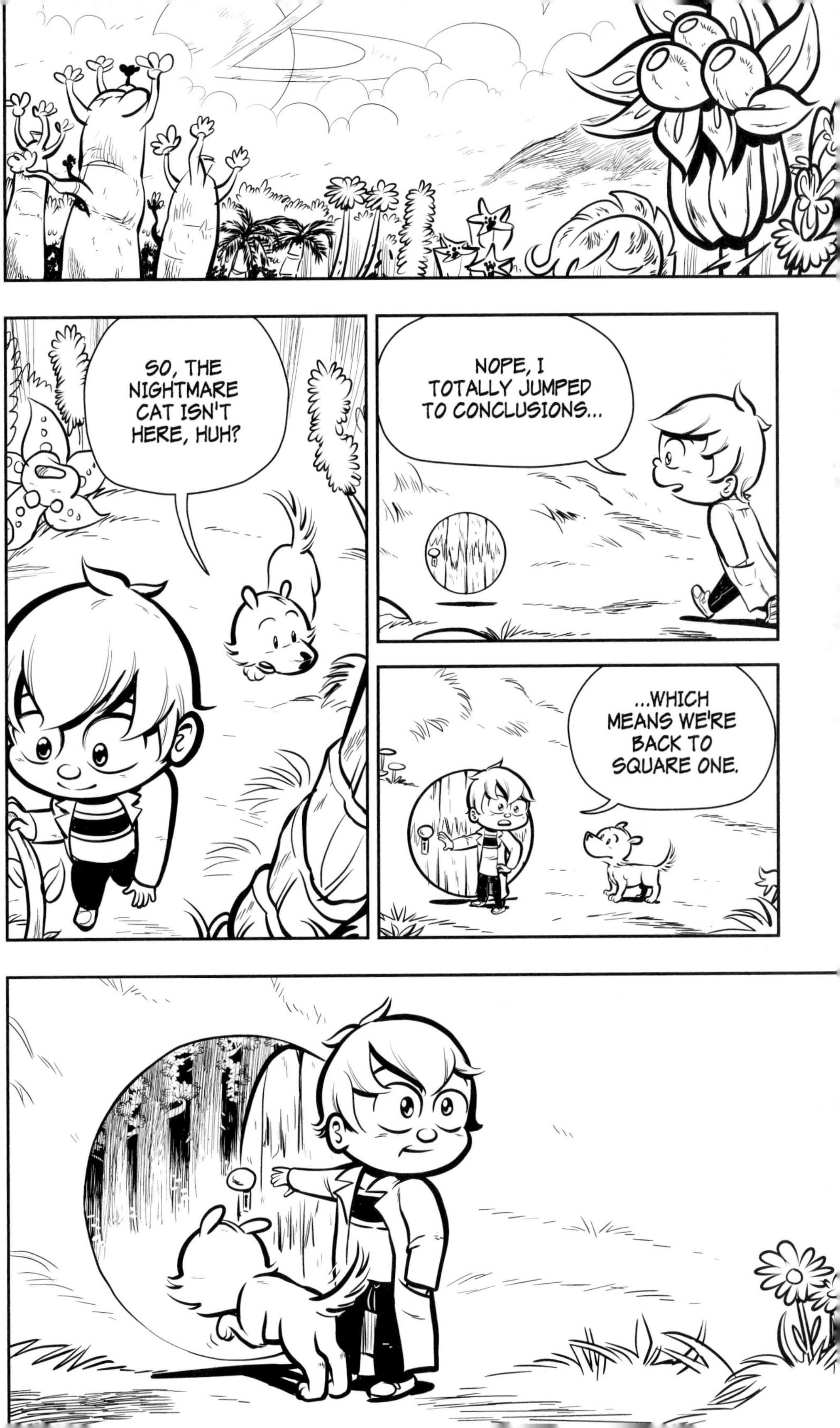
SO, THE NIGHTMARE CAT ISN'T HERE, HUH?
NOPE, I TOTALLY JUMPED TO CONCLUSIONS...
...WHICH MEANS WE'RE BACK TO SQUARE ONE.

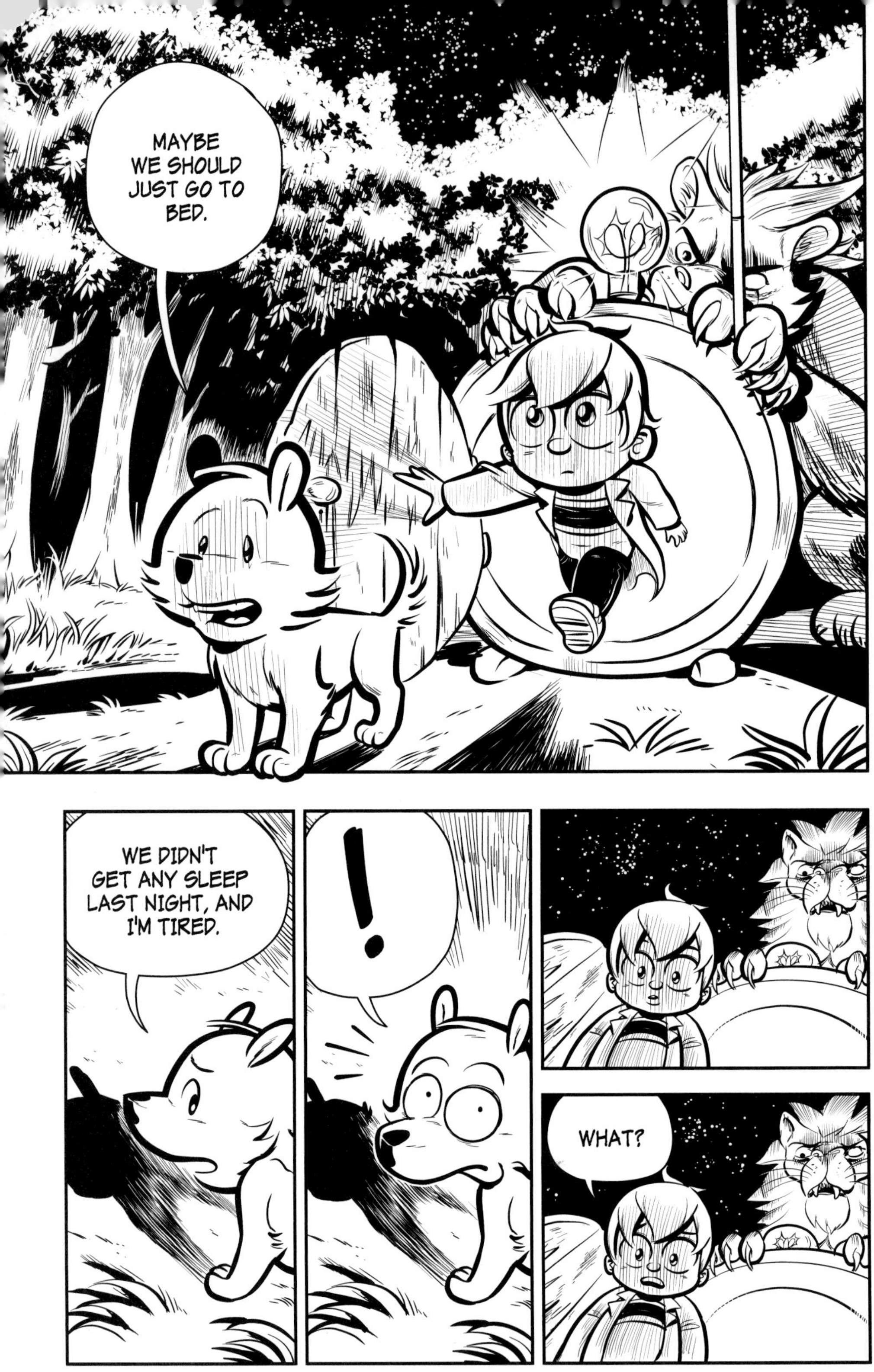
MAYBE WE SHOULD JUST GO TO BED.
WE DIDN'T GET ANY SLEEP LAST NIGHT, AND I'M TIRED.
!
WHAT?

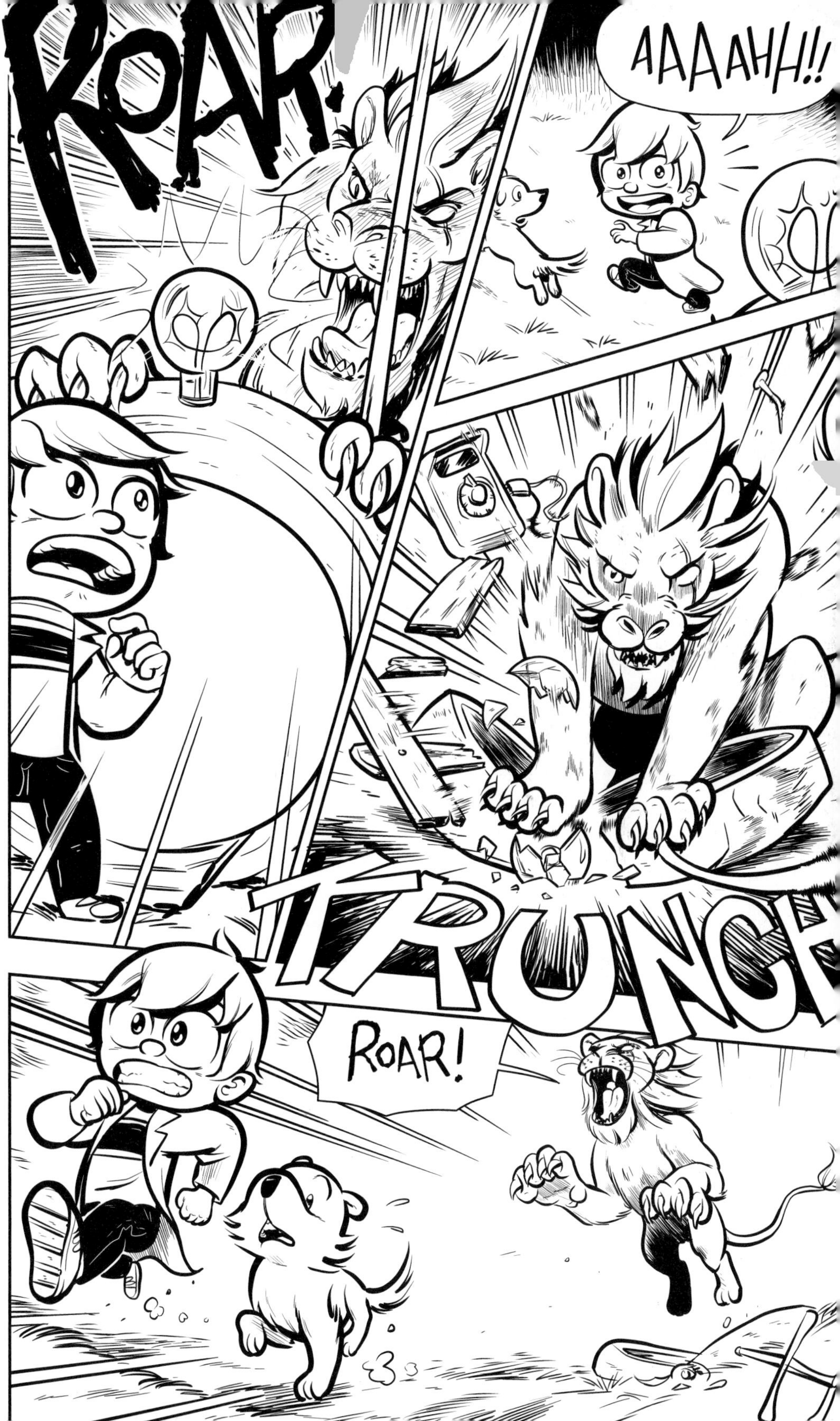
ROAR!
AAAAHH!!
TRUNCH
ROAR!

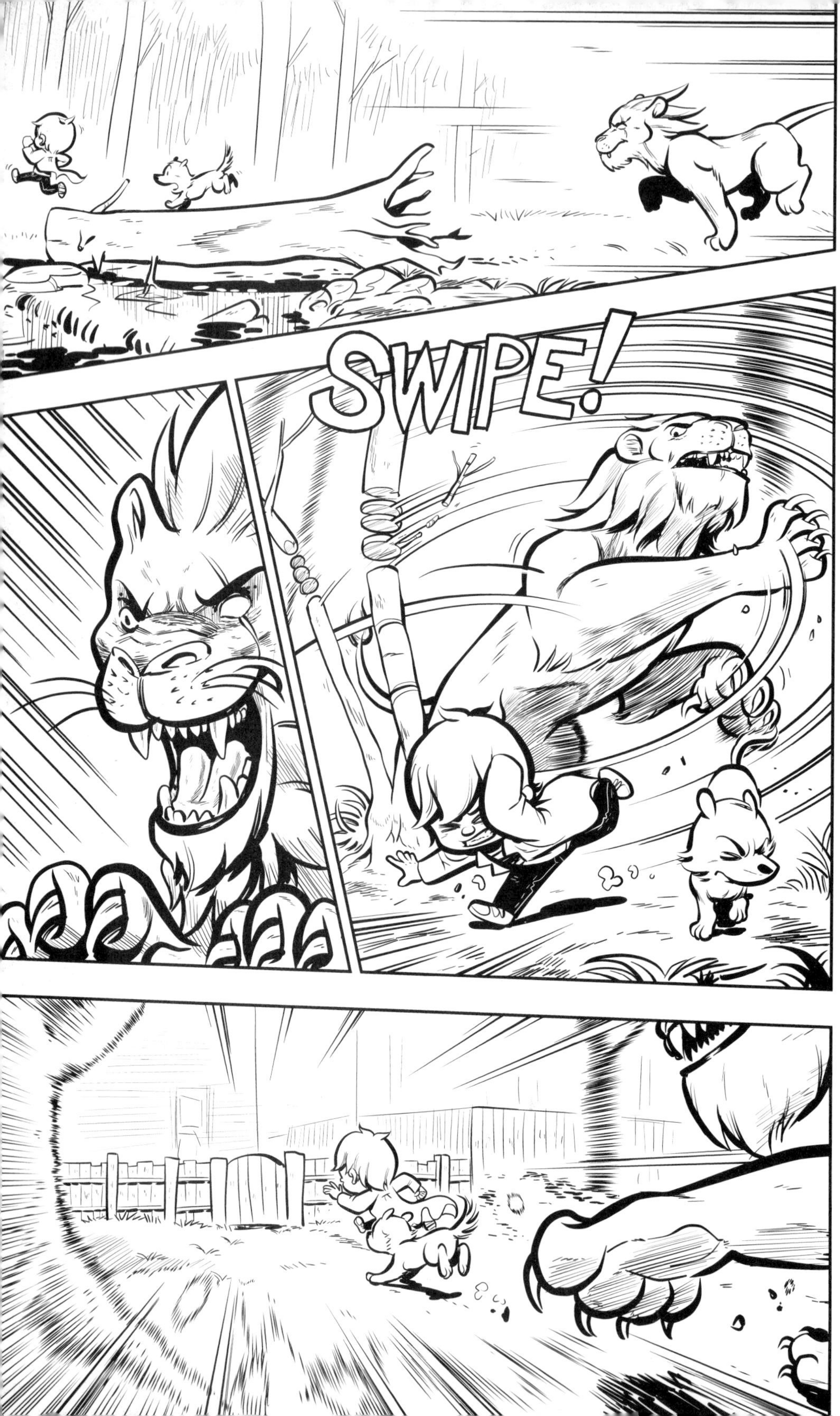
SWIPE!

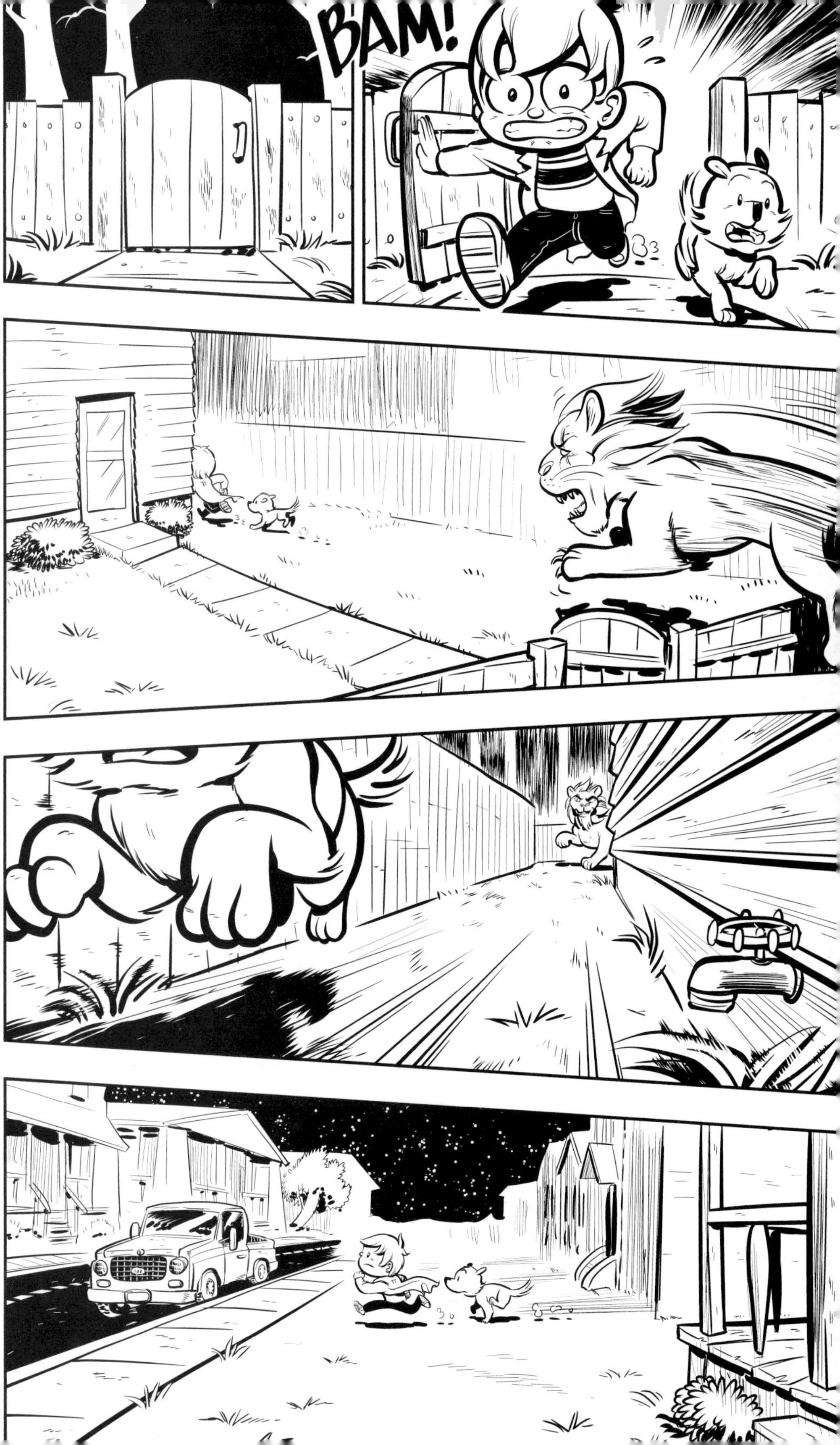
BAM!

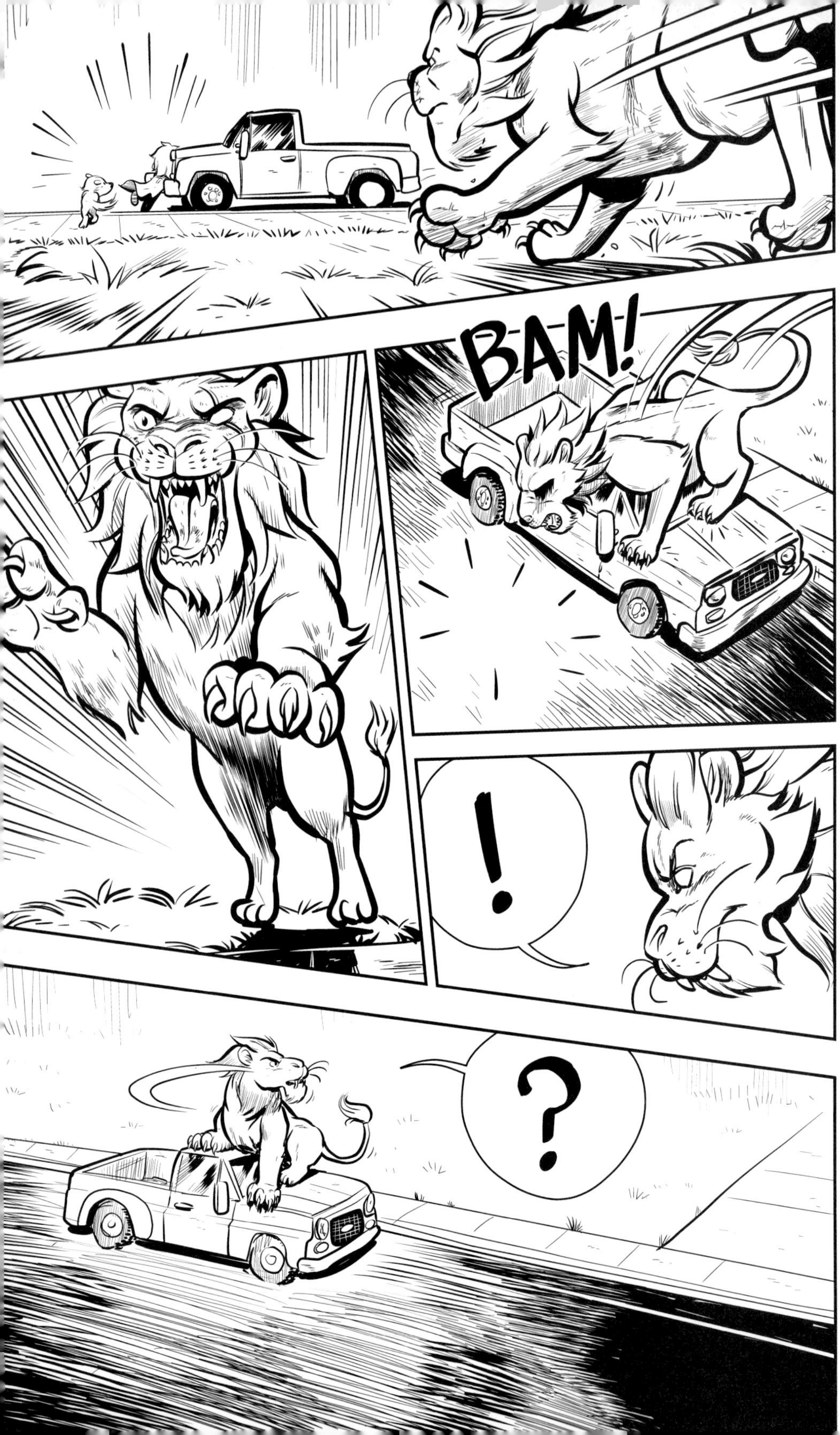
BAM!
!
?

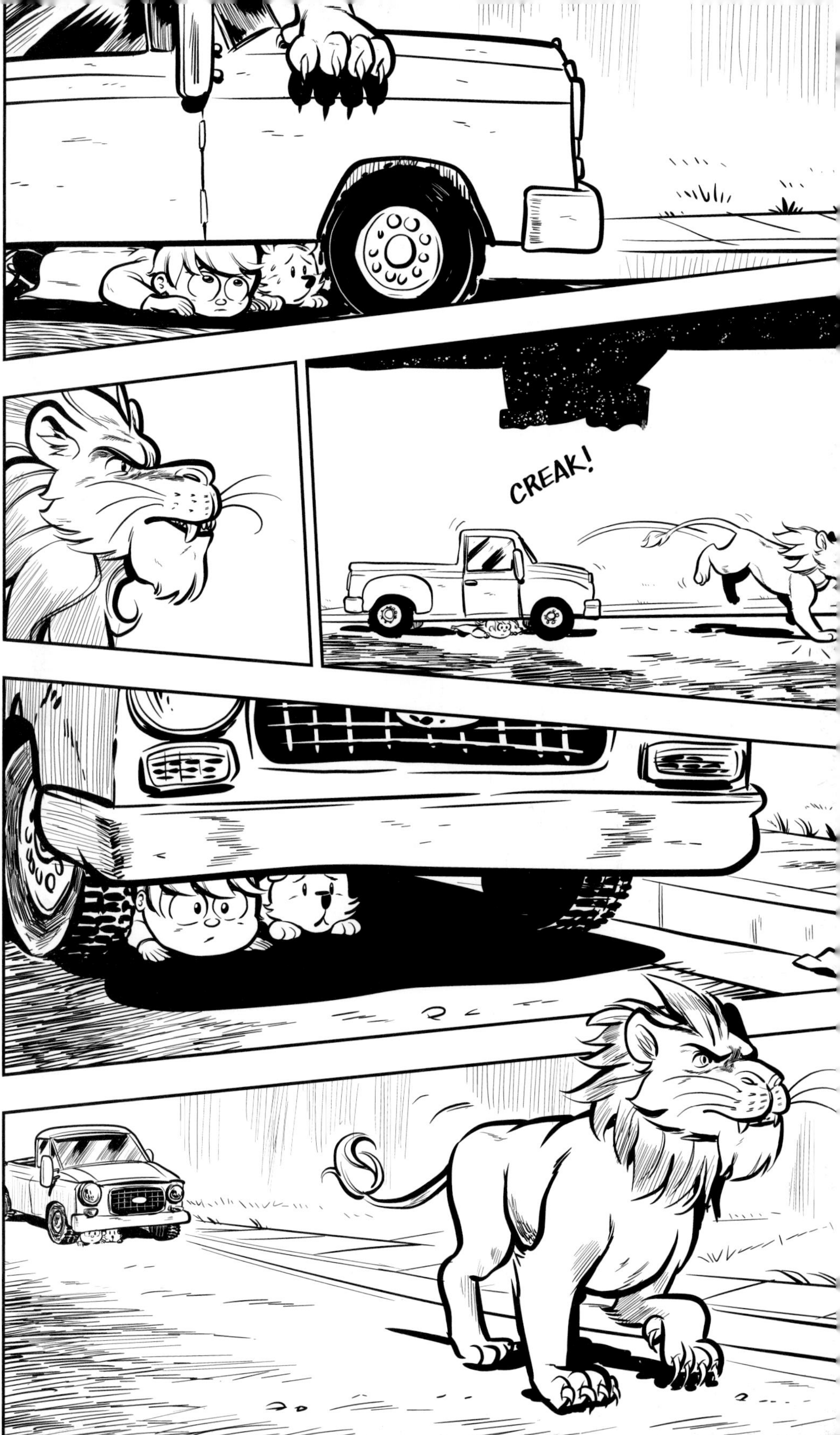
CREAK!

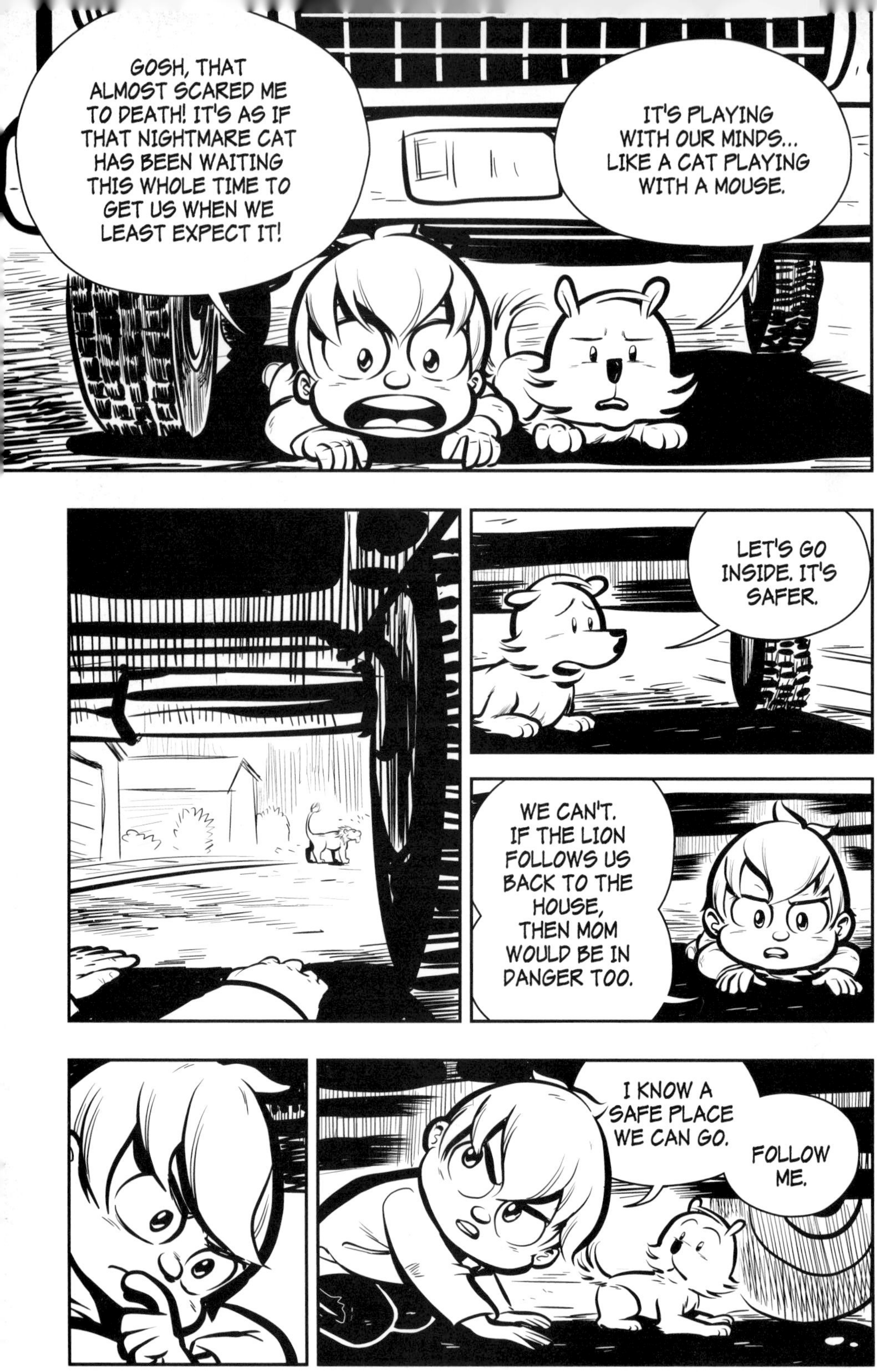
GOSH, THAT ALMOST SCARED ME TO DEATH! IT'S AS IF THAT NIGHTMARE CAT HAS BEEN WAITING THIS WHOLE TIME TO GET US WHEN WE LEAST EXPECT IT!
IT'S PLAYING WITH OUR MINDS... LIKE A CAT PLAYING WITH A MOUSE.
LET'S GO INSIDE. IT'S SAFER.
WE CAN'T. IF THE LION FOLLOWS US BACK TO THE HOUSE, THEN MOM WOULD BE IN DANGER TOO.
I KNOW A SAFE PLACE WE CAN GO.
FOLLOW ME.

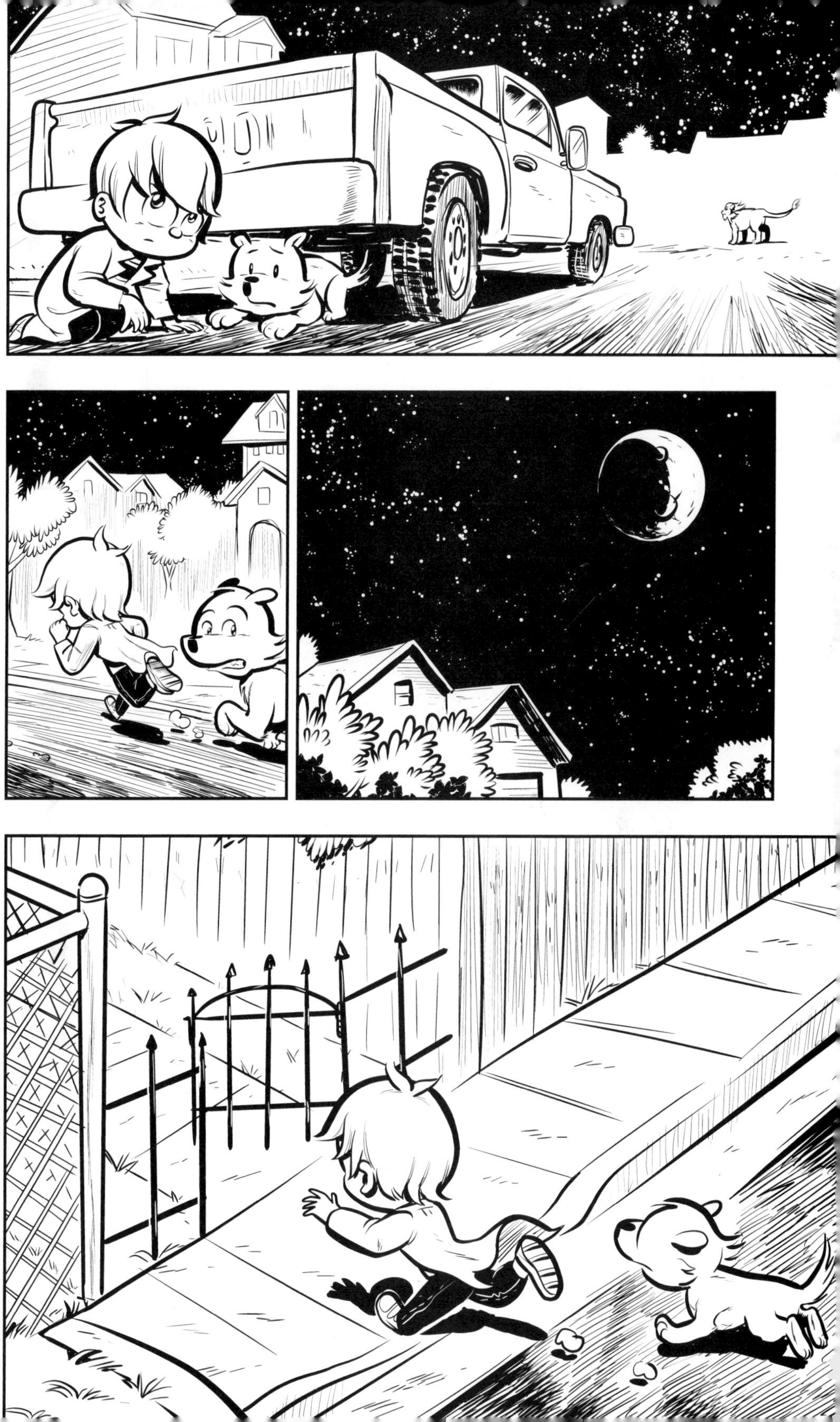

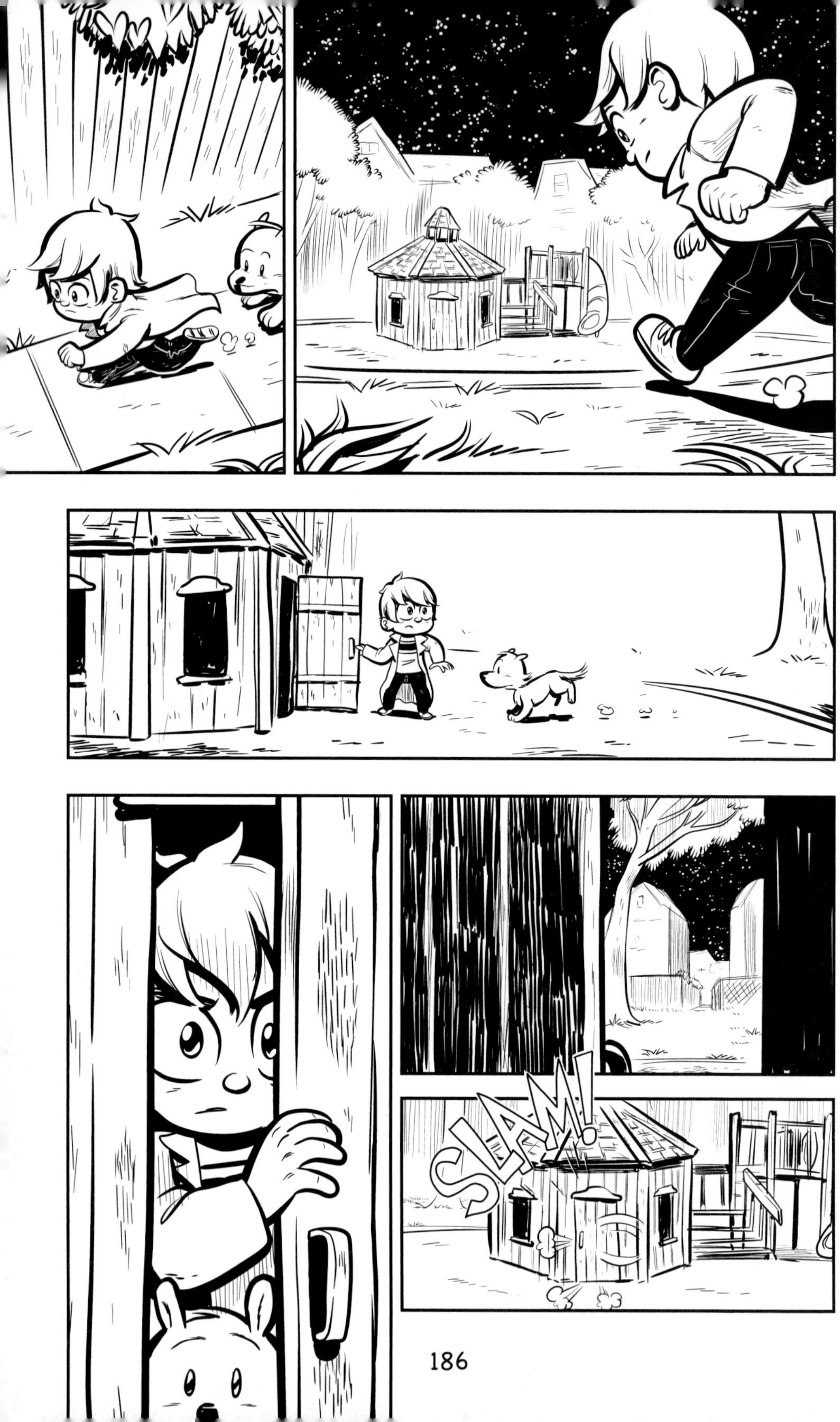
SLAM!

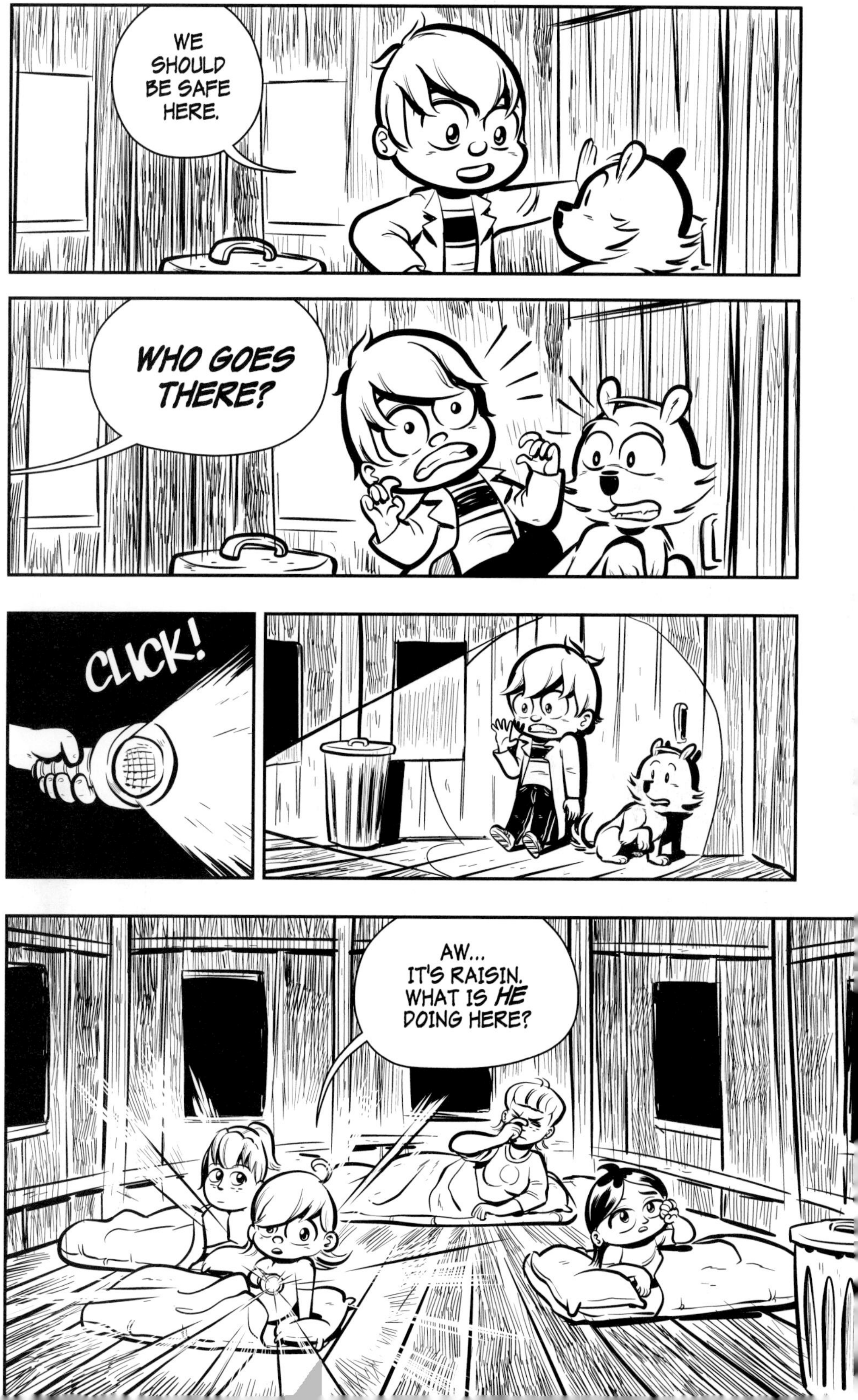
WE SHOULD BE SAFE HERE.
WHO GOES THERE?
CLICK!
AW... IT'S RAISIN. WHAT IS *HE* DOING HERE?

MAL?

I WAS JUST HAVING A DREAM ABOUT YOU...

HEH HEH

HI, MEGAN.

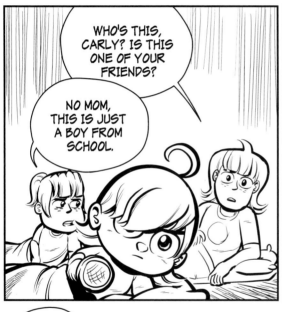

WHO'S THIS, CARLY? IS THIS ONE OF YOUR FRIENDS?

NO MOM, THIS IS JUST A BOY FROM SCHOOL.

WHAT ARE YOU GUYS DOING HERE?

WE'RE HAVING A CAMPOUT SLUMBER PARTY. WHAT ARE YOU DOING HERE, MAL?

UM...

ME AND CHAD ARE TRYING TO HIDE FROM THIS GIANT MONSTER LION.

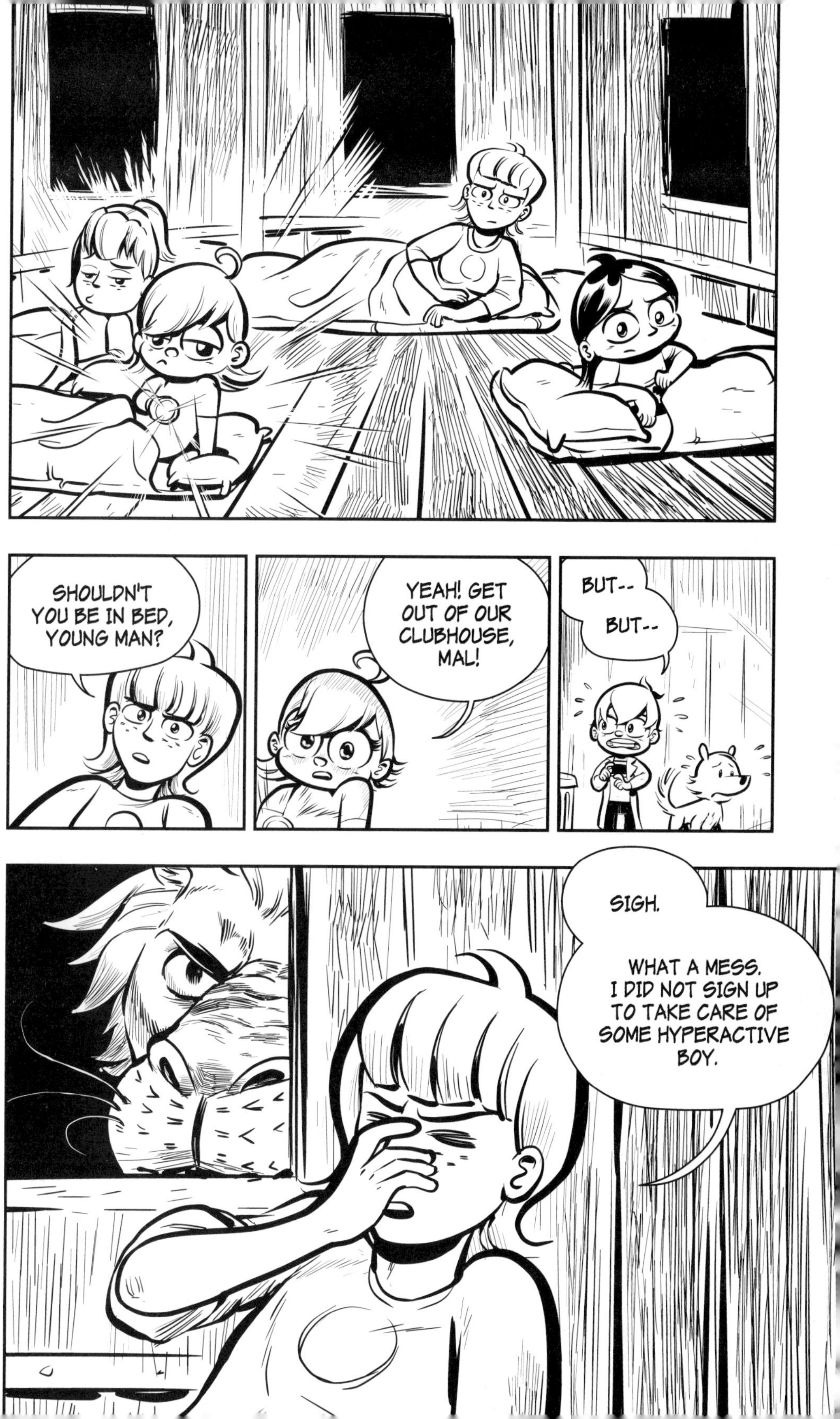
SHOULDN'T YOU BE IN BED, YOUNG MAN?
YEAH! GET OUT OF OUR CLUBHOUSE, MAL!
BUT--
BUT--
SIGH.
WHAT A MESS. I DID NOT SIGN UP TO TAKE CARE OF SOME HYPERACTIVE BOY.

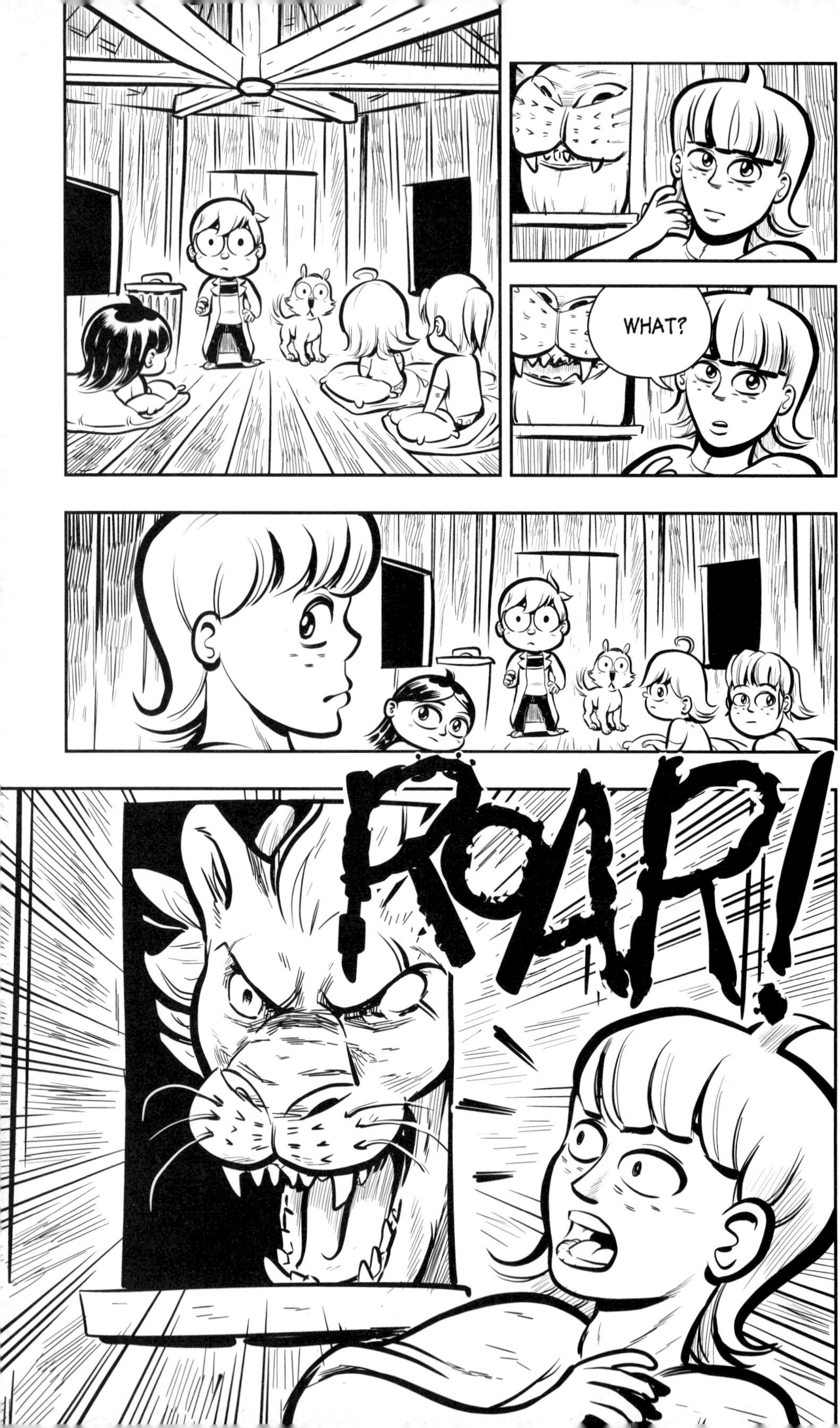
WHAT?
ROAR!

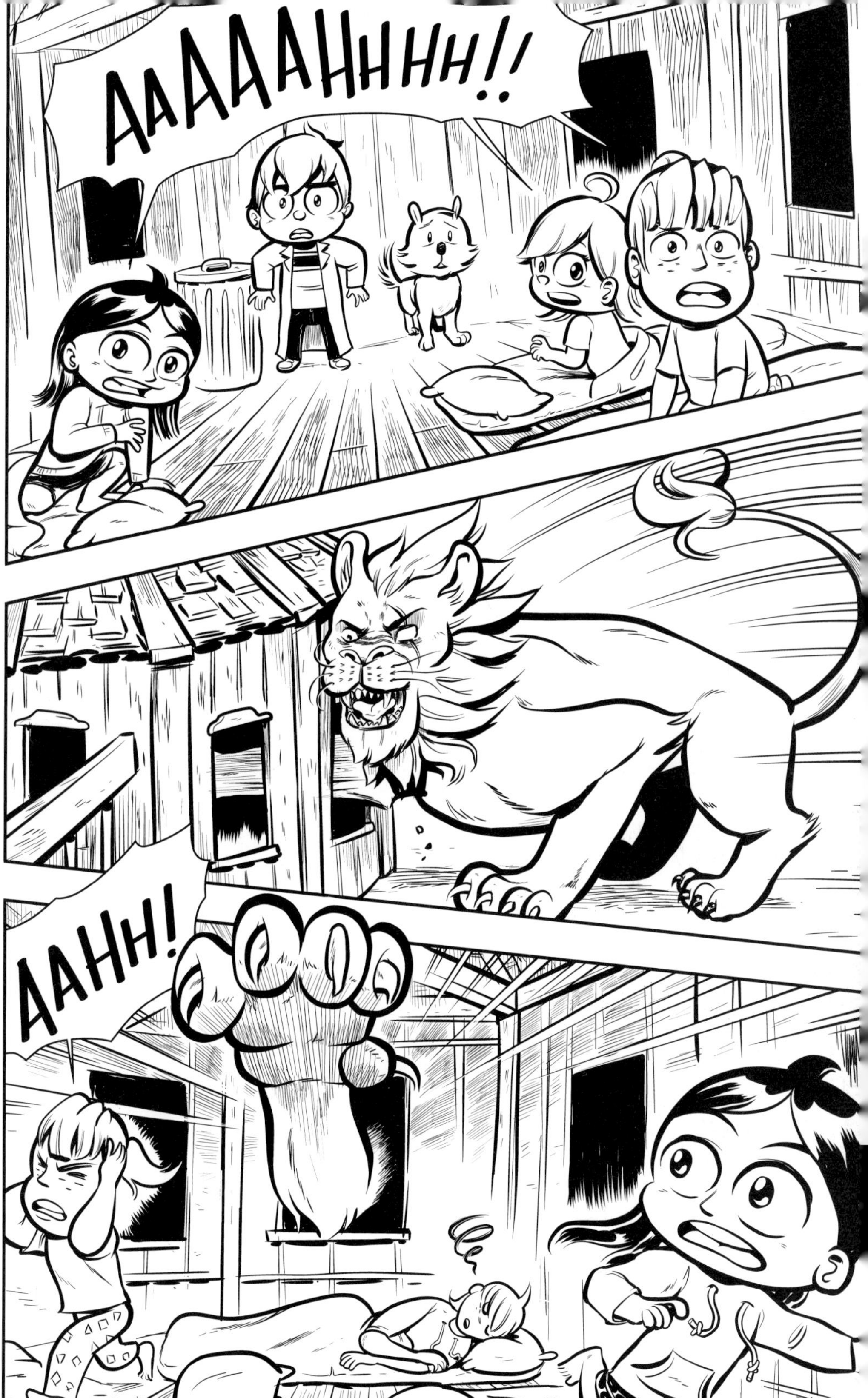
AAAAAHHHH!!
AAHH!

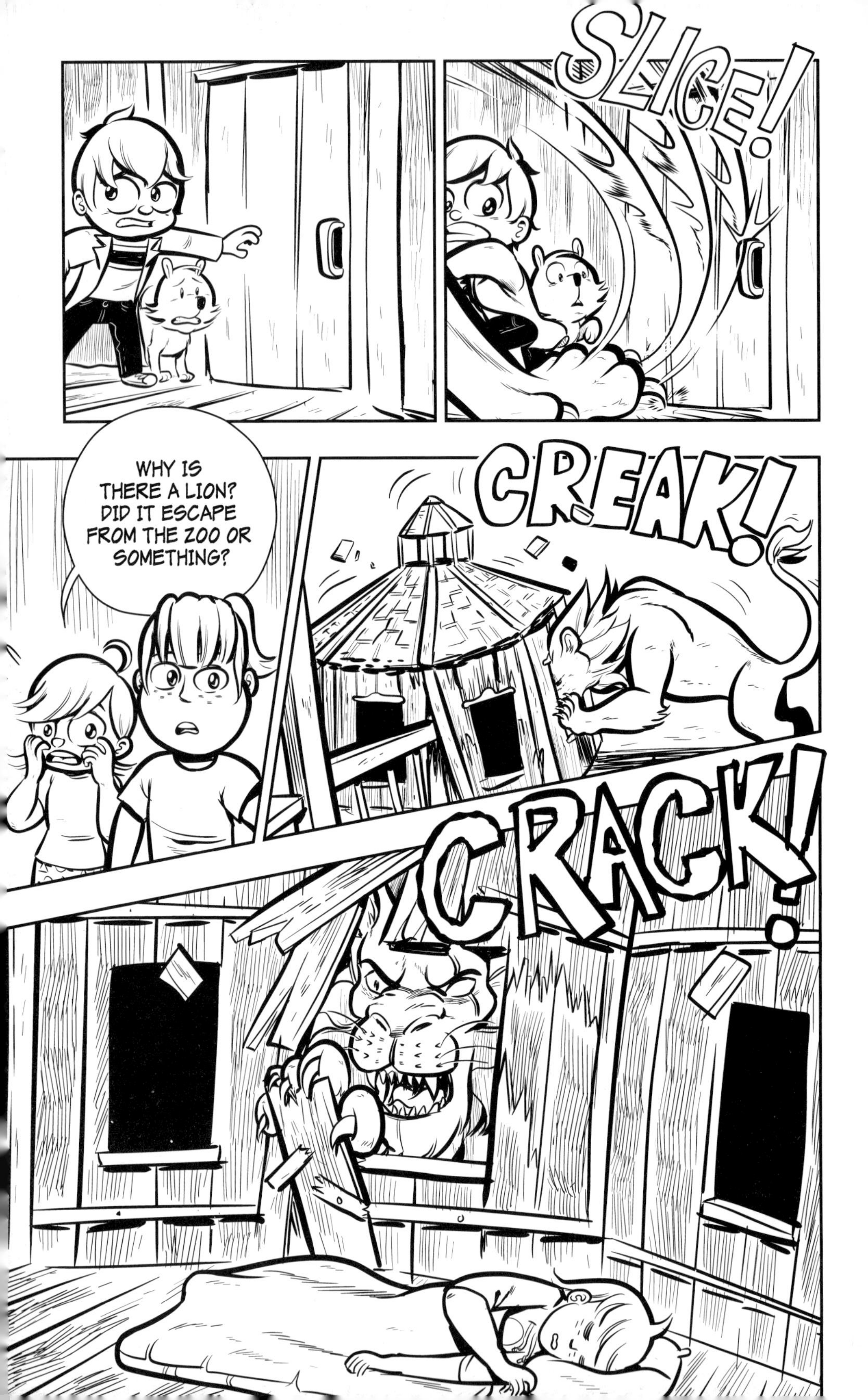
SLICE!
WHY IS THERE A LION? DID IT ESCAPE FROM THE ZOO OR SOMETHING?
CREAK!
CRACK!

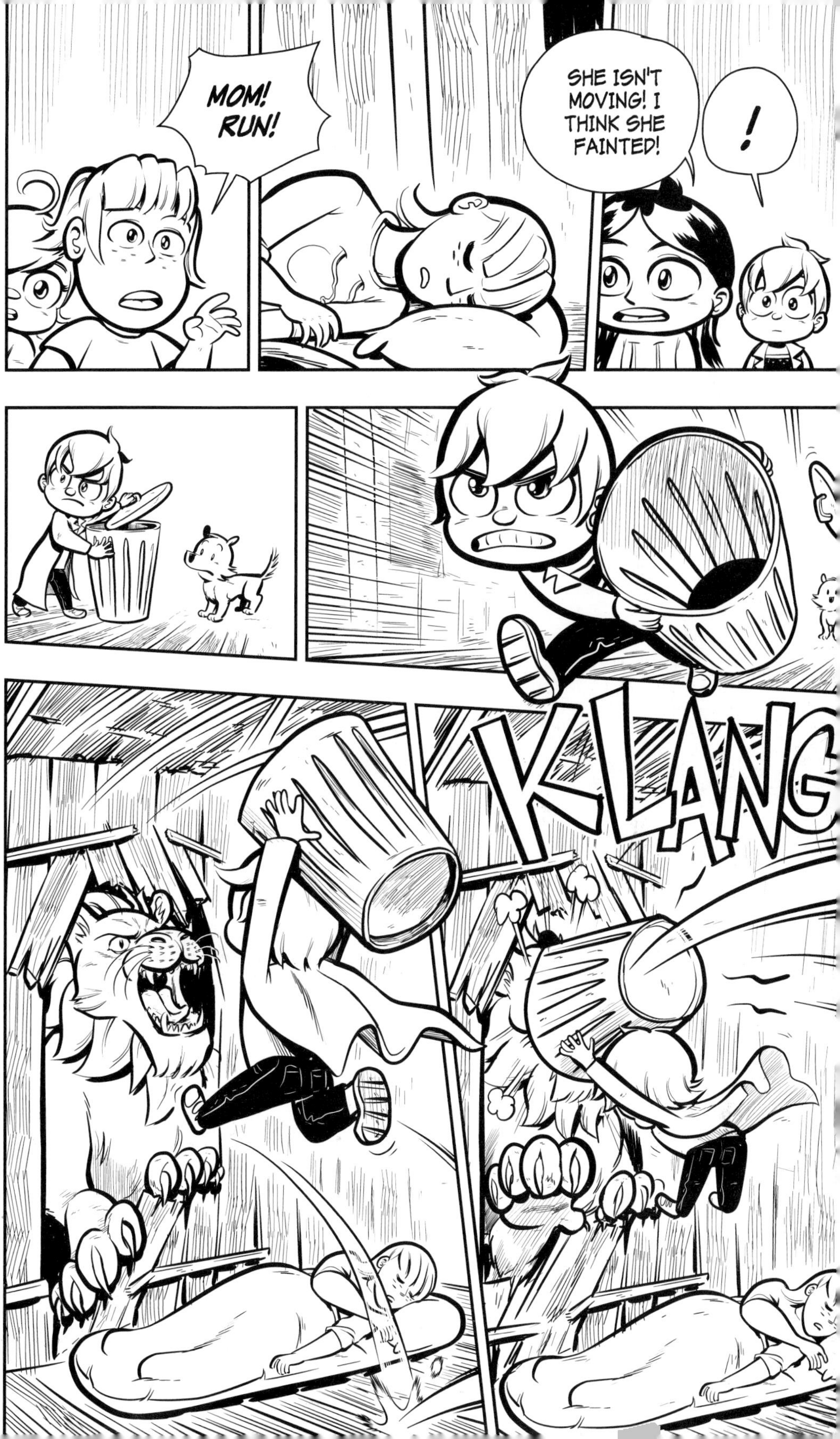
MOM! RUN!
SHE ISN'T MOVING! I THINK SHE FAINTED!
!
KLANG

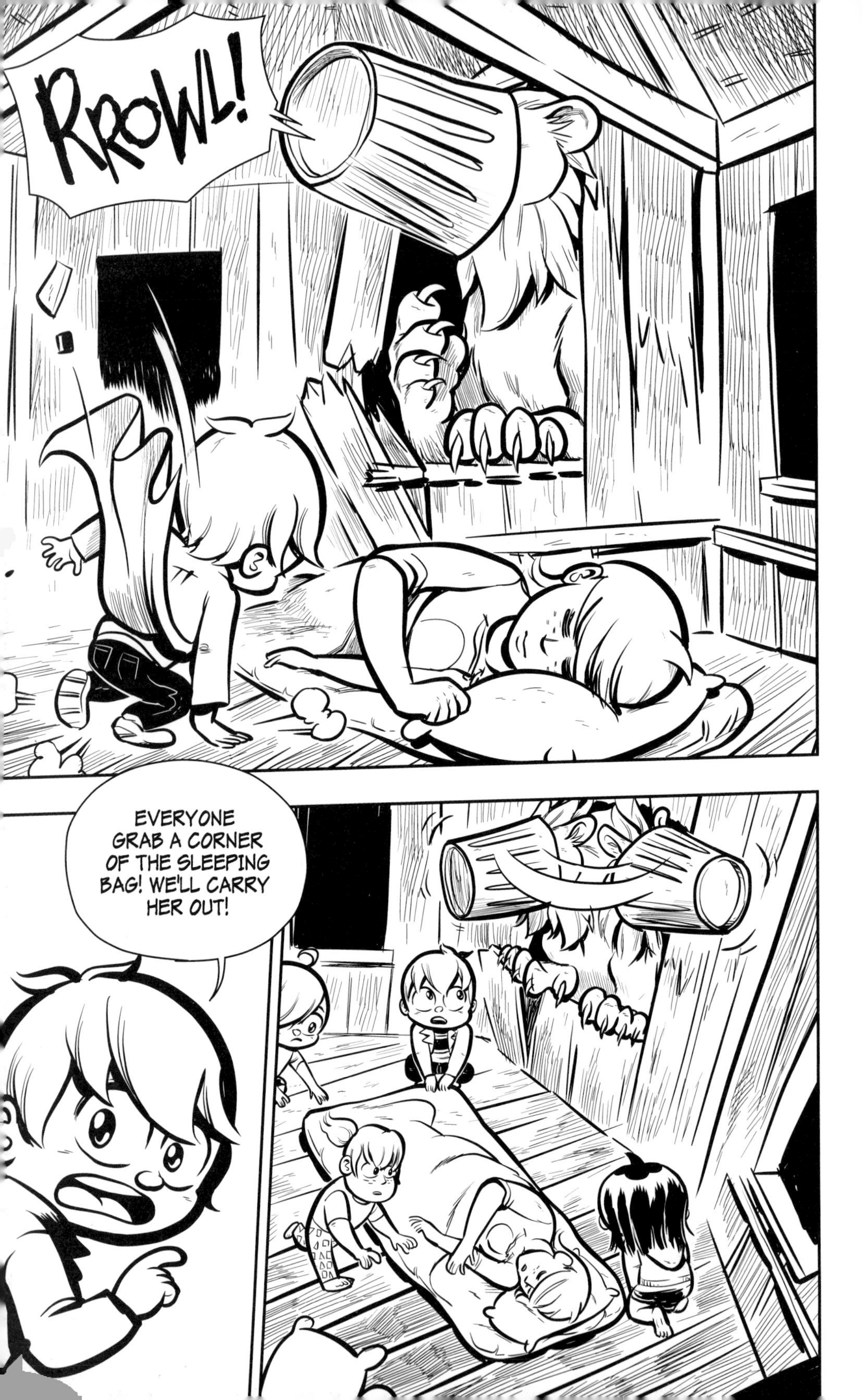
RROWL!
EVERYONE GRAB A CORNER OF THE SLEEPING BAG! WE'LL CARRY HER OUT!

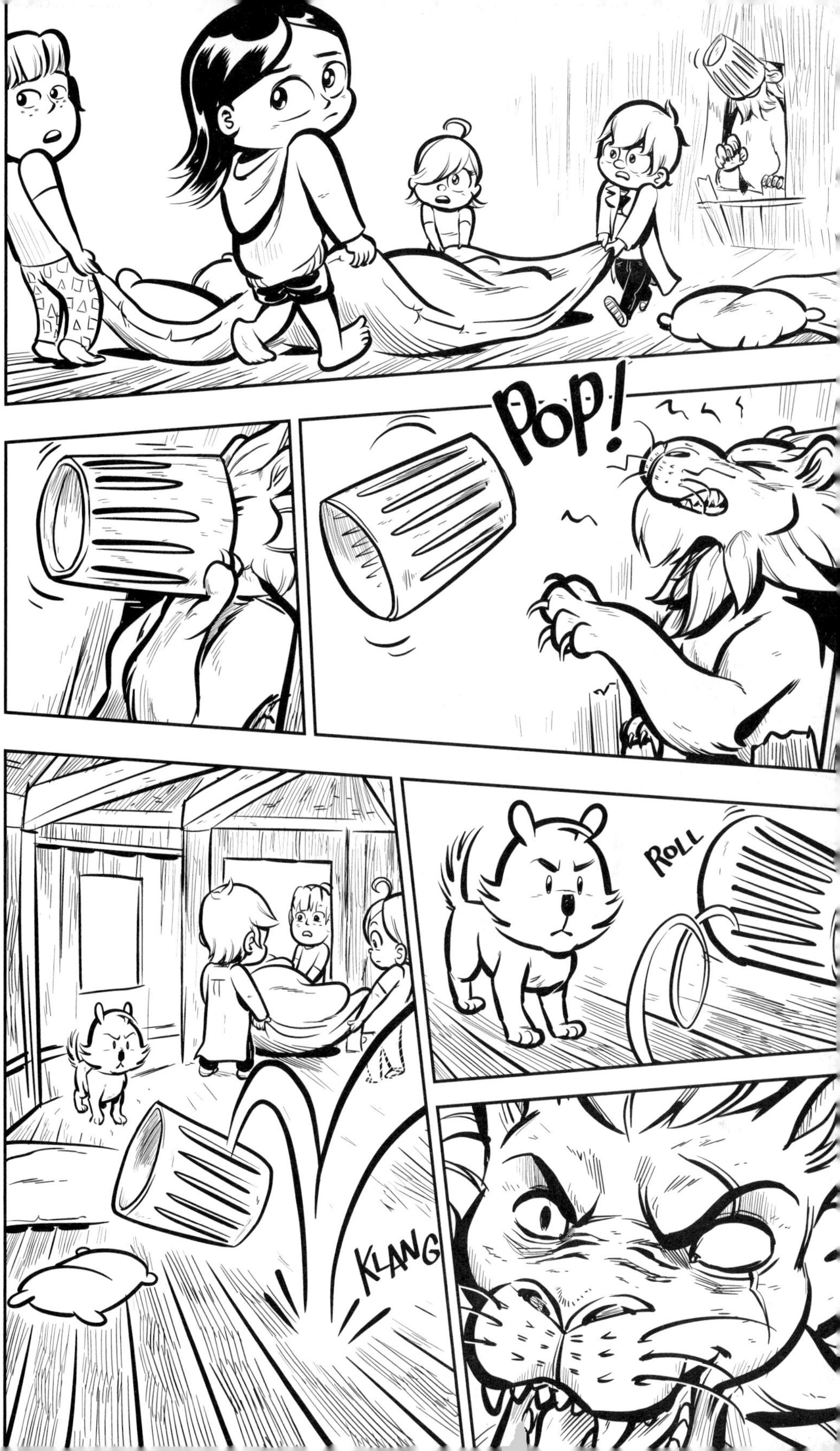
POP!
ROLL
KLANG

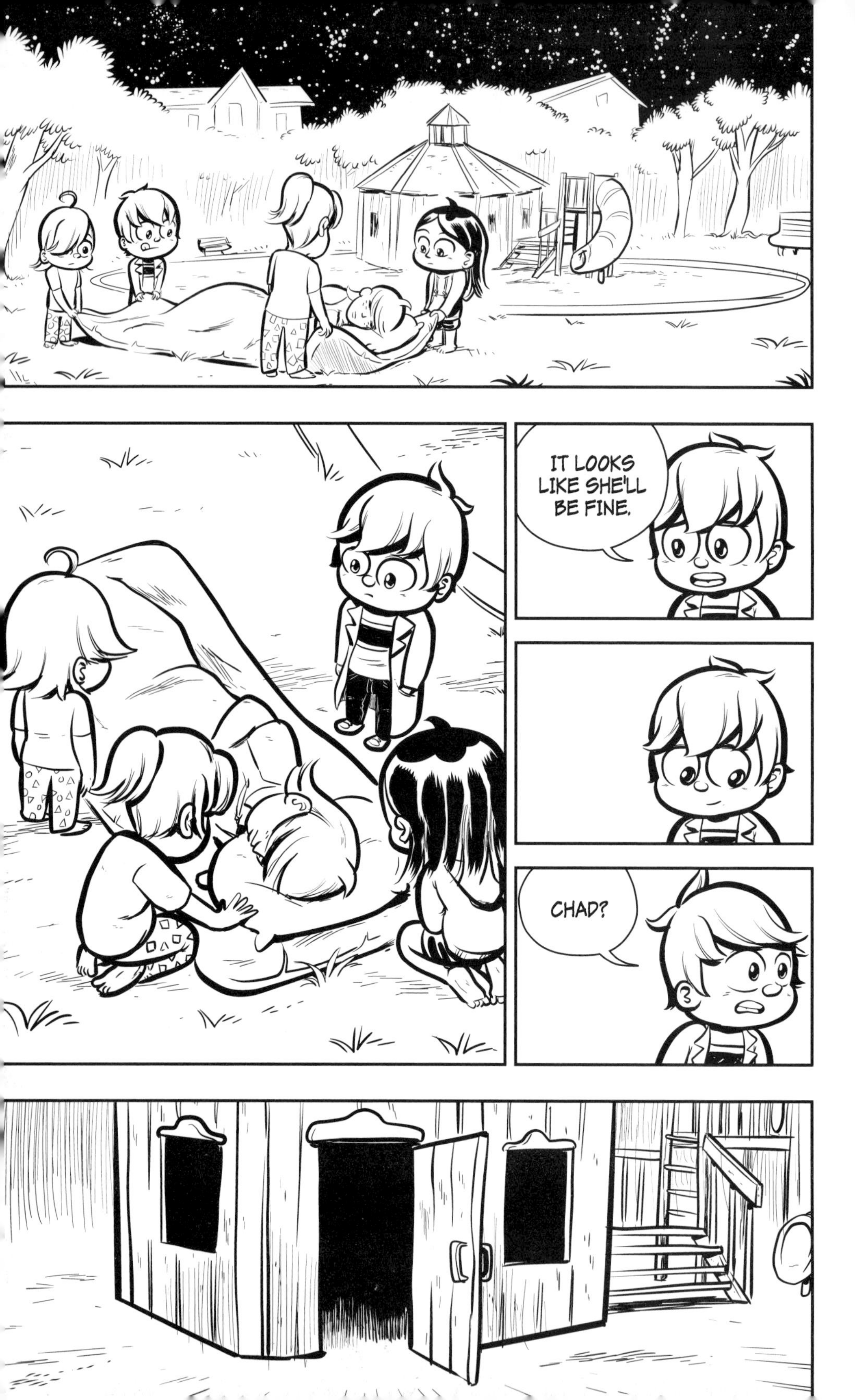
IT LOOKS LIKE SHE'LL BE FINE.
CHAD?

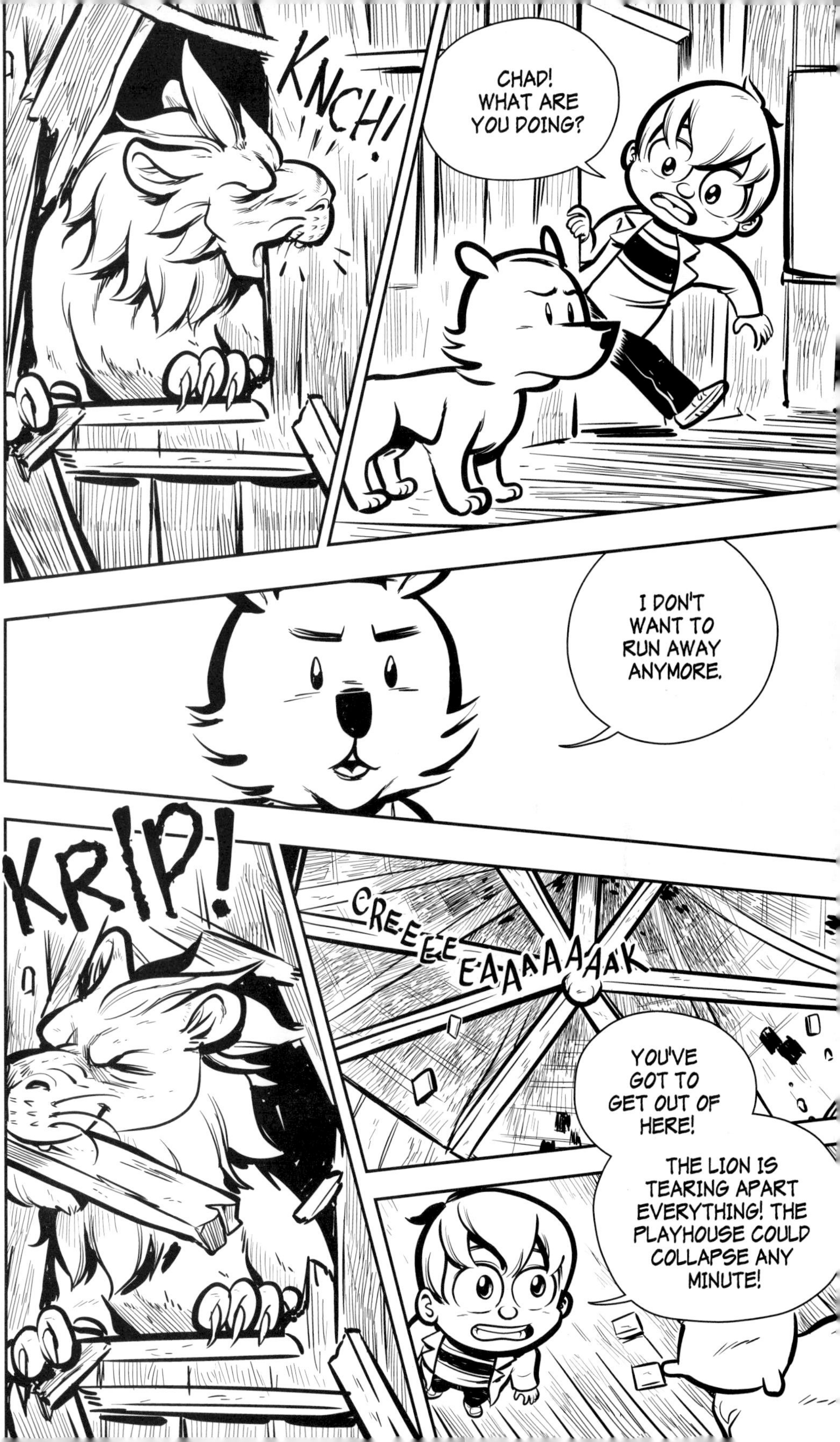
KNCH!
CHAD! WHAT ARE YOU DOING?
I DON'T WANT TO RUN AWAY ANYMORE.
KRIP!
CREEEEEEAAAAAAK
YOU'VE GOT TO GET OUT OF HERE!
THE LION IS TEARING APART EVERYTHING! THE PLAYHOUSE COULD COLLAPSE ANY MINUTE!

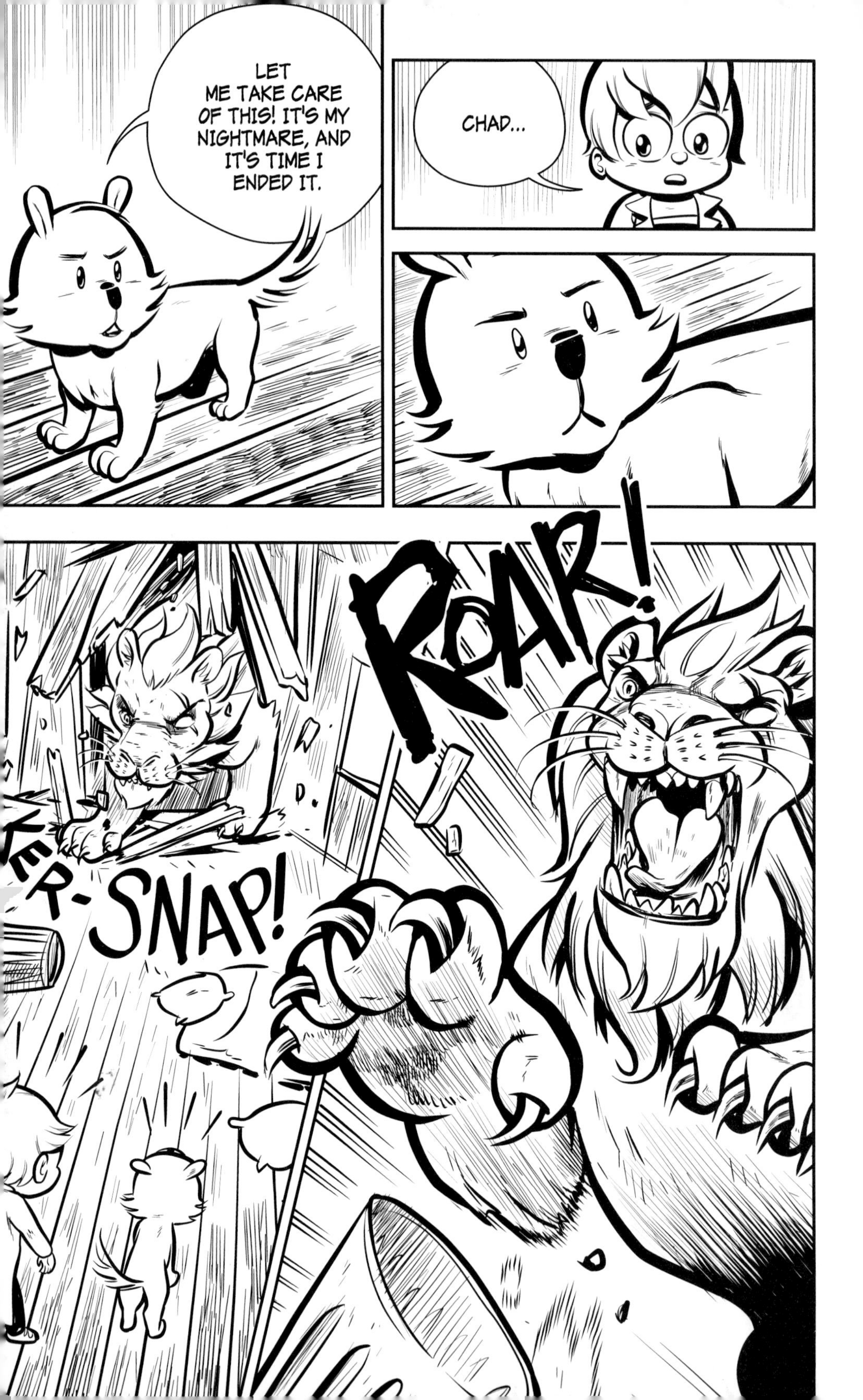
LET ME TAKE CARE OF THIS! IT'S MY NIGHTMARE, AND IT'S TIME I ENDED IT.
CHAD...
ROAR!
ER-SNAP!

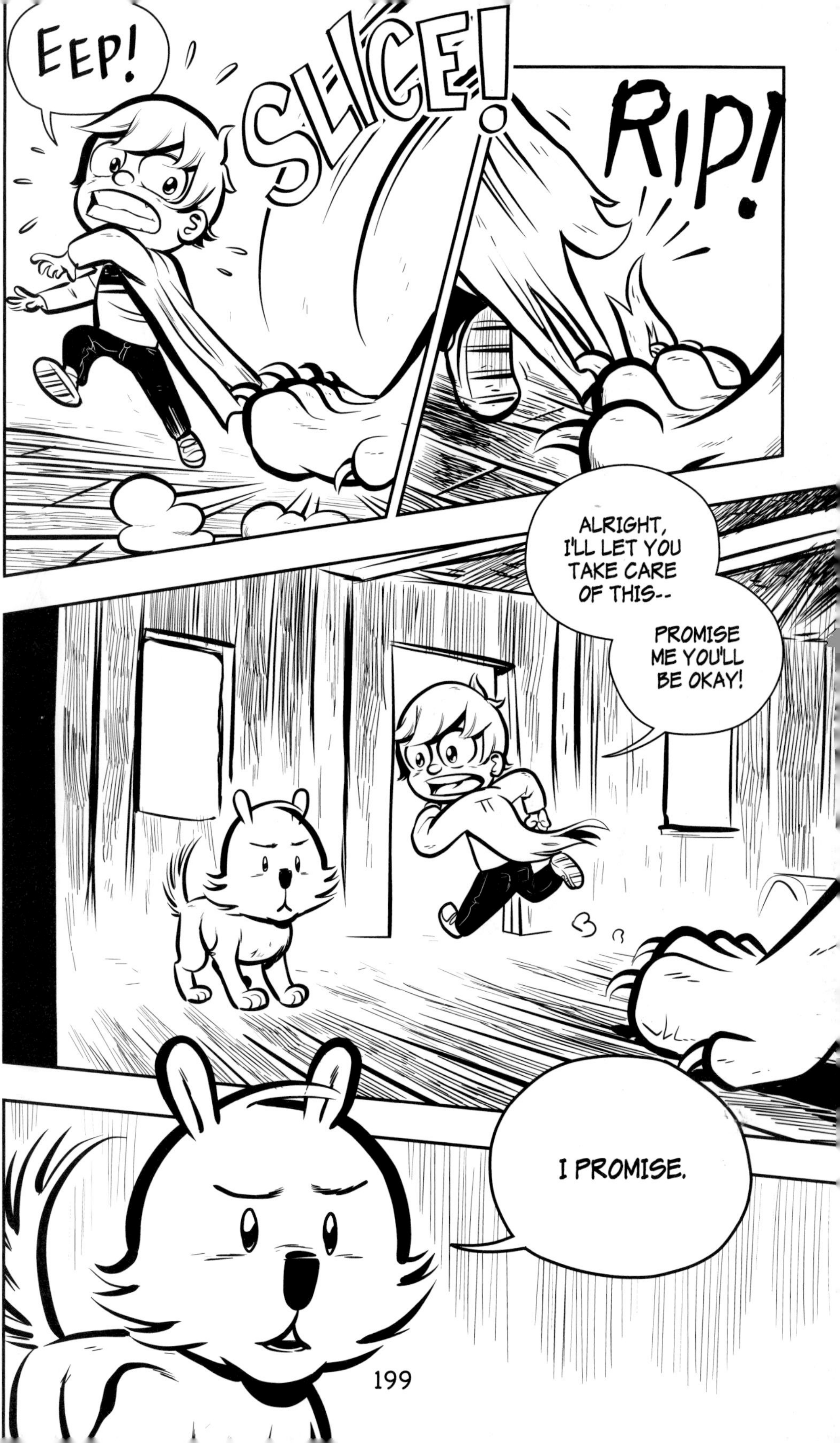
EEP!
SLICE!
RIP!
ALRIGHT, I'LL LET YOU TAKE CARE OF THIS--
PROMISE ME YOU'LL BE OKAY!
I PROMISE.

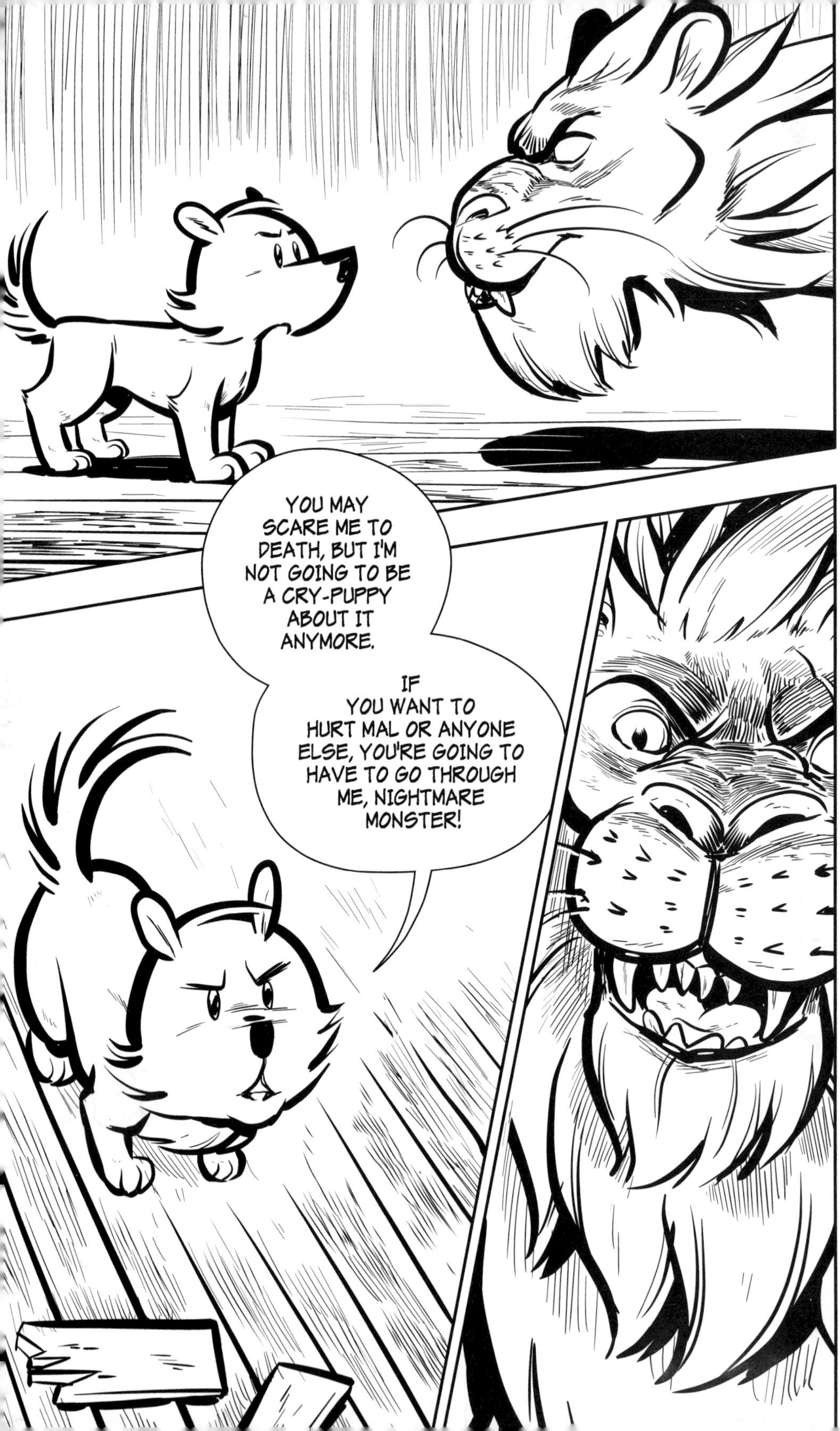
YOU MAY SCARE ME TO DEATH, BUT I'M NOT GOING TO BE A CRY-PUPPY ABOUT IT ANYMORE.
IF YOU WANT TO HURT MAL OR ANYONE ELSE, YOU'RE GOING TO HAVE TO GO THROUGH ME, NIGHTMARE MONSTER!

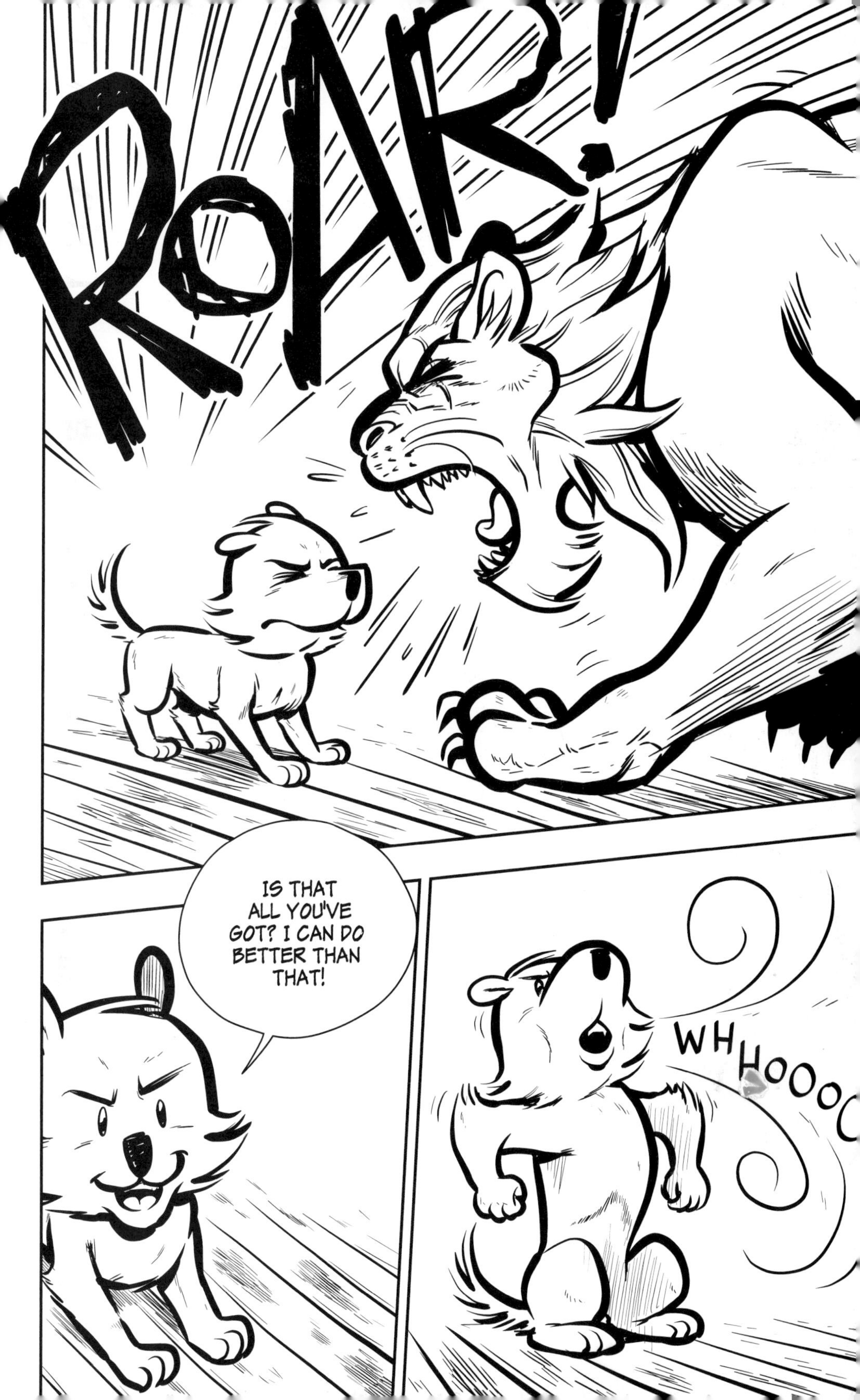
ROAR!
IS THAT ALL YOU'VE GOT? I CAN DO BETTER THAN THAT!
WHHOOOO

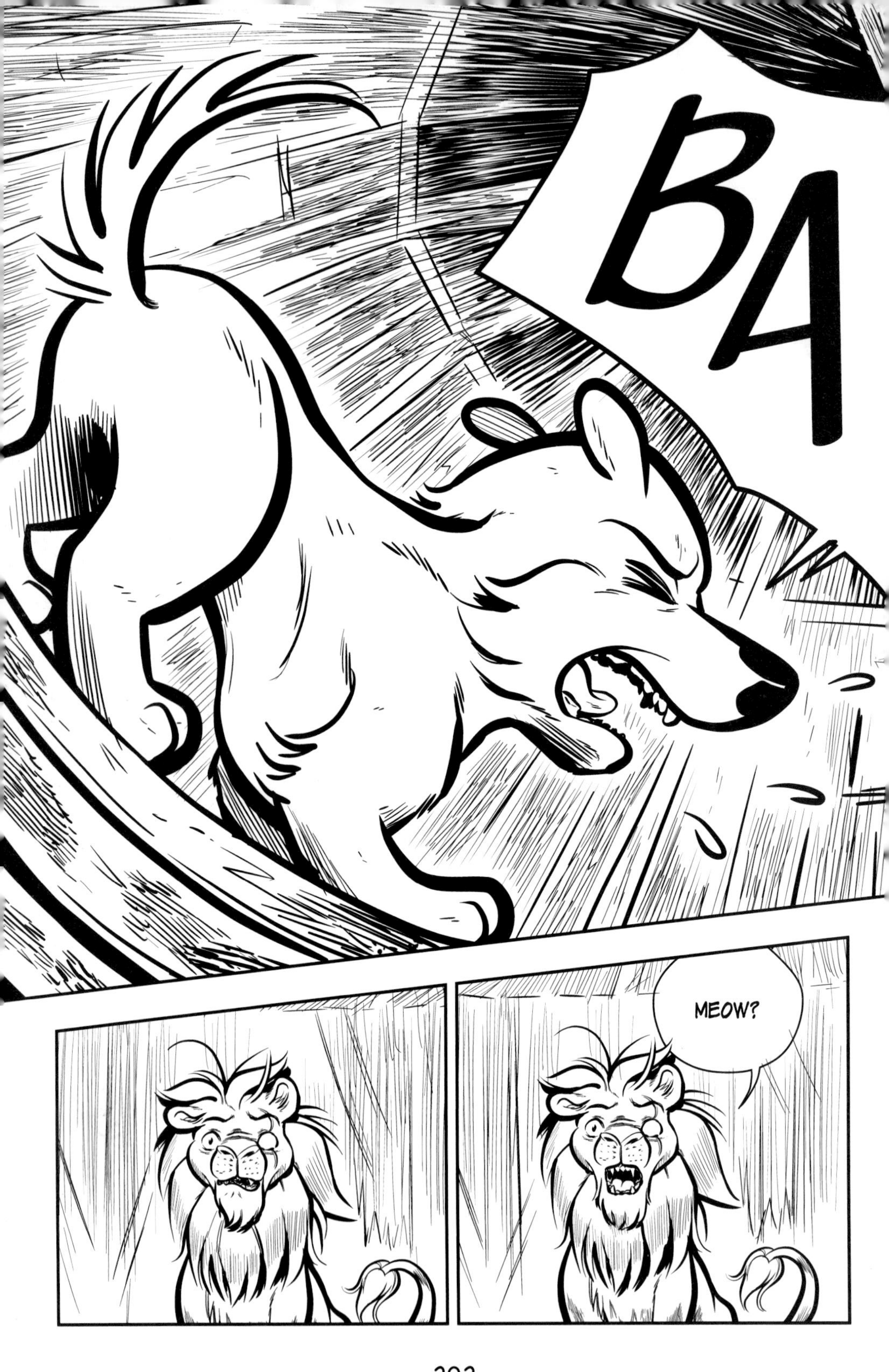
BA
MEOW?

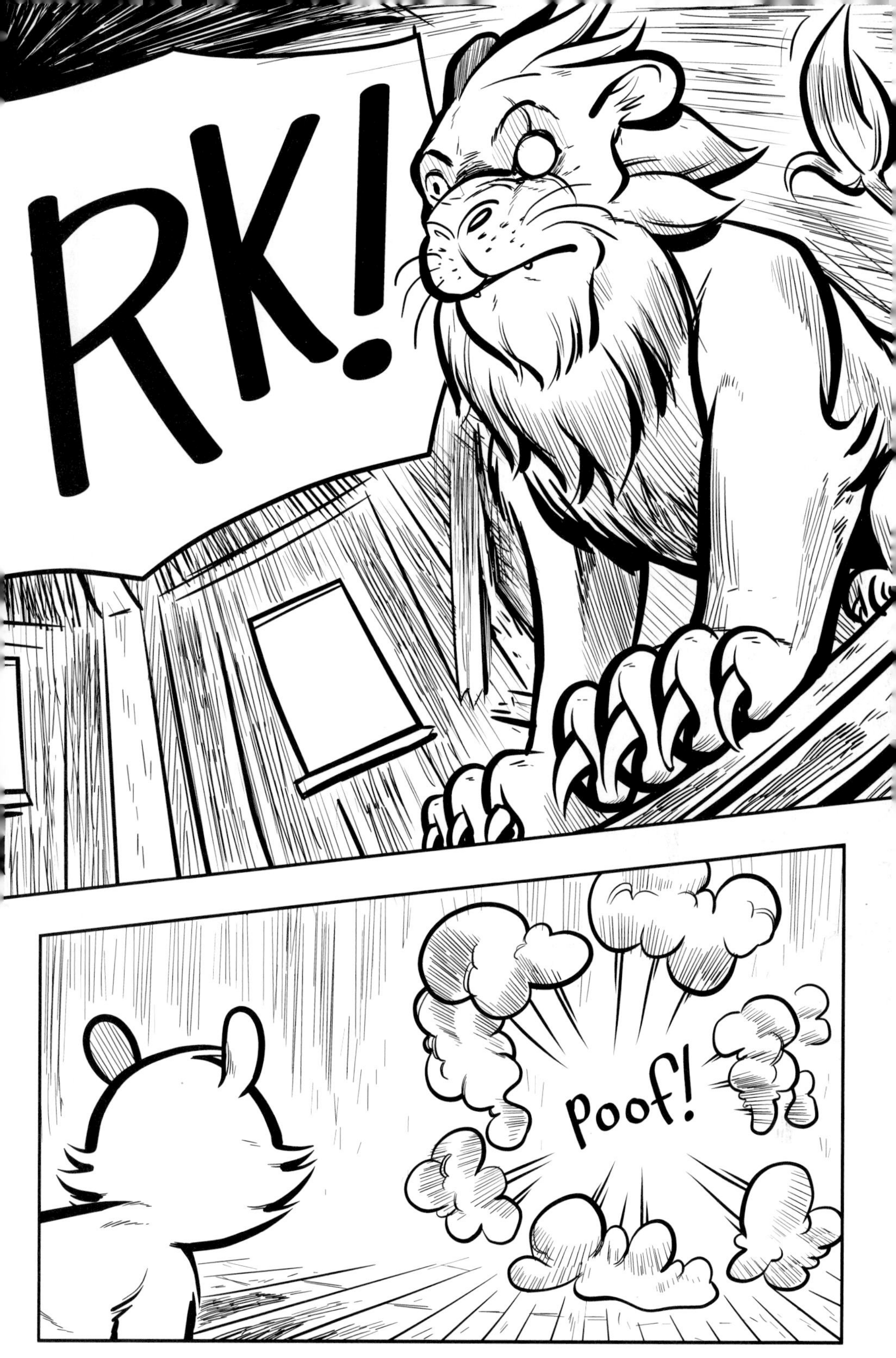
RK!
Poof!

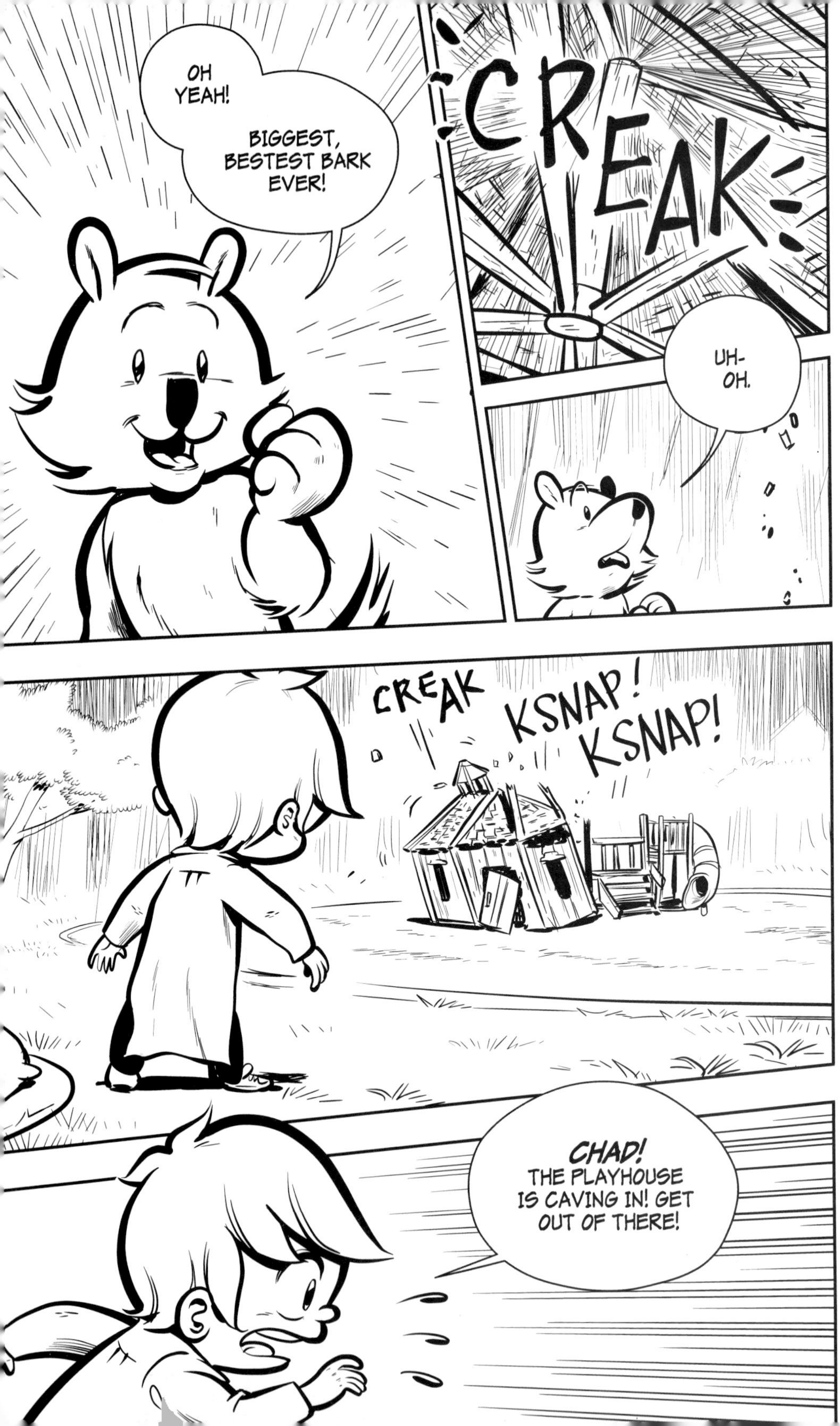
OH YEAH!
BIGGEST, BESTEST BARK EVER!
CREAK
UH-OH.
CREAK
KSNAP!
KSNAP!
CHAD! THE PLAYHOUSE IS CAVING IN! GET OUT OF THERE!

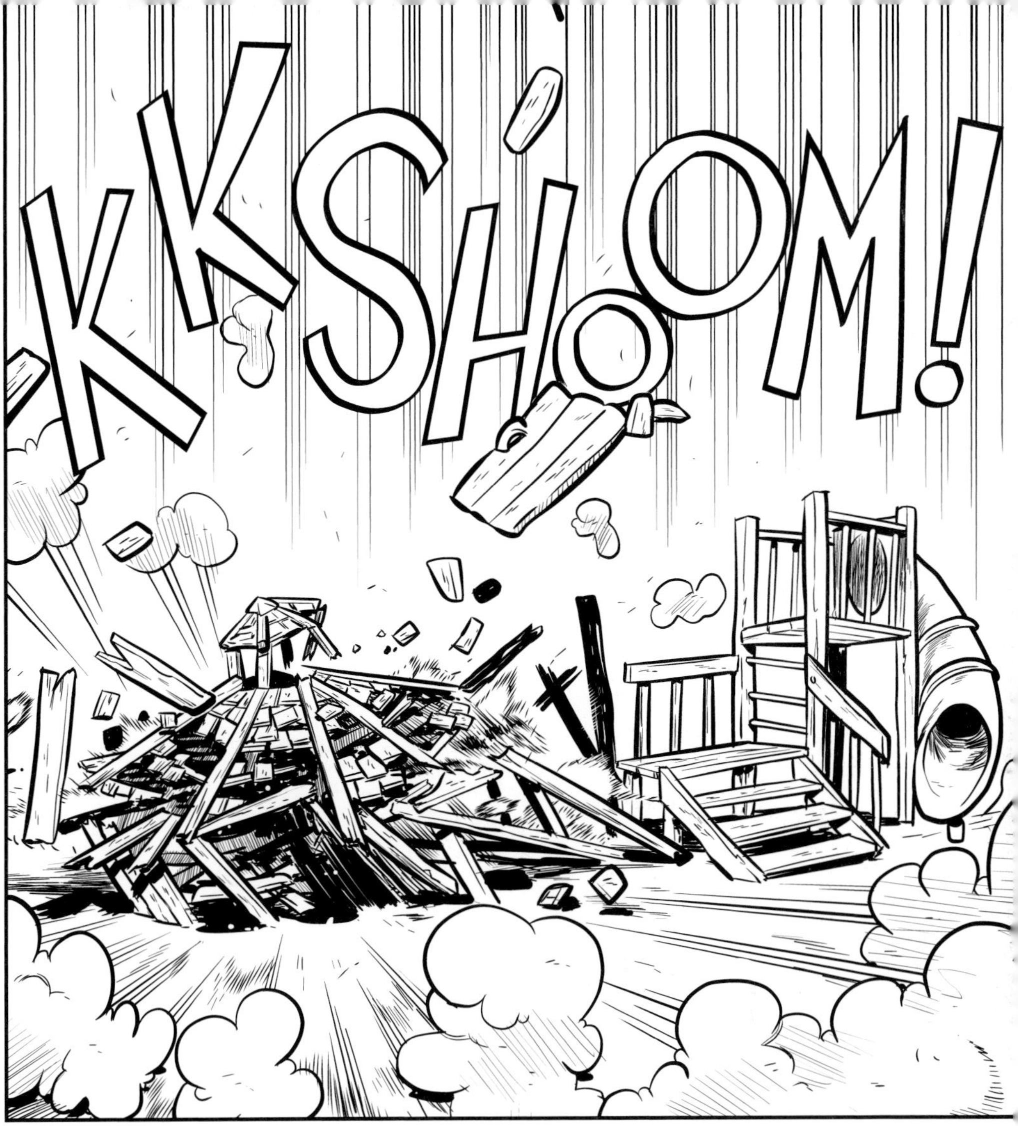
KKSHOOM!

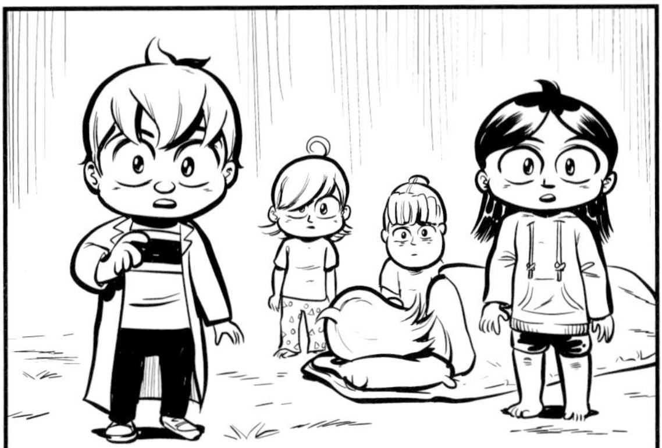

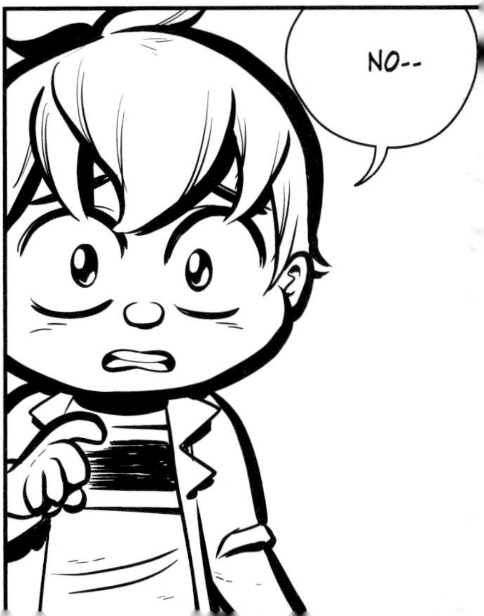
NO--

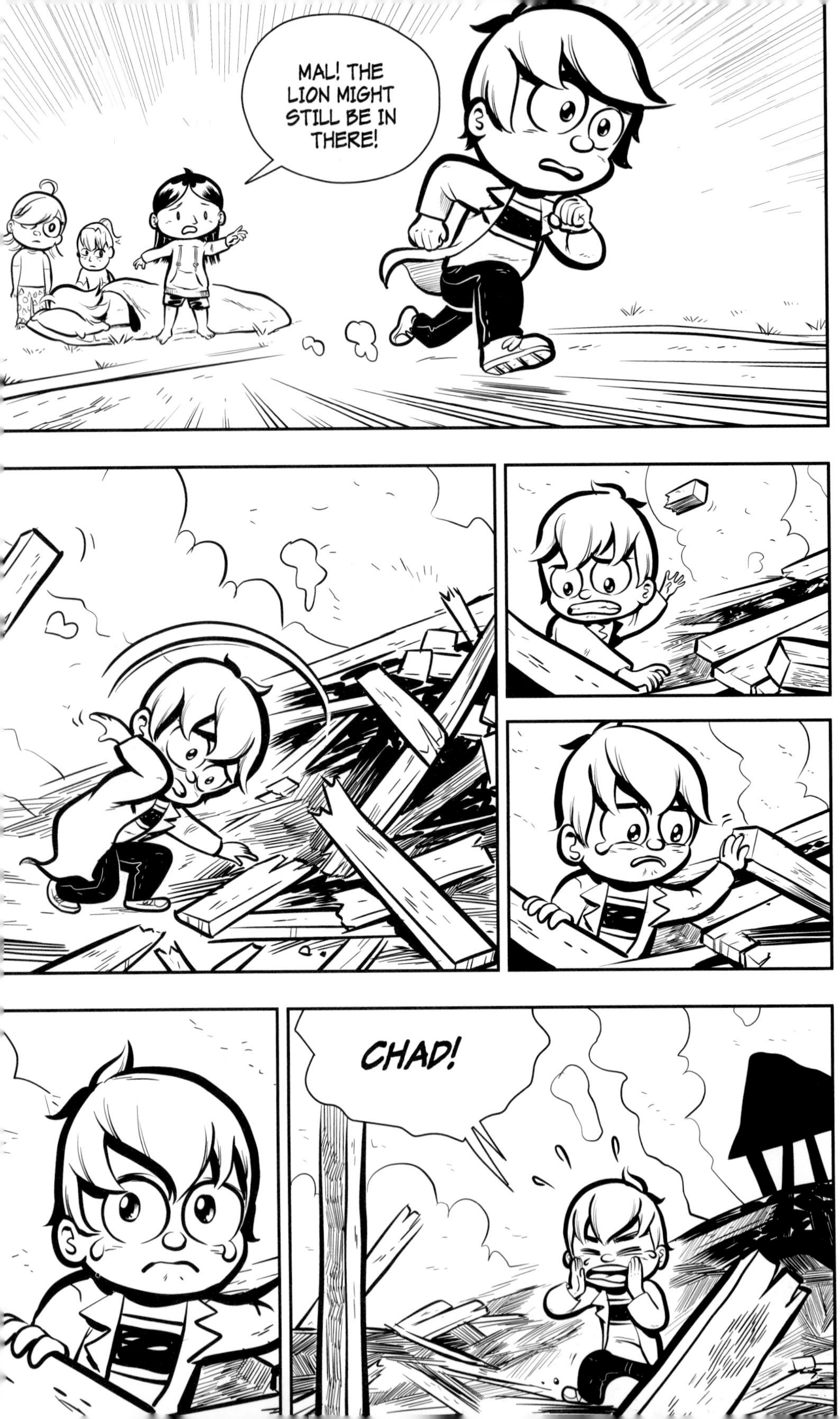
MAL! THE LION MIGHT STILL BE IN THERE!
CHAD!

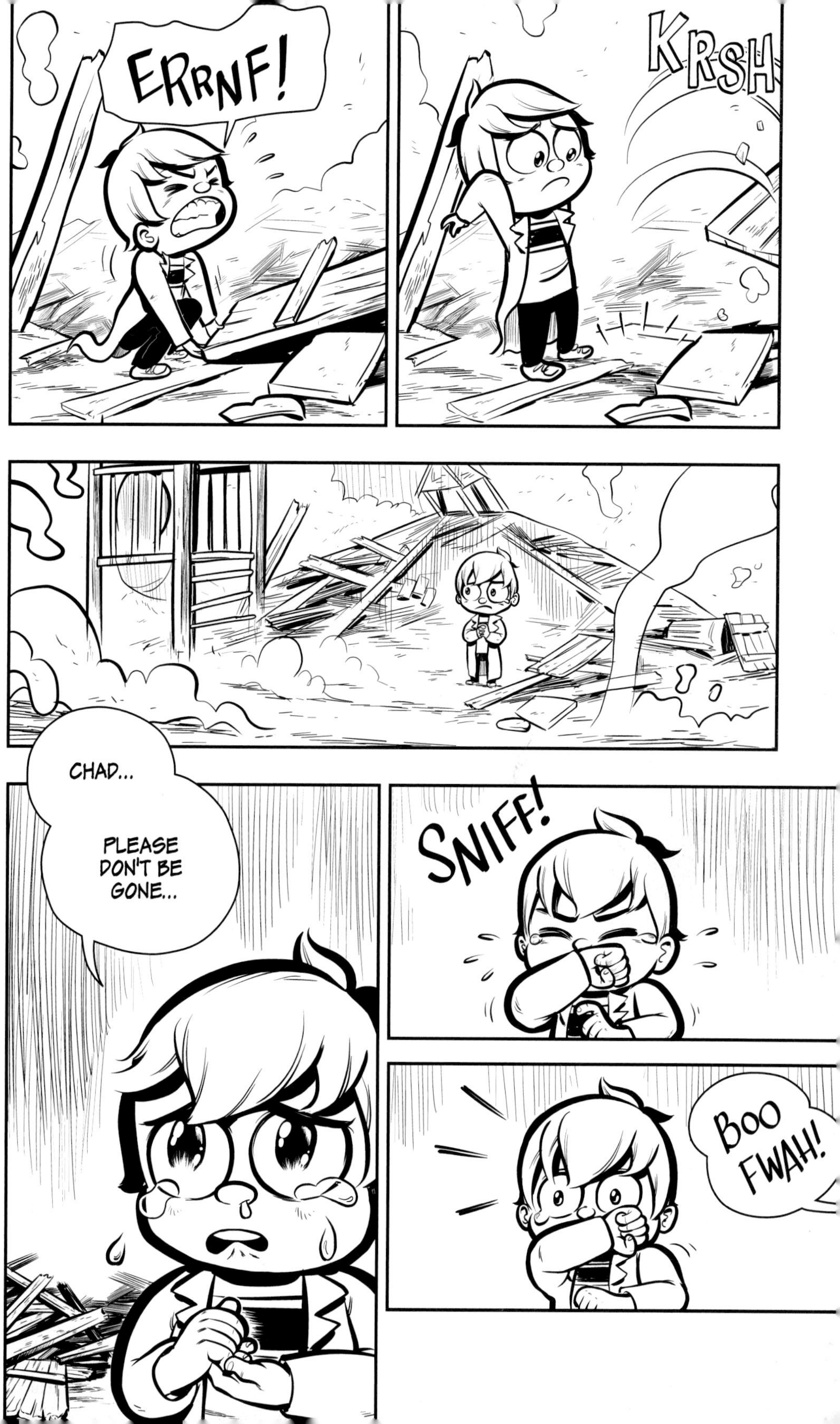
ERRNF!
KRSH
CHAD...
PLEASE DON'T BE GONE...
SNIFF!
BOO FWAH!

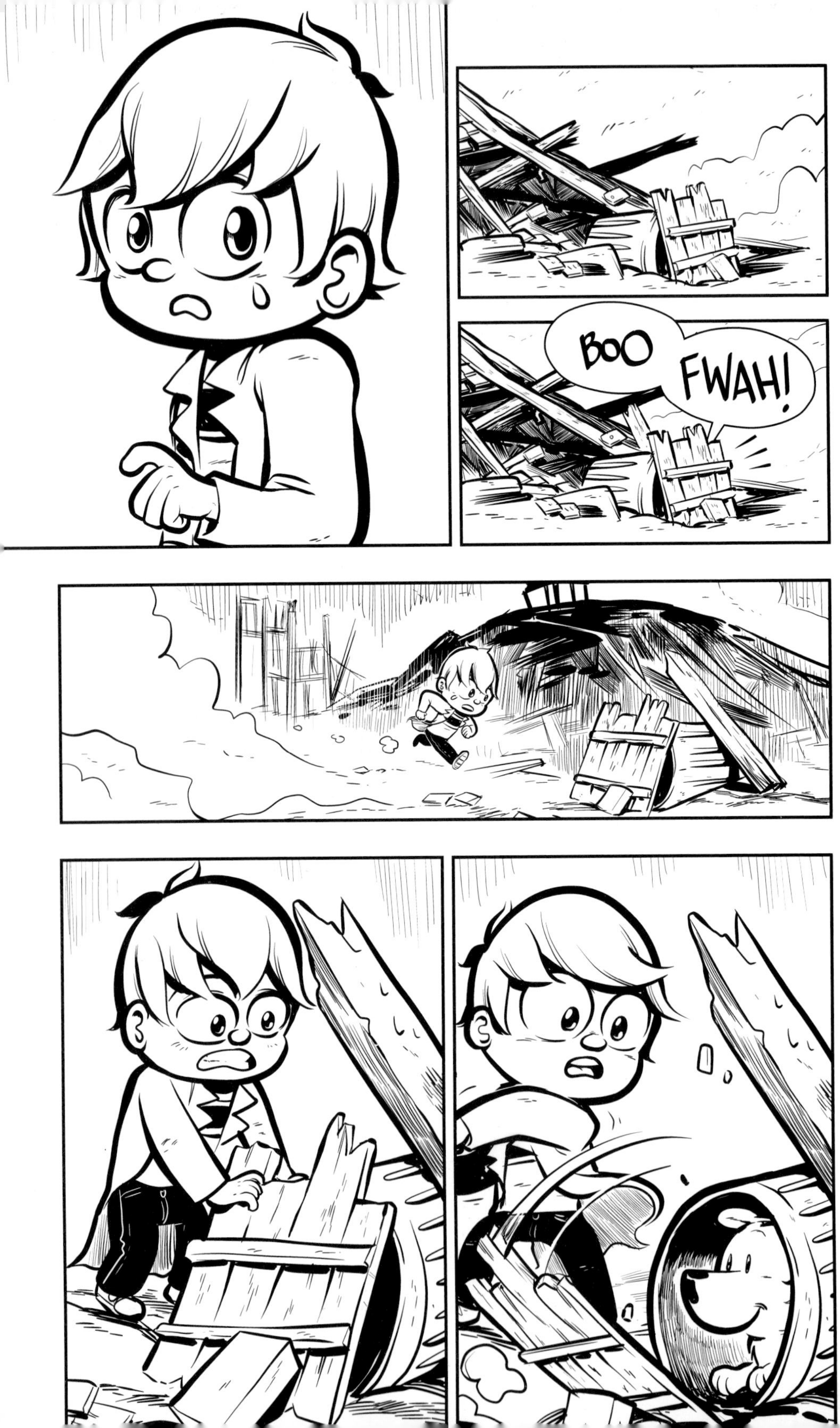
BOO
FWAH!

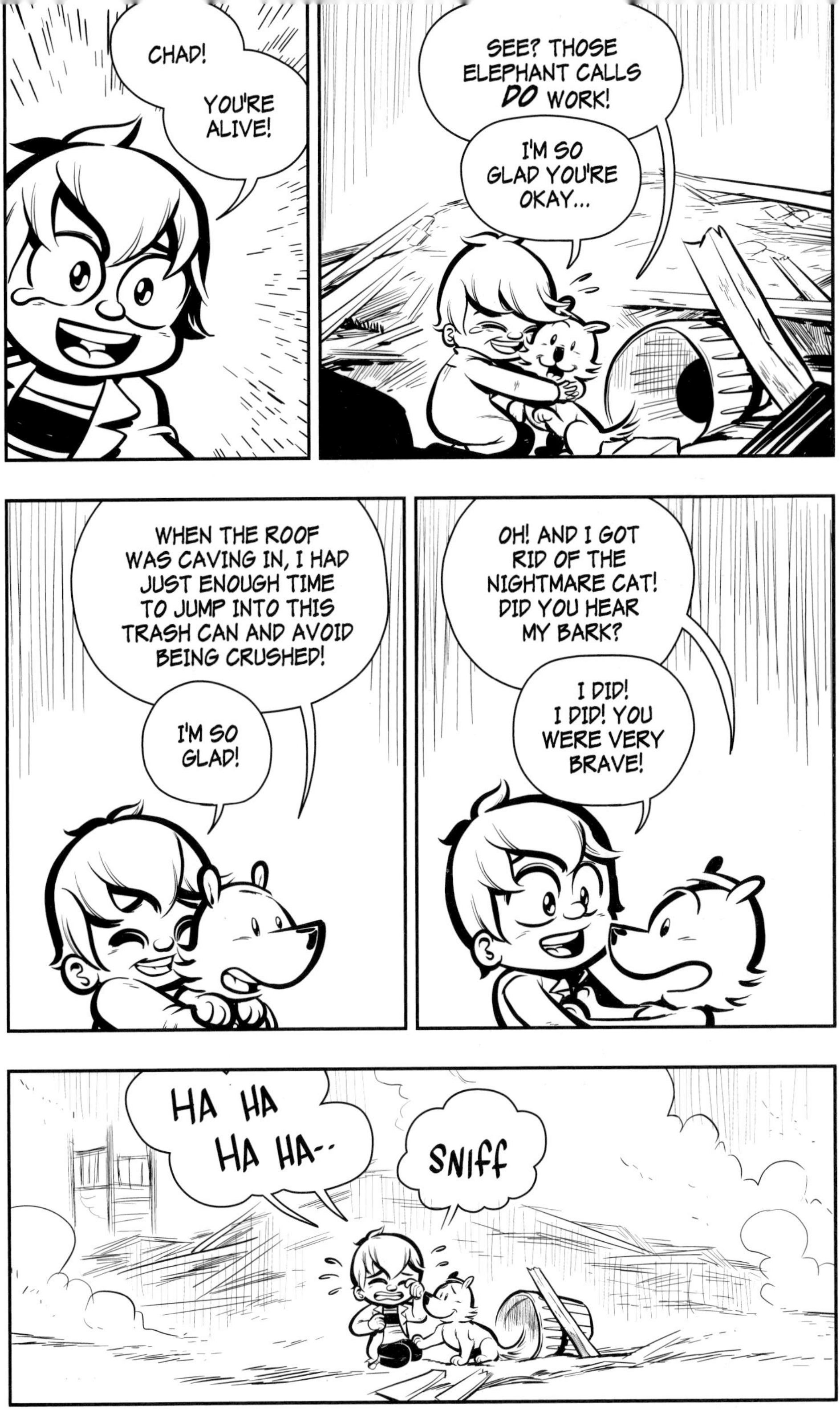
CHAD!
YOU'RE ALIVE!
SEE? THOSE ELEPHANT CALLS *DO* WORK!
I'M SO GLAD YOU'RE OKAY...
WHEN THE ROOF WAS CAVING IN, I HAD JUST ENOUGH TIME TO JUMP INTO THIS TRASH CAN AND AVOID BEING CRUSHED!
I'M SO GLAD!
OH! AND I GOT RID OF THE NIGHTMARE CAT! DID YOU HEAR MY BARK?
I DID! I DID! YOU WERE VERY BRAVE!
HA HA HA HA--
SNIFF

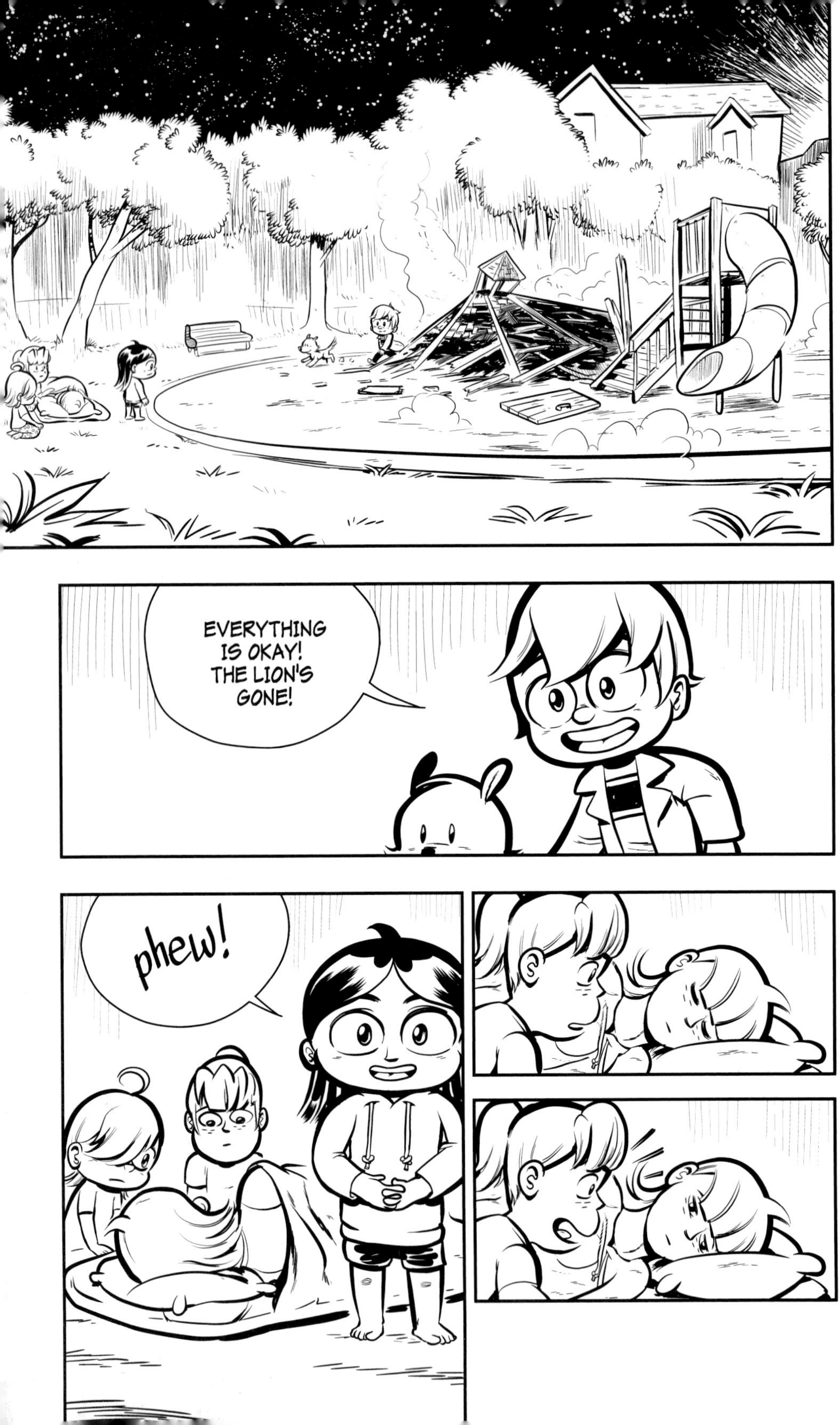
EVERYTHING IS OKAY! THE LION'S GONE!
phew!

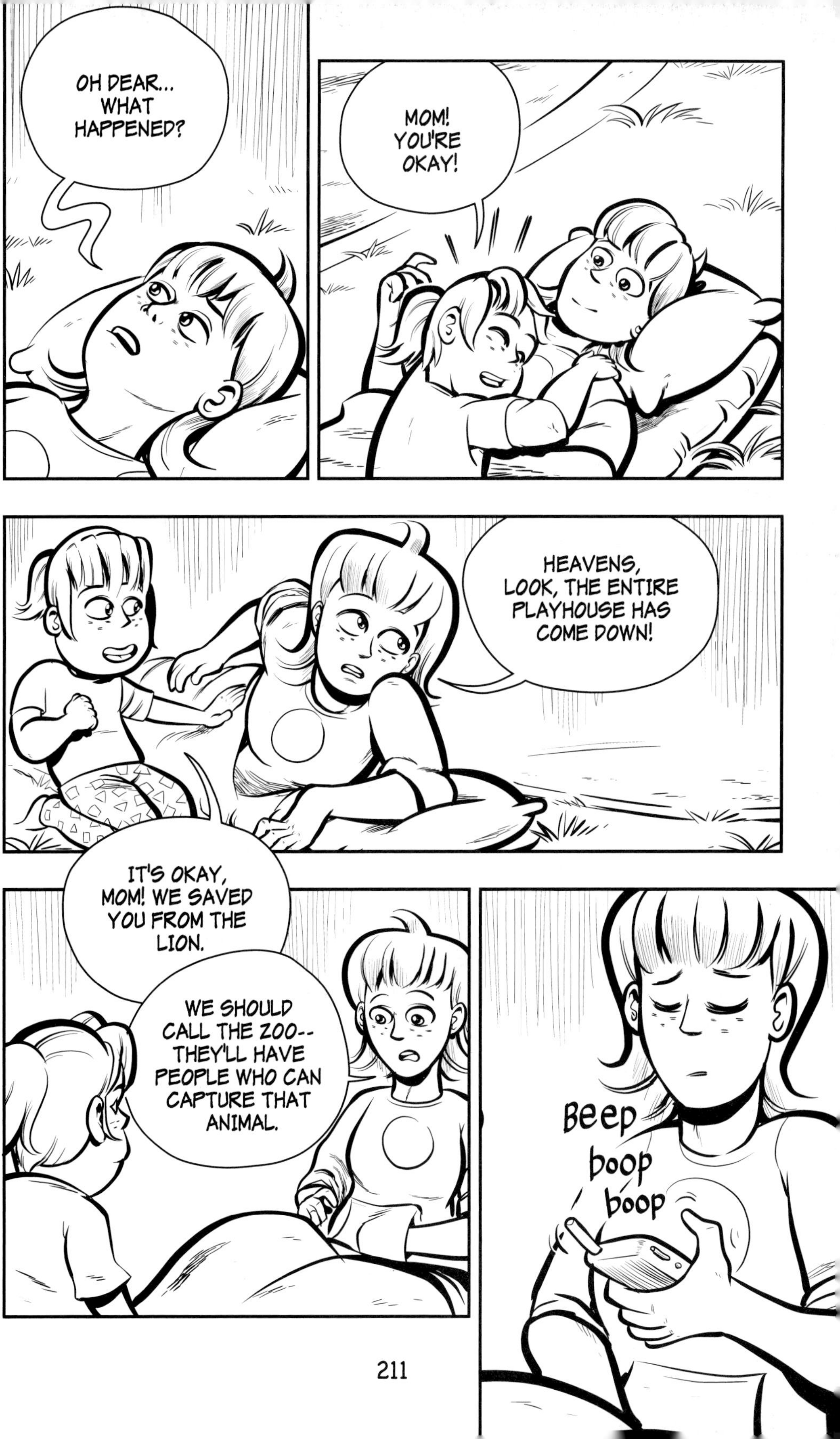
OH DEAR... WHAT HAPPENED?
MOM! YOU'RE OKAY!
HEAVENS, LOOK, THE ENTIRE PLAYHOUSE HAS COME DOWN!
IT'S OKAY, MOM! WE SAVED YOU FROM THE LION.
WE SHOULD CALL THE ZOO-- THEY'LL HAVE PEOPLE WHO CAN CAPTURE THAT ANIMAL.
Beep
boop
boop

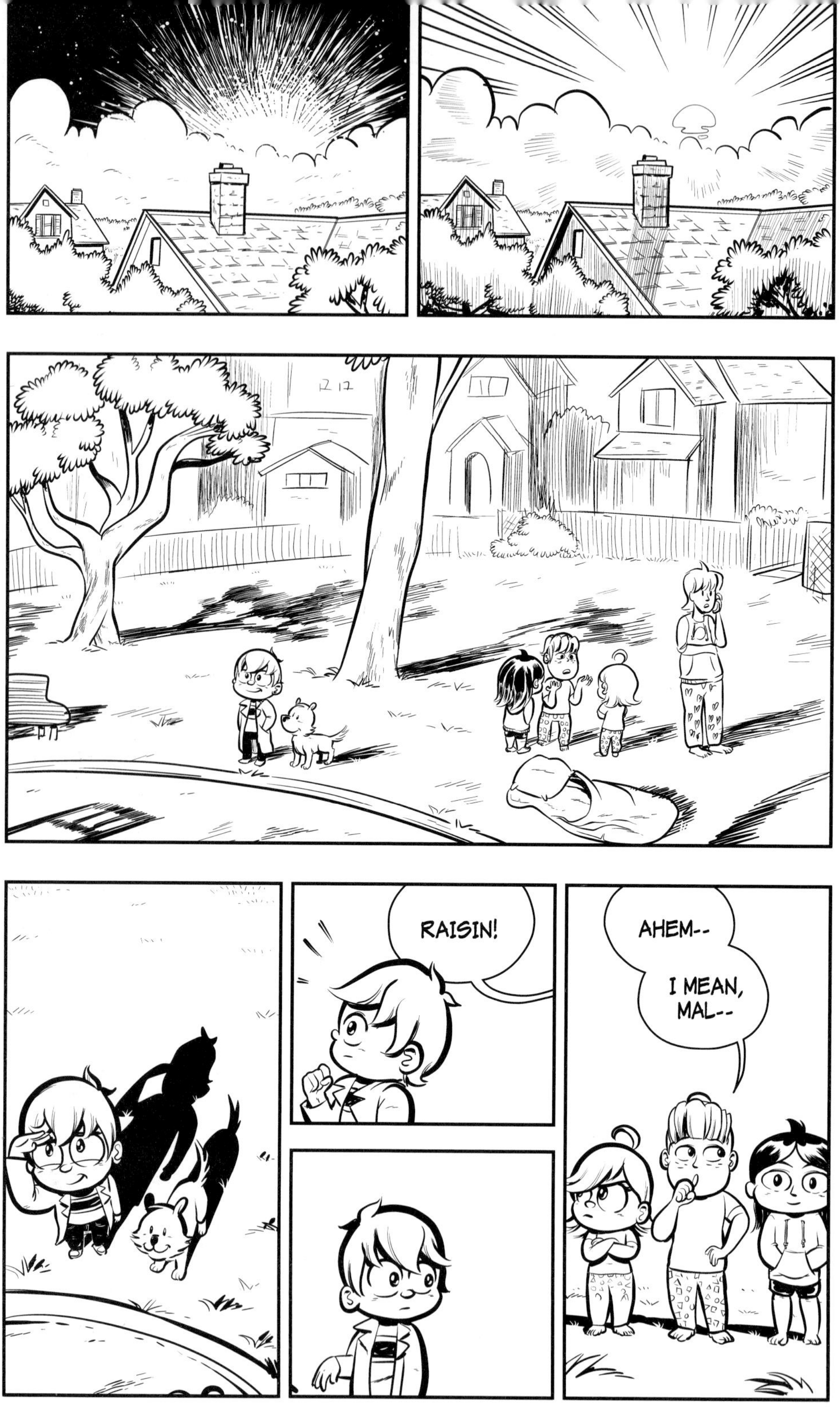
RAISIN!
AHEM--
I MEAN, MAL--

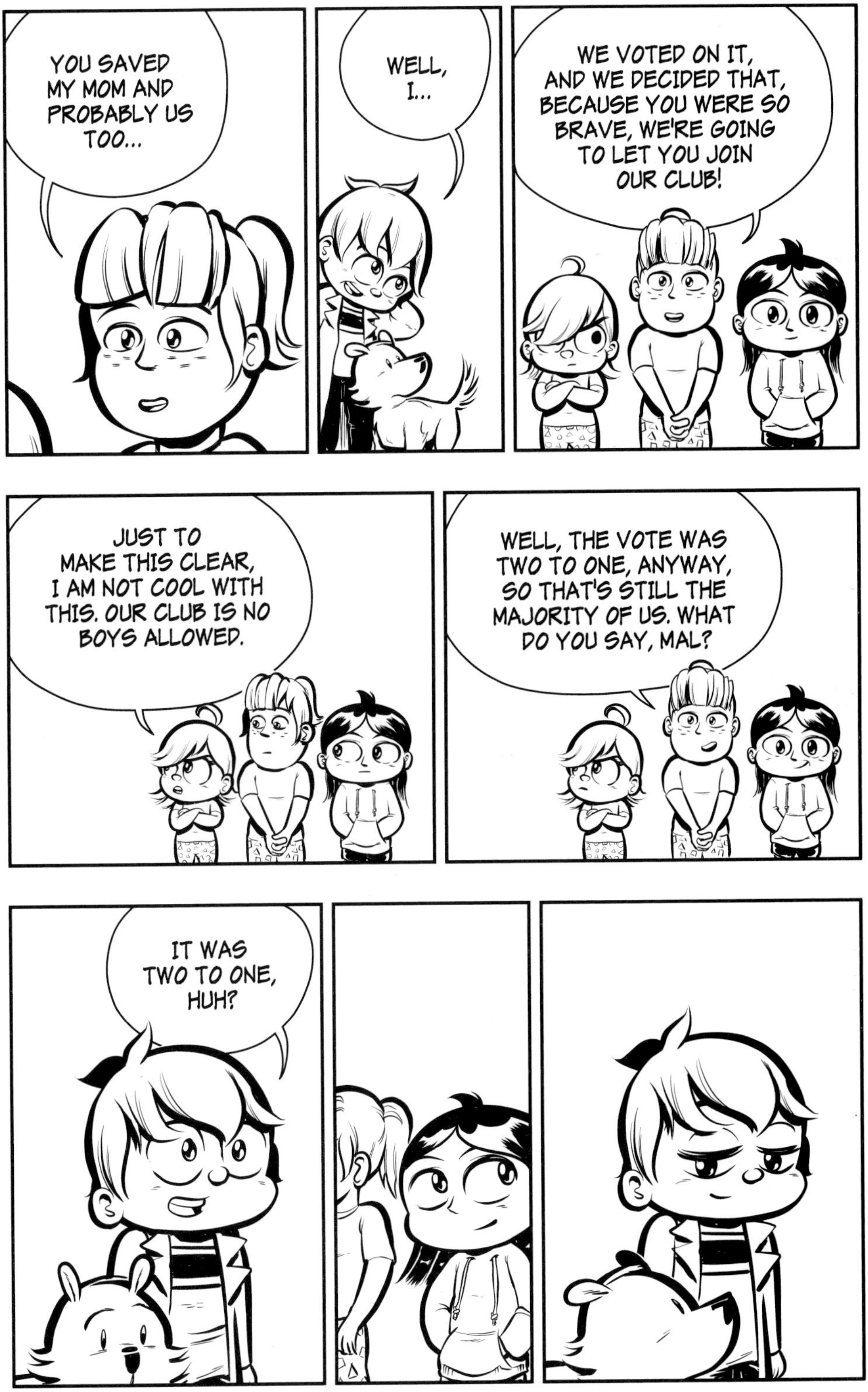
YOU SAVED MY MOM AND PROBABLY US TOO...
WELL, I...
WE VOTED ON IT, AND WE DECIDED THAT, BECAUSE YOU WERE SO BRAVE, WE'RE GOING TO LET YOU JOIN OUR CLUB!
JUST TO MAKE THIS CLEAR, I AM NOT COOL WITH THIS. OUR CLUB IS NO BOYS ALLOWED.
WELL, THE VOTE WAS TWO TO ONE, ANYWAY, SO THAT'S STILL THE MAJORITY OF US. WHAT DO YOU SAY, MAL?
IT WAS TWO TO ONE, HUH?

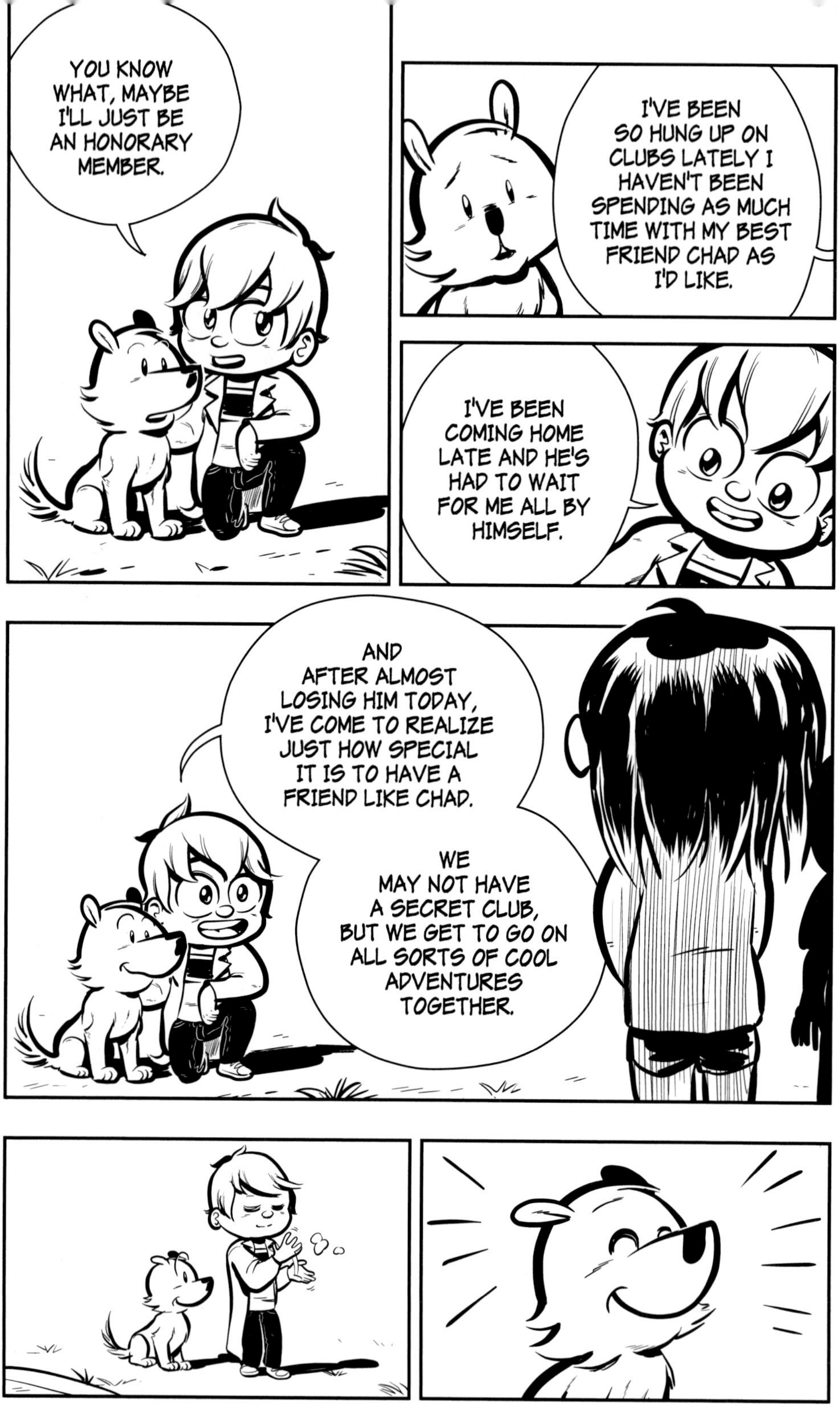
YOU KNOW WHAT, MAYBE I'LL JUST BE AN HONORARY MEMBER.
I'VE BEEN SO HUNG UP ON CLUBS LATELY I HAVEN'T BEEN SPENDING AS MUCH TIME WITH MY BEST FRIEND CHAD AS I'D LIKE.
I'VE BEEN COMING HOME LATE AND HE'S HAD TO WAIT FOR ME ALL BY HIMSELF.
AND AFTER ALMOST LOSING HIM TODAY, I'VE COME TO REALIZE JUST HOW SPECIAL IT IS TO HAVE A FRIEND LIKE CHAD.
WE MAY NOT HAVE A SECRET CLUB, BUT WE GET TO GO ON ALL SORTS OF COOL ADVENTURES TOGETHER.

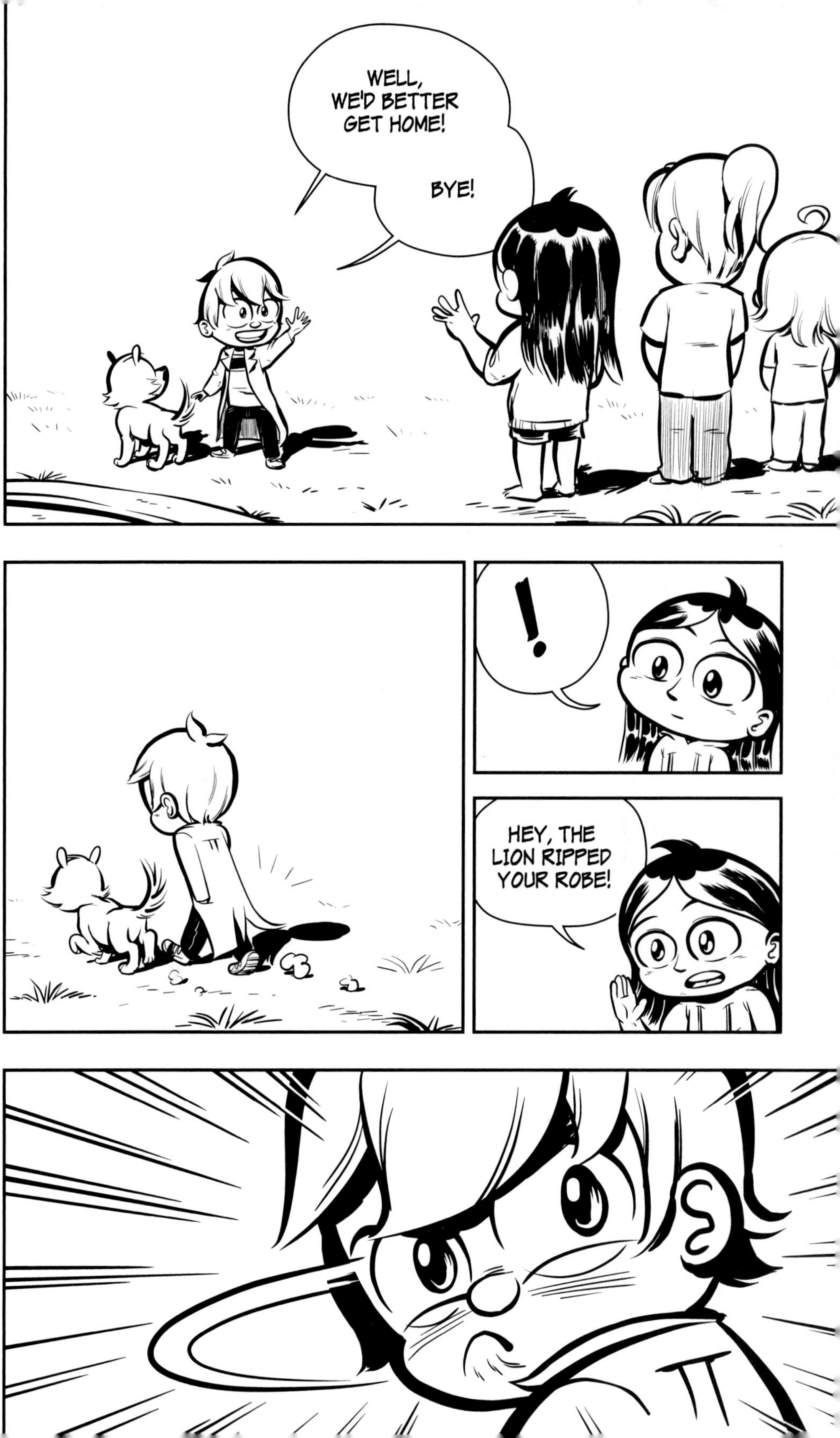
WELL, WE'D BETTER GET HOME!
BYE!
!
HEY, THE LION RIPPED YOUR ROBE!

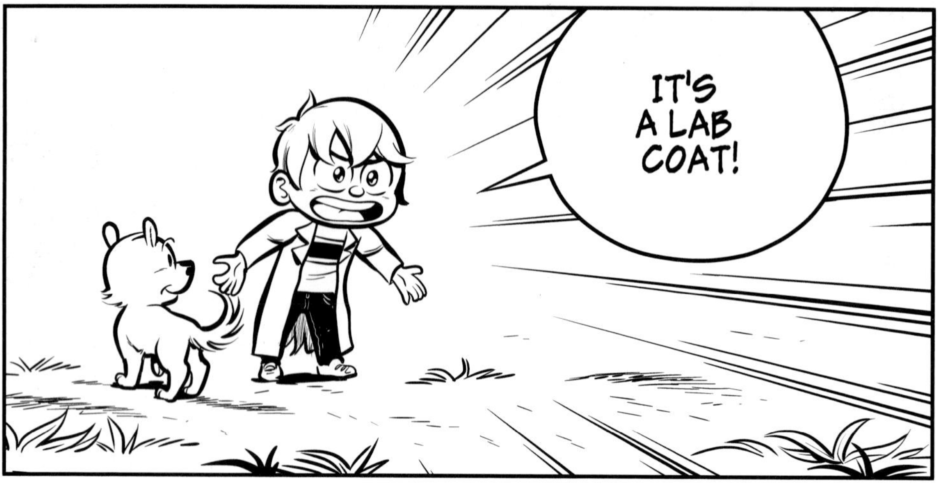
IT'S A LAB COAT!

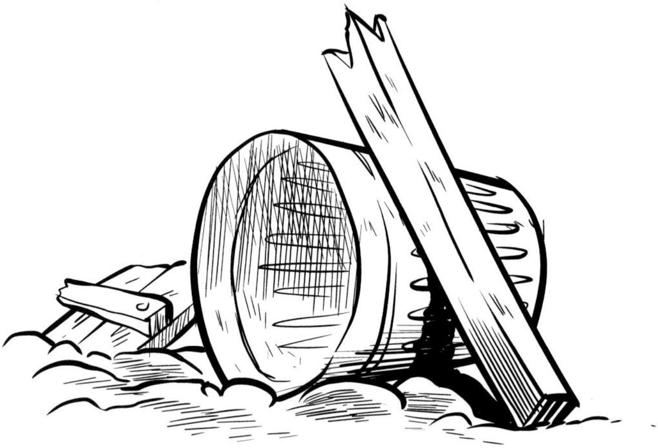

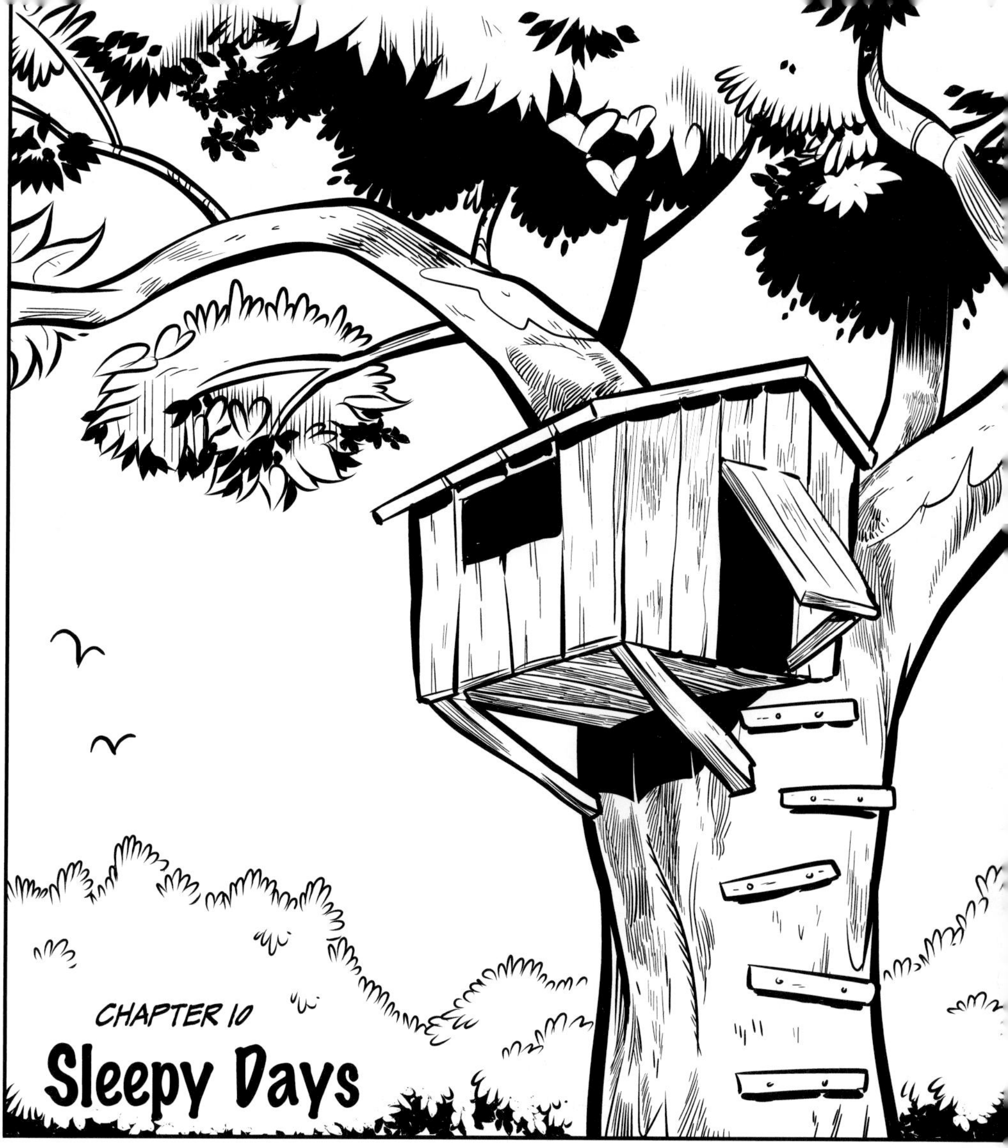
CHAPTER 10
Sleepy Days

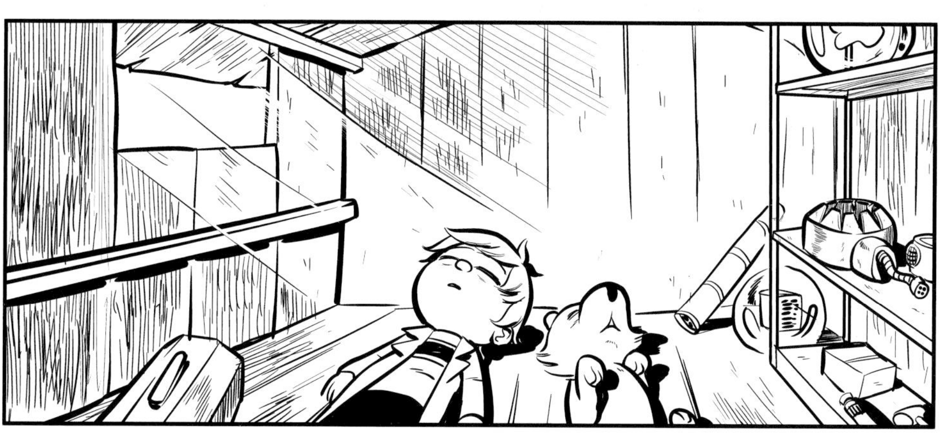

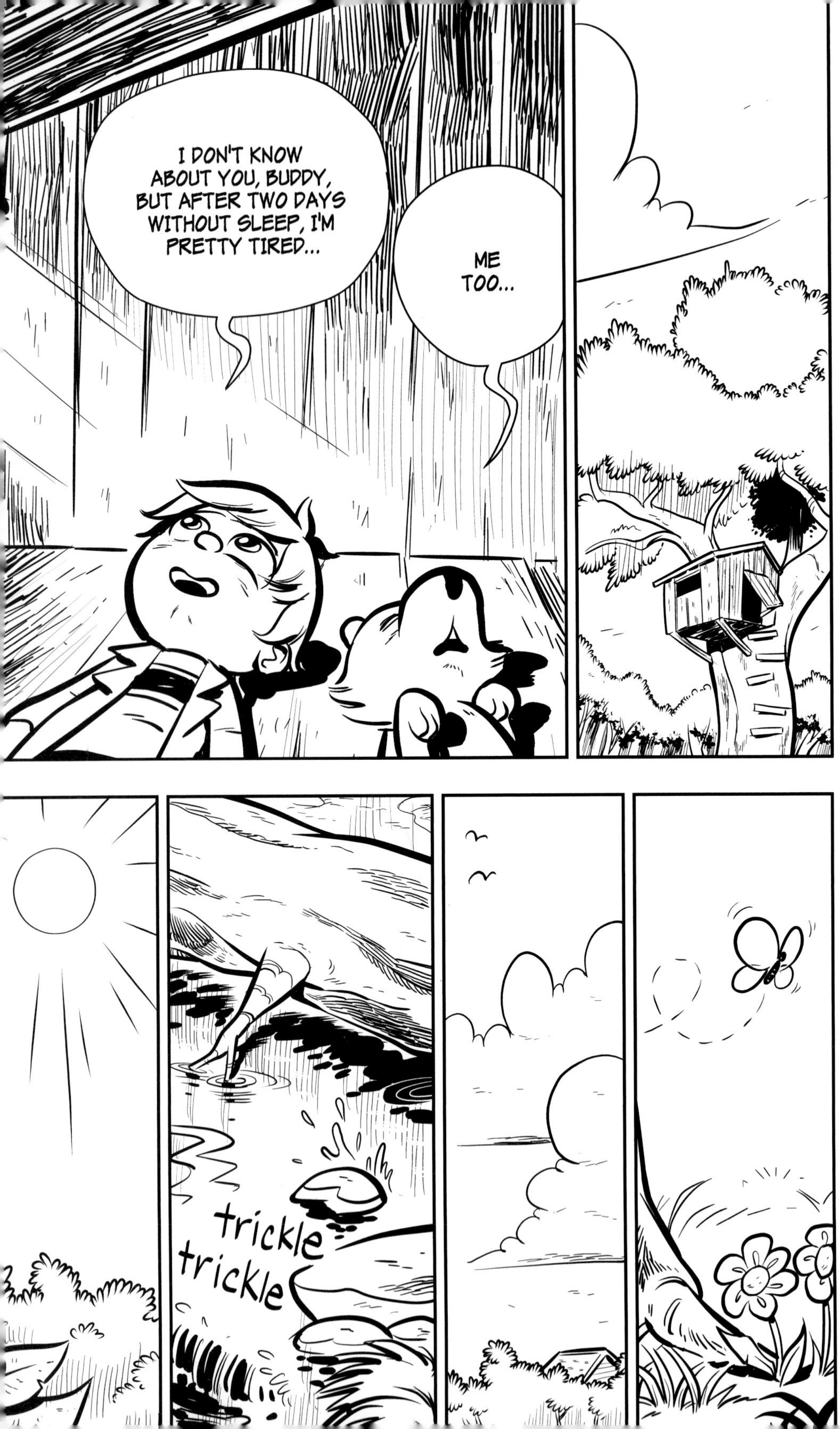
I DON'T KNOW ABOUT YOU, BUDDY, BUT AFTER TWO DAYS WITHOUT SLEEP, I'M PRETTY TIRED...
ME TOO...
trickle trickle

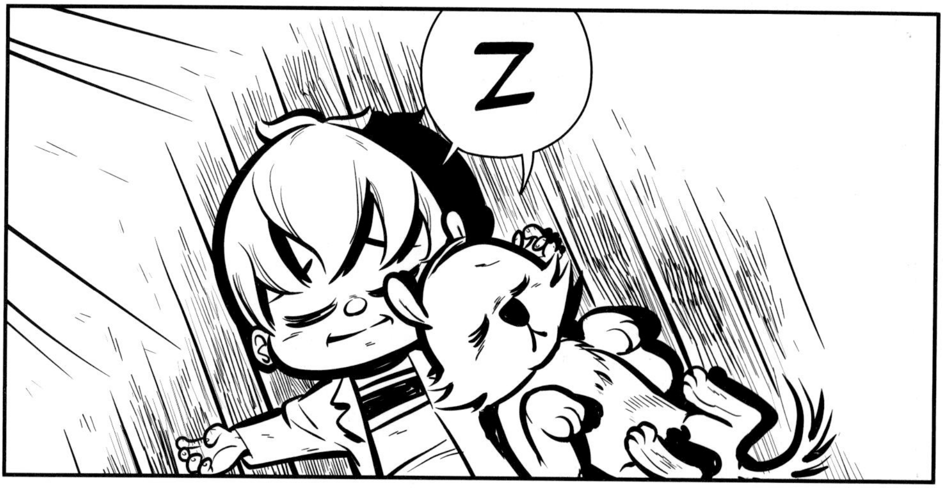
Z

the end

craving more Mal and Chad?

FEAR NOT.

www.MalandChad.com will tide you
over until the next all-new installment,
on its way from Philomel Books.

Stephen McCranie grew up drawing comics from an
early age. He eventually earned a Fine Arts degree at the University of
New Mexico. Stephen originally created *Mal and Chad* as a comic
strip for the UNM school newspaper. You can read this strip in its
entirety, as well as find other fun stuff, at the Mal and Chad website.

MOVIE BLOCKBUSTERS

Big-budget, spectacular films designed to appeal to a mass audience: is this what – or all – blockbusters are? *Movie Blockbusters* brings together leading film scholars to consider this most high-profile and culturally significant genre. Drawing on a range of critical perspectives, the book traces how and why the "event movie" has played such a large role in the popular imagination, tracing a path from the spectacles of the silent era to the effects-laden mega-hits of the digital age.

The contributors explain what the rise of the blockbuster says about the Hollywood film industry, address the work of notable blockbuster auteurs such as Steven Spielberg and James Cameron, discuss key movies such as *Jaws*, *The Jazz Singer*, *The Ten Commandments*, *Terminator 2*, and *Titanic*, and consider the various contexts in which blockbusters are produced, distributed, marketed, and consumed. In addition, the book considers the movie scene outside Hollywood, discussing blockbusters made in Bollywood, China, South Korea, New Zealand, and Argentina.